Praise for
A Nest of Sparrows

"Deborah Raney is a skillful novelist who weaves a powerful story that stays with you. *A Nest of Sparrows* is heart touching, authentic, and credible, with characters you care about, who live and breathe inside you. Once you start reading, this story won't let you go. You'll be sorry when the book's done, but take heart—there are other great Deb Raney books waiting for you!"

    —RANDY ALCORN, author of *Deadline* and *Safely Home*

"Deborah Raney's *A Nest of Sparrows* is a moving testament to the power of love. If you are looking for a story about family, about restoration, about home—as well as a story that's just plain engaging—this is it."

    —ANN TATLOCK, award-winning author of *All the Way Home*

"What a tender and moving novel! *A Nest of Sparrows* is cute, funny, tragic, and moving. Ultimately, it's a story of love on all levels: the love between parents and children, the love between a man and a woman, and foremost the love between God and his children. I was drawn into the story of this book and left with the message."

    —LINDA HALL, award-winning author of *Steal Away*
    and *Chat Room*

"We often read stories about a mother's heart. Deborah Raney paints a vivid picture of a dad's heart, better than any definition I've ever read. *A Nest of Sparrows* is a gripping portrayal of what family should be. An expertly crafted story with all the ingredients that make us laugh and cry—let go and let God."

    —YVONNE LEHMAN, author of forty novels, including
    Coffee Rings

"This is a heartfelt story of one man's struggle to keep the children he loves and the faith that keeps him strong. Deborah Raney's writing is always full of warmth and hope, and *A Nest of Sparrows* is no exception."

—JAMES SCOTT BELL, Christy Award–winning author
of *Breach of Promise*

"Wow—what an amazing, tender, touching story! *A Nest of Sparrows* grabs your heart from the get-go, delivering wonderful characters and an emotionally gripping story you'll love. By far Raney's best. Highly recommended! Do not miss this marvelous book."

—GAYLE ROPER, author of *Winter Winds, Autumn Dreams, Summer Shadows,* and *Spring Rain*

A Nest of Sparrows

A Nest of Sparrows

A NOVEL

Deborah Raney

WATERBROOK
PRESS

A NEST OF SPARROWS
PUBLISHED BY WATERBROOK PRESS
2375 Telstar Drive, Suite 160
Colorado Springs, Colorado 80920
A division of Random House, Inc.

Most scriptures are taken from the *New King James Version.* Copyright © 1982 by Thomas Nelson, Inc. Used by permission. All rights reserved. Also quoted is the *Holy Bible, New International Version*®. NIV®. Copyright © 1973, 1978, 1984 by International Bible Society. Used by permission of Zondervan Publishing House. All rights reserved.

The characters and events in this book are fictional, and any resemblance to actual persons or events is coincidental.

ISBN 1-57856-578-2

Library of Congress Cataloging-in-Publication Data
Raney, Deborah.
    A nest of sparrows / Deborah Raney.—1st ed.
        p. cm.
    ISBN 1-57856-578-2
    1. Custody of children—Fiction. 2. Motherless families—Fiction. 3. Women social workers—Fiction. I. Title.
    PS3568.A562N47 2004
    813'.54—dc22

                                    2003027714

Printed in the United States of America
2004—First Edition

10 9 8 7 6 5 4 3 2 1

To Jewel Fuson

With love.
For creating so many happy childhood memories.

Are not two sparrows sold for a copper coin?
And not one of them falls to the ground
apart from your Father's will.

MATTHEW 10:29, NKJV

Wade Sullivan glanced around the table as he expertly shuffled the dog-eared deck of cards. His old poker gang would have given him all kinds of grief about the images of Winnie-the-Pooh flipping by as he bent the playing cards into an expert arch, then tamped the deck on the tabletop and cut it again.

But it wasn't his poker buddies sitting around his dining room table tonight. He almost chuckled aloud to realize how drastically his life had changed in the space of twenty short months. If anyone had told him two years ago that his table would soon be routinely littered with crayons, animal crackers, and half-empty cups of strawberry Kool-Aid, he would have called them crazy.

"C'mon, Wade. Hurry up and deal." Eight-year-old Beau drummed his fingers impatiently on the table.

"Beau…" The boy's mother spoke his name low and aimed a warning glance his way.

"Sorry, Wade," Beau mumbled.

"It's okay." Wade winked at Starr across the table, tacitly thanking her for demanding Beau's respect. He knew she wasn't really upset. A pussycat lurked beneath Starr Parnell's stern expression.

They exchanged a secret smile, and something inside him melted. She was the sweetest, kindest woman he'd ever known. The one woman who'd finally succeeded in robbing him of the confirmed bachelor status he'd been so proud of all these years.

He counted out four cards and put them in front of Beau, then dealt around the table. Lacey and Danica, Beau's younger sisters, scooped up their cards and carefully fanned them out in their small hands, protecting them from their brother's roving gaze.

Starr's sister, Sophie, looked at her cards and let out a low growl.

"Sheesh, Wade, if you can't give any better than this, you'd better let somebody else deal."

He tossed a teasing smirk in her direction. "Be patient, Sophe. Your luck's bound to change."

"Not with a hand like this, it's not." She slapped her cards on the table and slumped back in her chair.

Wade laughed at his future sister-in-law's feigned moping and picked up his own cards. He'd grown up an only child, but at thirty-five he was getting a taste of what it must be like to be part of a big family. It felt good. He glanced up to see Starr watching him with that moony, I-am-so-in-love-with-you expression sparkling in her eyes.

Yep. It felt mighty good.

"Okay, Mr. Beau," he said, rubbing his knuckles gently over the boy's mop of blond hair. "You were in such a big toot. Get this round rolling."

Beau grinned and picked up a card from the pile. "Wake up, Aunt Sophie. Good cards comin' your way." The exaggerated lift of his brows gave him away as he tucked the card into his hand and passed the discarded one to four-year-old Danica.

In the center of the table, five of Wade's mother's old engraved stainless steel spoons were arranged like a giant asterisk, waiting for the free-for-all that would ensue as soon as one of them collected four matching cards.

Poker and solitaire had been the only games in Wade's repertoire before he'd met Starr. Now he played a mean game of crazy eights, go fish, slapjack—even old maid, when the little girls could talk him into it. Tonight it was spoons. And he had to admit, this was every bit as much fun as poker, and at least as rowdy. In fact, if a fellow wasn't careful, he could get beaned once the spoons started flying.

The cards made their way around to him, and he picked them up in quick succession. He nabbed the jack of spades to add to the two he'd dealt himself, but before he had time to pick up another card, Lacey crowed and grabbed a spoon from the pile. A tangle of arms and bodies flopped across the table as six people went for five spoons. When the grabfest was over, Wade was the one left spoonless.

"Sing a tune! Sing a tune!" The kids chanted, pounding the table in unison.

He rolled his eyes and heaved an exaggerated sigh. Striking a diva's pose he knew would draw grins, he clasped his hands in front of him and wailed one falsetto note. But when Starr flashed him the same stern look she'd given Beau a few minutes ago, he lowered his voice and crooned a few bars from a Randy Travis song they'd been playing on the radio lately. Since he was pretty much tone deaf, no one would have recognized his rendition without the lyrics.

He suspected Starr had added this crazy loser-has-to-sing-a-tune rule just to torture him. Still, whenever it came her turn to sing, it was worth every second of embarrassment he'd endured. Starr had a lovely, mellow voice that turned his insides to jelly. Just another of this amazing woman's myriad talents. How did he get so lucky?

He corrected the thought immediately. Luck had nothing to do with Starr Parnell's being in his life. She was a gift from God, plain and simple. A gift he hadn't known he'd needed until it had been given. Now he thanked God for her every day. Sometimes he didn't think he could breathe without her.

Starr tapped her fingers on the marble tabletop, gave the waitress an apologetic smile, and looked at her watch again. She'd been waiting for Sophie for almost an hour. If she didn't hurry up, they'd barely have time for a cup of coffee before she had to pick the kids up from school. And she hadn't had anything to eat since breakfast.

Five minutes later the bells on the coffee shop door clanked against the plate glass, and Starr looked up to see her sister sail in, breathless and flushed.

Sophie hurried over to the table and slid into the chair across from Starr. "Sorry. I had to run by the post office."

"It's okay. I've got to run at three, though."

Sophie looked at her watch. "Am I that late?"

Starr bit her tongue. Never mind that she'd wasted an hour of her one day off this week. Never mind that she had a dozen other things she should be doing. She loved her sister to pieces, but sometimes the girl drove her totally crackers.

Sophie shrugged. "You should have just gone ahead and ordered. I wouldn't have cared."

"Don't worry about it. You're here now." She signaled the waitress.

"Hey, look who just walked in." Sophie pointed toward the front of the shop.

Starr turned to see Wade heading their way. He gave her a smile that warmed her from the inside out. All her frustration vanished.

He bent to kiss her. "Hey, babe. Hi, Sophie." He dragged a chair over from a nearby table and sat down between them. "What are you ladies up to?"

"We should ask you the same thing," Starr said, cupping a hand over his cheek, loving the roughness of his five-o'clock stubble against her palm. "I thought you were working late."

"We are. But I had to pick up some supplies at the lumberyard, so I told Pete I'd grab us some sandwiches for supper."

"Mmm. Sounds good. I'm starving."

"You haven't even had lunch?"

"No…" Starr looked around the tiny shop for the lone waitress. "And if she doesn't hurry up and take our order, I'm not going to have time."

Wade looked at his watch. "I can pick the kids up if you want. We're working at that site out on Maple. It's right on my way. I'll just take them with me, and you can come out there when you're done."

She felt the weariness drain from her at the thought of a leisurely lunch. "You sure you don't mind?"

"Nah…I don't mind. You just enjoy your lunch."

The waitress came and took their orders. Wade ordered two sandwiches and then sat with Starr and Sophie until the waitress brought out his to-go bag.

"See you after a while," he said, standing and planting a kiss in Starr's hair. "Don't worry. I won't forget to pick up the kids."

She grinned. "Thanks."

He winked at her and walked out the door.

She looked at Sophie and sighed. "What did I do to deserve this, Sophie?"

Sophie shook her head. "I'm telling you, Sis, this is the calm before the storm. Run as fast as you can."

"Sophie! Quit. You don't mean that." Her sister had been burned too many times when it came to men.

"I know, I know… He seems like a keeper. But…you're sure this isn't too good to be true? I seem to remember you wearing that same sappy smile over Darrin."

Starr clenched her fists and dug her nails into her palms. "Wade's different, Sophie. You know that."

Sophie shook out her paper napkin and worried the edge of it. Her mouth twisted. "Okay…whatever you say."

It made Starr sad to realize that the roads Sophie had chosen in life had left them miles apart. Her sister didn't understand the difference faith could make in a man's life.

Still, sometimes Sophie's attitude made her second-guess herself. After all, she *had* been wrong about Darrin. Dreadfully wrong. But all she had to do to shake off the doubts about Wade Sullivan was to remember the first time she'd met him.

It wasn't long after she'd moved to Coyote. Dani was just a toddler, and feeling isolated and exhausted, Starr had hauled the kids to the café where Sophie worked. It was the middle of the lunch rush, and Sophie seated them in a booth behind Wade and his business partner, Pete Dolecek. The booth backs were high, and Starr hadn't paid attention to the strangers behind her until halfway through the meal little Dani crawled out of her booster seat and turned around to bounce on the bench seat. Before Starr knew what was happening, Dani reached over and yanked off Wade's Kansas City Chiefs cap and flipped it into her spaghetti sauce.

Starr blushed ten shades of red and managed to stutter an apology. She half expected Wade to fly out of the booth and cuss her out for not being able to control her bratty kid.

Instead, he winked at her and tugged playfully on Dani's pigtails. "Guess she's not a big fan of the Chiefs, huh?" he drawled. Then he burst into musical laughter. Dani giggled and lifted her pudgy little arms to him. Wade scooped her up as though he held babies in his arms every day. Sometimes Starr thought she'd fallen in love with him in that moment.

Sophie introduced them, and they ended up talking for ten minutes while Wade joked with the kids and bounced Danica on his knee. And somehow, when Wade left the restaurant, she and the kids had a date with him to Coyote's Fall Festival parade the following Saturday.

Starr felt the corners of her mouth lift at the memory, but her smile turned sheepish when she realized her sister was shaking her head and rolling her eyes at her.

"You are one hopeless woman," Sophie said.

Starr exhaled a breath of relief when the waitress finally showed up with their plates. She busied herself extricating silverware from her napkin and quickly changed the subject. "Oh, man, does this ever look good. I'll trade you a bite of my enchilada for some of that pasta."

"Deal." Sophie grinned and poised her fork over Starr's plate, and Starr knew things were back to a tenuous normal between them.

Starr blew a strand of hair out of her eyes, wiped her nose again, and tucked the tissue in her uniform pocket. She hoped she wasn't getting another cold. It seemed as though she'd had more than her share of flu and colds since she'd started working here at the nursing home. Still, she couldn't complain about her job. It was hard work, but the pay was pretty decent, and her schedule let her be home with her kids after school.

As if he'd read her thoughts, old Mr. Pedersen smiled at her across the day room.

"Going home?" he asked, leaning forward in the high-backed vinyl chair.

"Yep. Going home. Got to pick up my kids from school."

"What's that?" he said, cupping a hand to his ear.

It was the same conversation they had every night before her shift ended. She suspected he'd heard her just fine the first time, but she played along and went across the room to sit down beside him. She repeated her comment, louder this time.

"Well, you ought to bring those kids by sometime," he said.

"I don't know, Jake… They're a pretty rowdy bunch."

He looked around the day room at the three elderly women dozing by the window. He harrumphed. "This place could use a little injection of rowdiness."

Starr laughed and patted his arm. "Oh, I think you probably give us about as much as we can handle," she teased.

"I do my best." He tipped an imaginary hat. "And what about that young fella of yours?" he said. "I haven't seen him around for a while. He hasn't gone and called off the wedding, has he?"

"Oh no." She laughed, making a mental note to tell Wade he'd been dubbed a "young fella." He'd be tickled. "He wouldn't dare call it off."

"Well, tell 'im he'd have me to reckon with, if he did," Jake said.

"I'll tell him." She eased from the chair and looked pointedly at the clock over the nurses' station. "Well, I'd better run. You have a good night. I'll see you Monday."

"If I'm still here, you will."

She tried not to play favorites with the residents, but the spark in Jacob Pedersen's rheumy eyes made it difficult not to hold him in a special place in her heart.

"Oh, you'll be here," she told him, surprised at the catch in her throat. "This place wouldn't be the same without you."

He winked and waved her away.

Fifteen minutes later she had a car full of noisy kids and no idea what she was going to feed them for supper, let alone after-school snacks. Maybe she could talk Wade into picking up a pizza and joining them for dinner. She would be so glad when they could quit shuffling between two houses and make a *home* together.

She parked in front of the apartment building and herded the kids inside.

Dani tugged on the hem of Starr's uniform top. "Mama, can I play outside?"

"Not unless Beau or Lacey goes with you, baby."

"I'll go," Beau said.

"Do you have homework?"

"Just one page of math. I can do it later."

"Nope. You know the rules."

"Aw, Mom—"

"Don't even start with me, Beau Andrew. If it's only one page, you can finish it and still have time to play before supper, right?"

He huffed and stamped his feet and looked like he was going to argue with her. But instead he unzipped his backpack and flopped his math workbook on the table in the tiny kitchen.

This apartment had been a haven to her and the kids when they'd left Minneapolis for Kansas—*fled* Minneapolis was more like it. But she was so thankful her children were going to spend most of their growing-up years at Wade's house in the country.

No, our *house in the country,* she corrected herself. She still had to pinch herself to believe it was true. The old farmhouse had needed a lot of work. Wade and Pete had all the jobs they could handle in their contracting business, and the contractor's house was apparently like the proverbial shoemaker's shoeless children. It had been slow going, but the remodeling was coming along, and by the time they were married, it would be plenty livable.

Of course, a cardboard refrigerator box with Wade Sullivan would be plenty livable. She smiled at the thought and went back to her bedroom to change out of her uniform.

Two

Starr pulled into Wade's driveway just as the sun was rising over the hedgerow of red cedars. The instant she turned off the ignition, the kids freed themselves from their seat belts and scrambled out of the car. Hauling backpacks and McDonald's bags, they raced one another to the back door. Shadow, Wade's black Labrador retriever, romped to meet them and trotted behind, sniffing the brown paper bags bearing the golden arches.

"Mama got you a Egg McMuffin, Wade!" Danica shouted into the crisp March air.

Starr grabbed the tote with her painting supplies, and the paper sack that held Wade's breakfast, and started up the brick walk. Her gaze lifted to the second floor of the house she and Wade were restoring. She sure would be glad when August came and she could wake up in this house every morning beside the man she loved.

He stood holding the screen door open for her, looking droopy-eyed and disheveled—and handsome as all get-out.

"Good morning, sunshine," she said, standing on tiptoe to receive his kiss. She took in a whiff of the delicious aroma wafting from the kitchen. "Oh, good. I was hoping you made coffee. I didn't buy any. Here…" She held out the McDonald's bag. "Breakfast is served."

Wade peeked into the bag and inhaled an appreciative breath. Starr started up the back stairs to the kitchen where she could hear the kids fighting over their favorite juice cup. But Wade caught her elbow and pulled her back down. "Come here, you." He drew her into his arms, and she melted into his embrace.

"Thanks for breakfast."

"Mmm, who needs breakfast," she whispered into his cotton shirt. "How are you this morning?"

"Much better now," he said, pulling away and looking into her eyes. A piercing screech came from the kitchen. "Mooommm!"

Starr let out a low growl and disentangled herself from Wade's arms. "I'd better go mediate."

She stomped up the stairs and into the kitchen. "Okay, what is going on in here?"

"I had the blue cup first, and Beau grabbed it right outta my hand," Lacey accused.

"She did not," Beau shouted. "I called it before she even saw it."

"Beau, get your muddy shoes off the table! Good grief, were you born in a barn? Look at that mud."

"I had it first, Mom. I swear."

"We don't swear, Beau. And quit changing the subject. Feet. Down. Now."

Lacey took advantage of the diversion to pounce on her brother and wrest the coveted cup from his grip. Unfortunately, it had orange juice in it, which spewed across the table and splashed Danica full in the face. She opened her mouth and let out a high-pitched wail.

Starr grabbed the offending cup from Lacey's hands. "Give me that!" She stormed to the sink, dumped out the rest of the juice, and ceremoniously tossed the plastic cup into the trash can under the counter.

Danica's crying stopped instantly. All three children gasped as one. It was all Starr could do to keep a straight face.

"That was Wade's!" Beau said, mouth still agape. "You can't throw it away!"

"You just don't worry about the cup, buster. Now go get a towel and help Dani clean up." A dull ache started behind her eyes, and she rubbed her temples hard. "Lacey, get the dishcloth and wipe off the table. Don't miss any spots, or it'll be a sticky mess. And wipe up the mud from Beau's shoes while you're at it."

"What? Why do I hafta clean up *his* mess?"

"Just do it."

Wade appeared in the doorway. "What happened?" he asked over a bite of Egg McMuffin, seemingly oblivious to the fact that his kitchen was in total chaos.

"Mama threw your blue cup in the trash," Lacey tattled, hands on hips.

"Oh, she did, did she? Well, good for her. I'm tired of hearing you guys fight over it all the time."

Another collective gasp.

Wade winked at Starr over the top of the three towheads. She turned away, rinsing out the dishcloth, fighting to curb her laughter.

Wade clapped his hands. "Come on now, guys. Eat… Hustle up! I've got to get to work. Preferably sometime today."

Wade Sullivan had the patience of Job. Starr stood at the sink and watched this soon-to-be former bachelor attempt to round up her three children and herd them out the door.

Finally, with teeth brushed and faces washed, the kids lined up for their ritual kiss.

"Bye, kiddos. Have a good day at school." Starr kissed each cheek, waved, and ducked upstairs, anxious to get started on the project that was to be a surprise for Wade.

Halfway up she heard Lacey whine. "I can't find my backpack."

"It's probably out in the car, Lace," Starr hollered down the stairwell. "Did you bring it in with you this morning?" Without waiting for an answer, she went on up and walked into the bedroom she and Wade would soon share. She pried open a small can of moss-green paint and stirred it with a paint stick bearing the Coyote Lumberyard logo.

She heard Wade's heavy footsteps on the stairway and quickly put the paint down and went to greet him in the hallway, pulling the door closed behind her.

He cocked his head and tossed a suspicious look over her shoulder. "What are you being so secretive about in there anyway?"

She brushed a speck of lint from his T-shirt and let her hand rest on the broad plane of his chest. "Never you mind. If you guys would ever get out of here, I might get something done today and then I could show you my surprise."

"Okay, okay…we're going." He covered her hand with his own and gave it a squeeze, then leaned in and pressed his lips to hers. "Have a good day, babe. Don't work too hard. This is supposed to be your day off, remember?"

"Don't you worry about me. I'm having fun."

"You have a weird idea of fun, woman."

She gave him a playful shove. "Get. Go on. I'll see you tonight."

The screen door slammed one last time, and a heavenly silence descended on the old house. Starr sighed and smiled to herself. She touched the warm place on her lips where Wade's kiss still lingered. Then she went back into the bedroom and set to work.

Two hours later she heard the clock downstairs strike ten. She massaged her stiff neck, then wiped the last drips of paint from the narrow brush and balanced it across the top of the paint can. Climbing down from the ladder, she surveyed her handiwork. The uneven plastered walls of the bedroom wore two smooth coats of buttercream—the exact shade of the sunlight streaming in the windows on this March morning. And now her graceful calligraphy flowed in moss green across three walls, the lines from Robert Browning's poem awaiting her painted embellishments of dainty violets and ivy.

She scooted the ladder forward a few feet and swept a strand of hair away from her face. She loved this house. Loved everything about it—even in its naked, half-finished state.

She loved the keen of the Kansas wind as it whistled through the door sashes, and the way the old pipes clanked and sang after the hot water had run out. She loved the high ceilings and the way the rippled window glass left wavering patches of sunlight on the hardwood floors, like a mirage on desert sand.

Maybe it was all a mirage. This house, her life, everything. Maybe she would wake up tomorrow and it would all be gone. She'd be working like a dog and never making ends meet. Trying to explain to the kids why they were having hot dogs for dinner again. Why they couldn't go to the movies or skating or to a friend's birthday party—or *anything*—because there wasn't any money for tickets or skates or presents.

Maybe she'd wake up tomorrow morning to find that Wade Sullivan had been a figment of her imagination. That the man who loved her and adored her children had existed only in her sweetest dreams.

But the strong, sun-baked arms she'd felt slip around her this morning, the pale blue-gray eyes that held a certain spark whenever he spotted her across a crowded room, were too real, too concrete to be a mere dream. And even in her wildest imaginings, she'd never dreamed up anyone like Wade.

No, he was real all right. And the fact that he wanted to marry her made her want to fall to her knees in gratitude right here in the middle of this room—this room that would soon hold their bed, their love.

Oh, Father. Thank you. I love that man so much it hurts. Thank you, Jesus. Thank you for a real daddy for Beau and Lacey and Dani. The tears came then, as they did every time she thought about her blessings, about the glorious turn her life had taken after so many years of struggle.

Even if it wasn't for this stupid cold she was fighting, her head would probably still ache from all the tears she'd shed. It seemed funny that tears of joy would cause such pain. She pressed her fingers to her temples and kneaded the soft flesh beneath them. She couldn't seem to shake this headache. She'd found some sinus tablets in Wade's medicine cabinet downstairs and had been popping them for two days. She had taken one first thing this morning and another one about an hour ago, but, if anything, her headache was worse. Right now it felt the way it did when she ate ice cream too fast. Starr eased herself to the floor and leaned her chin on the low sill of the double-paned window, resting her forehead against the cool glass. As it always did, the view beyond took her breath away. The backyard was a lush green carpet that rolled down the gentle slope and disappeared into a copse of cottonwoods and elms that lined the banks of the Smoky Hill River. Summer was a breath away. And this would be the most special summer of her life—the summer she would become Mrs. Wade Sullivan.

Throbbing pain crawled through her brain to the back of her head. She made a cap of her hands and pressed her fingers hard against her skull, grimacing. Something wasn't right. She'd never had a headache like this. Maybe it was a migraine. She'd never had one that she knew of, but she'd heard they could almost knock a person out.

Or maybe the paint fumes were getting to her. Wade nagged her about proper ventilation when she worked with the paints and stains they used on the house. She tried to raise the sash, but she had no leverage from where she sat, and no strength in her hands.

She tried to stand and immediately slumped back to the floor. The ceiling spiraled overhead. She forced her eyes to focus on the fancy calligraphy she'd begun to paint around the perimeter of the room.

The poet's words expressed her love for Wade Sullivan so beautifully. Wade's face floated into her mind, and she felt the corners of her lips rise in a wan smile. She loved that man so much…so very much…

She tried to get to her feet again, but the room spun as though she were seeing it from a carousel. She sank to the floor. Why was she so dizzy? Why couldn't she stand up? Knifelike pain screamed through her head, excruciating now. A soft moan escaped from deep in her throat, and, for the first time, she was frightened by the raw power of her pain.

Then, as suddenly as it had come on, the headache left. Her heart fluttered weakly, and like a feather on a summer breeze, she had the sensation of being afloat, dancing on the updrafts, rising slowly toward the ceiling.

It didn't seem the least bit odd to be gazing down upon her own still, earthly form.

Oh, Father…be with my babies. Help Wade…

She turned away, and in the space of a breath, her spirit defied the bounds of the room's four walls, the roof of the house, then the limits of earth and the boundaries of the heavens themselves.

She became aware of a holy presence surrounding her, embracing her. And a beloved voice that spoke a name she did not know, yet somehow recognized as her own. She moved closer, into the arms of the One who beckoned. And in that moment she knew.

She was home.

Three

Wade shifted his weight to his left knee, laid down his roofer's hatchet, and pulled a bright red bandanna from the back pocket of his dust-caked blue jeans. Looking over the town from his vantage point on the peak of the roof, he mopped at his forehead, failing to halt a rivulet of perspiration before it stung his eye. The sun on his back reminded him that come June it would be hotter than blazes up here.

He stuffed the handkerchief back in his pocket and flopped another shingle into position. Fishing a handful of roofing nails from a pouch in his tool belt, he loaded them in his mouth. With the hammer end of the hatchet, he drove home half a dozen nails in rapid succession.

The shrill ring of the cell phone clipped to his belt spoiled his steady rhythm. Laying the roofer's hatchet down again, he rocked back on his heels and punched the phone's keypad. "Sullivan," he barked over the racket of his partner's hammering.

Wade heard the laughter of children in the background, then Beau's little-boy voice cracked over the line. "Wade?"

"Hey, buddy. What's up?"

"Mama's late again. Can you come and pick us up?"

"Did you try calling her cell phone?"

Wade could almost hear Beau wagging his blond head at the phone. "She didn't answer. I left her a message."

He glanced at his watch and frowned. School had been out almost forty-five minutes. Well, this wasn't the first time Starr had gotten so caught up in her painting that she'd forgotten to pick up the kids. "Tell you what," he said into the phone. "I'll call Aunt Sophie and see if maybe she can come get you. If she can't, I'll come myself. You tell the girls to wait outside with you, okay?"

"Okay."

Wade disconnected and dialed Sophia Braden's number. She

answered on the second ring. "Hey, Sophe. The kids need a ride. Apparently that sister of yours is in la-la land over at the house. I'm kind of tied up right now… Would you mind—?"

"Yeah, I can pick them up. You want me to take them out to your place?"

"No…just go ahead and take them home. Starr'll probably beat you there. If not, call me back. Thanks."

Wade hit End and dialed Starr's cell phone. It rang half a dozen times before her sweet voice came on the line. "This is Starr. Can't take your call just now, but leave a message, and I promise I'll get back to you quick as I can."

He turned the phone off before it could beep at him. That crazy woman. When she got a notion in her head, everything else just flew out the window. He could picture her now, balancing on the top of the ladder, her tongue tracing the path of her paintbrush, her mind a thousand miles away. In a few minutes she'd hear the clock chime in the foyer and she'd gasp, look at her watch, and suddenly remember she had three children who got out of school at the same time every day of the week. She'd say a few choice words, scramble down the ladder, dash out of the house, and drive like a maniac into town.

Wade chuckled to himself and dug out another handful of nails. If he didn't love the woman so much, she would've driven him halfway to loony and back by now.

Fifteen minutes later Wade's cell phone jangled again. He spit out a mouthful of nails and plucked the phone from his belt, wiping the metallic tang from his lips with the back of his hand. "Sullivan."

"Hey, Wade." It was Sophie. "I'm at Starr's place with the kids, but she's still not home, and I'm supposed to be at work in half an hour."

"Well, shoot-fire, where is she?"

"You're asking me?"

Wade smiled into the phone. "Yeah, yeah… Okay, I can wrap it up here. I'll stop by the house and see what's up, then one of us'll be right over to get the kids. Sorry about this, Sophe."

"Hey, it's not your fault."

Wade disconnected and shouted across the roof where his partner, Pete Dolecek, was fitting flashing around a chimney. "Hey, Pete, I've got to go pick up the kids. Do you mind cleaning up?"

Pete gave a half-salute and turned back to his work. Wade holstered his tools, climbed down the ladder, and jumped into his pickup. It took him ten minutes to get out to the house.

Wade had remodeled a lot of houses in his day, and he'd taken pride in each one. But none of them had ever contained every ounce of his hopes and dreams the way this one did. He drove around to the back and parked the truck. Sure enough. Starr's car was still there.

He tooted the horn and shaded his eyes, looking up to the second story. He couldn't see any lights on in the windows, but maybe it was still bright enough on the north side that she didn't need the light.

The back door was unlocked. Wade stepped inside. "Starr?" He walked through the entryway and up the short flight of stairs to the kitchen. "Starr?"

His work boots hammered across the hardwood floors in the living room. He started up the staircase. "Hey! You up here, Starr?"

He stopped to listen again. Usually sound carried like an echo in a canyon through these empty old rooms. But now it was eerily silent. "Hey, babe? Where are you?"

No answer.

The door to the master bedroom was halfway closed. When he'd left for work this morning, she'd hinted about a surprise for him. She'd fixed each of the kids' rooms up real pretty, painting a special poem or saying along the top of the wall like a border, and on the plaster ceiling in Lacey's room. She was probably doing something fancy to the master bedroom, too.

Starr had a real gift with a paintbrush. He'd tried to encourage her to do something more with her talent. He wouldn't be surprised if she could make good money just painting murals and borders for people. That seemed to be all the rage right now. To be honest, he didn't care much for all that fancy stuff on walls. But it was something Starr enjoyed. It would sure beat that nurse's aide job she had at the retirement home.

But whenever he brought up the subject, she brushed off his compliments. "You have to be a lot better than I am to get paid for that kind of thing, Wade. You're just prejudiced because you happen to love me."

Well, that he did. Nobody would argue that. Even when she pulled scatterbrained, thoughtless stunts like this, upsetting everybody's schedule.

He carefully pushed open the door to the master bedroom, knowing she could easily be atop a ladder on the other side of the door. "Hey, you…" The acrid scent of fresh paint assailed his nostrils. And something else. Something worse.

He stopped short.

Starr was lying on her back on the floor in front of the windows, her head turned away from him. If she was napping, she was in a deep sleep. He'd made enough racket to wake the dead coming up here. His heart thumped out an odd rhythm as he walked over to where she lay.

He bent over her. "Starr? Hey…wake up." The minute he touched her shoulder, he knew something was wrong. Terribly, eternally wrong.

He dropped to his knees beside her and gently lifted her head, turning her face toward him. Her face was drained of color. Her eyes were half open, but their vibrant blue had faded to a cloudy gray, and there was no flicker of life in them, nor in the pulse points he frantically sought for some spark of hope that she was still with him.

She was gone. He knew it as sure as he knew he loved her. His breath came in short gasps as he eased Starr's body back to the floor and brushed his palm over her eyelids, closing them. The blood pounded in his ears as he stood and whirled around the room, looking for some clue to what had happened. She wasn't lying close enough to the ladder to have fallen.

A small can of moss-green paint sat open atop the ladder's pail shelf, a congealed skin formed over its contents. The brush resting across the lid of the can was dry and stiff. Wade looked up toward the ceiling. The paint matched Starr's familiar, elegant script that snaked across the top of the walls. But he couldn't put the letters and words together in a way that made sense.

His breath grew more shallow and he felt lightheaded. *Oh, dear God. How can this be happening?* He looked at his watch. Probably no more than two minutes had passed since he'd walked into this room, but it seemed as if an eternity had elapsed. He turned to Starr's still form again and felt an irrational, desperate need to go to her, try to revive her—even though he knew it would be in vain.

He needed to call—who? The ambulance? It was too late for that. He ripped his cell phone off his belt and punched in 911. He heard himself telling the dispatcher where he was, that Starr was dead, that he didn't know what had happened. But even his own wobbly voice couldn't convince him this was real.

He hung up and slumped to the floor beside Starr. He put his hand on her head, felt the velvety texture of her pale corn-silk hair beneath his fingers. He was paralyzed. Unable to move, unable to think. Unable to breathe.

Oh, dear Lord… How could she be gone? How could he go on without her? What would he tell the kids?

He leaned his head back against the window frame and let his gaze travel up to the final words Starr had penned—words he knew were meant for him alone. Words that now pierced his heart like a dagger.

"Grow old along with me! The best is yet to be."

Four

Sophia Braden dropped the phone into its cradle and covered her mouth with her hands, trying to absorb the bombshell Wade had just dropped. Her throat constricted, and she struggled to catch her next breath.

A tug on her shirttail made her look down.

"Aunt Sophie? Was that my mama?" Danica looked up at her with woeful puppy-dog eyes—eyes so like her mother's. How did you explain something like this to a four-year-old? Sophie could barely make sense of it herself.

"No, sweetie"—she took a deep breath and put a hand on her niece's head, smoothing back the silky yellow hair—"that was Wade. He—" She swallowed back a sob that felt like a boulder. "He's going to pick you guys up in a little bit."

A glint of suspicion crossed Danica's delicate features, and she looked hard into Sophie's face, then ducked out from under her caress and ran back to the living room, where her brother and sister were watching a video.

What on earth was Wade going to tell these kids? And what would happen to them? No way in the world was Wade going to take on three kids and raise them. And she sure as Moses wouldn't do it.

Her big sister was gone. Dead. Sophie was jolted all over again by the thought. It brought back too many memories that were better left buried. But one thing couldn't be ignored. She was totally alone now.

What could have happened to Starr? Wade said they didn't know yet, but good grief, a twenty-nine-year-old woman didn't just drop dead for no reason. She and Starr had had their differences over the years, but in spite of it all, Sophie loved her sister. Starr was the only family she had left. Now she was gone too.

And where was her sister's God now? She strangled a derisive snort. If Starr had one fault, it was that she was always trying to cram her religion—her *faith,* she called it—down Sophie's throat. Well, it didn't take a psychologist to see that Starr had God and Wade mixed up. Just because things had finally gone right for Starr, just because she'd finally found a man who treated her like a princess and loved her brats as if they were his own, Starr was ready to jump up and shout *hallelujah* and give God all the credit. Well, where was God *now?*

Sophie hoped Starr knew...wherever she was.

Wade stood six feet from Starr's body and answered the questions the emergency personnel—and later the medical investigator from the coroner's office—threw at him. But Wade had no light to shed on what could have caused Starr's sudden death. Numb, he told them everything he could think of: She'd spent long hours working at the house, using all kinds of paints and varnishes. She'd been fighting a cold for several days, but that hadn't seemed to slow her down. No, she wasn't on any regular medications, though he thought she might have been taking something for the sinus headache. But he couldn't be certain. He racked his brain for anything else that might help and came up blank.

Finally they covered Starr's body and carried her from the house. Like an automaton, Wade locked up the house, climbed into his truck, and drove over to Sophie's place. He trudged up the sidewalk to the run-down apartment. It took supreme effort to put one foot in front of the other. How could he tell those kids their mama was dead? They'd had so many struggles already in their short lives.

He rang the doorbell. Almost immediately the door swung inward, and two featherweight little girls swooped on him. "Wade! Wade's here! Wade's here!"

Oh, Father, give me the words. "Hey, half pint." He hoisted Danica up with one arm and pulled her seven-year-old sister close with the other. "Hey, Lacey Daisy. Hey, Dani Banany."

Beau waited in the wings, with the newly acquired aloofness of an almost-nine-year-old. "Hey, buddy." Wade put up a hand for their ritual "give me five" greeting.

Beau slapped Wade's hand hard with his small palm, then dipped his head and tossed Wade a crooked grin.

"Where's Mama?" Dani asked, looking past Wade to the front door.

He felt his spirit falter. "Come here, guys." He started toward the living room, Dani still in his arms, herding the other two beside him. "I...I need to talk to you...about your mama."

From the corner of his vision, Wade saw Sophie grab the remote and switch off the television. She leaned on the doorjamb.

He sat down on the shabby sofa and pulled Danica close, breathing in the sweet baby shampoo scent of her hair. Beau and Lacey stared at him, waiting. What were they expecting him to say? Surely not the terrible, devastating words he was about to utter.

He cleared his throat and fought for control. "Something happened to your mama this morning. We...we're not sure what yet, but she had an accident—or maybe she was sick—we don't know for sure," he repeated. "The...the doctor is going to try to find out. But your mama...she's in heaven now."

"She died?" Beau's voice cracked, and his face contorted. He stood like a statue for a long minute before his angry outburst split the air. "No! You're a liar!"

Wade reached for him, but Beau wriggled out of his grasp and ducked between the sofa and the wall, whimpering.

"I'm sorry, Beau. We don't know why, but, yes,...your mama died. And she's in heaven with Jesus now."

"You're a liar," Beau spat again. "I hate you! I hate Jesus! I want my mama back!"

Danica began to whimper. "I want Mama. I don't want Mama to go up to heaven."

Wade held the little girl close, drawing strength from her birdlike weight on his lap. Her thumb went to her mouth—a habit that had been broken last year before she started preschool. He pulled Lacey into the circle. She snuggled close to him, dazed and silent.

Wade looked to Sophie, wondering why she didn't help him out somehow. Why didn't she go to Beau, try to comfort him. Or talk to the girls? But Starr's sister stood apart, removed from the scene. Wade reminded himself that Sophie had just lost a sister. They were all in shock.

Gently Wade eased the little girls from his lap and went to kneel beside the sofa where Beau crouched. He put a firm hand on the boy's shoulder. "Hey, Beau. C'mon, buddy, look at me."

Beau jerked away from his touch.

"Come on, Beau. I need your help here. I know it's tough. I miss your mama too. But we need to be strong…for the girls. Help me out here, okay?"

Beau sat stock-still, but Wade could tell by the way his sniffling quieted that he was weighing his words.

Finally Beau turned, still squatting on his haunches. He glared at Wade. "Why did she die?"

Wade risked reaching out to him again. This time Beau let him rest a hand on his shoulder. "I don't know, buddy. I don't understand it either. We're just going to have to be patient until the coron—" He stopped himself, not wanting to have to define the word *coroner* for an eight-year-old.

He started over. "We'll have to wait until the doctor examines her. Then maybe we'll know more about what happened. You sit with the girls for a minute, okay? I need to talk to your Aunt Sophie."

Beau nodded, his eyes glazed.

Wade motioned Sophie to follow him into the apartment's tiny kitchen. "What do you want to do?"

"What do you mean?"

"About the kids. Do you think it would be best if they stayed with you tonight?"

Sophie started wagging her head before Wade even got the question out. "I don't have room for three kids here, Wade. You can see that. Besides, I can't afford to miss work." She looked at her watch. "I've already lost almost two hours as it is."

"You're going back to work?"

"The bills don't pay themselves, Wade."

"Sophie, your sister just died. You're not going to work." How could she be so cold? She must be in denial. "I'll take the kids to Starr's and stay there with them tonight," he told her. "But we're going to have some decisions to make tomorrow…about the kids. We need to decide where they're going to stay…" Wade heard his sensible words, knew they were true, but there was a surreal quality about the very air in the room.

And yet, as each second ticked off the clock over Sophie's cluttered kitchen table, he was clouted with a startling new thought about the reality of what Starr's death meant for him: There would be no wedding in August. The big house he and Starr had restored would never hold all the love they felt for each other. The children were orphans. And the house had no purpose now.

Every room in that house had been lovingly created for one of those children. The names of Beau and Lacey and Danica were painted in Starr's hand on the walls of the rooms. Just like the mocking couplet that crawled across the wall in the room he and Starr should have shared come summer.

Oh, Starr…Starr light, Starr bright. He placed a hand over his chest in a futile effort to ease the terrible ache that throbbed there.

"They need *you* now, Wade. They ought to be with you." Sophie's words brought him sharply back to the present.

He nodded. "Yeah. Okay. I'll take them back to Starr's and stay with them tonight. Who…who do we need to call?" Starr and Sophie's parents were dead. The sisters had no other living relatives. "What about Darrin?"

Wade had never given the children's biological father much thought. He knew only the little that Starr had chosen to reveal about Darrin Parnell. The man had been abusive to Starr and neglectful of the children. They'd divorced when Starr became pregnant with Dani because Darrin insisted Starr have an abortion. Starr had cut off all contact with Darrin even before the baby was born. She'd told Wade she hadn't even wanted child support from a man who wished one of their babies dead.

But Parnell needed to know now, didn't he? Wade stepped into the living room and looked at the children huddled there. Would Darrin Parnell have a claim to these precious children? He shuddered at the thought. And for the first time his heart fully acknowledged that Beau and Lacey and Danica Parnell belonged to him—Wade Sullivan. He couldn't have loved them more even if they were his own flesh and blood. Over the two and a half years he and Starr had known each other, these kids had become his. Not once had he seen them as a liability Starr dragged after her. No. They were a windfall. Just one more wonderful asset that was a part of Starr. One more gift she'd bestowed on him when, unbelievably, she'd offered him her love.

"Darrin won't care," Sophie said, staring blindly past Wade, bitterness thick in her voice. "He doesn't deserve to know."

Wade looked at her. He agreed with Sophie. But still, they ought to let him know. "Okay…we'll worry about it after the funeral," he said. "Right now these kids need some supper in their bellies. And they need to be home."

Sophie just nodded. While Wade rounded up the kids and their things, Sophie grabbed her purse and car keys off the kitchen counter. "I'll be at work."

The ten blocks to Starr's apartment was the longest drive Wade had ever made. In his rearview mirror, he watched the kids lined up in the cramped backseat of his pickup. They sat buckled in, hands in their laps, eyes boring into the back of the bench seat in front of them. Any other time, he and Starr would have spent half the trip turned around in their own seats trying to shush the chatterboxes.

He pulled into Starr's parking space, jumped out of the truck, and leaned his seat forward to help the girls with their seat belts. Beau's eyes met his, and Wade cringed at the emptiness he saw there.

He gathered them all into the apartment. Beau immediately switched on the television.

"Hey, bud, turn that off, please. Let's get supper going. You guys go wash your hands, okay?"

Beau complied, following his sisters down the hallway to the bathroom. Wade followed but stopped in front of Starr's bedroom. He looked through the doorway. Her bed was neatly made, as always, and the faint, musky scent of her perfume assaulted him. His legs threatened to buckle under him. He leaned against the doorpost, gathering his strength, sucking in air.

He heard water running, then the kids straggled from the bathroom one by one.

He went back to the kitchen with them and doled out assignments. "Beau, you and Lacey get the dishes down. Dani, you can help set the table." He pulled open cupboard doors, one after another, looking for something easy he knew how to make.

He should have stopped for pizza, but in a town the size of Coyote, he was bound to run into someone he knew. The news of Starr's death would be hitting the streets by now, and he could not face the sympathy and questions it would bring. Not yet.

Besides, it seemed wrong somehow that they were going about the business of life—making supper, as though it were an ordinary day. What would people think if they could see him now, acting as if everything were the same, as if his whole world hadn't just crashed at his feet the way Starr had crumpled on that floor?

He pulled two boxes from the cupboard over the stove. "How does mac and cheese sound?"

"I'm not hungry," Beau said.

Wade tousled his spiked hair. "I know, bud. I'm not very hungry either, but we need to eat. The girls, too. Your mama wouldn't like it if you guys skipped supper."

He checked the instructions on the box and put a pan of water on the stove to boil. "See what you can find in the refrigerator to go with this, would you, Lacey?"

She tugged the door open and came out with a large container of applesauce cradled in both hands.

"Perfect. Did you put spoons on the table? We'll need spoons for that."

Lacey nodded. Wade wasn't sure how long he could stand to look into their hollow, grief-stricken eyes.

When the macaroni was finished, he scooped generous helpings onto Starr's everyday Melamine plates and helped the girls with their chairs.

"Let's pray," he said, stretching his hands out to Danica and Lacey on either side of him. It was something Starr had started, holding hands around the table while they prayed. It had made them seem like a family. Tonight it only emphasized the gaping hole she'd left.

He waited for the children to bow their heads, then did likewise. "Heavenly Father, this is…a very sad day for us—" His voice wavered and he willed it to steady. "We ask you to help us get through this time. Father, we know you loved Starr even more than we did. We know she's with you now, and for that we thank you. But—"

There was a loud scraping of chair legs on linoleum. He looked up to see Beau slide off his chair and run from the room. Lacey and Danica looked to Wade to see what he would do.

"It's okay," he said. "Beau just needs to be by himself for a while." He bowed his head again. "Help us, Jesus. Get us through these next hard days. Be with us. Amen."

"You forgot the food," Lacey said, nodding toward her plate of congealed macaroni.

It would have been funny any other night. But Lacey's voice quivered, and her blue eyes brimmed. Wade thought he would lose it if she let those tears spill over. Quickly he bowed his head again, trying to keep his tone light. "Um, sorry, Lord. I guess I forgot something. Please bless this food for the use of our bodies. Amen."

He raised his head but avoided looking into any Starr-like eyes. Shoveling a forkful of tasteless macaroni into his mouth, he watched Dani from the corner of his eye. She picked up her fork with her right hand, and with her left, she beaded a piece of orange macaroni on each tine. Starr was— had been—a stickler about manners. She would have corrected Dani sharply. But tonight Wade didn't have the heart.

Not tonight. Not on this first night that Danica Parnell was an orphan.

Five

*I*t was almost forty-eight hours before the coroner finally released Starr's body to the funeral home. Wade was told it might be weeks before the autopsy report would be available. Early the morning of the funeral, Wade lay on the sofa in her apartment. He hadn't been able to bring himself to unmake her bed. Besides, he didn't think he could stand to sleep in the room her scent permeated, where every place he turned was some sweet reminder of her. The faded, embroidered denim jacket she often wore. The collection of funky sandals lined up in her open closet. He'd often teased her about that, calling her Imelda Marcos.

A dusky half-light filtered through the curtains, and the birds twittered cheerily outside the window, but Wade could not enjoy their song. He tossed restlessly, trying to fathom what his life would be like now, trying to sort out the mystery of his beloved's death. Had Starr been overcome by paint fumes as several people speculated? Or had she suffered some sort of seizure or stroke? Maybe he should have insisted that she take a couple of days off, get some rest. But he'd been too busy with his own concerns. He *had* warned her about keeping the room well ventilated while she was paint-ing, but she never took his warnings seriously enough. He should have opened the windows himself. He should have made sure she was safe.

The whole nightmare of that dreadful day swirled through his head, and for the first time since he'd sat beside her lifeless body, he allowed the tears to flow. He rolled over on his belly and let the pillow soak up his tears and absorb his convulsing sobs, lest he wake the kids.

Finally the sun nudged him from his bed, and he went down the hall to rouse Starr's children and help them dress for this darkest day of their lives.

Starr would have approved of the funeral they planned. Wade made sure there were hundreds of the daisies she loved so much. The florist had brought vases full for the altar, and the casket was draped with a huge arrangement of the yellow and white flowers.

The girls wanted balloons. So at the graveside, Wade and Lacey and Danica handed out two hundred helium-filled balloons. Beau refused to help them and stood with his arms folded over his scrawny chest, his mouth set in a straight line, his eyes downcast.

When the last "amen" had faded, everyone let go of their balloons, and the pewter Kansas sky was soon dotted with cheery spots of red and blue, lavender and pink, yellow and green. The crowd standing around the funeral tent craned their necks and watched in silence as the balloons floated heavenward.

A few minutes later people began to disperse, some offering final condolences to Sophie, Wade, and the children. Sophie kept glancing nervously at her watch and finally edged her way to the drive where her car was parked. Wade had tried to convince her to ride with him and the children, but she'd insisted on driving alone in the procession to the cemetery. Now Wade realized that she was worried about making her shift at the café on time. Starr's sister was drowning her sorrow in her work. Wade made a mental note to talk to her about it later.

The lines of cars parked along the intersecting gravel pathways slowly dissolved, and as the last of the mourners drove away, an eerie quiet descended over the cemetery. In the distance, the haunting song of a mourning dove pierced the air. Wade waited with the children, watching the sky in silence until the last dot of color disappeared from view.

"Now Mama's in heaven," Lacey declared with a bob of her chin.

Wade didn't try to correct her theology. If it took soaring balloons for Lacey's seven-year-old mind to believe that her mama was with Jesus now, he wasn't going to argue the point.

But as cheerful as the balloons were, as comforting as Pastor Leonard's reading of the Twenty-third Psalm was, and as filling as the hot casseroles at the church dinner earlier had been, an overwhelming cloak of heaviness blanketed Wade now. The initial, numbing shock of Starr's death and the comforting ritual of the funeral were over. Now they had to go on. Now they had to find a way to live without the woman who'd anchored all their lives with her seemingly endless love.

He felt light pressure on his arm and turned to see Pete and his wife, Margie. "Hey, man."

The two embraced.

"Are you going back to…Starr's apartment, or on out to your place?" Pete asked.

His friends' grief-pinched faces had the same effect on Wade as had the hollow look in the children's eyes. He wanted to fix things, to erase that expression from all their faces. But he couldn't.

"I think…I'll take the kids out to my place," he said, suddenly sure of his decision. "They've all got their rooms out there. They were excited about moving. I think Starr would have wanted them to be there."

"Then that's where they should be," Margie said.

"Wade." Pete's tone presaged his words. "Are you sure you want to do that? It'll just make it harder when they go."

"Pete, I don't have a choice. I'm all these kids have now."

"What about Starr's sister? Surely she could take them in."

"No. Even if she could, it—" He cleared his throat and tipped his head pointedly in the children's direction, lowering his voice. "It wouldn't be a good situation."

"What about their father?"

Wade winced. "No. He's not involved. I don't even know where he is. I'm the only father these kids have ever known."

Pete put a hand on Wade's shoulder and squeezed. "What can we do to help?"

Wade struggled to clear his mind. He needed to think what to do next. "Well," he said finally, "we need to haul the kids' beds out to my house. Starr already moved some of their toys—so they'd have something to play with when she was working out there—but there's a lot of other stuff to move before they can stay."

"No problem," Pete said.

Beau shuffled up to them, eyes to the ground, and Margie put her arm around him. "We should get something in these little tummies first."

Wade nodded, grateful for someone to tell him what to do.

"We'll drive through McDonald's and pick up burgers for everyone," Pete said. "We'll meet you back at the apartment."

Again, Wade nodded. "Come on, girls. Beau…" He started toward Starr's car, shepherding the kids in front of him. He'd decided it would be easier to haul the kids around in the car, but they'd need his pickup to move the beds out to the house. It was going to be strange jockeying two vehicles back and forth. He realized this was just one of the thousand little details he would need to work out in the coming days.

Starting Monday morning, he would work his way down the list of things he had to take care of. He needed to check on Starr's insurance, get everything cleared out of her apartment, find out what he should do about transferring the title of her car, and turn her keys in to the nursing home.

And then there were all the little things she'd left undone at the house. He'd cleaned up the paint mess in the bedroom the day after they'd taken Starr's body from the room, but there were still little projects all over the house that she'd started and never completed. Already, he ached for her every time he walked by some hint of her handiwork and realized it would never be finished.

He'd been staying at Starr's apartment with the kids since that first night. But out at the house, he was still camped out on the sofa in the spare room downstairs. It had served as his bachelor pad in the two years since he'd gotten far enough along on the house that it was livable.

Pulling up in front of Starr's apartment, Wade braked and put the car in park. Without a word, the kids jumped out and raced for the door.

"Hang on, Beau. The door's locked, remember?"

"Gimme the key." Beau held out his hand, not meeting Wade's gaze.

Wade had tried to overlook the boy's surliness the past few days, but he wasn't going to put up with this forever. He held tight to the keys. "You want to try that again, buddy?" At some point the children were going to have to understand that their mama was gone and he was all they had now.

Beau scuffed the toe of his too-tight dress shoe on the concrete. "Can you give me the key"—there was a long pause—"please?"

That would have to do for now. Wade put the key ring in the boy's out-stretched hand. Beau went to open the door without acknowledging him.

The apartment had never seemed so empty, though it still carried the faint scent of Starr's musky vanilla perfume and the vanilla-bean scented candles she liked to burn.

"You guys get your clothes changed, okay? Pete and Margie are bring-ing us something to eat in a little bit, and then we're going to move some stuff out to the house and stay there tonight."

"We're gonna sleep at the big house?" Lacey looked surprised.

"I thought we would. Is that okay with you guys?"

"What are we gonna sleep on?" Beau croaked. "There's no beds there."

"Pete's going to help us move the beds after we eat." He hadn't thought to ask what the kids wanted to do. Maybe they wouldn't want to leave the apartment.

But even Beau seemed happy about the idea. "I can help tear down the girls' bunk beds, Wade. I helped Mama put 'em together, so I know how to do it."

"That'd be great, bud. And you girls can take the sheets off all the beds."

Lacey and Danica nodded soberly.

"Now go on. Get out of your good clothes. And don't forget to hang things up after you—"

But they'd already disappeared down the apartment's narrow hallway.

The scent of wood smoke hung in the air, and the moon was just rising over the cottonwood trees when Wade walked Pete and Margie out to their car.

"Thanks, you guys. I appreciate it."

"Let us know if there's anything else we can do." Margie patted his arm.

"Are you sure you can handle this, buddy?" Pete asked, deep concern in his voice.

Wade let loose a sigh that had been building for four days. "I don't have much choice but to handle it."

"Wade, maybe you should call Social Services. They can help with situations like this. I'm sure there's a family somewhere who would love to have these kids."

"That's not true, and you know it, Pete. The kids would probably get split up. I won't let that happen."

Pete looked at the ground. Wade knew his friend only wanted what was best for him. But what he'd told Pete was true. He didn't have a choice. He loved Starr's kids. He sure wasn't going to let anything happen to them.

And yet he'd never felt more inadequate in his life for such a daunting task. He was terrified they could read the fear in his eyes now.

Pete grasped Wade's shoulder. "You'll do what you have to do. God gives what you need when you need it and not before."

"Yeah. I know that." It came out sounding more sarcastic than he'd intended.

"It's true, Wade."

"I know, Pete. I do know."

"You're sure you don't want us to stay here tonight?"

"We'd be glad to stay, Wade," Margie said. "Amber is at my folks' for the night…"

"No. Thanks. I appreciate the offer, but you guys can't be here tomorrow, or the day after that. We…we might as well get used to it being just the four of us."

Pete nodded. He put an arm around Margie and turned toward the car.

"We'll be all right," Wade called after them. "Everything will be okay."

He wished he could believe his own words.

"Wade?" Lacey's voice halted him at the door to her bedroom.

"What, sweetie?"

"Do you think Mama can see us right now?"

He let his hand drop from the doorknob. He'd wondered the same thing himself as he'd tucked Lacey in only moments ago. In fact, he'd found himself whispering a plea for Starr to help him know what to do. He should have been praying, but it was Starr he wanted to talk to. She was the one who knew Dani's silly bedtime ritual, and what to do when Beau got testy, and whether Lacey should have more than one glass of water before bedtime. He didn't think he'd find the answers to those questions in his Bible.

Wade went to sit on the edge of her bed and smoothed the flaxen hair back from her forehead. "I'm not sure, Lacey. But I think your mama knows you're okay. I think she's probably happy we're all here together in this house she loved so much."

Lacey nodded, looking lost in the twin bed that was half of the bunk-bed set she and Dani had shared in the apartment.

Wade leaned back against the pillow, anchoring his six-foot-two frame with one foot solidly on the floor. He pulled Lacey to the crook of his arm and pointed to the ceiling. Reaching to the desk beside him, he flipped on her lamp. "Look up there."

Lacey followed his gaze to the ceiling, where a ribbon of Starr's fancy calligraphy meandered. "Can you read that?"

Lacey read the words in her sweet, whispery seven-year-old voice. "Cast all your care upon Him, for He cares for you."

"That's what your mama would be saying right now if she were here."

"I miss Mama, Wade."

"I know you do, sweetheart. So do I. But we've got to remember that your mama is in heaven now. She wouldn't want us to be too sad." It was a trite, simplistic thing to say, but it was all he had to offer.

Lacey nodded slowly and looked up at him with trusting eyes. "Okay."

He kissed her velvety cheek. "I'll check on you again before I go to bed, okay?"

"Uh-huh," Lacey nodded.

Wade rolled off the bed and knelt beside it, turning off her lamp before he tucked her in one last time.

He left the door open a crack and went across the hall to Danica's room. When his eyes adjusted to the darkness, he realized Dani was cowering in the corner of her bed, clutching her threadbare "blankie" to her mouth. He flipped on the light.

"Dani? Honey, what's wrong?" He sat on the edge of her mattress.

She took a shuddering breath and lunged into his arms. "I'm scared."

"Hey, it's okay. What are you afraid of?"

"I don't wanna be all alonesome. I want Lacey to sleep with me."

"But I thought you were all excited about getting your own room."

She sniffled in reply.

Wade gave her a hug and gently pushed her away from him. "Just a minute. I'll be right back."

He crossed the hall to Lacey's room again. Maybe he'd been wrong to take them away from everything familiar so soon. But in truth, the children had spent as much time at his house as at their apartment this past month while Starr had finished painting. He stuck his head in the door. "Psst…hey, Lace? You still awake?"

"Uh-huh."

"Dani's feeling kind of lonesome. What would you think if we moved the beds so she—"

"Yeah!" Lacey shot out of bed and wrapped her arms around his waist. "Can we do it tonight?"

He laughed softly. "I'll get Beau to help. Your room or Dani's?"

"Whichever one she wants."

"Thanks, Lace."

Wade went to knock on Beau's door, which stood slightly ajar. "You still awake, bud?"

"Yeah."

"Dani's scared to stay by herself. Would you mind helping me move her bed into Lacey's room?"

Without a word, Beau threw off the blankets and swung his spindly legs over the side of the bed. He followed Wade out to the hallway, where the girls were waiting, their matching nightgowns sweeping bare, sun-browned toes.

"I'll go get my tools and be right back."

He took the stairs down two at a time, and by the time he came back with his toolbox, Beau had already dragged Danica's mattress into Lacey's room and was attempting to pull the heavy bed away from the wall.

"You girls stay out of the way," Wade said. "Here...it won't take but a minute to get this frame apart. Then we'll need you to hold the doors open for us."

The girls trotted out of the room, arguing about who would hold which door.

Wade and Beau worked together in silence, unscrewing the headboard and footboard from the heavy bed frame. Beau worked adeptly, having helped Pete with this same chore earlier. When they finally had the thing apart, they hauled the sections across the hall. It was awkward, but Beau was surprisingly strong, and between the two of them, they managed to get the bed moved.

Wade watched him surreptitiously while they put the bed back together. It felt good to be working side by side with him, to have a concrete assignment to complete. By the relaxed muscles in Beau's jaw, Wade thought he felt the same way. But when the last screw was tightened and Wade reached out to him, Beau turned away, making a show of wiping his hands on his pajama pants.

Wade touched the slight shoulder briefly. "Thanks for helping, bud."

Beau gave a noncommittal grunt and left the room, closing the door behind him. Wade started after him but stopped with his hand on the doorknob. Best to let it go. He'd give it some time. Beau would come around. He turned to help the girls put the sheets back on Danica's bed.

When Lacey and Dani were settled in their beds, he gave them one last tuck, planted a kiss on each soft cheek, and started to leave the room.

"Wade?"

Lacey's high-pitched voice clutched at his heart. He turned to face her. "What, sweetie?"

"If you and Mama can't get married now, can you still be our daddy in August?"

His heart lurched. He and Starr had told the children that after the wedding this summer he would be their dad "for real and for always."

He went to sit on Lacey's bed. "I don't know, Lace... I hope so," he hedged. "You get some sleep now, okay? It's late."

The corners of her mouth turned down, and she closed her eyes. It wasn't what she wanted to hear, he knew. It wasn't the reply he wanted to give. Never in his life had he felt so bereft of answers. But these children had had too many promises broken in their short lives. He couldn't risk adding yet another to the list.

The drive-through at McDonald's was backed up almost to the street. From the passenger seat beside Wade, Beau mumbled under his breath. "We're gonna be late again."

"I think we'll be okay, Beau." Wade mentally kicked himself for not making them a good, home-cooked breakfast. He put an arm on the back of the seat and turned to look at his brood. Beau had a crust of dried food at the corner of his mouth. The girls' mismatched outfits and unruly hair stared back at him, accusing. Eight days into full-time fatherhood, and he was already failing miserably.

The car inched forward, and Wade looked at his watch for the tenth time in as many minutes. "Everybody know what they want?"

"I want the same thing I always get, Wade," Dani chirped from the backseat.

"I don't remember what that is, sweetie. You're going to have to tell me when it's our turn to order."

Lacey let out an impatient breath. "She gets a Egg McMuffin with no meat and a orange juice, remember?"

In spite of his effort not to echo the exasperation in her voice, his words came out loud and gruff. "No, Lacey, I don't remember. That's why I asked."

Beau leveled an icy glare at him. "You don't need to yell at her."

"I didn't mean to yell." Wade took a deep breath. "I'm sorry, Lace. But, hey, you guys are going to have to give me a break here. I'm not your mama. I can't remember everything." Even as he spoke the words, he cringed inwardly. Why did he have to go and say that?

The dead silence in the car let him know his words had hit their unintended mark. He looked in the rearview mirror and saw the girls' bottom lips puckering in identical pouts. Beau stared out the window, his demeanor grown colder, if that were possible.

But there wasn't time to apologize. The car in front of them moved forward, and he pulled up to the speaker. "Okay, guys, give me your orders."

Beau turned and reached over the back of the seat to nudge Lacey. "Tell him I want the number three."

Great. Now Beau was giving him the silent treatment as well. Wade felt as if he'd been slapped. *Doesn't the kid know I'm doing the best I can under the circumstances? Surely Beau is old enough to understand that I am hurting too.* But this was no time to address the issue. They *would* be late if he launched into a lecture.

For once, they got their food in record time, and amazingly everything on the order was correct. Momentary peace reigned in the car while the kids downed their breakfast and Wade navigated the streets to Beau and Lacey's elementary school.

In front of the school, he eased into the line of vehicles dropping off students—mostly minivans piloted by moms, Wade noticed. Lacey gave him the usual good-bye kiss, but Beau got out of the car without a word, pointedly avoiding Wade's gaze.

Wade waved at the boy's bowed back as Beau disappeared into the crowd of students on the sidewalk in front of the school. Wade let a heavy sigh escape his lungs. He'd thought maybe he and Beau had reached a truce the night they worked together moving the bunk bed into Lacey's room. But if anything, Beau had pulled further into himself.

The impatient toot of a horn brought him back to the present. Waving an apology to the car behind him, he pulled into the street and turned in the direction of Danica's preschool. He looked at his watch again. He'd missed almost a week of work and had taken off early every night this week. Now he was taking another day off to tend to some of Starr's business. Pete couldn't have been more understanding, but this couldn't go on forever.

He would call Sophie tonight and see if she could start picking the kids up from school and watching them until he got off at five. It would tick her off royally. She worked the late shift at the café and usually fell asleep watching her precious soap operas every afternoon. But if he was going to survive this single-parent thing, he could not miss any more work.

He pulled into the preschool parking lot and jumped out of the car. Danica was already unbuckled and out of her seat by the time he got around to the other side. Taking her hand, he started up the walk, noticing her thumb was back in her mouth again. Now he knew how Starr had felt with the weight of the world on her shoulders. How did *real* fathers know what to do in situations like this?

He put a hand on Dani's head as they walked toward the entrance to the school. The tangled mess of hair beneath his palm reminded him again of his inadequacy. "Hey, sweetie…" He reached and gently nudged her hand away from her mouth. "Remember?"

She wouldn't look at him, but at least her thumb remained out of her mouth.

They arrived at the door, and he knelt on the sidewalk in front of her. "You have a good day, okay?"

She peeked out from under too-long bangs and nodded solemnly.

He leaned to kiss her good-bye, and Dani lunged for him and wrapped herself around him, almost bowling him over. Though she didn't shed a tear, Wade could feel the desperation in the thin arms around his neck. *He* was barely surviving without Starr—barely eating, hardly sleeping, just going through the motions. How in the world was this little girl supposed to make it without her mama?

Was he being selfish to think he could raise these kids on his own? Was he crazy to even try?

Seven

The Coyote Manor Nursing Home was a beehive of activity this time of morning. The cloying antiseptic odor of the place made Wade's nose sting as he walked past the reception desk and down the corridor. He nodded to a couple of nurse's aides he recognized as friends of Starr's. They flashed him a now-familiar expression—the one that said, "Oh, you poor, poor thing." He was sick of it. Even if he agreed with the sentiment.

As he rounded the corner to the wing where Starr had usually worked, he was awash in a strange sense of anticipation. He half expected to see her come bustling around the corner looking like a teenager in her colorful uniform, her blond ponytail bouncing. Surprised by its power, he shook off the feeling. But the lump lodging in his throat threatened to choke him.

He cleared his throat and approached the nurse behind the desk. "Is Mrs. Houstead in her office?"

"I believe so. You can go on down."

Wade went down the hall to the administrator's office. The door hung ajar a few inches. He knocked tentatively.

"Come in," a gruff voice shouted.

He'd met Velda Houstead at a couple of office parties Starr had dragged him to. Not many people intimidated him—certainly not many women—but this one did. Big time. A fact Starr had found amusing.

He stepped into the tidy office and dipped his head in greeting. "Good morning."

"Hello, Mr. Sullivan." The woman rose to her full six feet and reached across her desk to shake Wade's hand before taking her seat again. "I suppose you're here about Starr?" She screwed up her face in a way that was almost comical. "We…we're sorry for your loss. She was a good woman."

"Thank you. Yes. She was."

Mrs. Houstead straightened in her chair and tented her hands in front of her, suddenly turning all business. "Now. How can I help you?"

Wade dug in the pocket of his jeans and produced a key ring with two small keys attached. "I thought I should return these. I think they came from here." He laid the keys on the desk. "And I wanted to check on… I think Starr said she had some insurance through the nursing home?"

"That's right." Mrs. Houstead opened a desk drawer and put some papers on the desk in front of her. She did not, however, offer them for Wade's perusal. "The only beneficiaries Starr named in this policy are her children," the administrator said, "and since the children are all minors, the policy can only be paid to the children's guardian."

"That would be me," Wade said with a slight nod.

"Of course you'll have to contact our insurance carrier, but they will need legal proof that you are the children's guardian before they can cut the check."

He nodded again. "Can you tell me…the amount of the policy?"

She pressed her lips into a hard line. "I'm afraid that information is only available to the legal guardian of the children." She slipped a business card from beneath the paper clip that secured the sheaf of papers and held it out.

He took it, glanced briefly at the insurance company's information, and sighed. "Well, I am acting as their guardian. As you may know, their only living relative is Starr's sister."

"Oh? It was my understanding that the children's father was still living. I assume he has been contacted?"

Wade tried to think how to answer her. "Actually, his whereabouts are unknown," he finally said. "Um…would you happen to know what it takes to make me 'legal'?"

She shook her head vigorously, as though he'd just asked something preposterous. "I'm sorry. I wouldn't presume to advise you in the matter. I assume you would need to talk to someone in Child Protective Services. But perhaps Starr's sister should be consulted. It would seem she is the logical one to raise the children." She leveled her gaze at him, and her dark eyes bored through him. "Let me be frank with you, Mr. Sullivan. The amount of the policy is nothing to get excited about."

Was this woman implying that he was only interested in the money?

It was not in Wade's nature to be rude, but Velda Houstead's brash demeanor would have incited rudeness in Miss Manners.

He stood and strode from the office before he could say something he would regret.

As he walked by the day room, someone called out, "Hey there, young fella!"

In a nursing home full of people with dementia, he supposed it wasn't unusual to hear shouting, but since he was the only "young fella" around, he turned to see an elderly gentleman waving at him from a chair in the corner of the room. The man looked vaguely familiar.

Wade went over to the chair and bent to speak to him. "Hello there."

"Sit down," the man commanded.

Wade was in no mood to humor a senile old codger, but he sat uneasily on the edge of the vinyl-upholstered chair the man was pointing to.

"Aren't you the young fella that was fixin' to marry Starr Parnell?"

Now Wade remembered. Starr had introduced him once when he'd come to pick her up from work. "Yes," he said. "I'm Wade Sullivan."

"Jake Pedersen." The man offered a frail hand.

He shook it. "Jake. How are you today?"

"I'm mad, that's how I am today."

"Oh? Why is that?" What had he gotten himself into? He looked around the room, wondering how he could make a graceful escape. But the man's next words startled him.

"I'm mad because I'm still sittin' here doing nobody no good, and that sweet girl of yours is lyin' in the ground while her babies go motherless. Don't seem quite right to me. Does it seem right to you?"

Wade gulped and looked at the tiled floor. "No, sir," he said finally. "It doesn't seem right. But…Starr's not lying in the ground. She…she's in heaven now."

"You really believe that?"

"Yes, sir. I do."

"Well, how do you account for a God who'd do that to her kids? And to you?"

Wade shot up a quick prayer, struggling to keep his emotions in check. Was this some kind of cruel test? He cleared his throat, deciding honesty was the best policy. "I don't know the answer to that. I just know that God hasn't changed. He…He's still good."

Jake harrumphed. "Don't reckon she'd agree with that, do you?"

Suddenly Wade felt defensive for Starr. "She *would* agree, sir. She loved God. More than anything else. She never put her trust in anything down here because she knew this earth wasn't all there is to life."

The old man thought for a minute. "You think that's why she always had that purty smile on her face?"

"Yes." Wade swallowed hard, realizing how true it was. "Yes, that's why."

"Well, maybe. But don't sell yourself short, son." Jake Pedersen winked at Wade. "I think you mighta had a little something to do with that smile yourself."

Wade grinned through his tears. "Thank you for that, sir." He stood and shook the man's hand again.

"You be good to those kids, you hear?"

Wade nodded again and escaped to the parking lot. He climbed into his truck, bent over the steering wheel, and wept.

Ten minutes later he was on the highway, driving too fast and trying to squelch the sudden assault of fears that pelted him. What if they wouldn't name him the children's guardian? In spite of what Velda Houstead had implied, he didn't care one whit about the insurance money.

Starr had made pitiful little at her nursing home job. He knew how tight it had been for her and the kids—how she'd lived paycheck to paycheck. After they'd become engaged, he'd often helped out with her bills when she came up short at the end of the month.

He and Pete usually had more jobs than they could handle. If they had to, they'd hire help and take on an extra remodeling job or two. Pete had been bugging him to do that for a couple of years now anyway.

No, it wasn't about the money. But what if they took the kids away from him? Mrs. Houstead had implied that Starr's sister would be the best one to raise them. The woman obviously didn't know Sophia Braden. Okay, maybe she'd do as good a job as he was doing so far. To be honest, he could understand why people might have a problem with a single man raising three little kids on his own. Shoot, *he* had a problem with it. But what other choice did he have? No way in the world was Sophie going to agree to take the kids. And if she didn't, and if they took the kids away from Wade, they'd put them in foster homes. Maybe even split them up. He could not let that happen.

He thought of Jake Pedersen's words at the nursing home earlier. *You be good to those kids, you hear?*

He drove on, tapping the steering wheel idly as his thoughts churned. Maybe it was best to let the insurance money lie for now. Just leave things as they were. He didn't know what it took to try to get himself named as a legal guardian, but there was no sense stirring up trouble and risking losing the kids. They would be okay. They'd get along somehow. It was just going to take some time to adjust, that was all.

Eight

Dee Thackery blew a wisp of bangs off her forehead and pulled another file from the stack on her desk. Sometimes it seemed as though she spent half her life behind this desk. As much as she loved her job, she hated all the paperwork. She understood why it was necessary, but she'd much rather be working with clients.

She heard footsteps in the hallway outside her office and knew without looking up that they belonged to Clay Two Feathers. Like Dee, Clay had come to St. Joseph's Children's Services three years ago, fresh out of college and proudly flaunting his brand-new degree in social work. Except Clay had his master's now, and Dee was still trying to scrape together the money to go back to school. They'd both had that bright-eyed, bushy-tailed eagerness when they started out. She wasn't sure about Clay, but she knew her own perception of the world had been tarnished by the reality of what she'd seen in three short years serving as a foster-care social worker.

Yes, she'd made a notable difference in a few lives. And most of the time she felt fulfilled by her work. But sometimes the hopelessness she saw day after day reflected in the eyes of the people she worked with—the children especially—caused her to lose sleep at night. And if things were this grim in little Coyote County, Kansas, right smack on the buckle of the Bible Belt, what must they be like in a city like New York, or even just up the interstate in Kansas City?

Clay popped his head into her office. Though his bronzed skin owed more to weekends in the sun than to his heritage, he wore his surname proudly, as testified by the dark braid hanging down his back, and the beaded headband bearing Lenape tribal symbols and two small wild-turkey feathers. Dee had heard the story of how Clay and his brother had caught and plucked that poor tom more times than she cared to remember.

"Hey, Dee-Dee, you doing anything for lunch?"

Dee glared at him. "Clay, please don't call me that."

"Dee-Dee? Oh, sorry. I forgot." He shrugged. "I don't mean anything by it."

"I know you don't, but please stop."

"Okay, okay."

She felt like she was back in junior high school. Maybe she should be able to just let it roll off her by now. But every time someone used that nickname—which was entirely too frequently, considering she was almost thirty years old—it brought all the sickening memories back again. She shook off the pall the remembrance cast over her. It wasn't Clay's fault. He couldn't know.

"So what did you have in mind for lunch?"

"I thought maybe we could hit the deli. Today is bierocks day. Plus I've had a hankering for their carrot cake."

"You know, for a skinny guy, you sure do think about food a lot."

Clay shrugged and gave her that crooked grin that sometimes made her wonder if maybe she shouldn't take him up on his bimonthly invitation to go out with him.

Dee slid open the bottom drawer of her clunky metal desk and pulled out her purse. "The deli sounds good. But you've got to promise you won't let me order dessert."

"Oh, come on. Live a little, Thackery."

"Yeah, if I 'live a little' much more, it'll take a winch to get me through that door."

Clay rolled his eyes. "Oh, please. What is it with you women, always obsessing about your weight?"

Dee slammed the drawer shut, put her computer in sleep mode, and slid from behind her desk. "Okay, okay. Subject closed." She grabbed her jacket off the hook on the back of her office door and ushered Clay out into the hall.

"Your car or mine?" she asked when they got to the parking lot.

"Depends. How much gas is in yours?"

"Under a quarter of a tank."

"You win. Yours it is."

She shook her head, laughing. "Man! I've got to learn to play my hand better than that."

The line at the deli wasn't long, and when it was their turn, Clay ordered two of the deli's signature beef-and-cabbage-filled rolls and a huge hunk of carrot cake with thick cream cheese frosting. Dee opted for the house salad and a Diet Coke.

Clay led the way to a booth in the back, and they put down their trays and went back to fill their glasses at the self-serve fountain.

When they were seated, Dee bowed her head briefly to bless the food. She looked up to see Clay watching her.

"Amen," he said with a sober nod.

Even though Dee knew Clay didn't share her faith, there was no disrespect in his voice. Dee actually enjoyed their friendly arguments. She could count on a fair hearing with Clay, and she tried to afford him the same. She always ended a debate with Clay Two Feathers exhausted, yet feeling that iron had sharpened iron and her own faith had deepened.

Dee lowered her voice, ever conscious of the need for confidentiality when speaking about clients. "So what's happening with Matty Blakesly?" she asked over a bite of iceberg lettuce. She knew Clay had agonized over the fourteen-year-old who'd become a client at St. Joe's after his stepmother accused him of abusing his younger half sister. Matty firmly denied the allegations and had been suicidal since entering foster care.

"Exactly nothing," Clay said. "Sometimes I get so frustrated with how slow this system works *when it works...*" He ripped off a bite of bierock and chewed, as if exacting his revenge on the whole Social Services system.

"Well, at least you know the holdup isn't on your end."

"Yes, and that'll be precious comfort when Matty blows his brains out."

"Clay!" She reached across the table and put a hand on his arm. "That's not going to happen. I've worked with the Jacobsens before. They're a good family. Very conscientious. I know they're keeping a close eye on him."

"Yeah, well, you wouldn't believe how closely I was being watched when I wrapped that rope around my throat."

Dee winced. Clay's reasons for choosing this line of work were similar to her own. He was just a lot more open about it. As he liked to say, he'd walked in the moccasins of many of his clients, and he was determined they would get a fairer shake than he had from the system.

"So what are you going to do? It's too late for him to go back home now. He'd be worse off there."

"I know. I know…"

"And what if he's guilty?"

"He's *not* guilty, Dee." The feathers in Clay's headband bobbed with the adamant shake of his head.

She couldn't tell Clay that she felt little sympathy for Matty Blakesly. She knew the aftermath of his particular sin too well. Instead, she shook her head. "You can't save them all, Clay."

"Yeah, well, I'm going to die trying."

"And I admire you for that. But think about it. How many hours did you put in last week? Fifty? Sixty?"

He kept his eyes on the table.

"You need to take a break."

He looked up, and a familiar playful glint sparked in his dark brown eyes. "Oh yeah! Look who's talking. Miss 'I don't have time to go to the movies.'"

"Okay, okay…touché." She rolled her eyes but couldn't hide a sheepish grin.

He cocked his head and studied her for a few long seconds. "So…how about it? That new James Bond film is showing in Salina."

She groaned. "Not James Bond. Puh-lease."

"Okay. A chick flick, then. You choose."

"Man, Two Feathers! How did we get from Matty Blakesly to this in ten seconds flat?"

Clay twirled an imaginary mustache, and his laugh was that of the sinister landlord he'd portrayed in Coyote's community theater melodrama last summer. It was contagious. And besides, it provided a welcome detour from the dangerous territory they'd been traversing moments ago.

The mailbox held three mail-order catalogs, a slew of bills, and not much else. For the hundredth time, Wade wondered how Starr had ever managed to support three kids on her paycheck. Standing at the edge of the drive, he riffled through the stack of envelopes. The red and white logo of State Farm caught his eye. Starr's auto insurance. This would be the second bill he'd paid since her death. And though the car was registered in Starr's name, he'd paid the insurance the last few months before she died. They'd slowly been merging their finances in the months before the wedding.

They'd never wanted to have separate accounts after they were married. "What's mine is yours," Wade had told her a dozen times. And she'd always echoed the words back to him. The memory helped a little to assuage the twinge of guilt that nagged at him over her car. He probably ought to check into the legality of continuing to drive it. But if he did that, would someone check into the legality of his having the kids? He didn't want to think about it.

He walked back up the drive to the house, Shadow yipping at his heels the whole way. "You hungry, boy?" He gave the dog's ears a good scratch, then went into the house and tossed the bills on the desk in the kitchen. He'd take care of them tonight after the kids were in bed. "Beau?" he hollered.

Beau appeared in the doorway from the dining room. "Yeah?"

"Did you feed Shadow yet?"

"Oh. Um…I forgot."

"Come on, Beau. You know it's important to feed him every morning. That needs to be done before you leave for school. He about ate me alive. Go…please."

Beau rolled his eyes, but he went to the back porch. Wade heard him scooping dog chow from the big plastic bucket. Things weren't great with Beau yet, but at least they were better. Still, Wade sometimes feared that those big, luminous eyes hid a sorrow so deep it would gnaw Beau from the inside out, and Wade wouldn't know until it was too late.

He sighed and rummaged in the cupboards to find something to make for supper. He'd cooked for himself half his life, but it was totally different trying to keep the bellies of three kids filled up. He needed to go to the library and check out some books on nutrition. He knew growing children needed certain kinds of food. He bought four gallons of milk every week and tried to make sure they at least had a glass of orange juice before they left the house in the mornings, but beyond that, he wasn't sure what they might be lacking in their diet. He'd started to buy some chewable kids' vitamins on their last trip to the grocery store but put them back on the shelf when he saw the price.

The cupboard over the stove yielded some spaghetti. He thought there was half a jar of Ragu in the refrigerator—if it didn't have mold growing on it yet. He set the package of spaghetti on the counter and put a pot of water on the stove to boil while he browned some hamburger.

With the sauce simmering and the pasta boiling, he poked his head into the living room. Lacey and Dani were still engrossed in a video. Starr would have a fit if she could see how much television the kids watched. But it seemed like a good escape for them. And he was careful what they watched. When things settled down a little and they were feeling more at home with one another, then he'd crack down. But right now he didn't have the heart. Let them have their distractions. He wished he could escape so easily.

"Hey, girls?"

Two flaxen heads popped up in unison. Two pairs of blue eyes looked expectantly to him. Eyes so like their mother's. His heart did a somersault.

"Could you girls come and help me set the table, please?"

Without a word, Lacey punched the remote control. The television went silent, and the girls followed him into the kitchen.

"Lacey, you put ice in the glasses. Dani, you can set the dishes and silverware around the table."

He got the glasses down for Lacey and set the bin from the icemaker on the table in front of her. He pulled four heavy pottery plates from the cupboard—Starr's good dishes. Her wedding dishes, Wade suspected, though he'd never asked, and she'd never offered.

Sitting in Wade's truck after a softball game, she had poured out the story of her nightmare of a marriage one night last summer. She'd told him how Darrin Parnell had started slapping her around when she was pregnant with Beau. It got worse after the baby was born, and Starr could no longer spend every minute waiting on the man hand and foot. The slapping had turned to full-fledged beatings after Lacey was born.

The last straw had been when Darrin ordered her to have an abortion after she'd discovered she was pregnant with Danica. She'd left him then, and after Dani was born, she loaded up her kids and moved to Coyote because that's where Sophia was. Sophie was all the family Starr had left.

Starr didn't want any child support from her children's father. She didn't even want him to know where she was. "I don't care if I never see him again," she'd told Wade that night, bitterness thick in her lovely voice. After that, she had rarely spoken of Darrin Parnell.

Wade had halfheartedly tried to locate the man after Starr's funeral. After all, he was the children's biological father, and he had a right to know. But Wade had found no records of a Darrin Parnell in the Minneapolis area. He hadn't looked too hard beyond that. In fact, that had been the end of his search and the end of any thoughts of Darrin Parnell—until now.

"Wade! The ba-sketti's bubbling out!"

Dani's screech brought him back to the present. Smiling at her comical pronunciation, he grabbed the pot, set it on a cool burner, and tried to separate the gummed-together spaghetti with a wooden spoon. The starchy water sizzled on the still-hot burner, and the kitchen filled with its pungent odor.

The back door slammed, and Beau came in from feeding Shadow. "What's burning?"

"Wash up, buddy. Supper's almost ready." Wade leaned across the counter to open a window.

Twenty minutes later, they sat at the round oak table, the clanging of forks against pottery underlining the dearth of conversation. "Can I be excused?" Beau asked, not quite meeting Wade's gaze.

"I guess so. If you're full. Clear your place, please."

Beau carried his plate and glass to the sink, then headed for the living room. The girls followed suit, and soon the bluish flicker of the television danced off the kitchen walls from the room beyond.

Wade was left alone at the table with a heart full of memories, a heart that seemed to ache more deeply with every setting sun. He looked across the table, envisioning Starr smiling back at him, her eyes filled with love. Would this terrible longing he felt for her ever subside?

He blinked, and the unsettling image faded, leaving her empty chair to mock him.

Nine

With an unwieldy bundle of shingles slung over his shoulder, Wade climbed the ladder. He flopped the heavy package onto the roof. Already at nine in the morning, it felt like a frying pan up here.

"Hey, Pete, what do you want for lunch?"

"Whatever you're buying."

"Ha! That's a good one."

Wade's partner stopped hammering and glanced at his watch. "Is it lunchtime already?"

"Nah, I just like to get my taste buds revved up early."

"Anything's fine. We haven't had Mexican for a while. That sound good to you?"

"Sure." Wade sliced open the package of shingles with his utility knife, trying to conjure the aroma of spicy picante and queso. Unfortunately, the pungent asphalt and tar odor overwhelmed his imagination.

"You want me to go get it?" Pete asked.

"No, I will. Beau forgot his homework, and I need to run it by the school."

"Again?"

Wade grunted in reply.

"A real Mr. Mom, huh?"

He ignored Pete, but his frustration must have been apparent.

Pete laid down his hammer, sat back on his heels, and turned to Wade. "Hey, man. How is it going? Really."

Wade released a sigh that had been building steam for weeks. "I'm not cut out to be a mom, Pete. Shoot-fire, I'm not sure I'm even cut out to be a dad. Beau forgets his homework half the time. I've gotten I don't know how many calls from the principal. I don't know what to do with the kid." He pulled a handkerchief from his pocket and swabbed the sweat from his forehead. "It was so easy when she was here. She…Starr knew how to handle the kids. She always knew what to say, what to do. I'm floundering around like a cat in a swimming pool."

Pete shrugged. "Hey, this has been rough for the kids. And worse for you. Give it a little time. They'll come around." Pete fit a strip of flashing around an exhaust vent. "Beau's still giving you trouble, huh?"

Wade nodded. "At least he's not lashing out at me anymore. But he's so quiet it scares me. I'd like to think it's because he's doing better, but I'm not so sure. I wish I knew what was brewing in that head of his. I keep trying to think how I would have handled it if I'd lost my mom when I was barely nine. I'd probably have been mad too. Especially if I didn't have a dad."

Pete turned to look hard at Wade. "The kids *have* a dad, Wade. You're their dad in every way that counts."

"Yeah, well…I thought so before Starr died. Now I'm not so sure."

Pete went back to hammering, but a few minutes later Wade felt his partner's eyes on him.

"So they don't talk about it? About their mama?" Pete said.

"Not much."

"Maybe they need to. I don't know spit about psychology, but when Margie's mom died, the counselor at school told us Amber needed to talk about her grandma."

Pete's mother-in-law had died several months ago, and Wade remembered him talking about how difficult it had been for their six-year-old daughter at the time.

"Margie helped Amber make a little scrapbook about her grandmother." Pete said. "And we visited the cemetery together. I think it really did help her get through the grieving."

"Yeah? I guess I could take the kids to the cemetery. We haven't been back since the funeral."

They went back to the tasks at hand, but he thought about what Pete had said. Wade hadn't encouraged the kids to talk about their mother. Partly because *he* didn't want to talk about her. It hurt too much. Not that Starr wasn't in his thoughts from the time the sun crept over the horizon until he finally tossed himself to sleep in the wee hours of the morning.

But somehow it had seemed foolish to deliberately inflict the pain—on himself or the kids—of recalling the sweet smile that made her cornflower-blue eyes sparkle, remembering her contagious laughter, aching for her gentle touch.

But maybe he was wrong. He made a mental note to stop off at the flower shop after work. They'd have time to go out to the cemetery before it got dark.

"Have you ever heard what happened?" Pete's voice interrupted his thoughts. "Why she died?"

Wade stared at the handful of roofing nails in his palm. How many hours of sleep had he lost over that very question? "No. The autopsy report still hasn't come back."

"Good grief, what's taking them so long?"

He shrugged. "Just your typical government red tape, I guess. They said it might take six to eight weeks. To be honest, I have a feeling that report isn't going to tell us a blame thing anyway."

Pete cocked his head and wrinkled his brow. "Why do you say that?"

"I don't know. Just a gut feeling."

Wade had wasted too much time wondering what the coroner would find. It would likely be some technical, medical mumbo jumbo he wouldn't understand anyway. Everybody who knew anything about what happened speculated that Starr had been overcome by the paint fumes in the house or that she'd suffered a stroke or heart failure. But why or how it happened didn't much matter anymore. Knowing what killed Starr wasn't going to bring her back.

The evening breeze whipped Lacey's and Danica's fine, pale hair across their faces, but as they trudged across the cemetery, the little girls' fists remained tightly clutched around the bouquets they'd brought for their mama. Wade turned to make sure Beau was coming. The boy lagged reluctantly behind their little procession, but he, too, carried a fistful of flowers.

Dani tugged at Wade's jacket and looked up at him with soulful eyes. "Does Mama know we're coming?"

He opened his mouth to reply, but Lacey relieved him of the burden.

"Sure she does," Lacey said. "She's in heaven looking down on us right now."

Dani stopped walking and turned her pixie face to the sky. "Here, Mama! Look what I'm bringin' you." Her thin voice floated away on the breeze as she waved the daisies above her head.

"She can't hear you, dummy," Beau spat.

Even from across the grounds, Wade heard the antagonism in Beau's voice. He turned and hurried back to where Beau was. Putting a firm grip on the slight shoulder, he kept his voice low. "Hey, bud. Let her be. Maybe your mama *can* see us. And even if she can't, if it makes Dani feel better to think so, then don't take that away from her."

Beau wriggled out from under Wade's grasp and walked ahead of him toward Starr's grave.

The mournful call of a turtledove filled the silence as the four of them made their way to the new grave at the far end of the Coyote Municipal Cemetery just outside of town.

After four weeks the weeds had carpeted the mound of dirt over Starr's grave in green. The tiny metal marker from the funeral home was dwarfed by the headstones and monuments dotting the rest of the cemetery. How much did one of these stones cost? Money was incredibly tight. He'd almost eaten through their wedding savings, and the stack of bills kept piling up at an alarming rate. He still hadn't checked into Starr's insurance, but he was terrified of the slippery slope he might tumble down once he started the whole process of making things legal with Starr's children.

He probably owed it to them to collect on the insurance they had coming from their mother's employer. Heaven knew the children were doing without because of his reluctance to take care of the matter. But they'd done without all their lives. In fact, they were living high on the hog now, compared to what Starr had told him about their life in Minnesota after she'd left Darrin.

He wondered what would happen to the money if no one ever tried to collect. Would it be put in a trust fund for the children? That would be good. Then, at least, they would have it to pay for college. Maybe he could call Mark Forester from church. He was an insurance salesman. He might be able to feel him out for an answer without putting his situation with the kids in jeopardy.

"Wade?" Lacey tugged at the hem of his jacket.

Monday morning, he would check with a monument company and see if it was something they might be able to afford. The children could help him choose the design. Maybe it would help them feel they were a part of their mother's memorial.

"Wade?" Lacey's voice, insistent now, forced his thoughts to the present.

"I'm sorry, honey. What did you want?"

"What should we do now?"

Wade hadn't thought about what they should say or do when they got here. *Help me, Lord.* Surely God was sick to death of his three-word plea.

The four of them stood in a little knot on the windswept knoll. Finally he put a hand on each of the girls' heads. "Do you want to put your flowers on your mama's grave?" he whispered. Dani bent and laid her offering on the mound of dirt. She looked to Wade for approval, and he nodded, afraid to speak over the lump in his throat.

Lacey followed suit, placing her bouquet beside her sister's and kneeling to arrange the yellow ribbon that held the stems together. She straightened and stepped back to stand in Wade's shadow, looking so grown-up he thought his heart would break.

Beau stood gazing across the cemetery, unmoving. Wade nudged him. "Beau?"

Beau tossed his flowers on top of his sisters'. Lacey quickly bent and arranged the three bouquets in a row at the foot of the mound.

Beau looked up over his shoulder at Wade. "Can I say something? For Mama?"

Wade raised his eyebrows in surprise and swallowed hard. "Sure, bud. Say whatever you like. That'd be nice."

Beau cleared his throat and bowed his head. "I miss you, Mama. I wish…I wish you could come back. But I know if you're with Jesus, you probably don't want to come back. So…well, I guess that's all. Except—"

Beau glanced over his shoulder, and Wade detected a spark of mischief in his hazel eyes. He hadn't seen that gleam since before Starr's death.

Beau bowed his head again. "Except," he went on, "Wade's not a very good cook, and we're back to havin' macaroni and cheese all the time."

"Yeah, Mama," Dani chimed, playful accusation in her voice.

Lacey giggled, then covered her mouth and looked over her shoulder at Wade.

He winked at her and stifled a chuckle. "It's true, Starr," he said, bowing his head again. "I'm not as good a cook as you were. We miss you, but—" His emotions took him by surprise and his voice broke. He cleared his throat and started again. "We miss you, babe, but we're doing the best we can. And…I'll try to do better about the macaroni."

"Amen," Lacey said too loudly. She clamped a hand over her mouth, but the giggles escaped anyway, and soon they were all laughing—even Beau.

Wade rubbed his knuckles over the top of Beau's head. "You little tattletale," he teased.

His joke might have seemed irreverent here at Starr's graveside. But Beau's satisfied grin and the girl's bubbling laughter rewarded him. And he felt that somehow Starr might be laughing along with them.

Wade flung propriety to the prairie winds. He picked Dani up and slung her over his shoulder like a sack of potatoes. "And you, too! I ought to make you eat macaroni for breakfast!"

"No way!" Dani said. But she squealed with delight.

"Me, too," Lacey cried, lifting her arms to Wade, a wide smile splitting her face.

He scooped her up and flopped her over his other shoulder.

Suddenly it was like old times. They were teasing and laughing the way they had when Starr had been the instigator. It felt wonderful.

And at the same time, it cut like a knife. Because Starr wasn't here to instigate. Wasn't here to enjoy their playfulness. How she would have delighted in their laughter now. Would he forever be aware of the huge void she'd left in their lives? And would these children be scarred for life because of their tragic loss? Would every joyful moment like this be tainted with the memory of the loving mother they'd lost?

Yet, for tonight, the gift of laughter had been returned to them. He would dwell on that and be thankful. He'd take life's sudden twists as they came, knowing he couldn't face anything beyond today.

Ten

Sophia Braden tossed her purse on the derelict sofa and flipped on the television. The insipid drone of an afternoon talk show immediately soothed her jangled nerves. She was wiped out. She'd worked a double shift again, her second in as many days.

She couldn't take much more of these long hours, but she could sure use the money. She glared at the phone as she passed by, willing it not to ring. *So help me, if Wade calls me to pick those kids up from school again, I'm going to scream.* Maybe she just wouldn't answer it. What would he do then?

Immediately, her thoughts heaped guilt on her. She slumped to the sofa and kicked off her shoes. She couldn't blame Wade. Taking care of the kids single-handedly, he had to be as tired as she was. Oh, she'd helped him out from time to time, picking them up from school or keeping them for an hour or two in the afternoon so he could finish up a job. After all, they were her sister's kids, and she felt some sense of responsibility for them. She blew out a breath. Heaven knew Wade didn't have to take them under his wing. There were other options for their care.

She still wondered about his motives sometimes. But unless Starr had won the lottery or something and failed to tell Sophie about it, she couldn't imagine what would motivate a free man to take on three kids who didn't share one drop of his blood. Watching him over the last few weeks, she was starting to believe that Wade Sullivan might be the real deal.

She hadn't liked the man when Starr first started going out with him. Of course, in her twenty-seven years, she could count on half a hand the men she liked. Or at least the ones she trusted. But Wade had eventually grown on her. He'd been good to Starr.

Not like that good-for-nothing Darrin Parnell. She'd known he was trouble the minute she'd laid eyes on him. She knew his type all too well. She'd even tried to warn Starr, but her starry-eyed sister hadn't listened to her. She'd been duped by Darrin's good looks and charm. She'd fallen for his whole sorry act, and by the time Starr realized what a bum the man was, he'd given her three little mouths to feed and a few broken bones to remember him by.

Sophie had moved to Coyote before things got so ugly between Starr and Darrin. She hadn't realized how bad it was until Starr showed up on her doorstep in Coyote, bruised and battered, scared to death, kids in tow, having driven straight through from Minneapolis.

Sophie wanted to believe Wade Sullivan was different. She'd known him longer than Starr had. Wade and Pete came into the café for lunch at least once a week. She'd thought Pete was cute—until she found out he was married. Very happily married. Wade had made that quite clear when he recognized that she was flirting with Pete. At first she'd thought Wade was trying to turn her attentions his way. After all, he was one of Coyote's most eligible bachelors. But it soon became obvious that he'd only been defending his friend's honor. He wasn't interested in her—or in anyone else, it seemed. Rumor had it that Wade rarely dated and was perfectly content to remain single the rest of his life.

Sophie had actually been the one to introduce Wade and Starr, though not with any hint of an agenda. She'd sure never dreamed Starr would end up with the guy.

It turned out Wade, like Starr, was one of those semireligious freaks. Went to church every Sunday, talked about God like he actually knew the guy. Sophie was leery from the start. It all seemed a little too weird to her.

But she had to admit she'd never seen Starr so content. And unless her sister had become an Oscar caliber actress, Sophie thought Starr had been truly in love with Wade.

Not that it mattered now. Starr was dead. So much for happily ever after.

May was half over, and summer came in earnest on a wave of eighty-degree days. Wade and Pete were building a great room and master bedroom addition onto a Tudor-style house twenty miles outside of town. It was a fun project and a lucrative one, but the added commute each day meant the kids were in day care that much longer.

Sophie volunteered to keep them for a while after school and drop them off at day care before she started her evening shift. Most nights it was after six before Wade picked them up from the center.

Martina Blackwell, who ran the Coyote Childcare Center, had been very understanding of his situation, but after two weeks of picking up the children after the center was officially closed, he could sense she was growing impatient. He'd apologized till he was blue in the face, but Marty had a family of her own, and it wasn't fair for him to expect her to neglect her own kids while she took care of his.

More than anything, he hated that he only saw the kids for a few minutes as he hurried them through supper and tucked them into bed, only to get up and rush them off to school the next morning.

The only good thing he could see in the whole lousy situation was that the long hours and hectic schedule gave him little time to think about Starr. He'd lived almost two months without her now. Sometimes it seemed like forever.

On this warm day in May, Wade and Pete straddled the rafters of the addition, hammering away in companionable silence. The Kansas sun pierced a cloudless blue sky, baking the earth and them with it. Across the blacktop road, the wheat was already beginning to turn gold.

Wade had planned to knock off at five tonight. Beau had basketball practice, and the coach had scheduled a scrimmage with another team. It would be a good chance to spend some time with the kids. But when five o'clock hit, he and Pete were so close to finishing this phase of the project that he ignored his nagging conscience and kept hammering. By the time he parked in front of the day-care center on Coyote's Main Street, it was close to six-thirty. He'd be lucky if he had time for a shower before Beau's game.

He pulled open the front door and walked through the entry hall into the large playroom. A smile tugged at the corners of his mouth when he spotted Dani bent over a child-size table in the corner, her pixie face a mask of concentration.

As if sensing his presence, she looked up from the puzzle she was working. "Wade!" She snapped one last piece into place and ran over to wrap her arms around his knees.

"Hey, Dani Banany! Careful, sweetie. I'm all dirty. How was your day?" He rubbed his knuckles affectionately over the top of her head. "Where're Beau and Lacey? We need to hurry. Beau's got basketball tonight."

"He's out on the playground. I dunno know where Lacey is."

"Well, get your things. I'm extra late tonight, so we need to hustle."

Wade hurried through the back entrance to the playground. Beau and Lacey were both on the swing set, but when they spotted him, they jumped off and ran to meet him.

"Get your stuff, guys," he told them. "We need to grab some supper and get home. Your scrimmage starts in less than an hour, bud."

He looked up to see Marty Blackwell watching them through the large window in her office that overlooked the playground. He gave her a sheepish wave.

A pained expression pinched Beau's face. "Um…you're s'posed to talk to Miss Marty before you leave."

Wade cocked his head. "What about?"

Beau looked at the ground.

"Did you get in trouble?"

"He hit Taylor Bishop," Lacey volunteered.

"Shut up, Lacey!"

Wade put a hand on Beau's shoulder. "Hey…look at me. Is that true?"

Beau nodded reluctantly.

"Beau, why would you do that?"

He looked up at Wade, narrowing his hazel eyes and jutting out his chin. "That stupid Taylor was making fun of me!"

"Well, you don't haul off and hit somebody just because they're making fun of you."

"Yeah, but he said—"

Wade squeezed Beau's shoulder firmly. "Okay, okay…we'll talk about it later. Let's go see Miss Marty." He turned to the girls. "You two wait for us in the playroom."

He led Beau to Marty's cluttered office. Wade knocked on the doorjamb. "Marty?"

"Hi, Wade. Come on in." She looked at Beau and nodded a greeting. "Hello, Beau," she said, her tone turning stern. Sweeping away a stack of picture books from two straight-backed chairs in front of her cluttered desk, she motioned for them to take a seat.

"Did Beau tell you what happened?"

"Well, sort of. He hit a boy?"

The teacher nodded, looked at Beau, then back to Wade. "Yes, he hit Taylor Bishop. I've already talked to Beau about this, and he apologized to Taylor. But this isn't the first time this has happened."

Wade turned to Beau, who suddenly found something fascinating outside the window overlooking Main Street. Wade hadn't heard about a previous incident.

"I'm sorry, Wade," Marty said, "but if this happens again, I'll have to dismiss Beau from the day care. I'm sure you understand why we can't have other parents worrying about whether or not their children are safe here."

He cleared his throat and placed his palm on Beau's head. "I understand. We understand. It won't happen again. I can assure you of that."

She smiled and pushed back her chair, then rose and dipped her head before looking up at Wade. "I...I know this has been a very difficult time for you. It...takes some adjusting. I'm sure it will all work out, but...I'm sorry, Wade, you have to start getting here before six o'clock. I can't keep making an exception for you. And besides, it makes an awful long day for the kids."

Wade nodded, feeling like a child who'd been slapped on the wrist. "I know. And I'm sorry. I haven't been fair to you. Or the kids..."

"We'll see you next week, then." She bent to shuffle some papers on her desk and looked pointedly toward the door.

He stood, acknowledging her dismissal with a nod. He guided Beau out the door, and they went to gather the girls from the playroom.

On the way out of town, Wade stopped at the drive-through at McDonald's and ordered cheeseburgers to take home. The kids sat like robots in the backseat. They didn't even try to talk him into french fries or milkshakes.

They ate in the car on the way home, and when they pulled into the driveway, Wade gave out assignments. The kids did their chores without complaint. Wade kept an eye on the clock and tried to think what would be an appropriate punishment. He knew what Starr would have done. She would have made Beau miss his ball game. But it killed him to think of it. Truth was, he was as excited as Beau about the scrimmage. Before things got so crazy, he'd practiced for hours with Beau on the wobbly hoop outside the garage, passing the ball and working on shooting drills.

But the more he thought about it, the more he knew it was important for Beau to acknowledge that what he'd done was serious and that it would cost him something valuable. Besides, they were already going to be late.

Wade helped the kids clear the table, and while they put the dishes in the dishwasher—as much as it pained him—he went to call Beau's coach.

Eleven

Wade was exhausted. It had been another long day at work. He'd talked Sophie into keeping the kids on her only night off, and he and Pete worked till almost dark, trying to finish a roof before they got rained out.

It was already past bedtime when he picked the kids up from Sophie's, and they had been fighting like bantam roosters ever since. The kitchen sink overflowed with dirty dishes, and the house was a virtual pigsty. Wade had tried without success to get the girls to clean up the dolls and the hair ribbons strewn all around the dining room.

Beau had forgotten to feed the dog again. Wade sent him out to take care of Shadow while he attempted to herd two whiny towheads up to bed. He shot a quick prayer heavenward. "Don't let me kill anybody tonight, Lord." He prayed loud enough so the girls could hear him. And he tried not to let their raised eyebrows and exchanged glances get to him.

"But, Wade, I still have to finish my homework." Lacey's shrill soprano grated on his last nerve.

"You should have thought of that while you were watching television all night," he barked.

"But if I don't turn it in tomorrow, I'll have to stay after."

"Then you'll have to stay after." Why were they giving second graders homework anyway?

Lacey stomped a bare foot on the hardwood floor. "You're mean!"

"Sorry you feel that way. Now get moving."

Dani raced up the stairs and stood at the top of the landing watching them. Wade put his hands on Lacey's shoulders and pointed her in the same direction. He heard the back door slam and the shuffle of Beau's tennis shoes on the kitchen tile. "Come up right away, Beau."

"I know, I know. I'm coming." He muttered something unintelligible under his breath.

Had the kids acted like this with Starr? He couldn't remember. He tried to conjure up her image and failed. The realization pierced his heart. She hadn't been gone three months, and already he'd lost the nuances of her smile, her voice.

"Isn't she, Wade?" Dani's voice broke through his morose thoughts.

"What?" he snapped, immediately sorry when he saw her mouth turn down in a frown. "What did you say, Dani?"

"Isn't Lacey going to get in trouble if she does her homework in bed?"

"That's none of your business, Dani." He ushered the girls into the bathroom. "Now quit being a tattletale and brush your teeth."

Dani folded her arms across her chest and stuck out her bottom lip.

Oh, good. Now he had all three of them mad at him.

He got the messy, well-squeezed tube of toothpaste out of the medicine cabinet and handed it to Lacey. "You ladies brush your teeth. I'll go see if Beau is ready for bed."

As if on cue, Beau burst into the bathroom.

"Hey!" Lacey and Danica shrieked in unison.

"Get out, Beau! We were in here first," Lacey said, giving her brother a shove.

"So? You don't own the bathroom." Beau shoved back.

Wade stepped between the two camps. "Cut it out, you two. Beau, why don't you go get your pj's on first, and then you can have the bathroom to yourself."

Beau rolled his eyes and started out of the room, but a split second later, he popped his head back in. "Wade, I—"

Lacey lunged for the door and tried to slam it on her brother. Wade yanked her by the arm and pulled her away, but at that same moment, Beau hurled his weight at the other side. The wooden plane of the door swung into the bathroom with full force. The room exploded with a popping sound. Wade didn't realize what had caused the noise until he saw Dani lying in a heap on the floor, the pale green carpet turning red beneath her head.

Lacey screamed.

Beau clapped his hands over his mouth. "I didn't mean to! I didn't mean to," he cried, his eyes big, his voice climbing an octave. "It was an accident. Honest."

"Get out of the way!" Wade shouted. The children stood motionless between him and Dani. He pushed them aside and knelt on the floor beside her. By now she was moaning softly. Wade had never been so grateful to hear a child's cry. "Dani? Are you okay, honey?"

He knew head wounds often bled profusely, but he didn't like the size of the crimson stain beneath her. Turning her over, he tried not to gasp. Her whole face was covered in blood. Its brackish scent pricked his nose. As one, Beau and Lacey inhaled sharp breaths. Lacey started to cry.

"Hey," Wade whispered, locking eyes with Beau. "Take Lacey with you and go get me one of those extra large Band-Aids out of my medicine cabinet downstairs."

"Is she gonna die, Wade?" Lacey's voice quivered.

"No. She's not going to die. Go on now. Help Beau find the Band-Aids."

Wade reached up and grabbed a washcloth from the towel rack. It was a fancy embroidered one that Starr had hung there just for looks. Starr would kill him for getting blood all over her nice linens. He winced at the absurd thought, immediately dismissing it. Oh, if only she *were* here to rake him over the coals for it. To tell him what to do. She would have known how to handle this.

Cradling a whimpering Dani on his lap, he reached over the sink and ran warm water on the washcloth. He wrung it out as best he could and wiped off her face, trying to locate the wound. Pushing back a blood-soaked strand of blond hair from her pale forehead, he discovered an inch-long gash right at the hairline. He dabbed gingerly at the wound and cringed when it gaped open. A Band-Aid wasn't going to do the trick this time. This definitely needed stitches.

He heard a clatter on the stairway. Beau and Lacey rushed into the room, breathing hard. Beau held out a box of supersize bandages.

Wade covered Dani's forehead with the blood-soaked washcloth and tried to keep his voice level. "You guys go get your shoes on. I think we need to have the doctor take a look at Dani's head."

The two stood still as stones, eyes glued to their sister.

"Go on now. It'll be okay, but Dani might need stitches."

It was the wrong thing to say. Beau and Lacey gasped, and Dani cried harder.

Wade pulled her close, barely aware that his white T-shirt and the lap of his jeans were streaked with blood. "It'll be okay, sweetie. I'll stay with you while the doctor gets you all fixed up." He turned to her siblings. "Beau. Lacey. Get your shoes and meet me in the car."

They raced out of the bathroom, and he heard their bare feet slapping on the wood floor in the hallway. He peeled the wrapper from a Band-Aid and laid it upside down on his denim-clad knee, but when he pulled the washcloth away to apply the bandage, blood immediately seeped from the wound and trickled into her eyes. He swabbed at her face and tried again, but finally he gave up on getting a bandage to stay. He pressed the wash-cloth to her head. "Here, sweetie." He took her hand and placed it over the cloth. "Hold this here, and don't let go."

She complied without a word.

"Hang on now." Holding her close to his chest, he grabbed on to the sink with his other arm and pulled himself up. Cradling her against him, he went down the hallway and into the girls' room. Lacey had one foot up on the edge of her bed, tying her tennis shoe.

"Do you know where Dani's jacket is?"

Still working on a knot in her shoelace, Lacey motioned toward the rocking chair with her elbow. Wade pulled the little pink windbreaker from the arm of the chair, stood Dani in front of him, and helped her put her arms in the sleeves. The washcloth was almost soaked through with blood.

"Do I hafta get a shot, Wade?" Dani's voice was thin and wavering.

"I don't know, honey. Let's just wait and see what the doctor says. Everything will be okay." He lifted her back into his arms and turned to Lacey. "Hurry up, Lace. We'll be in the car, okay?"

"I'm coming." She picked up her other shoe and limped after him.

Wade ran down the steps and headed out the back door with Lacey right behind him.

Beau was already waiting in the car. "Is she gonna get a shot?"

Wade shook his head pointedly and aimed daggers at Beau over the top of Dani's head. Beau apparently got the message and slumped back into the seat.

Wade slid Dani from his lap onto the passenger seat and fastened her seat belt, then checked to make sure Lacey was buckled in beside Beau.

"You doing okay, Dani?" he asked as he flicked on his headlights and backed the car around.

She only nodded, still clutching the washcloth tightly to her forehead, but Wade didn't like the pallor of her skin or the blue tinge around her lips. He put the car in drive and pressed hard on the accelerator.

Twelve

With Danica in his arms, Wade motioned for Beau and Lacey to sit in the row of uncomfortable-looking metal chairs in the waiting area outside the emergency room. The place was relatively quiet on a Tuesday night. An elderly man sat looking at magazines and checking his watch. A janitor pushed a dust mop down the corridor leading to the hospital proper. Behind wide double doors, Wade could hear a child crying over the whir of some medical instrument. The calming voices of medical personnel floated beyond the pass-through at admissions.

He carried Danica up to the admissions desk.

The nurse glanced up from her computer. "Oh dear. What happened here?"

"She was on the wrong side of a swinging door," Wade said, offering the woman a grim smile.

The nurse leaned over the desk. "Let's see what we have."

Wade read her nametag: Faye O'Donnell. Cradling Dani in his right arm, he gently removed the washcloth from her forehead.

"Oh yes." Nurse O'Donnell nodded dispassionately. "That will need a couple of stitches. It's going to be a few minutes, though.

Dani turned her face to Wade's chest, whimpering. "I don't wanna get stitches."

He stroked a hand over her hair. "Shh...it'll be okay."

The nurse thrust a clipboard into Wade's free hand. "If you could fill out these forms while you wait. And I'll need to make a copy of your insurance card."

"Um...she doesn't have any insurance."

"Oh?"

"She was insured under her mother's policy, but"—he looked at the floor—"her mother...died."

"You haven't transferred her to your policy yet, is that it?"

Wade hesitated. He didn't want to get into this with a stranger.

"Maybe I'm misunderstanding," the nurse said, as if reading his mind. "You're her father, right?"

"No...actually...I'm not."

"Oh." The woman's eyebrows shot up again, and her tone became brusque. "We will need to get permission from her parent or legal guardian before we can treat her."

Wade rubbed at a spot on the carpet with the toe of his boot. "I'm her guardian. I'll give permission." It wasn't a lie. He *was* the kids' guardian. As Pete had said, he was their father in every way that counted. He just hadn't made it legal. He wondered how much they'd stick him for an emergency room visit.

"How did you say this injury happened?" A note of suspicion had crept into the woman's voice.

From the fringe of his vision, Wade saw Beau stiffen. He looked at Beau and tried to communicate with the lift of his brow that he wasn't going to rat on him. Beau's narrow shoulders rose as he took in a deep breath, then bowed his head.

"It was an accident," Wade explained. "The kids were getting ready for bed, and Dani just happened to be standing in front of the bathroom door at the wrong time. It was an accident," he repeated, not looking at Beau.

The nurse gave no response as she rolled her chair back from the computer desk. With Dani still in his arms, he bent to watch through the low pass-through window as the nurse disappeared into a curtained alcove of the emergency room.

Wade straightened and went to sit across from Lacey and Beau, who were quietly looking at magazines. Dani was limp in his arms, and he rubbed a hand over her cheek to assure himself she had only dozed off. He filled out the forms, then took the clipboard to the admissions desk.

A few minutes later, Nurse O'Donnell stuck her head through the double doors. "You can bring her in now, Mr. Sullivan."

Brother and sister looked up at Wade expectantly.

"You two be good out here now, you hear me? This might take awhile. And stay put."

They nodded solemnly.

When Wade stood, Dani started awake and began to whimper. Carrying Dani in his arms, he followed the nurse through the doors and into one of the partitioned alcoves. She left them there without another word, closing the curtain behind her. A younger nurse came in to take Dani's temperature and blood pressure. She allowed Dani to remain on Wade's lap while she took her vitals and recorded the results.

They waited another ten minutes before a young female physician peeked into the room. "Danica Parnell?"

"Yes," Wade replied. "Right here." He held Dani out like an offering.

"Why don't you set her up here on the examining table." The doctor's nametag read SARAH WELLING, M.D. Wade didn't think the girl could be a day over thirty. But he liked her bedside manner. Her smile was genuine as she knelt to meet Dani's gaze.

"May I take a look?" she asked Dani after glancing over the chart.

Dani nodded warily and pulled the washcloth away from her forehead.

The doctor inspected the wound. "Ooh, looks like that door got you good."

Dani nodded, warming to the young woman a bit.

"Here, I'll take that washcloth. Oh, that's a fancy one." Dr. Welling turned to Wade and winked. "Did you have to grab the prettiest washcloth in the house, Daddy?"

Dani grinned. Wade shrugged and smiled back, although the physician's remark made him think again, painfully, of Starr.

While the kind doctor lined Danica's forehead with a neat row of spiderlike sutures, Wade let Starr's daughter grip his hand until it hurt and scream until he didn't think he could stand it. He let the guilt wash over him, knowing it was deserved. He tried without success to swallow the bitter taste in his mouth. *I'm sorry, Starr. I'm so sorry...*

Twenty-five minutes later, he and Dani emerged from the treatment room. She had a large bandage and a happy-face sticker to show for her trouble, and Wade had the promise of a medical bill he'd be doing well to pay off before Christmas.

The kids were all asleep in the backseat of the car by the time Wade pulled into the driveway.

Wade carried Danica up and tucked her into bed. He sat a while, patting her back. She was asleep in minutes, her soft breathing a profound relief. He prayed sleep might come as easily for him.

But it was not to be. After a hot shower, he settled in on the sofa bed in the den. The monstrous old Hide-A-Bed was six inches too short for his tall frame, but it had been his "cot" since the day he'd started restoring this old house. The master bedroom upstairs sat empty and waiting for him to move into it, but he still couldn't bring himself to occupy the room he should have shared with Starr for the rest of his life. The door remained closed on the four walls that bore Starr's last ironic message to him: "Grow old along with me! The best is yet to be." Even the thought of it mocked him now.

Wade sighed in the darkness and trained his eyes on the high ceiling overhead. A tear slipped down his stubbly cheek, and for a moment he couldn't think where the dampness had come from. He swiped at his face. How long would thoughts of Starr still bring him so quickly to tears?

"Oh, Starr," he whispered into the emptiness, "I'm failing miserably. I don't know how to be a father to these kids. I need you. I need you so bad." He turned his desperate plea into a silent prayer.

The clock in the foyer chimed a muted *bong, bong, bong…* Midnight. *Oh, God, help me. I miss her so much.*

"Couldn't you give us at least a week, Karen?" Dee Thackery struggled to keep the desperation from her voice. "I honestly don't know where the kids would go at this point. You know what a shortage we have—"

She held the phone away from her ear as the caller cut her off with an unrelenting, desperate "no."

"All right, all right. I understand. Someone will be out to pick up the children tomorrow morning. Around ten. Please have their things ready."

Dee eased the phone back into its cradle and sat staring into oblivion, wondering where in the world the two preteen siblings who had been living with the Xaviers would go.

Next to paperwork, these kinds of challenges were Dee's least favorite part of her job.

She'd worked successfully with this particular foster home for almost two years now. Ben and Karen Xavier had taken in more than a dozen children during that time, often having three or four foster children under their roof at any given time. But Willy and LaShondra Green were high-maintenance children, and the Xaviers felt they were jeopardizing the other child in their care—and taking time away from their own family. Now Dee was stuck finding new placements for two children who were not easy to place.

She put her computer to sleep, stood, and stretched. Sighing, she went across the hall and poked her head into Clay Two Feathers' office. "Hey, I'm in a major pickle."

Clay looked up from his computer. "Oh yeah? What's wrong, can't decide what to have for lunch?"

"I'm serious, Clay. I need some advice."

He took his hands off the keyboard and gave her his full attention.

"Karen Xavier just called, and she wants us to come and get the Green kids."

He looked at her askance. "Right now?"

"Tomorrow," Dee said, recounting her conversation with Karen. "I have no idea where we're supposed to put those kids."

Clay shook his head. "Man, that hurts to lose the Xaviers. You don't think they're getting out altogether, do you?"

"No. They still have Kimbra Johnson. It's just… Well, you know what the Green kids are like. I can't really blame them."

"No…that's for sure."

"You don't have any brilliant suggestions, do you?"

He drummed a ballpoint pen on the top of his desk. "What about Lonni Barker?"

"Full to overflowing."

"That new family over on West Douglas…the ones with the seven-bedroom house?"

Dee shook her head. "Same thing."

"Doesn't leave many options, then, does it?"

Reading his thoughts, she rubbed her temples and sighed in frustration. "Clay, I'm not letting these kids go to Vickridge."

Vickridge Children's Home was a last resort as far as Dee was concerned. The institution was well-staffed and well-run, but it housed mostly incorrigibles—older kids who were all too proficient teachers for any innocents unfortunate enough to land there. No way was she subjecting Willy and LaShondra to that place. They had enough problems as it was. She'd take them home with her first.

Clay shrugged, but the look he gave her conveyed empathy. "I don't know what to tell you, Dee. I wish I could help."

"I know," she sighed. "I'll figure something out. I just needed some moral support."

Clay looked at his watch. "It's almost lunchtime. How about I support you morally over a cheeseburger from Junie's?"

"I can't, Clay. I've got to figure out where I'm going to put these kids. I guess I'll call Betty Graffe at SRS and see if she has any ideas." Did Clay even detect the exasperation in her voice? Sometimes the man was too laid back for his own good.

Clay pressed his palms on the edge of his desk, pushed his chair away, then raised well-muscled brown arms in a languorous stretch. "Dee, you've got to eat sometime. Go call Betty, alert Jim at Vickridge if you need to, then give me a buzz, and I'll take you to lunch. I'll go with you to pick up the kids tomorrow if you want."

It wouldn't break her heart to have Clay along for support, but it wasn't exactly kosher office procedure for both of them to go on a call. Besides, she knew Clay had ulterior motives. She'd encouraged him more than she should, as it was, accepting lunch invitations and even a movie date once. She loved the man as a friend, but she was afraid he saw much more than friendship in their future.

"Thanks, Clay, but—no thanks."

She felt a rush of guilt for the look of dejection that washed over his face.

He heaved a sigh and rolled his chair back up to his desk. "Suit yourself." He slid out his keyboard drawer and started typing.

Dee stared at him for a long minute, started to say something to smooth things over, then changed her mind, and turned toward the door.

She went back across the hall and plopped down in her chair, pulling the telephone close. She had enough problems without worrying about Clay Two Feathers.

Thirteen

The queue at the pharmacy was half a dozen customers long. When it was finally Wade's turn, he paid for the cough syrup and practically ran out to his pickup.

It always made him a little nervous to leave the kids home alone—even if it was just for a few minutes. But Lacey's cough had definitely gotten worse since yesterday morning. He didn't think she was running a fever, and she didn't seem to be in pain, but he wanted to nip this in the bud. He didn't want to go through another hassle with the hospital about the insurance.

Wade headed out of town with a sigh of relief. A few minutes later, as he pulled into the driveway, his pulse quickened as he noticed a white Chevy Cavalier parked in front of his house. Anyone who knew him always came in the back door at his place.

A little dart of alarm went through him when he noticed that the Cavalier's license plates bore the word "Official" over the distinctive design reserved for state-owned vehicles. What was going on? Had something happened to one of the kids? He'd been gone longer than he intended. He glanced at his watch and cringed. It had been almost thirty-five minutes. But surely if anything was wrong, the kids would have called him on his cell phone. He pulled the phone from his belt and checked to make sure it was turned on. The display screen flashed reassuringly.

He parked the truck around back and went in the entryway, taking the short flight of steps up to the kitchen two at a time. When he opened the door, the smell of last night's scorched macaroni and cheese hit him, and he noted with chagrin that the kids had not cleaned up the kitchen like he'd asked. The sink overflowed with dirty dishes, the counters were littered with the makings of supper, and he crunched this morning's Frosted Flakes with every other step.

Voices floated from the living room, and he went to investigate.

A dark-haired woman of about fifty was perched on the edge of the sofa, leaning in toward Lacey and Danica, who nodded solemnly at her. Beau sat apart on Wade's recliner, watching impassively.

Wade cleared his throat. The woman started and jumped to her feet. "Oh…hello, Mr. Sullivan." She stuck out a hand. "I'm Betty Graffe with Coyote County Social and Rehabilitation Services."

Wade deposited the package from the pharmacy on an end table and offered his hand tentatively. His face must have revealed his confusion because the woman said, "You don't have any idea why I'm here?"

Wade shook his head. Had someone reported that he'd left the kids alone? But who would have known? He'd only been gone half an hour. He'd heard of other people who left children younger than his alone for hours at a time after school. "Is there a problem?" he finally asked.

She ducked her head briefly, turned her back to the kids, and lowered her voice. "Our office received a call that there might possibly be children in need of care at this residence. We are obligated to check out such reports. I wonder if you can shed any light on why a report might have been made?" She wet her lips and waited.

"I don't understand," Wade said. "Who made the call?"

"I'm sorry. We're not allowed to give out that information." She flipped a page of the yellow legal pad she carried and referred to a sheet of paper tucked inside. "The report I have was filed on June 4. The caller apparently had some concern about the fact that your children are without health insurance, and there was some question about the cause of an injury one of the children was treated for."

Someone from the hospital emergency room must have reported him. Wade was sure the social worker could see his heart pounding through his shirt. "Everything's fine here. I can assure you the kids are well taken care of." His mind raced. What had the "informant" told SRS?

"I'd like to visit with the children for a few minutes," Ms. Graffe said, her legal pad ready for note taking. "Alone, if I could, please."

"It looks to me like you've already done that," Wade said.

"Actually, I was waiting for you to get back." She looked accusingly at her watch, then met his gaze. "Could I have a few minutes with them, please?"

Wade looked at the floor and wagged his head. "No. I'm sorry, but I'm not comfortable with that. Anything you have to ask them you can ask in front of me."

"Mr. Sullivan…we find that children usually feel more free to speak honestly if their parent"—she looked at him pointedly—"or guardian… isn't present."

His stomach clenched. "What exactly are the accusations against me?"

"Oh, I didn't mean to imply that any accusations have been made—certainly not against you, personally. Someone just expressed concern that perhaps the children were not being properly cared for and—"

"Well, if that was the accusation, then it *was* against me personally because I'm the one caring for them." He struggled to keep his temper in check and tipped his head toward the knot of towheaded children staring up at them with curious faces. "I think you can see they are doing fine."

She nodded concession. "Mr. Sullivan, I realize that many times when SRS makes a home visit, people fear we are here to remove the children from the home. I can assure you that is not why I am here today. Please, Mr. Sullivan, it will make things much easier if you'll just allow me to speak with the children. It won't take but a few minutes."

Wade felt something akin to panic rise within him, but he looked pointedly at the kids, who were taking in the exchange with wide eyes. "I'll be right out here." He indicated the wide arched doorway leading to the combination dining room and kitchen. "Please…be gentle. Especially with this one"—he reached to cup a hand over Dani's head—"she's tender-hearted."

Betty Graffe held up her palm and shook her head. "Of course, of course… It's not my intention to upset anyone."

Wade cleared a pile of wrinkled, clean laundry off one end of the sofa and motioned for her to be seated.

"Hey, guys, Ms. Graffe is going to ask you some questions, okay? I'll be right in here." He hooked a thumb toward the dining room, but lingered for a long minute before leaving the room. He turned off the fan whirring in the corner, then sat down at his desk near the doorway with a clear view to the living room. Idly shuffling some papers on the desk, he caught the social worker's eye. He wanted her to be fully aware that he intended to listen to every word.

He couldn't see the children's faces from where he sat, but he watched Ms. Graffe's profile as she leaned in toward them, her pen poised.

"I'm a social worker," the woman said in a teacher's patient voice. "Do you know what that is?"

Silence. But Wade could picture the little girls' shiny bangs swinging as they shook their heads. And even without seeing Beau's face, he could detect the studied indifference in his demeanor.

"My job is to help children and make sure they are safe," Ms. Graffe continued. "I have a few questions I need to ask you, and then if you have any questions for me, you can ask afterward. So you might be thinking of some questions for me, okay?"

Ms. Graffe sat back. "Do you live here with Mr. Sullivan?"

"We live with Wade," Dani said.

From his seat at the desk, Wade couldn't help but smile. He saw the social worker's cheekbones rise in a grin, as well. But just as quickly her expression turned serious again.

"Now, who all lives here in this house? You three children and Wade?"

"Uh-huh," the children chorused.

"Anybody else? What about your mommy?"

"She died," Beau spat out, sounding angry all over again.

"Oh, I'm so sorry. When did she die?"

"Mama and Wade were gonna get married, and he was gonna be our daddy," Lacey said between raspy coughs. "Now Wade's sad all the time."

Wade felt his throat tighten. He thought he'd hidden his feelings from the children better than that.

"I'm sure he is sad. What about your daddy?"

"Wade's gonna be our daddy." Dani said.

"I mean your real daddy. Your birth father. Do you know what a birth father is?"

Silence.

"Was your mommy married before?"

"We're not s'posed to talk about him," Beau said in a monotone.

"Oh? Why not?"

"He wasn't nice to our mama," Beau said, his voice almost a whisper. Wade had to strain to hear.

Ms. Graffe leaned closer. "Oh?"

"He hurt Mama. He hit her all the time."

"Oh, my! I'm sorry to hear that. Did he ever hit you or your sisters?"

"He never even saw Dani," Beau said. "Mama got us away from him before she was born. He was mean."

Wade was shocked to hear how much Beau remembered.

"Does he sometimes visit you…here at Wade's?" Ms. Graffe asked.

"Uh-uh," Lacey said. "He lives far, far away."

"I see. Well…how do you like living with Wade?" She turned toward the archway and sneaked a glance at Wade.

He met her gaze head-on.

"It's okay. He's cool." This from Beau.

Wade was surprised and pleased to get this vote of confidence from what was, of late, an unlikely source.

"Wade's nice," Danica said.

"Does Wade have a girlfriend?"

Wade saw three heads wagging in response.

"Our mama was his girlfriend," Lacey offered. "But now she's in heav—" Her words were lost in another deep fit of coughing.

Betty Graffe gave her a look of concern, but she made no comment and went on with her questions.

"Can you tell me where Wade works?"

"He fixes up houses and roofs and stuff," Beau said.

"And who takes care of you while Wade is at work?"

Beau gave an impatient sigh. "We go to school while he's at work."

"And after school?"

"Sometimes we go to day care, and sometimes we go to Aunt Sophie's." It sounded as though the usually uncommunicative Beau was warming up to the interrogation.

"When I got here today you were alone in the house. Does that happen a lot?"

Danica recited the rules. "We hafta be good and stay in the house and not talk to strangers."

"But you answered the door and let me in," Ms. Graffe reminded them.

"Are you gonna tell Wade?" Lacey whispered, in a way that told Wade she'd been the one to let the woman in.

The social worker ignored the question. "How long were you here by yourselves before I came this afternoon? Have you been alone since you got home from school?"

"Aunt Sophie picked us up from school," Beau said.

"Oh. Well, does Wade leave you here by yourselves very often?"

"Whenever we hafta stay by ourself he always says"—Lacey notched her voice down an octave in imitation of Wade—" 'I'll be back in fifteen minutes. You guys call my cell phone if you need me.' "

"I see…" Betty Graffe riffled the pages of the legal pad and made a few notes. "Can you tell me what happens when you get in trouble?"

"You have to go to the principal's office," Beau said.

She smiled. "No, I mean when you get in trouble at home. With Wade."

"He's strict," Beau snorted.

"What do you mean by that?"

"He doesn't let you get away with anything. We have to do what he says. And do our chores."

"What happens if you disobey—if you do something you're not supposed to?"

"We get in trouble," Dani piped up.

Good for you, Dani girl. Don't make it too easy on the old gal.

"What does that mean exactly—in trouble?"

"Huh? It means *in trouble.*" Beau's tone of voice suggested he thought Ms. Graffe might be a few aces short of a full deck.

"What I mean is, if you get in trouble, do you get punished? Like… do you get sent to your room or—"

"Oh yeah…" Beau said, vibrato in his voice. "Stuck in your room for the whole day."

"And extra chores," Lacey said.

"Or a spankin' if you're really bad," Dani added.

"Not me," Beau said. "I'm too big for spankings."

"Don't count on it," Wade hollered from his place at the desk.

"Hey!" Beau sputtered, obviously unaware Wade had been listening in. But the feminine chuckle that followed made Wade hopeful he'd wormed his way into Betty Graffe's good graces.

But her next question sent a flash of heat through his core.

"Danica, I noticed you have a bandage on your forehead. Can you tell me what happened?"

Wade heard Beau's sharp intake of breath, and his heart went out to the boy.

"I got hit by the baffroom door," Dani said.

"How did that happen?"

Silence.

"Do you remember what happened?" Ms. Graffe prodded.

"Uh-uh," Dani said. It sounded as if her thumb had gone into her mouth.

Wade jumped up from the desk and went to stand in the archway. "Ms. Graffe, could I speak to you for a minute please?"

Her brows shot up, but she laid her legal pad on the sofa and went to meet him in the dining room.

He lowered his voice. "The kids were messing around getting ready for bed, and Beau shoved the bathroom door open. He didn't know his sister was on the other side. He feels bad enough about it as it is. I assure you it was an accident, and I'd appreciate it if you wouldn't say anything else about it."

The social worker nodded, but Wade couldn't read her expression. She went back into the living room and talked with the children for a few more minutes, asking about the sleeping arrangements in the home and what kinds of things they ate.

Finally she came out to the dining room. "Would you mind taking me on a quick walk through the house?" she asked Wade.

Taken aback by the request, he shrugged and held out an arm Vanna White style. "Be my guest."

Fourteen

The social worker walked slowly through the downstairs rooms of Wade's house, as though she were a potential buyer at an open house. What was she looking for? Did she think he had a torture chamber hidden in the pantry? Wade led her back out to the living room.

She glanced around the room, peeked into the spare room where Wade slept, then indicated the stairway at the end of the room. "May I?"

"Go ahead."

"Oh. Well…I'd feel more comfortable if you'd show me around."

Wade shrugged. But with the children in tow, he led the way up the stairs. The four of them stood clustered at the top of the stairs, looking at one another in silence as they listened to the staccato of Betty Graffe's shoes on the hardwood floors. They watched as she walked systematically from room to room, poking her head into each before emerging, apparently satisfied.

"Are we in trouble?" Lacey whispered to Wade.

The hoarseness in her voice reminded Wade that he hadn't had a chance to get any cough syrup down her. Wade put a hand on her shoulder. "No. Everything's fine. It's like Ms. Graffe said: They just want to be sure you kids are safe." He wished his thudding heart would take a cue from the calmness he managed to plant in his voice.

"Do they go to *everybody's* house?" Beau asked.

Wade dodged the question, putting a finger to his lips as the social worker's footfalls echoed down the hallway.

Betty Graffe followed them downstairs to the front door, then turned to give Wade a tight smile. "Thank you, Mr. Sullivan. I know things come up, but…you really shouldn't leave the children alone—especially out here in the country. They're still just a little young for that, even if it is only for a short time."

He didn't acknowledge her condescending warning.

Lacey started coughing again, deep barks that hurt him to listen to.

Betty Graffe looked at Lacey with concern in her eyes and knelt down to the little girl's eye level. "That sounds like a mean cough. Do you care if I check your forehead for a fever?"

Lacey nodded shy approval. The woman laid the palm of her hand gently on Lacey's forehead. She spoke quietly to Wade over Lacey's head. "It feels like she might be running a fever. Have you had her to the doctor about that cough?"

Anger rose in Wade, and he replied through gritted teeth. "I was out getting medicine for her when you arrived. Are you about finished here?"

She leveled her gaze at him, her tone turning frigid. "She really ought to see a doctor."

Wade took a deep breath and forced a civil tone. "I took her temperature this morning before she went to school, and she wasn't running a fever then. The cough just started yesterday, but I'll watch it closely."

"That's good. Now, do you have any questions I might answer before I leave, Mr. Sullivan?"

"I have a lot of questions, but I don't think you're going to answer them."

She drew back and put a hand to her throat. "Well…I'll certainly try."

"I just want to know why somebody thought I wasn't taking good care of the kids."

"I don't know what this particular person's reasons were, but most likely they simply wanted to make certain the children are safe. Can you think of anyone who would make a report like this for malicious reasons?"

He shook his head, anxious to be rid of her.

Lacey started coughing again.

Betty Graffe took Wade's cue and moved toward the front door, putting a hand on the doorknob. Then, seeming to change her mind, she turned back to him. "I'm satisfied that the children aren't in any danger, but I would like to make some recommendations that I think will be helpful to all of you. First of all, you should get Lacey to a doctor and make sure that cough isn't anything serious. If insurance is a concern, then you should probably check into getting some coverage on the children." Her eyes softened. "Lacey mentioned that you are sad all the time. That's completely understandable after what you've been through, but the children have had a serious loss in their lives too, and they need to know they can depend on you."

He nodded and gave a noncommittal grunt.

"I would like to check back with you just to see how things are going in a week or so. Would it work if I came around six thirty, say, a week from tonight?"

He shrugged. "Sure. I guess so." He was not crazy about the thought of an ongoing relationship with this woman.

She jotted a note on her legal pad, and Wade opened the door for her. He waved a terse farewell as she headed for her car.

After the Cavalier disappeared down the blacktop, Wade closed the front door and looked down to see that his hands were trembling. Composing himself, he turned to the children and made his voice bright. "Who wants to eat at the café tonight?"

The distraction worked its magic, as Wade knew it would. The children danced around him, excitedly reciting menu choices that didn't include macaroni and cheese or Happy Meals.

That night Wade lay on the sofa bed in the spare room, watching the moon spread patches of gold over his blankets. As disturbing as Betty Graffe's visit had been, the overriding emotion it wrought in him was fear. For the first time, he faced the facts head-on: Someone might actually be able to come and take the children from him.

He looked toward the ceiling. *I can't do this alone, God. You've got to help me.*

Immediately he was enveloped by a tangible sense of God's presence, and he knew he was not alone. At the same time, he was hit with the finality of Starr's death. She wasn't coming back. The life he had with Starr's children now and for the future would be whatever he made of it. And though he hated to give Betty Graffe any credit, she was right: He needed to be strong for the kids.

Maybe he had been in denial like Pete said. Pete and Margie had told him it was part of the grief process. He'd written the notion off as a bunch of psychobabble. But maybe they were right.

There were things that needed to be done—should have been done long ago. For the children's sake and for Starr's, he had to pull himself together.

The kitchen was still in chaos the next morning, but in spite of the anxiety over the visit from SRS, things looked better in the light of day.

Wade smiled as he surveyed the scene: Lacey and Dani still in their pajamas, Beau dressed, but with a cowlick the size of Texas and a face that looked like it hadn't seen a washcloth in a week.

The three of them slurped milky spoonfuls of Cap'n Crunch and stared at each other across the table. His family. His own little family. Who'd have ever thought it of the incorrigible bachelor he'd been? He could scarcely remember that man.

"Come on, you guys, finish up here, or you're going to be late for school. Do you girls have your clothes picked out?"

"I do," Dani said over a mouthful of cereal. "But Lacey doesn't."

"I do too," Lacey shouted.

Though her voice was still a bit raspy, the medicine seemed to have worked its magic. Wade hadn't heard her cough once last night, and he'd been awake enough of the night to know.

"Do not," Dani shot back.

"Stop lying, you—"

"Girls!"

That one word quieted them. They settled back over their cereal bowls.

Wade went to the phone in the living room and dialed Sophie's number. She finally answered on the tenth ring.

"Hey, Sophe. Sorry if I woke you up. I wanted to let you know that I had a little visit from SRS last night."

"What?"

He told her about Betty Graffe's visit. "I think everything is okay, but I thought you should know, just in case they call you or something."

"Are you worried?"

"No. Not really. But I'm taking the day off. I need to take care of some stuff. Talk to the insurance agent…"

"Yeah…okay. Well, what am I supposed to do if SRS calls?"

"Just tell the truth. I don't think they're going to call, Sophie. I…just wanted you to know. Just in case…"

Wade hung up, making a mental list of the things he needed to take care of. The kitchen was quiet now, and he could hear his brood upstairs, tromping back and forth to the bathroom, slamming doors, and shouting occasional warnings to one another. The typical sounds of morning in this house.

Yes, they were good kids. And unless he was totally missing something, they were thriving. Sure, they missed their mother something fierce. They wouldn't be normal if they didn't. But they were making the best of it.

Beau was a concern, but he was older and understood the ramifications of his mother's death better than the girls did. And he had difficult memories of his father that the girls did not. It was perfectly understandable that he was struggling.

He went to pour a second cup of coffee. Looking around the kitchen, he cringed, seeing it as Betty Graffe must have seen it on her little tour of the house yesterday. One more thing to add to his to-do list.

Maybe he was fooling himself into thinking he had what it took to make a home for three children. Sure, love counted for something—and he loved these kids with everything in him—but love couldn't clean the floors or make a home-cooked meal or pay the insurance.

The front doorbell interrupted his conflicted thoughts. He glanced at the clock over the stove. Nobody came calling this early in the morning.

Hoping the children hadn't heard the bell, he put his coffee mug in the sink and went into the living room. He couldn't help but think of the official state car that had been parked in his driveway last night. Pushing the drapes aside, he looked out. The car parked in front of the house was an older-model maroon Monte Carlo. He unlocked the front door and opened it.

A man in a white dress shirt and tie stood there with a shiny leather briefcase in hand. Wade rarely had salesmen call out here in the country, but it looked like he was about to be offered the deal of the century.

"Can I help you," Wade asked, his mind racing to think of an excuse to get the peddler off his porch.

The man ran a hand through neatly combed hair. "I've come for my kids."

Fifteen

Wade stood with his mouth agape, staring at the stranger on his porch.

"I've come for my kids," the man repeated.

The words hit him like a cement truck. He'd never seen photographs of Starr's ex-husband, but this had to be him. Wade could discern Beau's defiant attitude in the sharp gaze of the man's hazel eyes. Even his hair, like Beau's, was the color of old straw. There was no doubt this was Beau Parnell's father. And Lacey's. And Dani's. Wade's stomach churned.

"You *are* Wade Sullivan, aren't you?" the man asked, shifting the weight of the briefcase in his hand.

"Yes…I'm Wade. And you must be Darrin Parnell."

"That's right. I've come for my children," he said again, taking a step toward Wade and straightening to his full height.

Wade, too, stood taller, taking small satisfaction in the fact that he was a good three inches taller than Parnell. His mind scrambled for some magic words that would make this man disappear from his porch—from his life. "I'm sorry…" *Give me the words, Lord. What do I tell him?* He cleared his throat and started again. "I'm sorry, Mr. Parnell, but the children live with me now. You gave up your rights to them long ago."

The hazel eyes darkened and narrowed. "Don't tell me what my rights are, Sullivan. I know my rights, and I want my children."

Wade glanced back into the house, praying the kids would stay upstairs until he could get rid of the man. He stepped out onto the porch, forcing Darrin Parnell to take two steps backward. "If you think I'm going to hand these kids over to you knowing what I know about you, you're crazy."

"And just what is it you think you know about me?"

Wade pulled the front door closed and lowered his voice. "I know you abused their mother. I know you wanted her to get rid of her baby. Do you want to hear more?"

The reminders seemed to take some of the starch out of Parnell. He took another step backward, glancing over his shoulder, presumably to gauge where the edge of the porch was. But his voice held venom as he jabbed a finger in front of Wade's face. "The only thing you need to know is that those kids are my flesh and blood, and I'll do whatever it takes to get them back."

"Then I suggest you get started." Wade despised the tremor in his own voice.

Parnell glared at him. "I'm not going to make a scene in front of the kids, Sullivan, but you haven't heard the last of me. I'll have the sheriff out here after school, and I expect you to have their things packed and ready to go. And while you're at it, I'll need the bank accounts transferred over to my name."

A glimmer of hope sparked in him at the words. "There are no bank accounts, Parnell. If that's what this is about, you can go back to Minneapolis. I have Starr's car. You're welcome to it. It's all she left."

"That's a lie, and you know it. I heard Starr worked at some nursing home around here. Insurance is my business," Parnell said, "so don't try to tell me she didn't have a life insurance policy through her employer."

He must have talked to Sophie. Had she led him straight out here? His mind raced, trying to think how to respond.

Wade had no desire to reveal to this man that he'd been too paralyzed by grief and fear to try to collect on the policy on the children's behalf. The less Parnell knew, the better chance Wade had of taking care of all this before the man could make good on his threats. If he lost the kids over his inaction, he would never forgive himself.

Wade felt the rumble of footsteps on the stairway inside the house and heard Beau calling his name. He reached behind him for the door handle, leveling his gaze at Parnell. "Get out of here before I call the police."

Darrin Parnell stood firm, his eyes boring a hole in Wade. Before Wade could turn and escape into the house, the doorknob was jolted from his hand, and the door flew open behind him. Wade turned to see Beau standing there, his hair slicked to one side, the stubborn cowlick standing at attention. Beau looked from the man on the porch to Wade, then back again, to stare into the face of the father he hadn't seen in almost four years.

Parnell suddenly turned into a candidate for Father of the Year. "Beau! Hey, buddy! How's it going?"

Beau seemed scarcely able to squeak out a word, but when he finally did, that one word cut to the quick of Wade's heart.

"Dad?"

"Beau? Is it you, boy?"

Wade watched as Beau took a tentative step toward Darrin Parnell, his biological father. The man met him more than halfway and knelt down to pull him into a fierce bear hug. Wade swallowed the bile that rose in his throat.

Beau pulled away quickly, his face a mask of confusion. "What are you doing here?"

"I came to get you and your sisters...to take you home with me."

"But—"

Parnell smothered Beau's words, drawing him close again, holding the tousled head tight to his broad chest. "We'll worry about the details later. You go on to school, and I'll be back this afternoon to pick you and the girls up."

Beau pulled away. "But...where are you taking us?"

"Home, son. Back home to Minneapolis."

"But...what about Wade?"

A flicker of malice crossed Parnell's face. "We'll talk about it later. Right now I'm going back into town to take care of some things."

Beau looked up at Wade with an expression that Wade thought must mirror the bewilderment and fear in his own eyes.

The front door exploded open again, and the girls charged out onto the porch. As one, they stopped short when they saw Parnell, who was still kneeling on the porch with his arms around their brother.

Lacey and Danica looked up at Wade, their doelike eyes asking him silently whether this stranger was friend or foe.

Beau turned to the girls. "It's our dad," he said simply.

Parnell shifted on one knee and reached out to gather the girls in with Beau. But they both drew back, scrambling to Wade's side to cling to his legs.

Wade put a hand on each blond head. "It's okay, girls. Beau's right. This is your father."

Parnell struggled to his feet. "Hi there. You probably don't remember me." He stretched his arms toward them awkwardly, but the girls retreated again and hid behind Wade.

Of course they don't remember you, Wade thought bitterly. *Lacey was a baby when they escaped your cruel clutches. And you never met Dani. She wouldn't be here if you'd had your way.* It was all he could do to keep from giving his thoughts voice. But he bit his tongue and pulled the girls closer. "We'll talk later," he told Parnell pointedly.

"Yeah. Right," the man grunted.

Without meeting Parnell's gaze again, Wade turned and herded the children into the house. Inside, he closed the door firmly behind him.

"Was that really our daddy?" Lacey asked. Her puckered brow tugged at Wade's heart. "Yes, honey. It was. Come here, all of you."

He glanced out the window, watching Parnell's car leave the driveway in a cloud of dust. When the car turned onto the main road, Wade led the children over to the sofa. "Sit down here for a minute. I need to talk to you guys."

"But we're gonna be late for school," Beau protested.

Wade took a deep breath and massaged his temples. "I don't think you're going to school today," he said.

"Why not, Wade?" Dani looked up at him, her big blue eyes pools of puzzlement.

He didn't have an answer. Every instinct told him to pack a suitcase, load the children into the car, and drive as far south as Starr's car and his bank account would take them. "Listen, guys. Your father has come all the way from Minneapolis and he…he wants to spend some time with you."

Beau's eyes narrowed. "He said he wanted to take us back there."

"I know, I know." Wade paced to the window that overlooked the drive, then back to the sofa. "Do you want to do that, Beau?" he asked suddenly. "Do you want to go with your dad?"

He'd never considered that the kids—Beau especially—might wish to be with their father. He dismissed the thought as quickly as it had come, regretting he'd given it voice.

"No," Beau said, rubbing the toe of his tennis shoe on the corner of the rug. "I don't want to see him unless you can come too."

"Well, *I* don't—" Lacey's words were eaten up by a spasm of coughing that sent a chill through Wade. "I don't wanna go," she said, when she finally caught her breath.

"Me either," Dani said. Her lower lip quivered, and she burst into tears.

"Hey, hey…it's okay." Wade scooped her onto his lap and cradled her in his arms. "It's going to be all right. I'm not going to let anything happen to you guys."

"Why can't you go with us, Wade?" Beau asked.

"It just…" He scrambled unsuccessfully for an answer that would make sense to a nine-year-old. "It doesn't work that way, bud. I have my business with Pete to take care of. And the house. I can't just up and leave," he finished lamely.

"Then I don't wanna go with him. Can't he just visit us here?"

"I don't know, Beau. I don't know." He thought for a minute. "Maybe…maybe it would be best if you guys go to school today, after all. Yes…" Gently, he slid Dani off his lap and stood. "Go get your things. I'll take you to school."

"We're already late," Beau said.

"I know. I'll explain to your teachers."

All three of them stared at him.

"Well? Come on… Go get your stuff. It's okay, guys. I'll have everything sorted out when you get home."

Reluctantly the children moved toward the kitchen, gathering jackets and backpacks along the way. But Wade could see they didn't fully understand—or fully trust—his words. He shot a desperate prayer heavenward that by this afternoon he could give them an honest reason to trust him.

With its gleaming mahogany-paneled walls and high-dollar furnishings, the waiting room of Locke & Locke, Attorneys at Law, looked like something straight out of a fancy architectural magazine. Classical music wafted at a barely audible volume from invisible speakers in the ceiling.

Wade sat on the edge of a burnished leather sofa rubbing his hands together, taking in the elegant space, and breathing in the rich scent of fine leather. Rather pretentious for a lawyer in a tiny county seat, he thought. The sofa alone probably cost more than he made in two months. How would he ever afford the attorney's fees?

But he had no choice. Feeling like a coiled spring, he pushed himself off the sofa and went to the narrow window that overlooked the parking lot. "God," he whispered, "You've got to let me keep my kids. Please, Lord, I can't lose them."

The *tap-tap-tap* of the receptionist's typing stopped abruptly, and he realized his whisper had blossomed several decibels. Biting his tongue, he paced the length of the room half a dozen times before sinking back onto the sofa. He buried his hands under his thighs on the smooth leather of the sofa and willed himself to sit still. His prayer became a silent litany. *Please, God. Please, God. Please…*

Finally the receptionist called his name. He rose and followed her down a long corridor and into an office as swank as the reception room.

Frank Locke finished signing some papers on his desk, then looked up with a white-toothed smile and pushed away from his desk. He stood half-mast and reached across the desk to shake Wade's hand before sitting back down. "Please…have a seat. How can I help you, Mr. Sullivan?"

Wade took the chair the lawyer indicated. He cleared his throat and took a deep breath. "I need to find out how to get custody of my fiancée's three children." He cleared his throat again and swallowed hard. "She died in March. The kids have been with me ever since, but I…never bothered to get legal guardianship of them."

"I see," said the attorney, putting an elbow on his desk and resting his chin on his fist. "Are there other relatives who might want custody of the children?"

Wade looked at the floor and scuffed his shoe on the plush carpeting. "That's why I'm here. Their father showed up unexpectedly on my doorstep this morning, wanting to take the kids back to Minneapolis."

Frank Locke leaned back in his chair, as though dismissing him. "Well, I'm sorry, Mr. Sullivan, but that's most likely his right as the children's biological father."

"You don't understand." Wade sat forward and rested his elbows on Locke's desk. "Starr—the children's mother—divorced him more than four years ago. The girls don't even remember him. The man has never paid one red cent of child support."

"But now he suddenly wants to take the children to live with him?" Locke sounded skeptical.

"So he says. He's never even met the littlest one. He tried to force Starr to have an abortion when she found out she was pregnant with Dani. He was—"

"Wait," Locke interjected, holding up a hand. "How old are the children now?"

Wade ticked off names and ages. "He abused Starr for years. Beat her."

Locke looked up with interest. "Did he ever harm the children?"

It was an angle Wade hadn't thought of. For one desperate moment, he was tempted to lie. Starr had told him she finally got out of the marriage because she was afraid the children would be Darrin's next targets. Wade had always taken that to mean Parnell had never laid a hand on the kids. He told the lawyer as much now.

"I see. Unfortunately, it might be better for you, Mr. Sullivan, if he *had* abused the children. Of course, that would be difficult to prove unless the police were involved."

Wade's hopes rose another notch. "I know the police were called to the house in Minneapolis at least one time. Starr's sister made the call."

"Did the sister witness the beatings?"

"I'm not sure. She saw the results. I know that."

"Would she be willing to testify to that fact? And perhaps to his treatment of his children?"

"I think she would. She lives here in Coyote now. Sophia Braden is her name."

Locke slid a gray legal pad in front of him, took a slender pen from his shirt pocket, and wrote for several minutes. Wade tried to make out his notes across the desk, but the lawyer's handwriting looked like some sort of cryptic shorthand.

"What is Mr. Parnell's occupation?"

"He was working for an insurance company last Starr heard. And I remember he said something about insurance being his business." Wade remembered the fancy briefcase Parnell had been carrying this morning. "He was in sales, I think. But like I said, she hadn't heard from the guy in over four years."

Frank Locke raised an eyebrow. "Is there an insurance settlement or an inheritance or some financial motive that might be prodding Mr. Parnell's sudden interest in the children?"

The thought had crossed Wade's mind, but he hesitated to broach the subject now for fear it would expose his own negligence. "I know Starr had a life insurance policy with the nursing home she worked for. I...I never really pursued it. I didn't figure it would amount to much."

The attorney clicked the pen absently. "Apparently Mr. Parnell thinks otherwise. You don't know how much the policy is worth?"

Wade shook his head.

"What we need to do is file a guardianship action in district court. At the least, we can hope for the judge to order that the kids be placed in your legal custody. Since they've been with you since their mother's death, chances are good the judge will be receptive to that. But the biological father will have to be notified of your filing, so we must assume he will protest it."

"And what if he does?"

"Then it will go to court. If we can prove he abused the children or even that he was abusive to their mother, the judge will probably at least give you temporary custody. But if this guy wants to fight it, I have to warn you that the courts tend to favor the biological parent."

A thread of fear crept up Wade's spine. "But Parnell's coming for the kids today. In just a few hours. What if he tries to take them? Forcefully?"

"Believe me, that would only help your case, Mr. Sullivan. He'd be a fool if he tried. But if you truly think he might be abusive, to be on the safe side, it might be best if the children are...uh...not there when he arrives."

Where could he take them? Wade thought of Sophie but dismissed her immediately. That would be the first place Parnell would look. But Pete and Margie would take the kids for the night. They'd be safe there.

Sixteen

Sophia Braden blew a strand of blond hair off her forehead and went to get the coffeepots. It wasn't even eleven-thirty, and the café was already swarming with customers. From the looks of the sea of polo shirts and sunburned noses, there must be a golf tournament in town. She was way behind on refills, and her tips would prove it if she didn't get a move on. Lydia was on a smoke break, and, like a fool, Sophie had agreed to cover her section. She was going to have to take up smoking again just so she could get a break now and then.

With one hand, she grabbed the handles of a pot of decaf and a half-full carafe of regular, and headed for Lydia's tables.

"Anyone care for more coffee here?" she asked a foursome of senior citizens in a heated discussion about the golf game they'd just finished.

"Well! There she is," one silver-haired gentleman crowed. "We thought you'd forgotten about us, pretty lady." He winked and reached out to put a hand on her waist.

Sophie didn't think she'd ever get used to having old geezers flirt with her, but she pasted on a smile. "I'm so sorry. We're shorthanded this morning. Can I get you fellas any dessert?"

They all waved her off, patting their ample bellies. She finished pouring coffee and moved to the next booth, whose occupant was engrossed in today's issue of the *Coyote Courier*.

"Can I refill your coffee, sir?"

The sandy-haired man folded the paper slowly and looked up at her with a knowing smile on his face.

Sophie gasped and involuntarily took two steps backward, almost losing her grip on the coffeepot.

"Hello there, Sophie."

"Darrin!" she whispered. "What are you doing here?"

"Motherless children need their father."

Sophie's mind churned. She knew Wade had tried to contact him after the funeral, but he'd said he had only run into dead ends.

"They already *have* a father, Darrin. The kids are with Starr's…husband," she lied. "They're happy where they are. Just leave them be."

"Sophie, you know I can't do that. I owe it to the kids. Starr would have wanted them to be with me. You know that."

She'd forgotten the velvety timbre of his voice. He'd put on a little weight and his hair was longer. He looked good.

He reached out and touched her arm, his deep-set eyes searching hers in a way that made her squirm inside. She pulled her arm away, sloshing coffee out onto the already stained carpeting. The man had something up his sleeve.

"You liar," she hissed, "Starr would have wanted you to burn in—"

"Save it, Sophe." He held up a hand. "Sorry, sis, but your memory's obviously a little messed up. Those drugs'll do that to you, you know?" He sneered and scooted his coffee mug to the edge of the table. "I'll take half a cup. Decaf, thanks."

Boiling inside, Sophie resisted the urge to overflow his coffee cup into his lap. "What do you want from me?" she sneered.

"I want you to help me get my kids back."

"Assuming I even wanted to do that, what could *I* do?"

"Convince this Wade guy it's for the best that the kids come with me. Maybe you could turn him in for abusing the kids or something?"

Sophie snorted. "You've got to be kidding! If I turn anybody in for abuse, it sure ain't gonna be Wade Sullivan." She set the heavier coffeepot on Darrin's tabletop and took a tablet from her apron pocket. She leafed through until she found his ticket. She ripped it off, wishing it were his head. "Leave those kids alone. Wade's a better father than you ever thought about being."

Darrin drained his coffee mug and set it down hard on the saucer. "You know, Sophie. I'd think you'd want to help me in any way you could."

She glared at him. "What's that supposed to mean?"

"I think you know. I'd hate to have to drag out our little stories from the good old days back in Minneapolis."

Sophie's heart lurched to a stop before it started pounding double time. "You don't scare me, Darrin Parnell."

Keeping his eyes locked unnervingly on hers, he dug into his wallet, fished out a dollar bill, and flung it onto the table. "Have a nice day, Sophe." He slid out of the booth, purposely bumping into her, then swaggered away without looking back.

She stood, trembling, and watched him walk out to the cashier's desk in the entryway. She had lied again.

Darrin Parnell scared her to death.

Wade pulled out of the attorney's parking lot and slipped his cell phone from his pocket. He punched in Pete's number, tapping out a nervous rhythm on the steering wheel while the phone rang four times…five…six. "Come on, Pete. Pick up…pick up."

Pete's voice finally came on, but it was via the metallic echo of his voice mail. "Pete, it's Wade. Give me a call the minute you get this. I've got big trouble with the kids."

He punched End and started to dial Margie's work number. Pete's wife was a nurse at the Coyote County Hospital. He hated to call her at work, but he didn't know what else to do. He would have bet his life Darrin had already tracked Sophie down by now.

Suddenly a terrifying thought struck him. *What if Parnell has gone to the school and taken the kids out?* He didn't think the school would release them to a stranger, but if Beau or one of the girls told them Parnell was their father… He jammed his fingers on the phone's keypad and dialed the school.

"Coyote Elementary. This is Judy. How may I direct your call?"

"Judy, this is Wade Sullivan. The kids are there, right?"

"Your kids…? As far as I know."

Wade could tell he'd confused her. "Nobody came and got them?"

"No…I don't think so." He heard her cover the receiver and repeat his question to someone in the office. Her voice came back strong on the line. "They're all in school today, Wade."

"Good." He heaved out the word on a sigh of relief. "If anyone should show up later asking for them, don't let him talk to them."

"Is everything okay?"

"I...I can't really say right now, Judy. Just don't let anybody take them out of school. I'll be there to pick them up as soon as school's out."

"Okay...I hope everything's all right."

"Yeah. You and me both."

He tried Margie at the hospital again. The front desk put him through. "Margie, it's Wade. I'm sorry to bother you at work, but I've got an emergency here."

"What's wrong, Wade? What's happened? Is Pete okay?"

"Oh no. I'm sorry to scare you. Pete's fine. He's just not answering the phone."

"What is it, then?"

"It's a long story, but...Starr's ex is in town trying to get the kids back."

"Oh, Wade, no!"

"Yes, I'm afraid so. Could the kids stay at your place tonight? I have a lawyer looking into things for me," he told her, "but it might take a couple of days before I have anything legal on my side."

"Sure, Wade. Of course. I'm supposed to work the evening shift, but Pete said he'd be home by six. Is that soon enough, or do you want me to try to get off?"

"No, no...don't do that. But I might try to reach Pete and have him come home a little earlier. I have a feeling Parnell—the kids' dad—is going to be on my doorstep again at four o'clock, and I want to be there when he shows up."

"Well, if you can't get hold of Pete, just give me a call on my cell. I'll carry it with me." She gave him the number.

"Okay. Thanks a million, Margie."

"I'll be praying. And the kids can stay as long as they need to. Amber will be thrilled for the company."

"Thanks, Margie."

As he drove home, he prayed he'd find a message waiting from Frank Locke. Was it too much to hope that the attorney would tell him it was all taken care of and he could send Darrin Parnell packing when he showed up to collect his kids?

No. Wade knew better. Something—a familiar inkling too strong and reliable to brush off—told him this was just the beginning of what might well be the fight of his life.

Seventeen

The Monte Carlo pulled into Wade's driveway right on schedule at four o'clock. Wade was waiting on the front porch, his palms sweaty but his resolve firm.

Parnell got out and leaned over the roof of the car, glaring at Wade. "Well? Where are they?"

"They're not here." Wade stepped off the porch and went to stand on the opposite side of the sedan. "You should know I've filed for legal guardianship of the children. If you have any questions, you can contact my attorney."

A muscle twitched in Parnell's jaw. He leaned over the sedan. "And you should know, Mr. Sullivan, that you're not the only one who has a lawyer. I just spoke with *my* attorney, who assures me I have every right to my own flesh and blood. I'll contest your filing, and, if necessary, we'll get a court order forcing you to turn my children over."

"Go right ahead and get that court order," Wade told him, relieved that his voice came out sounding more confident than he felt. He jabbed a finger in Parnell's direction and ground out his words. "Those kids will leave Coyote with you over my dead body."

Parnell sneered. "I think you underestimate the law, Sullivan. If you knew anything about it at all, you'd know that in this country the courts almost always rule in favor of natural parents."

"And that's as it should be," Wade said, "assuming the natural parents are fit to have custody. I'd think you'd realize—if you knew anything about the law at all—that in this country, abusive, neglectful parents almost always lose the right to raise their children." Wade was winging it, and way out of his comfort zone, but he wasn't about to let Parnell have the upper hand.

"Where are my children?" Parnell blurted.

"They're someplace safe."

Parnell came around to the front of the car but stopped short of the porch. "I'm warning you, Sullivan. You're only digging a deeper hole for yourself. I could have you arrested for kidnapping."

"My lawyer doesn't seem to think so. The kids are in a safe place on his advice."

Darrin Parnell narrowed his eyes and pounded an impotent fist on the hood of the car. Without further comment, he went back around to the driver's side and slid behind the wheel. He slammed the car door, revved the engine, and threw the car into reverse. Wade had to dodge the spray of dirt and gravel the sedan kicked up as it careened backward down the drive. Halfway down the curving lane, the car made a hasty three-point turn, then lurched out onto the blacktop, leaving gaping, muddy ruts at the edge of the lawn.

A mindless soap opera droned on the television, and Sophie draped herself over the threadbare sofa. This job was going to kill her yet.

She was just dozing off when a thunderous pounding on her door caused her to shoot upright, her heart thumping like a drum. She looked at the clock over the bookcase. It wasn't yet five, still bright outside. What was going on?

The pounding came again, louder.

"I'm coming, I'm coming," she muttered. She ran her fingers through her hair and tried to rub away the sleep marks she knew must line her face.

She started to open the door but suddenly felt unaccountably cautious. She moved her hand from the doorknob and went quietly to the kitchen. Pulling the curtain aside, she blew out a stream of air. Darrin Parnell was standing on her doorstep.

She went back to the door, unlocked it, and opened it a crack. "What do you want?"

"Let me in, Sophie. I need to talk to you."

"I told you, I've got nothing to say to you."

"Let me see my kids."

"What are you talking about?"

"Don't play dumb with me. I know they're here."

"No. They're not."

He shoved the door into her, knocking her backward. He stepped inside and slammed the door shut behind him, towering over her menacingly.

"What do you want?" she repeated, taking a step back.

"Sit down," Darrin ordered.

Sophie remembered his temper well enough to know she was better off doing what he demanded. She slid onto a barstool at the narrow kitchen counter.

Darrin strode down the hall to the back of the apartment, pushing open doors as he went.

He came back to the kitchen and stood close enough she could smell his wintergreen chewing gum. "Where are they?" he demanded.

"I told you, Darrin. I don't know. I haven't talked to Wade for a couple of days," she lied.

He grabbed her forearm and wrenched it. His eyes held a terrifying gleam—one she remembered vividly.

He gave her arm another twist. "You lying little—"

"Ouch! Stop it, Darrin!" Pain sliced through her elbow.

He inflicted one last painful squeeze before releasing her. "Where would he have taken them?"

She backed away, rubbing her forearm. "Darrin, I swear, I don't know where they are. Have you been out to Wade's place? Are you sure they're not out there?" She backpedaled, desperately trying to buy time. She didn't know where the kids were exactly. That much was true, though she could guess where Wade might have taken them.

"No. They're not out there. But don't worry. I'll find them."

Sudden anger supplanted Sophie's fear. "And what are you going to do when you find them? The kids are happy with Wade, Darrin. If you really cared about them like you say, you'd leave them be."

"And what would you know about it, Sophie?"

She didn't respond.

"I'm taking them back with me. I don't care what anybody says. They're my kids, and I'm not leaving this town without them."

"Good luck, then," she shot back.

His eyes narrowed to slits. "What's that supposed to mean?"

She swallowed hard and glared at him. "Just so you know, the SRS was out to Wade's yesterday, and they assured him everything looked good. They'll be on Wade's side."

"I thought you hadn't talked to him," he said.

She ignored his challenge, chagrined at being caught in her lie. "They did one of those home studies or whatever they're called. Wade passed with flying colors, so he's got SRS to back him up," she repeated. As soon as the words were out, a startling thought came to her. She eyed him suspiciously. "It was you, wasn't it. You're the one who reported Wade."

"Reported him? What do you mean?"

"To SRS? Did you turn him in?"

Darrin's head came up. "Wait a minute. Let me get this straight. SRS paid a little visit to Sullivan because somebody turned him in?" A smug smile came to his face. "Oh, that is rich. That is just rich," he said, running his toe along the dented metal strip dividing the living room carpet from the kitchen linoleum.

"He's got the state behind him, Darrin. Good luck fighting that," she said, uncomfortably aware that her words fell flat.

Darrin cocked his head and scrutinized her. "What are you saying? Is Sullivan trying to adopt the kids? Legally?"

"Yes...that's it," she said. Maybe that would shut him down.

"It's probably the only way he can get to her money."

She laughed bitterly. "Starr didn't have any money. Thanks to you, she had three kids to feed by herself."

He ignored her, and when he spoke again, it was as though he'd forgotten she was in the room. "Starr would have had a life insurance policy where she worked... She surely wasn't foolish enough to put it in Wade's name."

Sophie didn't know if her sister had an insurance policy or not. Shoot, she didn't even know if she had one herself through the café. She'd never been good with business stuff the way Starr had. But Wade had never mentioned a policy, and she knew the kids were costing him a bundle.

It was ironic. Finances weren't Wade's forte, and Starr had always said that was the one thing Darrin was good at. He was a good salesman. And he knew how to work the system. They'd had a nice house in Minneapolis. Before she left Darrin, Starr had been able to buy nice clothes and get her hair done whenever she felt like it. Sophie had been jealous of her sister's good fortune.

Until the first time Darrin put Starr in the emergency room. Starr was so angry, she'd told Sophie she wished he would die so she could collect on all the life insurance he'd amassed. Though she'd never said as much to her sister, at the time Sophie wondered if Darrin had a big enough policy out on his wife that he might someday decide she was worth more to him dead than alive.

Darrin's voice broke through her dark thoughts. "If that woman ever learned anything from me in all the years I tried to put some sense into her head, she probably had a nice little policy or two squirreled away. No doubt Sullivan's already tapped into those."

Again, his voice drifted, and Sophie knew he wasn't really speaking to her anymore.

"Starr was living paycheck to paycheck, Darrin. Wade was pitching in with some of the bills. He's struggling to pay them all now."

"So he tells you."

"What's that supposed to mean?"

"Think about it, Sophie. It's probably all a big act. You're the *last* one Sullivan is going to tell if Starr was worth a hundred grand. He would know you'd be trying to get your sticky fingers on it. God knows you can't support that habit of yours on what you make as a waitress, and besides—"

"Shut up, Darrin. I don't do that stuff anymore."

He held his hands palm out and grinned. "Okay, okay. So you said. But think about it, babe. You think he's going to advertise it if he struck it rich off Starr? No. He's probably sitting out there in that nice big house of his, biding his time, watching the interest rack up."

"Wade's not like that," Sophie said. But she heard the lack of conviction in her own voice. It had never crossed her mind that Starr had left anything but liabilities when she died. According to Wade, even her car still had a lien on it.

According to Wade.

Darrin's comments set her mind awhirl. Maybe Wade wasn't being totally up-front with her. Maybe he had collected on some insurance and, as Darrin suspected, just didn't want her to have any claim to it. Heaven knew every man she'd ever known had lied to her face. Did she really think Wade Sullivan would be any different?

Eighteen

A furnace blast of heat met Dee Thackery when she opened her car door. Spring had been a mere blip on the calendar this year, and it was looking like a long, hot summer ahead.

Sliding behind the steering wheel, she turned the key in the ignition and punched the air conditioner on. It would barely cool off the interior of the car before she got home, but there was something psychologically satisfying about seeing that little glowing light marked AC.

She eased out of St. Joseph's cramped parking lot and onto the quiet, tree-lined street. Maybe she'd stop by Sonic on the way home and get something cool to drink. She quickly dismissed the idea, remembering that Clay Two Feathers had mentioned doing the same. The last thing she needed was to encourage that man, although she had to admit Clay had been a sweetheart lately.

He'd been someone to lean on when she found out Willy and LaShondra Green were being sent to the children's home, in spite of all her efforts to find them an alternate place to stay after foster care fell through.

Dee understood how difficult it was to be foster parents. There were many reasons why it sometimes just didn't work out. And with the increase of government regulations, foster parents were becoming more difficult to recruit all the time.

Turning onto her street, Dee instinctively began her ritual of taking inventory of her blessings. Seeing her house at the end of the narrow, brick avenue was always a good reminder. Her bungalow was no more than a cottage, really, but it was perfect for her. Anytime she started to doubt God's care for her, she needed only to remember the way events had fallen into place for her to move to Coyote, to live in that house, and to work at the job she loved.

These days, she had a lot to be thankful for. Her life had pretty much been a mess from the time her parents divorced when she was nine. Her mother had remarried just months later to a man Dee would later learn had been waiting in the wings. She'd seldom seen her dad after the divorce, and she'd missed him terribly.

But her stepfather was a charmer, never raising his voice to her and always spoiling her with new clothes and trips to the mall or the amusement parks Dad had never seemed to have time for.

Mick Cranston had eventually won Dee over. But the summer she'd turned eleven, Mick's attentions had turned into something she didn't understand. The clothes he bought her seemed more suited for someone older. And he was always touching her and hugging her—but not the way other girls' fathers hugged them. Mick's hugs and caresses made her feel like she'd done something wrong.

The busier Mom got at her job, working late two or three nights a week and most Saturdays, the more Mick's affections turned to Dee. By the time she was old enough to realize what was happening, Mick had taken liberties with her that she would regret for the rest of her life.

Finally on her thirteenth birthday she got up the courage to tell her mother. At first her mom refused to believe her, but finally Peg Cranston couldn't deny the evidence Dee presented. Dee never knew what transpired between her mother and stepfather after that, but the abuse stopped immediately. When her mother divorced Mick less than two years later, Dee felt equal parts relief and guilt.

She had escaped—barely—with her virginity. And for that she was grateful. On good days, she could almost appreciate her past, for it had led to her future. God had used the tragic circumstances of her childhood to instill in her a deep compassion for children who suffered at the hands of impostors pretending to be parents the way Mick had pretended to be her father.

As she'd worked toward her degree in social work, she'd learned many things that helped her cope with what had happened to her. Through the counsel of the campus pastor and his wife, Dee had discovered a faith that enabled her to forgive Mick—and her mother. And now she found real meaning in helping children through similar trials.

Sadly, she'd seen it over and over again in the three short years she'd practiced her profession. Sometimes the enormity of it all overwhelmed her. But if all the tears she'd shed, all the doubts she'd harbored, could save even one child from a fate like her own, it had been worth it.

Pulling into the driveway, she shook her head to clear away the disquieting thoughts. Where had those come from in the midst of her litany of thanks? The bottom line was that God had taken the worst thing in her life and used it to bring about the best.

She pulled under the shade of the carport at the side of the house, turned off the ignition, and rolled her window down a few inches against the heat. She gathered her briefcase and bag from the backseat of the car, then went in through the side door.

Phog, her smoke-colored tomcat, greeted her in the kitchen with a comical meow that sounded more like a dog's yap.

"Hey, buddy, did you miss me?"

The cat wove in and out between Dee's feet, leaving a haze of gray fur on her good white pants.

"Phog! Aargh. Cut it out." She brushed at her pants to no avail, but she couldn't muster enough fury in her voice to make the cat do anything but purr and rub harder against her.

Dee laughed and gave him a good scratching under the chin. Going into the kitchen, she deposited her briefcase and purse on the desk chair and went to lift the lid off the Crockpot. The spicy twang of her homemade barbecue sauce filled the kitchen. She'd invited her elderly neighbors for dinner tonight. Donald and Jewel Frederick had unofficially adopted her as the granddaughter they'd never had. Dee looked at the clock over the stove. The dear couple would be there in an hour. She'd better get a move on.

Yes. She had much for which to be grateful.

Almost a week went by, and Wade lived every day of it on the knife-edge of fear. Every time the phone rang or whenever he heard a car drive by, his heart jumped. But the only place Darrin Parnell showed up was in Wade's recurring nightmares.

He seriously considered taking the kids out of state somewhere until this all blew over. But he couldn't very well leave Pete high and dry with the business, and Frank Locke probably would have advised him against leaving town. It might be perceived as an attempt to kidnap the children. According to Locke, until they had an edict from the judge, Wade needed to tread carefully where the kids were concerned.

Wade called Frank Locke's office almost every day during his lunch hour, only to be repeatedly assured that the guardianship action was in process—whatever that meant—and that he would be notified the minute there was anything new to report.

The kids spent three days with the Doleceks before Wade decided he wasn't about to let Parnell dictate their lives. He thanked Pete and Margie, packed up the kids' things, and took them home. The kids didn't even gripe when he made macaroni and cheese for dinner.

It was after eleven before Sophie finally got her last rowdy table out the door. She clocked out and went to retrieve her purse from under the counter.

"Hey, Lydia," she hollered across the dining room, where her coworker was refilling the saltshakers. "You need a ride home tonight?"

Lydia screwed a metal lid on a shaker and looked up at Sophie. "Uh-uh. Thanks anyway, but Bobby's picking me up."

"You better watch it, girl. Next thing you know you'll find yourself married to that guy."

"Hey, I can dream, can't I?" Lydia quipped, echoing the song winding down on the jukebox.

"Sure you can. Just remember, sooner or later you've gotta wake up." Sophie waved. "See you tomorrow. Don't do anything I wouldn't do."

"Ha! That leaves the field pretty wide open."

"Hey! Not nice."

Lydia laughed and waved off Sophie's good-natured protest.

Searching her purse for her car keys, Sophie headed out the door. The parking lot was still littered with a few cars, most likely late-night patrons of the liquor store next door. It amused Sophie to see people park "undercover" at the café before casually moseying over to buy their hooch.

She walked around the south side of the building where her old Plymouth was parked. Clouds blocked the moon, and the shadow of the building darkened the parking lot.

She hoped her car would start. It had been acting up lately. She'd have Wade take a look at it. He owed her anyway, for all the baby-sitting hours she'd put in lately. Now that school was out, it seemed he was always wanting her to pick up the kids from day care or to baby-sit them while he ran by a work site.

She didn't blame him for being a little paranoid ever since Darrin Parnell had showed up on his doorstep. Wade had warned her not to open the door to Darrin when the kids were at her apartment, but she hadn't bothered telling Wade about the visit Darrin had paid her. She was pretty sure the guy was all blow and no go. There wasn't a life insurance policy in the world worth taking on three little kids. At least that's how she saw it.

She fumbled for the door handle and threw her purse across to the passenger seat. She eased into the driver's seat and fit the keys in the ignition, but when she tried to pull the door shut, she met with resistance. Her pulse quickened.

She caught a whiff of wintergreen and looked up to see Darrin Parnell grinning down at her. He leaned over her door, elbows out, arms flexed like he was God's gift to women.

"Sheesh, Darrin! You scared the spit out of me. What are you doing still hanging around here?" It was an effort to keep her voice steady. It had been over a week since the weasel had practically beaten down the door to her apartment. She'd started to think he'd gone back to Minneapolis.

"You can't get it through your head, can you? I'm serious about getting my kids back."

"Darrin, I—"

"No." He cut her off. "I know you think it's just about the money, Sophie. You think you know me. I know you've never had much use for me, but if there's one thing you have to believe, it's that I love my kids. It about killed me when Starr left and took them away from me. For the last four years, I've done nothing but dream about them—about getting them back."

This was not a side of Darrin Parnell she recognized. She'd never heard him be so passionate about anything. It struck her that maybe this was the side of the man that had drawn her sister in. But she had to wonder how he reconciled the whole issue of wanting Starr to get rid of Danica with the words pouring out of his mouth now. Sophie opened her mouth to say as much, but he cut her off again.

"Wait," he said, backing away from the car and holding up both hands, palms out. "Let me speak my piece."

"Okay, okay." Sophie slid from behind the wheel, shut the car door quietly, and leaned back against the side of the car, arms folded over her stomach.

Darrin paced in front of her, kicking at the gravel that covered the lot. "You don't understand what it's like trying to support a family. Starr spent money as fast as I could make it, and what she didn't spend, the kids gobbled up in formula and diapers and whatever else Starr thought they had to have. She didn't understand the value of money. She didn't appreciate how hard I worked so she could live the way she did. Carma's not like that."

Sophie straightened and tilted her head. "Carma?"

An almost shy grin crossed Darrin's face. "My fiancée. As soon as I get this custody thing worked out with the kids, we're getting married."

Lucky girl, Sophie thought sarcastically. "Does this…Carma know you're dragging three kids back with you?"

Darrin glared at her. "Not everybody hates kids as much as you do, Sophie. Carma's excited about the kids. She's good with kids."

"Yeah, I bet."

He shook his head and gave a scornful laugh. "You've still got issues, don't you, chick?"

"Yeah, I've got issues all right. One of which is that I've got to work an extra shift tomorrow, and I can't do it on zero sleep. Do you mind telling me why you were out here stalking me? I need to get on home and get to bed."

"I need your help, Sophie. Sullivan is going to fight me for the kids. I know he is. I don't think he has a prayer, but I'm getting the impression he's pretty well liked in this town. I want to be sure I have your support."

She gaped at him. "You've got to be kidding. After everything you did to my sister, you have the gall to think you'd have my support?"

Darrin took a step toward her, reached out, and stroked a hand down her shoulder. "Hey, Sophe...come on." His voice turned velvet again. "That's all in the past. You're surely not going to hold a grudge. I know Starr forgave me."

"What makes you think that?"

"She always forgave me. That's just the way she was."

He was right. Sophie was surprised by how much the realization hurt. "Yeah, well, even if it's true, I'm not Starr. What you did was unforgivable."

"Hey, come on, babe. This isn't like you." He put a hand on her cheek, then trailed his fingers through a strand of hair that had come loose from her ponytail.

She moved away, scooting along the side of the car. "Get your hands off me. I can't believe you'd even ask me to help you."

He whirled away from her, kicking a hunk of gravel into the vacant street. "What is your problem!" he shouted. Then, looking furtively around the parking lot, as though aware that he might attract unwanted attention, he took a deep breath and turned his back to her, wringing his hands, obviously trying to collect himself.

When he turned around, the malice she remembered all too well was in his eyes.

"Do I have to draw you a picture, Sophie?" The velvet was gone from his voice.

"What are you talking about?"

"I already told you. Did you really think I was going to let this ride? It was bound to catch up with you sooner or later, babe."

She swayed and rested her back against the car again, praying it would hold her upright. "What do you want from me?" she spat. "Why don't you just go back to Minneapolis?"

"Can't do it, babe. You might as well face it. Your past has done caught up with you." His shoulders shook in a callous, noiseless sneer.

Sophie felt the heat rise to her face. "Just shut up. You don't have anything on me. You don't even know me anymore. Things are different. I'm not into that stuff anymore."

"Yeah, well, I'm not sure the judge is going to buy that. I've heard they can prosecute these things years and years after the fact. That is, if they have a witness to testify. And by George, I do believe there's a witness."

The look he gave her turned her stomach and set her mind crawling with ugly images. Things she'd spent the last four years trying to erase.

She'd done some terrible things. But it had been a good five years since she'd so much as broken the speed limit. Surely what Darrin said wasn't true. Could he really turn her in after all this time? He'd been a witness, that was for sure. And knowing him, he probably had half a dozen of the old gang ready and willing to testify against her if she didn't cooperate with him.

She crossed her arms and tried to rub away the goose bumps that had risen there. "What do I have to do?"

Nineteen

"No, Darrin," Sophie said. "I won't do it."

"I don't think you have a choice." A muscle twitched in Darrin Parnell's cheek. The faint rays of the distant streetlight caught the flash of anger in his eyes.

"I don't have to listen to this. I'm not the naive girl you used to push around." Sophie turned and started to open her car door, her hands trembling.

The next thing she knew, she was staggering backward into the stuccoed wall of the café. A blade of pain sliced through her jaw.

She watched helplessly as he drew back his arm again. "Darrin, no! Stop it!" Cowering against the side of the building, she raised an arm to protect herself.

The gleam in his eyes went dim. "Don't you tell me what to do."

As if in slow motion, he raised a clenched fist and came at her again, this time landing his punch full in her face. Pain screamed through her head. She huddled in the shadows against the wall and waited for the next blow. It came with startling precision. Practiced precision, she realized with a shudder.

Blood gushed from her nose and ran down her throat, gagging her. Her tongue worried a sharp bit of something—a chip off a tooth, or a pip of gravel he'd kicked in her face—and she put a hand to her jaw. She spat onto the asphalt, alarmed at the amount of blood. Looking down, she saw that her white uniform blouse was spattered with blood too. She spat again, trying to rid her mouth of the metallic taste.

How had their discussion escalated into such brutality? One minute they were arguing and the next thing she remembered, she was in a heap on the ground with Darrin towering over her.

She'd never been in such pain. But strangely, for the moment, her thoughts weren't for herself. A mixture of regret and sorrow flooded her.

How had Starr endured batterings like this month after month, year after year, often in front of little Lacey and Beau?

Beau. No wonder the kid was having problems. No wonder he struck out at the other kids in school the way he did. He'd seen it modeled by the man who was supposed to be his hero.

Even as Darrin's next blow connected with her right temple, Sophie's heart went out to her nieces and nephew with new understanding. They had been through so much in their short lives.

And she had done nothing to stop it. She'd been too wrapped up in her own little world, her own prison of pain; she'd been too busy trying to deaden the hurt—first with alcohol, then with a succession of increasingly destructive drugs. And, she realized with anguish, too busy consorting with the very one who was the cause of all Starr's suffering.

She slid down from the wall and curled up into a ball on the asphalt that skirted the back of the café. Darrin kicked her in the small of her back, and she cried out. But this time it wasn't for the physical pain he inflicted on her; it was for the agony of realizing the part she'd played in her sister's life of tragedy.

She lay in a heap, silent, waiting for Darrin to strike again. But in a half-conscious haze, she heard his footsteps retreat on the gravel lot, heard his car door slam, and an engine rev. Tires squealed, and he peeled out of the drive.

Was she going to die in this lonely parking lot? She deserved to.

Oh, God. Oh, God. Her own thoughts startled her. Not because the words were unfamiliar. She'd used them as a curse since she was a little girl imitating her parents. But this time the words were a prayer. Where had that come from? She didn't even believe in God.

Had Starr really believed all the stuff she'd said about God and forgiveness? If only she could know that her sister had been right. Starr had been so sure of God's existence, so certain heaven awaited her when she died, so sure even of God's personal interest in every detail of her life.

But if God was so interested in Starr—so loving and caring—why did he let her die in the first place? Why didn't he take *her* instead? Sophia Braden had no one in this world to mourn her when she was gone. Why did God choose to take her sweet sister who had three little children who needed her desperately right now?

God? God, if you're out there, you don't make any sense to me at all. If you're really a God of love like Starr always said, you sure have a funny way of showing it.

She heard a car pull into the lot, and the heartbeat that had slowed to a snail's pace in her chest quickened. Had Darrin come back to finish the job? Her head told her she should get up and run. Get in her car and flee. But her body wouldn't obey. She felt paralyzed.

The car stopped and there were voices, shouting, coming closer. Now speaking in her ear. She couldn't understand what they were saying, but they were friendly voices. That much she knew. Her muscles went slack with relief. She opened her mouth, but she couldn't make her thickened tongue form a single intelligible word.

The message light was blinking on the cordless phone hanging over the desk in the dining room. Wade punched the caller ID, and Frank Locke's name flashed on the display.

He looked out to the kitchen where the kids were doing the supper dishes and turned the volume down low enough so they couldn't hear. He hit Play.

"Wade, this is Frank Locke. I need to talk to you. Please call my cell phone at your earliest convenience."

He jotted down the home phone number Locke recited, dialed it, and then carried the phone into the spare room.

"This is Wade Sullivan. You have news for me?"

"Yes, Wade. As we expected, Darrin Parnell is challenging your petition for guardianship and has filed for full custody of his children."

Wade bit his lip until he tasted blood. "So what do we do now?"

"We wait for the judge to make a determination. He'll probably issue a temporary order for custody."

"You mean it's possible he could…award the kids to Parnell?"

"It's possible, but not likely. If everything checks out with you, and especially if court services turns up Parnell's run-ins with the police, Judge Paxton will likely find it in the children's best interest to remain with you—at least until the hearings can be set for the case. But that's weeks, probably months, down the road."

"What if things don't check out? What if the judge talks to SRS?"

"What do you mean?"

"Well, what if he finds out SRS came out to my house?"

"I thought you said the social worker was satisfied with what she found on the home visit?"

"She said that. I mean, she made some recommendations…things I'm supposed to take care of. But I've done all that."

Locke cleared his throat. "Were you given a written recommendation?"

"I'm not sure what that means. They gave me some papers—more like a pamphlet. It told what SRS does and explained what they were looking for when they came to the house. That's all."

"But nothing with specific instructions pertaining to you and the children? Dates to complete those by?"

"No. She just talked to me about it."

"And what did she suggest you do?"

"She thought Lacey ought to see a doctor. She's had a bad cough," he explained. "The school nurse checked her the next day and said she seemed fine. Her cough's almost gone now." Wade ran a hand over his stubbly jaw, trying to remember what else Betty Graffe had said. "She wanted me to check into health insurance for the kids. I already called about getting them added to my policy."

"Good…good…" Locke said, sounding relieved.

"And she mentioned something about not leaving the kids home alone anymore."

"They were home alone?" Locke seemed as alarmed as he'd been relieved seconds earlier.

"She came while I was at the pharmacy getting medicine for Lacey's cough. They were only alone for a few minutes."

"But you don't leave them by themselves ordinarily?"

"No…not very often. Not if I can help it. But still, it can't look good to have this SRS visit on my record, can it? Can we find out what they put in their report? What if the judge finds out I haven't had insurance on the kids all this time? The social worker is supposed to come back and check up on things in a couple of days. What if she's not satisfied with what she finds?" He paced the floor, phone to his ear, raking a hand through his hair over and over again.

"Relax, Wade." Frank Locke's voice changed gears again and took on a soothing tone. "I don't think there's anything to worry about at this point. I'll keep you posted as things progress. We've done all we can do for now. Just…be extra careful from this point on. Make sure you pick the kids up on time from day care, keep the house in good shape, make sure they're getting well-rounded meals, that kind of thing."

Wade nodded.

"Do you attend church? Take the kids to Sunday school?"

Wade looked at the floor. "We used to…before their mother died. It's…been a while."

"It might be a good idea to get plugged in again somewhere. This judge seems to be impressed by that sort of thing."

Wade nodded again, taking mental notes.

"And whatever you do," the attorney went on, "no spankings or harsh discipline. Don't do anything that could be misinterpreted as abuse. It's important that in the eyes of the court you are the epitome of fatherhood."

Wade nodded. "Okay…sure…"

"I'll call when I have any news."

"Okay."

"Oh, one more thing…" The hesitancy in Locke's voice was unmistakable. "I found out Starr Parnell did have a life insurance policy through her employer. It's a pretty hefty one, considering her income."

"Oh?"

"Seventy-five thousand dollars. The children are the beneficiaries, but the money could be paid to their court-appointed custodian."

"I see." Wade let the implications of the attorney's news soak in. "That explains a lot."

"It might."

Wade didn't respond. He clicked off the phone, walked back to the dining room, and replaced the handset in its cradle. He had dared to hope Parnell might drop the whole thing and go back to Minneapolis. Now there was no denying that this wasn't all just going to go away. And in the midst of it, *he* was supposed to suddenly become the epitome of fatherhood?

He went and stood in the doorway to the kitchen, watching the kids—*his* kids—finish up the dishes. The kitchen was clean and tidy, the product of a full Saturday of housecleaning and laundry. They'd all worked their tails off to keep it clean since then. He would impress Betty Graffe's socks off if it killed him. And it just might.

He looked past the kids to the coatrack by the back door. Beau's baseball glove was lopped over the peg bearing his name in his mama's calligraphy.

A wave of nausea rolled over him, but he clapped his hands and injected artificial cheer into his voice. "You know what, guys? Those dishes can wait. Let's go play some catch before it gets too dark."

Their gleeful laughter was the best medicine he could imagine.

The following afternoon Wade was waiting in line at the lumberyard, shooting the breeze with Charlie McCauley, when his cell phone jangled. He tried to ignore it for a couple of rings while Charlie finished a story.

Finally the old man waved him off. "Aw, go ahead and get it… You young people with your crazy gizmos. Time was, a fellow went to work to get away from the telephone."

Smiling an apology, Wade fished the phone out of his pocket and turned away from Charlie. "Yeah, this is Wade."

"Wade?"

"Beau?" He looked at his watch. It was after five. "Hey, bud. Where are you?"

"At day care."

"Aunt Sophie hasn't picked you up yet?"

"Uh uh."

"She didn't call?"

"I don't think so. Miss Marty said to call you."

He gave an angry shake of his head and stepped out of the queue. "Okay. I'll be right there. You guys stay put. If Sophie comes before I get there, tell her I'm on my way." Wade clicked off the phone and tucked it back in his pocket.

Charlie stepped aside and motioned for Wade to take his place back in line. "Thanks, but go ahead, Charlie. I've got to run. Tell Lurene I'll come back later and get my order, will you?"

As he weaved his way back to the front of the store, he dialed Sophie. A recording told him her number had been disconnected or was no longer in service. She must not have paid her phone bill again.

He ran out to the pickup and broke the speed limits racing to the daycare center. Beau and the girls, along with four or five other kids, were waiting in front of the building with one of the teachers. At least he wasn't the last one to pick up his kids.

He could've wrung Sophie's neck. She knew how important it was to get the kids on time. He'd depended on her. She knew he was skating on thin ice with this whole situation with the kids.

He leaned across the seat and opened the passenger side door. "Hi, guys. Hop in."

Dani climbed onto the running board, and Wade offered a hand and pulled her up into the cab beside him. Beau and Lacey clambered in behind her.

"Buckle up," he told them.

"Can you drive faster," Beau said. "I'm missing my show."

"Sorry, bud. I need to run by Aunt Sophie's."

"Oh, good. I can watch my show there."

"No. I want you guys to wait in the car. I just need to talk to her for a minute. And then I've got to run out to a site and talk to Pete before we go home."

"Aw, come on," Beau moaned. "It'll be over by then."

"Sorry." Which program did Beau consider "my show"? It bothered him that he didn't have a clue.

They drove to Sophie's apartment on the other side of town. Her car wasn't in her parking space. Maybe she got called in to work early. She could have at least let him know.

"Stay in the truck," he warned the kids. "I'll just be a minute."

Despite his pounding, nobody came to the door. He leaned against the railing on Sophie's stoop, keeping an eye on the truck. He pulled out his phone and dialed the café.

The owner's cheery voice came on the line. "Coyote Café."

"Hey, Berta. Is Sophie in yet?"

There was a long pause. "Oh, Wade. Didn't anybody call you?"

"Call me?" He didn't like the quaver in Berta's voice.

"You really don't know?"

"Know what?"

"Lydia's new boyfriend found Sophie unconscious outside the café last night."

"What!"

"I'm sorry, Wade. I figured Lydia called you."

"Where is she now? Is she okay? What happened?"

"Lydia and Bobby took her to Lydia's place, and she stayed there last night. I imagine she's still there. Fred told her and Lydia both to take the night off."

"Yes, but what happened? Was she…passed out?" Sophie had fallen off the wagon once a couple of years ago, but Wade was pretty sure she hadn't had so much as a sip of anything stronger than Fred and Berta's famous homemade root beer since then.

"Somebody beat the snot out of her," Berta said.

"What?" Wade slumped against the railing. "Somebody beat her up? Who?"

"She told Lydia she doesn't remember, but… You don't know if Sophie was seeing somebody, do you?"

"No…not that I know of, anyway. Did anybody call the police?"

"Sophie wouldn't let them. At least that's what Lydia said. I tried to tell Fred we should report it, but he doesn't want to meddle." Berta looked at the floor. "It...it would be bad for business if word got—"

"Where does Lydia live?"

"Up on Sixth Street. She has that apartment over Johnny Seldridge's house."

"Okay. The kids and I will head over there."

"Wade—um..." Berta cleared her throat. "You might not want to take the kids with you. Lydia said she looks pretty bad."

Twenty

Wade drove to Sixth Street and parked in the drive beside the old Victorian house. After everything Frank Locke had said, it made him nervous to leave the kids in the truck, but it would be too upsetting to them if Sophie was wounded as badly as Berta made it sound.

"You guys stay put. I won't be long." He lowered his voice an octave and shook a finger at them. "And I mean it. You stay in this truck."

"Whose house is this?" Beau asked.

"A friend of Aunt Sophie's," he said, rolling down his window and making sure the passenger side window was open as well.

Dani tilted her head and looked up at him. "Hows come we can't go in, Wade?"

He ignored the question and jumped out of the truck. "I won't be but a couple of minutes," he said, slamming the door.

The entrance to Lydia's apartment was at the back of the house. Wade followed the sidewalk around and climbed the steep stairway to the landing.

There was a doorbell, but he opened the screen door and rapped on the inner door instead.

After a minute, Lydia opened the door a crack. "Wade—"

"Where is she? Why didn't somebody call me?" He put a hand up to push open the door, but Lydia held it wide and led the way to the small kitchen at the back of the apartment. The place smelled of mold and stale cigarette smoke.

Lydia poked her head into the kitchen. "I'll be in the living room if you need anything, Sophe."

She stepped aside and let Wade through.

He took in a sharp breath.

If he'd seen Sophie on the street, he wouldn't have recognized her. She sat at the small dinette table, cradling a steaming mug in her hands. Her upper lip was puffed up like a water balloon, and there were eggplant-colored circles under her eyes. She had a butterfly bandage over a cut on one cheek, and by the cautious way she held herself, he guessed it wasn't just her face that had taken the beating.

He took a halting step toward her. "Sophie? What in the world happened?"

She started crying, silently, her shoulders heaving, tears streaking her swollen face.

Wade didn't think he'd ever seen Sophia Braden cry. He wasn't sure how to react. He pulled out the chair beside her, took the mug from her hands, and set it on the table. Even her hands were bruised. Feeling awkward, he wrapped his large hands gently around hers.

"Who did this to you?"

She shook her head, still unable to speak.

"Why didn't you let Lydia call the police?"

A flame came to her eyes. Was it fueled by anger—or fear?

"I just want to forget about it, Wade. I'm fine. It's no big deal."

"No big deal! Look at you! Who did this?" he repeated.

"I…I don't know."

Something wasn't right. Sophie wasn't telling everything she knew. Suddenly Darrin Parnell's image flashed through his mind. "It wasn't Parnell, was it? He hasn't been around again, has he?"

"No!" Sophie said, a little too quickly. "I…I told you, I don't know who it was." Her words were muffled, coming through swollen lips.

"Well, what did he look like? Did he get your purse? Your tip money?"

She shook her head.

"Sophie…you honestly don't know who it was? Do you think it was a customer from the café? Did anybody at your tables hassle you last night?"

She pulled her hands away and picked up her mug, wincing as the hot liquid reached her lips. "I told you, I don't know who it was." Her voice had taken on an edge.

He pulled a pencil and notepad bearing the lumberyard's logo from his shirt pocket. Lowering his voice, he said, "Well, tell me what you do know. What did he look like?"

"Forget it, Wade. I'm okay. I don't want this to go anywhere. Just leave it be."

Wade shook his head slowly. She was as stubborn as her sister. He looked at Sophie again and saw Starr's eyes staring back at him. And for the first time he comprehended what Starr must have gone through at Darrin Parnell's hands. What made men do such things?

Like Sophie, Starr had never wanted to talk about it. She'd even used the words "no big deal" once with Wade. Only once. He'd told her emphatically that it *was* a big deal.

He jammed the pencil and pad in his pocket and pushed back his chair. "The kids are waiting in the truck. I've got to go. You staying here tonight?"

"Probably."

"Are you afraid?" He looked at her hard and saw something unreadable flit across her battered face. "Is there more to this than you're telling me, Sophie?"

"No, Wade. Just go."

He stared for a moment. "Okay, then."

He turned and walked back through the apartment, giving Lydia a terse nod as he passed.

Something didn't feel right. If he had to guess, he'd say Sophie was lying about not knowing her attacker. He thought about Berta's question about a new boyfriend.

He hoped Sophie hadn't fallen in with a bad crowd again. He knew she'd taken Starr's death harder than she let on. She was all alone in the world now. That couldn't be easy. It would be tempting to find solace in the bottle and the pills again. He understood that, and his heart went out to her. He felt bad that he hadn't seen this coming.

Still, this was the last thing he needed to deal with on top of everything else.

"It's not good, Wade." Frank Locke looked up from his massive mahogany desk, rested his elbows on the polished surface, and steepled his fingers.

"The judge has directed the county attorney to file a CINC petition on behalf of the Parnell children."

"I don't understand. Sink? What does that mean?" Wade didn't like the somber tone in his attorney's voice.

"C-I-N-C. It stands for Child In Need of Care. This isn't good," he repeated. "It means the judge is turning the children over to the custody of the state—SRS."

"Custody? But what does that mean exactly?"

"It most likely means they'll put the kids in foster care."

Wade exploded. "Foster care? But why?"

Locke held up a hand. "Just temporarily. The judge apparently determined that neither of you—you or Parnell—has been proven competent to raise the children."

A flush of heat crawled up his neck. "That's crazy! Not competent? You mean they'd send the kids to live with strangers?"

"Sometimes that is in the best interest of the children."

"Well, not this time. You don't believe that, do you?"

Locke shook his head, but Wade wasn't sure he saw the conviction he needed from this man who was supposed to be his ally.

"Did he even try to find out about Parnell?"

"Believe me, if he hadn't, the kids would be with Parnell right now. You've got to understand the way the system works, Wade. There's a big push for family preservation in these situations. Anytime there's a possibility the courts can keep—or in your case, reunite—children with their natural parents, that is going to be their primary goal."

Locke took a pencil from a mug on his desk and absently drew geometric shapes on the legal pad in front of him. "You should know that… Judge Paxton lost a custody battle for his own son years ago, so he's probably going to come out pretty strong for keeping these kids with their father."

"But he's supposed to be impartial!"

"Sure he is. And he's a good judge, Wade. But you can talk about impartiality all you want… People can't help their experience shaping what they believe. I just want you to know what you're up against if you decide to continue pursuing this."

Wade combed unsteady fingers through his hair. "Isn't there anything you can do?"

"I could move for another judge, use the peremptory challenge. But that's a roll of the dice. We could end up with someone worse."

Wade shrugged, defeated. "What choice do I have? I am not going to let those kids spend one day with that man. I know what he's capable of."

"Then we have our work cut out for us."

Wade pushed his chair away from the desk and rose to pace the plush, rose-colored carpet. "So what happens now? When will the kids have to go?"

"Probably right away. I've got a call in to the SRS office."

"Right away? You mean like this week?"

"Maybe today…"

Wade glared at him in disbelief.

"I'm sorry," Locke said. "It depends on how soon they can get all the papers in order. I'm checking on it. I'll let you know as soon as I know anything. But you might want to explain to the kids what will be happening."

Wade felt as if he'd been struck by a two-by-four. "How the—" He stopped pacing and bent over Locke's desk, gripping opposite edges, wanting to heave the thing across the room. "How can I explain what I don't understand myself?"

"We're going to fight this, Wade. We're going to get your kids back for you. If Parnell is as bad as you say, there's no way he's going to end up with those kids."

Wade's mind raced. "But what do I do in the meantime? Can I still see them?"

"Most likely. You need to understand that every decision is going to be determined by what is deemed best for the children. It's highly likely the judge will grant you visitation rights. Probably supervised visitation, you understand? More than likely once a week."

Wade staggered back a step and glared at Locke. "You're telling me I can only see the kids once a week? And somebody is going to be breathing down our necks every minute? You can't be serious! Dear God! This can't be happening!" He pounded a fist on the desk, causing Locke to rear back in his chair.

Wade put his head down and rubbed his temples, trying to compose himself. After a long minute he looked up. "I am begging you. You can't let them send the kids to live with some stranger. They've just lost their mother. This will kill them."

Locke pursed his lips and shook his head slowly. "I'm sorry."

"Come on. Please. This makes no sense at all. This is not right." He threw his hands up, trembling, out of words. He'd never felt so powerless. "What if…what if they went with a neutral third party? Somebody they know. My business partner… Pete and his wife, Margie. There has to be some other way. There *has* to!"

By the way Locke closed his eyes and leaned back in his chair, Wade knew his suggestion was absurd.

"Those wouldn't be neutral parties," the attorney said finally.

"Then…what about Starr's sister. The kids could stay at Sophie's. Surely Starr's only sibling has a right to the kids."

"I thought you said she wasn't an option. That she wouldn't be *willing* to take them even if she was fit to parent them."

A disturbing vision of Sophie's swollen, bruised face filled his thoughts. But in spite of his nagging suspicion that she was in trouble again, he felt a spark of hope ignite. "At least they know her," he told Locke. "At least then I could still see them every day." Maybe he *could* talk Sophie into taking the kids for a while. He could supervise and make sure the kids were taken care of, even keep them at his house most of the time. Nothing would have to change.

Frank Locke doused the flame of hope. "I'm afraid it's too late for that now, even if Sophie were willing. Once SRS is involved, the kids become their wards, and all decisions concerning their well-being are up to the state. Besides, from what you told me before, I'm not sure Sophie would be deemed any more fit to care for the children than Parnell."

Wade knew he was right. And for a minute he hated Sophie for it.

Twenty-One

The hosts of the video bloopers show exchanged inane banter as the credits rolled. Wade eased Dani off his lap, unearthed the remote from the couch cushions, and turned off the television. He tried to ignore the knot growing ever tighter in his gut. He'd put it off as long as he could. Now it was half an hour past the kids' bedtime, and Wade had yet to let them know that tomorrow night they would be sleeping at some foster home. The energy drained out of him at the thought.

"Okay, kiddos," he said, ruffling Dani's hair, "time to get ready for bed. Everybody go get your pj's on and brush your teeth, and then come back down here. There's something we need to talk about."

Beau raised his eyebrows, and a look of hopeful expectation washed his sun-browned face. When he and Lacey exchanged glances, Wade realized his forced cheerfulness had them thinking they were in for a treat.

"No," he said soberly, shaking his head. "This is serious."

"Uh-oh," Beau said, rolling his eyes. "What'd we do now?"

"You're not in trouble, either," Wade said. "Just go get ready and then we'll talk." He corralled the three of them into a huddle and gave them a gentle shove in the direction of the stairway.

They raced up the stairs, and Wade listened to the everyday sounds of his house—the patter of the kids' bare feet on the hardwood floors, the creaking of the house's old pipes as the kids turned the water on and off, the lilt of their thin voices wafting downstairs. He'd taken it all for granted. Now he recognized it as music. A melodic air that had changed keys and been transposed to a dirge before he'd made time to appreciate the happy tune.

He walked through the living room, picking up empty popcorn bowls and dirty glasses and carrying them out to the kitchen. The sink was already full of lukewarm sudsy water, so he put the dishes in to soak.

Standing at the sink with his hands immersed in the lukewarm water, a wave of bitter nostalgia came over him. This was it. This part of his life was over. Tomorrow night—and God only knew how many tomorrows after—he would stand at this sink and wash one plate, one glass, one fork, one spoon. The kids would be gone, and the house would echo with the din of their absence.

His knees buckled, and he slumped over the sink, supporting his weight on his elbows. *Oh, God...how am I going to tell them. I can't do this. Don't make me do this. Help me, Lord.*

Never had he wanted so desperately to pretend everything was okay. Never had he wanted so much to go tuck each of those precious kids into bed and kiss them good-night, like it was an ordinary day.

The clatter of three sets of footsteps on the stairway jolted him. He stood up straight, dried his hands, and swabbed his forehead with the dishtowel.

The kids came to the kitchen and stood before him expectantly. They smelled of soap and toothpaste and sunshine. He breathed it in, wanting to remember all of it.

"In there," he said, slanting his head toward the living room.

They filed in and lined up on the couch. As he followed them through the house, he turned off the lights in the kitchen and dining room, leaving the house in darkness.

He flipped on a lamp and pulled a straight-back chair out from the wall. He set it backward in front of them, straddling it, resting his elbows on its back.

Three well-scrubbed faces stared up at him.

Lord, I can't do this. "Okay, guys. I need to talk to you about something important."

As though their movements were choreographed, they all leaned forward and tipped their chins up a notch.

Any other time, Wade would have laughed, but now he just wanted to get this terrible moment over with. "You guys know something's been going on...with your dad showing up here and with all my visits to the lawyer. Well, your dad... He wants you kids back. He thinks it would be best if you went to live with him. I'm not so sure that's a good idea. Your dad has had some problems and…well, I told my lawyer about that, and we're talking to the judge to try to decide what would be best."

The kids sat like statues, their eyes trained on him. He wished he could know what they were thinking. How much could they even comprehend of what he was saying? Especially little Dani.

He shifted on the chair and continued. "It takes a long time to decide things like this, and the judge thinks it might be best if you guys go stay with another family while we try to work everything out."

Beau wrinkled his brow. "What other family?"

"Well, I don't know yet. It would be a foster family. Do you know what that is?"

"Luke Hammell has foster parents. Is it like that?"

"Yes, I'm sure it is. And I bet he's pretty happy with his foster parents, right?"

Beau shrugged. "I guess."

Wade cleared his throat. "Foster parents are just ordinary moms and dads who open up their home for kids like you to stay for a while until the grownups get everything straightened out and decide what would be the very best thing for the kids."

"But why can't we just stay here while they decide?" Lacey said. "All our stuff is here. I don't want to go."

Wade leaned over the chair back and patted her arm. "I know, sweetie. I don't want you to go, either. But that's what the judge thinks would be the best. We don't really have a choice. Once a judge makes a decision, it's pretty hard to change his mind."

"How long do we hafta stay with foster parents?" Beau asked.

"I honestly don't know, bud. Hopefully not long."

"Like a week?"

Wade looked at the floor before he met Beau's gaze. "Probably longer than that. But we'll see. We'll just have to take it one day at a time."

"When do we hafta go there?"

"Well, that's why I wanted to talk to you. Remember the lady—the social worker—who came to see us that night?"

Three heads nodded in unison.

"She's going to come and pick you up tomorrow and take you to the foster home."

"Tomorrow?" A look of horror spread over Beau's features.

Dani looked at her brother and her face crumpled. "I don't want to go tomorrow, Wade."

"Can't we wait and go later?" Lacey said, her voice rising a pitch.

"How come you never told us?" Defiance sparked in Beau's eyes.

"Well…I really just found out myself, bud." He swung the chair aside and knelt on the floor in front of the couch. "Hey…I don't like this any better than you do. But maybe the judge is right. Maybe it will be good for you to be with a nice family while we get this all straightened out. I'm going to have to go to lots of meetings and stuff, and you'd have to stay at day care or with a sitter. Maybe it's best this way." He couldn't look them in the eye while he spouted things he didn't believe.

Beau folded his arms over his chest. "I'm not going."

Wade put a hand on Beau's knee. "I'm sorry, buddy, but you don't have a choice."

"Then I'll run away."

"Beau…"

The boy slithered out from under his touch and ran up the stairs. Wade let him go. He'd give him some time to cool off and talk to him later.

He took Beau's place on the couch between the girls and wrapped an arm around each one. "Do you guys understand what I'm telling you?"

He felt their heads nod against him, and a giant lump rose in his throat. He pulled the girls close and swallowed hard. "No matter what happens, I love you guys, okay? You'll always be my Lacey Daisy and my Dani Banany."

Ordinarily, the silly pet names would have produced a giggle, but now the girls just nodded harder against him.

"You know that, don't you? I couldn't be more proud of you. And I couldn't love you any more than I already do."

"I love you, too, Wade," Dani whispered.

"Me, too," Lacey echoed.

"And hey, the judge said we can see each other sometimes. So you be thinking of all the stuff you want to tell me, okay?"

"Is it gonna be a long, long time, Wade?"

"I don't know, Dani. I hope not." He sighed and gave them one more squeeze. "You guys better get to bed now. I need to go talk to Beau."

They slid off the couch, and he scooped them into his arms and hoisted one over each shoulder. He carried them up the stairs, and for a fleeting moment, they recaptured the playful, familiar joy of their bedtime ritual. Wade tried to savor every second.

He tucked the girls in, kissed each one good-night, and turned out the light, forcing himself not to think about the fact that this might be the last time he would have the tender privilege to do these things.

He went down the hall to Beau's room. He was curled up in bed facing the wall, his covers thrown off. Wade sat down on the bed beside him and put a hand on the slight shoulder. "Hey? Can we talk?"

No response.

"Beau, I know you don't like this. Believe me, I don't like it either. I hate it. I'd do anything to keep you with me. But this is one of those things we just have to accept. We can't do anything about it, so we may as well make the best of it."

Beau drew his knees up closer to his chest and let out a breath.

Wade waited for a response. "I need you to be strong for your sisters. They're younger than you are, and they probably don't understand everything that's happening. But you guys need to stick together. Lacey and Dani are going to depend on you to keep your chin up. Do you hear me?"

Met with silence, he went on. "It's not like we'll never get to see each other, you know. We get to have a visit once every week or two, maybe even—"

"Every week or two!" Beau scooted from under Wade's hand and sat up in bed with his back against the headboard. "I thought we were only going for a couple of weeks?"

"That…that's not what I said, Beau. I said I didn't *know* how long it would be. I hope it'll only be a couple of weeks, but the truth is, it probably takes longer than that to get stuff through the court system…for the judge to decide what's best for all of you."

Wade reached out and squeezed Beau's foot affectionately. "I…I want to tell you what I told the girls awhile ago. I couldn't be more proud of you. I'm going to miss you like crazy. I love you, buddy, and I'm going to—"

"You don't really mean that." Beau narrowed his eyes. "You're lying."

Wade drew back. "Of course I mean it."

"No you don't!" he shouted. "If you really loved us, you wouldn't let them take us to that stupid foster home. You'd do something!"

Wade let loose a weighty sigh. "Beau, there's nothing else I can do. I hired a lawyer to try to keep this from happening. Do you know how much lawyers cost? I swear to you I did everything I knew to keep you with me. I don't know how else to explain it."

"We don't swear," Beau said in a monotone. They were his mama's words. Starr's words.

"You're right," Wade said, aching at the memory. "I'm sorry. But I *did* do everything I could. Do you believe that?"

Beau scooted down and plopped on his back, arms under his head, staring at the ceiling.

"We'll talk about it some more in the morning, okay? You need to get to sleep now. I do love you, Beau. With all my heart."

It nearly broke him to walk out of the room. He had worked so hard to earn the boy's confidence. Steadily, over the weeks, he'd been gaining ground, and now this. How many times could a kid's trust be dashed before he just gave up?

He checked on the girls one last time, then went down to get ready for bed.

Twenty minutes later, lying on the sofa bed, he couldn't fall asleep. He relived every moment from the day Starr's kids had come into his life. He smiled at the remembrance of Dani flipping his Chiefs cap into the spaghetti at the café.

But his smile soon turned into a sob. "Oh, Starr," he whispered into the darkness, "how did this all get so messed up, babe?"

He hiccuped and rolled over on his belly, burying his face in the lumpy pillow. He tried to pray, but no words would come—except the one that had become his desperate watchword over the past weeks: *Help*.

Wade started awake and rolled over to look at the alarm clock. One o'clock in the morning. He sat up in bed, holding his breath, listening. He'd thought he'd heard a sound, but everything was quiet now. It must have been a dream. The air conditioner kicked on, and its distant drone lulled him.

All over again, the truth of what would happen in a few short hours punched him in the gut. A heaviness settled on his chest. He closed his eyes, praying sleep would rescue him.

A crash from the vicinity of the kitchen brought him upright in bed again. Heart thudding, he climbed out of bed and peered out into the hallway. He crept through the living room, avoiding the spots on the floor that he knew would creak.

The house was dark, but a bluish patch of light reflected off the floor in the kitchen. The light from the mercury lamp in the yard. The back door must be open.

"Hey!" Wade hollered. "Who's there?"

The *bang* of the back screen door answered him.

Shadow started barking. Frantically, Wade looked around for a weapon. Finding nothing, he ran through the kitchen and into the back entryway. The door was still swinging. Whoever it was, they were gone now. Heart in his throat, he raced back through the kitchen and took the stairs two at a time.

He flipped the light on in the girls' room. They both stirred beneath their quilts but slept peacefully. Nothing seemed out of place in their room.

He turned out the light and went down the hall to Beau's room.

The bed was empty except for the rumpled blankets. Beau's pillow was on the floor.

Wade flipped off the light and went down the hall to the bathroom. Empty. He ran back to Beau's room, not turning on the light, peering out the window that overlooked the driveway. Shadow's barking had stopped, and everything was quiet outside.

In the faint glow of the night-light, Wade noticed that Beau's dresser drawers were open, T-shirts and shorts spilling over the edges, as though he'd been searching for something.

Wade started down the stairs. Maybe Beau had forgotten to feed Shadow again. Twice before, he'd discovered the boy outside late at night—though never this late—trying to take care of the forgotten chore before Wade found him out. He'd probably been too hard on the poor kid.

He went out the front door onto the porch. Shadow didn't come running as he usually did. Wade whistled and called for him. No response, but a movement out on the road that ran by the house caught his eye.

Twenty-Two

Wade trotted out onto the driveway and stopped, squinting into the deep night shadows.

A hundred yards down the road, a slight boy and a dog were silhouetted against the pale moonlit sky.

He cupped his hands around his mouth and shouted. "Beau!"

The two figures moved faster. Beau appeared to be dragging something. Wade watched as the boy put a hand on Shadow's head and turned briefly to look back at the house. Wade could make out the outline of a suitcase in his hand.

"Beau! Wait!"

Wade ran back into the house and hurriedly slipped on his jeans and a pair of tennis shoes that sat by the back door. Back in the heavy night air, he sprinted down the driveway and onto the road.

Beau and Shadow had almost reached the crossroad, but they were no longer running. Out of breath, his chest aching, Wade finally caught up with them.

Beau kept walking, but Shadow pranced joyfully around Wade, letting out little yips of pleasure at this nocturnal adventure.

"Beau. Wait. Listen to me. Where are you going?"

Shoulders slumping, Beau stopped in the road, refusing to look at Wade. "I don't know." His voice cracked.

"Hey…come here." Wade went to his knees and pulled Beau into his arms. "Running away isn't going to solve anything. Believe me, I've thought about it myself."

Beau pulled away and looked him in the eye. "Really?"

Wade turned up the corners of his mouth in a dismal smile and nodded.

"Where were you gonna go?"

"I don't know… Same place you were, I guess."

Beau cocked his head, looking skeptical. "But what about us?"

Wade wrestled with how much to say. Finally he sighed. "I would have taken you with me."

He struggled to his feet, and they stood together in the middle of the dirt road, listening to the night sounds.

"You really would have run away?" Beau asked, his voice rising a pitch.

"I really wanted to. I wanted to take you and Lacey and Dani and just go someplace where nobody would bother us anymore. I didn't want to risk losing you. Not ever. But if I'd done that, Beau, I could have gone to jail. Do you understand?"

Beau nodded, his lips pressed into a thin line.

"It would have been like kidnapping. That's why I'm letting them take you tomorrow. I want to obey the law. That way, when the judge says we can all be together again, we'll never have to worry about losing each other again. Do you understand what I'm saying?"

Again, Beau nodded solemnly.

"Come on back home," Wade whispered, putting an arm around Beau's shoulders and gently turning him toward the house. "It'll be okay. I'm not going to let anything happen to you. Everything will work out okay."

In the dim cast of the summer moon, Beau looked up at him and searched his eyes. "Do you promise, Wade?"

Wade swallowed hard and nodded. "I promise," he whispered.

A chorus of cicadas started up. *Chirrup-chirrup-chirrup.* For a few minutes, they stood side by side on the road, man and boy and dog.

And as they walked back up to the house together, Wade pleaded with heaven not to make him a liar.

Even in the light of morning, the whole thing seemed surreal. Wade fixed eggs and pancakes for breakfast, and the kids ate in silence. He didn't trust himself to keep one bite down, so he stood by the stove and kept fresh pancakes frying on the griddle.

"Can I have a bunny rabbit, Wade?" Dani asked.

"I'll see what I can do," he said, a lump clogging his throat. He poured out a circle of pancake batter and, with a flourish of the bowl, attached two long blobs of batter to form ears. It was a treat Starr had fixed for them on special occasions.

"Me, too, Wade," Lacey said over a mouthful of scrambled eggs. "I want a bunny rabbit too."

"Hang on, Lacey Daisy. There's only room for one bunny on the griddle at a time."

"How about you, Beau. You feel like rabbit for breakfast?"

Beau shook his head almost imperceptibly and sat silent, moving his eggs around on the plate with his fork.

Wade looked at the clock. He had less than two hours left. A rising tide of panic caused him to lean on the counter and struggle for a breath deep enough to clear his head.

He flipped Dani's pancake and slid it onto her plate. He buttered it and helped her drizzle syrup over it. The sweet maple aroma seemed vile to Wade on this morning.

Checking to make sure the stove was off, he wiped his hands on the dishtowel. "You guys come on upstairs when you're finished. I'm going to go up and…get your things ready. And don't touch the griddle. It's still pretty hot."

He went upstairs and dragged his big suitcase down from the top of the linen closet in the hall. Wade took it into the girls' room and started pulling clothes from the dresser they shared. The sweet clothesline-fresh scent of their things wafted up from the drawers, and he brought a neat pile of folded clothes to his face and breathed in, memorizing the fragrance.

When the dresser was empty, Wade took the suitcase down the hall to Beau's room and transferred his things from the smaller suitcase he'd packed last night. He refolded the messy clump of clothes along with the rest of the contents from Beau's dresser, and placed them neatly beside the girls' clothes in the large case. Somehow it made him feel better to have all their things together in one place.

Though Frank Locke had assured him the agency had a foster home willing to take all three children, Wade still had a nagging fear that they would somehow be split up. It was hard enough to think of them being sent to live with strangers. If they shipped Beau off somewhere by himself—or, God forbid, one of the girls—Wade was afraid he might do something he'd regret. He'd promised Beau that everything would be all right, that he wouldn't let anything happen to him. It was a promise he intended to keep.

He heard Beau's footsteps in the hall and looked up. Beau came and stood in the doorway, watching him pack.

"Hi, buddy."

Beau eyed the empty dresser. "How come you're packing everything? All of it?"

"Well…I don't know what all you might need." Wade's mind raced. He wished he'd thought to leave some of Beau's clothes in the dresser. It would have been such a simple thing. Now Beau probably thought Wade was anxious to be rid of him.

"There's still some of your stuff in the laundry," he said finally. "We'll leave that here. It…it'll be waiting for you when you come back." He shouldn't be planting seeds of hope where he couldn't be sure a promise would bloom, but he couldn't leave Beau wondering either. *Don't make a liar of me, Lord. Please…*

Wade put the lid of the suitcase down and started to zip it. He wished he could add his own clothes and pretend they were just going on a little trip together. Disneyland maybe. Or Six Flags. Why hadn't he done those things with the kids? They'd missed so many opportunities over the past months—opportunities that might never come again.

He pushed the thought away and motioned for Beau. "Hey, bud, come and help me, will you? This thing's about to blow."

Beau didn't laugh at his sorry attempt at humor. But he came and held down each corner while Wade tugged on the zippers. Silently, they worked their way around each side of the case until the zippers met in the middle.

Wade picked up the heavy bag and set it by the door. Then, without a word, he pulled Beau into his arms. Beau returned the hug, wrapping his arms around Wade's waist. They stood that way in the middle of the room saying a wordless good-bye.

Finally he pulled back and ruffled Beau's wayward cowlick. "You better go brush your teeth, bud."

Wade followed Beau down the hall to the bathroom and cleared the kids' toiletries from the medicine cabinet. He helped them load their favorite toys into a large duffel bag, and the four of them went downstairs to wait.

At exactly nine o'clock, Wade heard the crunch of gravel on the drive. The kids looked at one another, then at him.

"Well...this is it," he said. He stood and started for the door. Lacey and Danica followed him. He put a hand on the doorknob, then turned and knelt in front of the girls, motioning for Beau to join them. He didn't want to say this last good-bye in front of strangers.

Beau came reluctantly, and Wade enveloped the three of them in his arms. "I want to pray with you guys before you go."

They bowed their heads as one.

Don't let me break down, Lord. Keep my voice steady. He cleared his throat loudly and swallowed a bitter lump of sorrow. "Father, be with these kids wherever they go. Keep them close to you. Watch over them and keep them safe. I...I'm going to miss them, Lord. Please, Father, bring us back together soon...real soon. In Jesus' name, amen."

Lacey tucked herself tighter under Wade's arm.

The jangle of the doorbell pierced the air, and Wade rose to open the door. A suffocating summer wind sucked the cool air from the living room, seeming to take the air from his lungs with it.

"Good morning," Betty Graffe said cheerfully. The wind whipped her hair, revealing strands of gray. "It's a hot one today, isn't it?" She looked from Wade to the children and back. "Well. Is everyone ready?"

Wade stood by helplessly as Ms. Graffe and another woman from SRS—someone the social worker introduced as a family support worker—packed the children's belongings into the trunk of the county vehicle. The kids stood on the porch and watched.

Wade pulled Betty Graffe aside. "Will you take them directly to the foster home?" he asked.

"We'll transport them to the agency, and they'll go to the foster home from there." She looked at him for a long moment. "They'll be well taken care of, Mr. Sullivan. You don't need to worry about them."

He nodded.

"Okay, children," she said, "It's time to go. Let's get buckled up."

The family support worker took Dani by the hand and led her around to the other side of the car.

Dani waved, seeming suddenly shy. "Bye, Wade."

He lifted a hand and pasted on a smile, unable to speak over the catch in his throat. An overwhelming sense of loss flooded him.

Betty Graffe made sure Beau and Lacey were buckled in. Before she closed the door, she motioned for Wade.

"If you'd like to say good-bye…"

He knelt on the gravel beside the car, welcoming the pain as the sharp rocks cut into his knee. "I'll see you guys soon. You be good, okay?"

The girls nodded solemnly.

"I love you Lacey Daisy. I love you Dani Banany. Beau, I love you, buddy."

Wade stood and Ms. Graffe started to close the door. Beau looked at his lap, then suddenly yanked off his seat belt.

He pushed the door open and tried to climb from the car. "I forgot to feed Shadow!" he yelled, panic in his voice.

"Hey, hey…" Wade knelt beside the car again, refastening the buckle around his waist. He patted Beau's knee. "It's okay, buddy. I'll feed him. You…you can take care of him when you come back, okay?"

He looked at the three of them, lined up on the backseat of the car, and he knew he had to get out of there. He gave Beau's leg one last pat and held up a hand in farewell, forcing a smile that felt obscene on his face. "I'll see you guys in a few days, okay?"

Wade closed the back door of the car carefully, and Betty Graffe went around and got behind the wheel. Beau put a hand on the window, and

even behind the reflections in the glass, Wade could see the agony contorting the boy's freckled face. He was grateful he couldn't see the girls.

The car backed slowly around, then headed down the narrow lane.

Wade stood watching, his hand still raised in a feeble wave, until the
car disappeared from sight.

Then he slumped onto the porch steps and wept.

Twenty-Three

Dee Thackery pulled into the Xaviers' driveway, swinging wide to miss a tricycle that had been abandoned on the edge of the curb. She cut the engine and leaned over the back of the driver's seat. She cleared a rumpled pile of papers off the backseat to make room for the three children she was picking up for a visitation.

Dee was grateful that Ben and Karen Xavier had agreed to take these children. She wasn't sure she could have placed them together, otherwise. It broke her heart whenever siblings had to be split up, especially when the kids were as sweet as these three angels.

When Dee had phoned Karen earlier in the week, it sounded as if the adjustment was going well. After the challenges they'd faced with the last kids, Dee felt certain God had seen to it that Ben and Karen's next experience was a good one. She'd breathed a heavy sigh of relief when she hung up the phone.

She didn't quite know what to expect this morning. Often, the first visitation after children had been removed from a home took place at St. Joseph's or on neutral territory. But Ben Xavier had mentioned that the Parnell kids were really homesick, and they were especially lonesome for their dog, so she'd arranged to take them to the country house where they'd lived with their mother's fiancé since her death a few months ago.

Dee had supervised a visitation with the Parnell children's birth father just last Friday, and in spite of the fact he hadn't been a part of the children's lives for several years, she felt the visit had gone quite well. Though he had a distant history of drug use and spousal abuse, the father appeared to have changed. He seemed genuinely caring and conscientious. She admired the way he had taken it slow with the kids—especially the little girls. He had let them interact with him at their own pace and hadn't tried to force anything.

The fiancé had been reported to SRS for possible neglect, so the judge had ordered the children into the care of Child Protective Services, granting both men supervised visitation rights. Uncharitable though it was, she already had an idea in her mind of the kind of man who would fight Darrin Parnell for custody. She knew that image was mostly to blame for her nervousness about today's visitation. She shook off the sudden memory of her stepfather.

Steering her thoughts to the moment, Dee locked the car and went up the walk to the Xaviers' front door.

Karen answered the doorbell almost immediately. She welcomed Dee into the sunny foyer where the Parnell children were lined up on an antique church bench.

"Hi, Karen. Thanks for having them ready." Dee knelt slightly to the children's eye level. "Good morning. Don't you all look nice. Are you guys ready to go for a visit?

"Are we gonna go home?" the littlest girl asked.

Dee couldn't tell if it was apprehension or eagerness that made her voice quaver. "Well, we're going for a visit... Out to the farm where you used to live."

"We still live there," the boy said, folding thin arms over his chest. "And it's not a farm. It's just in the country."

"Oh, sorry," Dee said, flashing Karen a covert grin.

"Everybody ready?" She held the door open as they filed out to the car. "Thanks, Karen. See you in an hour or two. I'll make sure they have lunch before I bring them back. Hopefully the guy'll feed them, but if not, we'll hit McDonald's on the way back."

She helped the children buckle up in the backseat, then went around and got behind the wheel. Glancing down at the directions she'd jotted down, she mumbled, "Let's see... It's off of Raphael Road. I think that's west of town."

"Yeah, it's west," the boy piped up from behind her. "Six miles west on Thirty-seventh Road. It's 3303 Thirty-seventh Road."

"Thanks. Beau, isn't it?" She knew the answer, had it on the papers on the seat beside her, but it was a good way to make conversation.

"Yeah," he grunted in reply, slumping lower in the seat.

She caught the girls' eyes in her rearview mirror. "Okay, I know one of you is Lacey, and one is Danica, but I get mixed up which is which."

"I'm Lacey," the older sister said. "And she's Dani."

Three miles past the Coyote city limits, Beau perked up. "It's four more houses," he told Dee, leaning across his sister to the center of the backseat to look through the bug-splattered windshield.

His voice rose, and he pointed to the left. "There! That's it. Right up there. Better slow down. You're gonna miss the turn. Everybody always misses the turn 'cause the trees hide our driveway comin' from the west."

Dee hit the brake pedal, and the wheels ground on the blacktop. She eased the car onto the long, curving drive. The traditional curved-top mailbox at the end of the lane bore the name Sullivan. She glanced in her rearview mirror again and saw the kids had loosened seat belts and were all piled against the right rear window, practically atop one another. Beau had his nose pressed to the window, and the girls were shoving to see around him.

"Look, you guys," Beau said, "Wade took down the birdhouse."

"I wonder where Shadow is?" Dani said.

"Wade probably tied him up so he wouldn't knock *her* over." Lacey hooked a thumb in Dee's direction.

"No, he's probably huntin' for birds down by the river," Beau said.

Dee stopped in front of the house and put the car in park. "Well... here we are."

Wade walked through the house for the hundredth time, straightening pictures on the wall, brushing invisible dust from the tabletops, and checking out the window to see if they were here yet.

He'd never been so aware of the way his home might look to an outsider. Every dish was put away, the porcelain sinks sparkled, and the hardwood floors gleamed. He'd even plumped the pillows on the couch in the living room. It was something he'd always teased Starr about because she fluffed them five times a day, only to have them flattened again every time someone sat down, which was, after all, what couches were made for.

The thought of Starr brought the usual quick smile and subsequent plunge into melancholy that it always did. And something new today: the stark realization that the reason his home looked so neat and tidy was the absence of her children. The life, the spirit of this house had gone with them, and right now, Wade would have traded the shiny surfaces and Pine-Sol scented air for all the dirty dishes and muddy floors and cluttered tabletops three kids could generate.

He brushed off the depression. His kids were coming today. He wanted to be upbeat for them, wanted this to be a good time together. But after two weeks, he missed them so badly his heart ached from the emptiness.

Of course their visit would be supervised. What would it be like to have someone hovering over them, listening to every word they said, watching every expression of affection? He reminded himself that he needed to remain civil to the social worker who came with the kids. He couldn't give them any reason to take away this one privilege he still had with his kids. Frank Locke had said that after today, he should get to see the kids every week until the hearing.

They had not been able to get a date until the fall. It seemed unbelievable that a small Kansas county court could be so logjammed they'd make a man wait weeks—maybe months—on end to get his children back.

Darrin Parnell had been furious about that. He had gone back to Minneapolis temporarily, promising to bring back his fiancée—a fact that Frank Locke was none too happy about. "It would help if there was a mother figure in your life for the kids, Wade. I know you can't just go out and buy a wife, but it's something the judge will definitely consider. Maybe we can somehow make the aunt look like mother material?"

When Wade pooh-poohed the idea, Locke had said, "Well, we need *something*, Wade. This bachelor father scenario isn't going to fly."

Wade sensed his desperation. But he couldn't make promises for Sophie.

The crunch of tires on the gravel drive pulled Wade from his reverie. They were here.

He looked toward the ceiling, noticing a cobweb he'd missed in a far corner. He closed his eyes. *Oh, Father, please be with us today. Be with the kids. Help them to understand what's happening. Don't let me get emotional. Help us to make memories they won't forget. Please, God…don't let them forget me.*

It was a prayer he'd prayed a hundred times in the days since that SRS car had driven out of his driveway carrying his children, their faces pressed against the window. It was a selfish prayer. He knew that, but he didn't care. Though it was a blessing, under the circumstances, it frightened Wade to remember that Lacey had no memory of the man she'd called Daddy for the first three years of her life. Even Beau, who'd been five when Starr fled from Darrin Parnell, had scant memories of his father. Would Dani forget Wade the same way? He couldn't bear to think of it.

He went into the living room and pulled back the curtain. A blue Ford Taurus stopped in front of the house, then pulled forward again and slowly drove around back. Wade could almost hear the kids telling the driver that nobody ever used the front door.

Shadow barked down by the river. Out of habit, Wade started to head out the back door to assure the callers he was friendly. Then he heard the muffled sounds of the kids' joyful greetings and the slam of car doors. Their laughter was the sweetest music he could imagine.

The front doorbell rang. The kids must not have been able to persuade this social worker that it really was okay to use the back door.

Walking through the living room, his heartbeat matched the staccato of his boots on the hardwood floor.

He'd barely turned the knob when the door flew open.

"Wade!" He was instantly bowled over by the three little people he loved more than life itself. They brought him to his knees—both physically and emotionally—and for a split second Wade was terrified he would collapse in a tearful heap on the floor beside them.

Instead, a mantle of peace settled over him. He wrapped his arms around all three of them, memorizing the sweet fragrance of their hair and the exquisite softness of their skin.

Finally he pulled back and looked at them, one by one. "Hey, you guys! You're looking good."

"That's 'cause we all had to take a baff and wash our hair before we could come home," Dani told him, hands on hips, head tipped charmingly to one side.

Wade ruffled her bangs. "Well, you look good…and you smell good too."

She giggled.

Wade didn't miss her reference to "home." He wondered if the kids understood that this was just a visit.

"Can we go out and play with Shadow?" Beau asked.

Wade struggled to his feet and, for the first time, acknowledged the social worker who'd stood, silently watching their reunion.

He put out a hand and forced a smile. "I'm Wade."

"Yes, I know. Dee Thackery." She offered a polite smile but seemed to ignore his outstretched hand.

Wade dried his damp palms on his blue jeans and dipped his head. "I'm not really sure how this is supposed to go. Is…is it okay if the kids play outside?"

She gave a slight shrug. "Sure. We can all go out there."

So that was how it was going to be. They would all have to stay together so she could monitor his every move and make sure he didn't harm these children he loved like his own flesh and blood. He felt the anger rising, but forced it down and pasted on another smile.

Wade looked at his watch. He'd been told he'd have an hour with the children, and already almost ten minutes had hurtled by. He didn't want to waste another minute. "Okay, then. We'll go out the back door." He turned to Beau. "You want to play some catch?"

"I didn't bring my mitt. How 'bout Frisbee?"

"Good idea," he said with false enthusiasm.

Lacey looked up at him with a puzzled expression on her pixie face. He looked from Lacey to Beau and Dani and saw the same hint of confusion in their eyes. It struck him that in his zealousness to impress the social worker with what a good daddy he was, he was behaving like an idiot. And the kids were on to him.

He shot up another prayer. *Just let me be myself, Lord. Don't let me waste another minute.* He blew out a sigh, which garnered the same quizzical look from the social worker. Well, never mind her. This day was for him and his kids. She was just along for the ride.

He grabbed a couple of Frisbees off the shelf over the coatrack, where Beau's mitt used to hang, and led the way outside.

Shadow met them at the door, and the girls lit on the dog like butterflies on wildflowers, running their hands over his massive black head and cooing sweet words in his ears. Wade's heart overflowed with love and joy at their reunion, no matter how brief.

Beau ran backward down the knoll that sloped to the river, arms open for Wade's toss. Wade zipped a Frisbee to the boy, then turned to the social worker, who was still standing by the back door. "I can get you a lawn chair if you like."

"Oh no. That's all right. I'm fine."

"Well, you can have a seat there on the stoop. I swept it off this morning."

"Oh. Thanks." She moved to the steps and sank onto the bottom one, stretching her long, khaki-clad legs in front of her.

Her hair caught glints from the sun, and Wade couldn't help but think of all the times it had been Starr stretched out on those steps, watching the children play. Dee Thackery's hair was a few shades darker than Starr's, and she wasn't as tall and lanky, but she had the same delicate feminine quality about her. For some reason, he found it unsettling.

Wade was thankful when he had to run back down the hill to snag Beau's errant throw. He winged the Frisbee back and stood watching Beau, marveling that the kids were back with him.

The wind caught the Frisbee, and Beau ran headlong toward the river.

"Oh!" The social worker jumped up and cast an anxious glance toward the riverbank. She cupped her hands around her mouth. "Don't go too close to the water, Beau!"

Wade turned to watch her, curbing a smile. "It's okay," he shouted. "He knows. The kids respect the river."

"Oh. Okay." Seeming reluctant, she sank back onto the step.

Beau retrieved the Frisbee and whipped it back in Wade's direction.

Catching a breeze, the disk sailed over Wade's head, sending him back up the hill toward the house.

Lacey and Danica met him by the porch, Shadow in tow. "Can we play too, Wade?" Lacey asked, scratching the dog behind one ear.

"Sure. You'll have to spread out a little bit, though. And you might have to fight Shadow for it." He reached down to scratch the other velvety black ear. "Isn't that right, boy? Huh? Isn't that right?" he cooed at the dog, as though it were a baby.

Wade felt himself relaxing. This wasn't as bad as he'd imagined. Dee Thackery hadn't tried to orchestrate things or make him feel inadequate. She stayed in the background, seemingly a neutral observer.

Lacey let out a little gasp. "Wade! I almost forgot." She came to stand squarely in front of him. Hands on her hips, she tipped back her head and opened her mouth wide.

"What?" He cocked his head to one side, not sure what she was doing.

She closed her mouth, glared at him, then rolled her eyes. "I lost a tooth! Didn't you even notice?"

He knelt in front of her. "Really? Open up. Let me see."

"Aaahhhh…"

"Well, I'll be. You sure did." He rested a hand lightly on her shoulder. "Did the tooth fairy come?"

"Uh-huh. She only left me a quarter, though."

"Well, hey, times must be tough in Tooth Fairyland. That's pretty cool, though, squirt. Are you getting hungry?" He turned to the social worker. "It's a little early, but I fixed some lunch."

She glanced at her watch. "Actually, they should probably eat now. I need to take them back in half an hour."

Out of habit, Wade looked at his watch too. "Okay. It won't take but a minute to get things on the table.

"Beau! Girls!" he called. "Come on in. It's time for lunch." He made his voice light, but Wade felt like he'd been punched in the stomach. His time with the kids was almost over.

Twenty-Four

Wade pulled a bowl of potato salad from the refrigerator and handed it to Lacey. "Here, sweetie. Would you put this on the table? And you and Dani can set the table. We'll need five places." He motioned for Beau. "Bring the other chair in from the living room, would you, bud?"

"Oh no…" Dee Thackery held up a hand and shook her head. "That's all right. I…I won't be eating with you."

"Please, I've fixed plenty."

She squirmed uncomfortably, but Wade could tell she was reconsidering.

"Please," he repeated. "You have to eat anyway, right?"

She offered a weak smile. "Well…all right."

He took two tall glasses from the cupboard, along with three brightly colored plastic drinking cups. "What would you like to drink?"

"Oh…just water is fine."

"I have lemonade."

"You gotta try the lemonade," Lacey said. "Wade makes good lemonade."

"No thanks. I'll just have water. Is there anything I can do?"

Wade opened the refrigerator and brought out a platter of ham-and-cheese sandwiches. He handed it to her. "You could put these on the table… Oh, Beau, grab a bag of chips from the pantry, will you?"

Dani looked at the plate of sandwiches and put her arms akimbo. "You mean you didn't make macaroni and cheese?"

Wade opened his mouth to respond, then caught a teasing glint in her blue eyes. He burst out laughing. "You little rascal," he said, giving her nose a gentle pinch.

Dani giggled, and Dee Thackery shot Wade a puzzled glance.

"She used to give me the dickens about making macaroni and cheese for every meal," he explained.

"Oh." The social worker gave a polite but obviously forced laugh.

"Apparently you had to be there," he said, grinning. He turned to survey the table. "Well, I think we can eat."

He motioned the social worker to the chair Beau had carried in. The kids gravitated to their regular places, leaving him and Dee Thackery side by side at the round table. He didn't miss that she inched her chair closer to Lacey's before she sat down. He moved his own chair a few inches in the opposite direction, not wanting her to feel uncomfortable. He wondered what she'd been told about him.

He took his seat. Immediately, Dani grabbed his hand. Lacey reached for the social worker's hand, and Beau wrapped his fingers around Dani's.

Wade cleared his throat and looked to his left. "Um…we…hold hands around the table when we say grace," he explained.

Feeling awkward, he put his hand on the table, tacitly inviting her to take it. She turned and took Lacey's hand but seemed not to notice Wade as she bowed her head, keeping her right hand in her lap.

"Beau, would you like to say the blessing?"

Beau shook his head and blushed. "No. You."

"Okay." Wade bowed his head. "Heavenly Father, thank you for this time together. Thank you for this food you've provided. And please bless our guest. Amen." After the words were out of his mouth, he felt a little foolish. She wasn't exactly a guest. She was a "monitor," an overseer who—when he thought about it—had been assigned to pass judgment on him.

Catching himself, he pushed the disquieting thoughts away and took a gulp of lemonade. He set his glass down and took the plastic wrap from the sandwich platter. "Can you start this around, Dani? Lacey, please pass the potato salad to Ms. Thackery."

Dani tipped her head to one side and wrinkled her brow. "Hows come you call her Ms. Thackery? Her name is Dee."

Wade and Dee exchanged awkward glances, then spoke at the same time.

"Well, because that's—"

"You could call me Dee."

They laughed together self-consciously.

"Then Dee it is," Wade said. "Ms. Thackery *is* kind of a mouthful."

He cleared his throat. "So, hey, you guys…how's everything going—at the foster home?" He turned to Dee. "Is it okay if I ask that?"

She suddenly turned all business. "Sure. They're getting along just fine. The foster parents said there haven't been any prob—"

"May I ask the kids?" he said, realizing too late how rude he sounded. She pulled back and stared at him. "I'm sorry. I was just trying to answer your question."

He nodded and attempted a smile of apology, which she ignored.

"I just…I'd rather hear it from them," he said, painfully aware he was likely not making the good impression on her that he needed to for the sake of the kids. He turned to Beau. "Are you feeling okay about how things are going, bud?"

"Yeah, I guess so," Beau said, wiping a dollop of mayonnaise off his chin. "Jason's cool. And Ben's okay…but he's not around much."

"Jason?"

"Jason is Ben and Karen's son," Dee interjected. "He's in high school."

"I see." He hoped she wasn't going to jump in and answer every question he asked the kids. He turned pointedly to Lacey. "Lace? Everything going okay with you?"

Lacey nodded. Wade waited for the animated report he'd come to expect from the chatty seven-year-old, but she just shrugged and went back to munching on her sandwich.

"How about you, Dani Banany?"

Dani opened her mouth to answer, but Lacey suddenly leaned forward and glared at him. "Hey! You didn't call me Lacey Daisy!" She stuck her lower lip out in a genuine pout.

He put a finger to his lips. "Shh… Dani was talking. Wait your turn —Lacey Daisy."

Her lips turned up in a satisfied smile, and she popped a potato chip in her mouth.

Wade reached over and patted Dani's arm. "Okay, sweetie, what were you saying?"

"I forget…"

"You were going to tell me how you like it at the foster home."

"Karen's nice."

"Good…good." He wasn't sure what he'd wanted to hear, but learning that everybody was nice, that everything was going fine, and that there were seemingly no problems at all somehow didn't comfort him the way it should have.

"So…everybody's doing okay, then?" he said.

Three heads nodded solemnly around the table.

They ate in silence to the tune of forks clunking against pottery and ice tinkling in glasses. Wade thought about their answers and realized with shame that he'd actually hoped the kids might be just a bit miserable without him. Of course he was glad they were safe and well cared for. But it hurt a little that while he'd been consumed with loneliness and homesickness for them, they seemed to be weathering the separation quite well.

More than anything, he hated the fact that they had a life apart from him. That they were making memories and sharing experiences that had nothing to do with him.

He looked around the table and noticed the plates were almost empty. "Who's ready for dessert?"

Beau's eyes lit up. "What is it?"

"Nothing too exciting. Just ice cream. But I have caramel sauce and chocolate syrup to put on it."

"Me!" Lacey crowed.

"Me, too!" said Dani.

"Would you like some?" he asked Dee.

She took the paper napkin from her lap and wiped the corners of her mouth. "No, thank you."

The woman seemed determined to remain aloof. Wade pushed back his chair and went to take the tub of ice cream from the freezer. He stood at the kitchen counter, digging out ice cream that had frozen rock hard.

"Is there anything I can help with?" Dee asked from her place at the table.

"Oh. Well…if you'd like to open the toppings and put them on the table…"

She came over to the counter and stood awkwardly at his side.

He reached into an overhead cupboard and handed her a jar of caramel sauce. "The chocolate syrup is in the door of the fridge. And you'll find spoons in that drawer." He nodded in the direction of the utensil drawer.

"You're sure you wouldn't eat just one scoop?"

"No...I'm sure. This is a little early for me to be having lunch."

"I know. It's early for me, too. But...I thought it would be good to have lunch here...for the kids, you know. I...didn't realize the time would go by so fast."

She nodded noncommittally and took the ice cream toppings to the table.

He followed her, juggling four bowls of ice cream.

"Here we go," he said, plopping a bowl in front of each of the kids.

For the next few minutes it was pleasant chaos as arms crisscrossed the table reaching for various sauces and toppings.

Wade helped Dani spoon her ice cream into bite-size chunks.

Dee sat with her arms folded primly, watching them.

"Can I stir, Wade?" Beau asked. The kids had always loved stirring their ice cream into a thick milkshake consistency, but Starr had made a rule that it wasn't allowed when they had company.

"Let's not," Wade said, arching an eyebrow toward Dee.

"Aw, c'mon, Wade...she's not company."

"Beau." Wade spoke firmly and shook his head. "Not this time."

Beau moped a little, then dug back into his ice cream.

They ate in silence. When the last spoon clattered into the bowl, Dee looked pointedly at her watch and then at Wade. "I really do need to get them back."

"Already?" Wade looked up at the clock on the wall above his desk even as the clock in the foyer began to chime. It was straight-up noon. His heart sank.

"We hafta go back?" Dani asked. "But we just got here. I wanna play with Shadow some more." Her face crumpled. Tears sprang to her eyes, and she climbed down from her chair and ran to Wade.

He let her crawl onto his lap and wrapped her in his arms. "Hey, Dani girl, it's okay. You can play with Shadow when you come next week."

"That's too long."

"I know…I know," he said, brushing a strand of straw-colored hair from her tear-dampened cheek. He kissed the top of her head. "I'll miss you."

She snuggled close against his chest, and Wade flashed a look of frustration at Dee Thackery. She didn't acknowledge him but began clearing dishes from the table.

He felt bad. It wasn't Dee's fault his kids had been taken from him. And he needed her in his corner. Frank Locke had warned him that Dee's recommendation, based on what she observed of his interaction with the kids, would carry tremendous weight at the upcoming hearings that would decide legal custody for the children.

He patted Dani's back and slid her to the floor. "You go wash your hands, okay? Then we'll go out and see Shadow again before you leave."

She sniffed and rubbed her eyes, then started for the bathroom. Lacey followed.

Dee carried a stack of dirty plates to the sink.

"You don't need to do that," Wade said, taking them from her. "I can take care of them later."

"Well, okay. I really do need to get the kids back."

"I know. I'm sorry… I didn't mean to be…difficult."

She waved him off and carried the potato salad and the nearly empty sandwich platter to the kitchen counter.

"Beau, go check on the girls, will you? And wash your own hands while you're in there. Hustle up, okay?"

Beau obeyed, seeming to sense the tension in the air.

When the kids emerged from the bathroom a minute later, Wade had the leftovers safely put away in the refrigerator.

"Everybody ready?" Dee asked. "Let's go get in the car."

"We hafta tell Shadow good-bye," Beau reminded her.

"Make it really quick," Dee said.

"I'll call him," Wade said, starting for the back door. Dee and the kids followed him into the bright sunshine. He whistled for the dog. Shadow came running up from the riverbank, prancing around them, panting and drooling.

The three of them knelt by the dog, petting him and talking to him in high-pitched voices.

"Bye-bye, Shadow," Dani said, sounding close to tears again.

Beau patted the dog's neck. "See you next week, boy."

Wade saw Dee glance surreptitiously at her watch.

"Okay, guys," he said. "It's time to go. Shadow will be waiting for you next week." He looked at Dee, hoping he hadn't spoken too soon. "Is that all right? Can they come out here again next week?"

"I think that should be fine," she said. "Same time?"

He hesitated. "Um…this is a really bad time of day for me, with work and everything. Could we possibly make it either early in the morning or late afternoon? My partner and I are working on a remodeling job about twenty miles outside of town," he explained. "It's a little hard to get back and forth. It would really help if we could change the time."

"I'll have to check my schedule. I'll give you a call."

He couldn't read her expression, but he put up a hand. "Well, if it doesn't work I can figure something out. With my job."

"I understand," she said. "Well, we'd better go." Dee put a hand on each of the girls' shoulders and gently turned them toward the waiting car. "I'll let you know."

Five minutes later, Wade stood alone in the drive, watching as the trail of dust Dee's car kicked up faded to nothing.

Twenty-Five

Wade stood in the drive, shading his eyes, seeing only an empty road. Dee Thackery's car had disappeared from sight, carrying away the most precious cargo imaginable. He whispered a prayer for the kids, then trudged to the end of the lane and flipped down the arched door of the mailbox. Inside, the usual stack of catalogs and bills were neatly bundled with a rubber band.

He stripped off the elastic and leafed through the envelopes as he walked slowly back up the drive. The sun's fiery rays bored through the thin fabric of his cotton shirt, but he was in no hurry to go back into the dead silence of the house. He culled the obvious junk mail from among the catalogs and letters and tucked it under his arm, ready for the trash bin.

When he reached the porch, he sat down on the wide steps and sorted through the rest of the mail. There was the electric bill—probably sky-high now that he'd turned the air conditioner on. And another notice from the hospital about Dani's emergency room bill he still owed on.

The monthly State Farm bill in its distinctive red and white envelope was there. It still gave him a moment of pause every month to see a letter addressed to Starr. With the kids gone he hadn't used Starr's car much. He probably ought to sell it. But he hated to open what could be a real can of worms. Though he'd been writing the checks for Starr's auto insurance for several months now, everything was still in her name. He had no idea what was involved in getting it changed. He'd probably find out when it came time to pay the tags and taxes in November.

He sighed and added the bill to the "deal with later" pile. He picked up the only remaining letter, a regular number ten business envelope. He had to read the return address twice before he realized what he was holding. In spite of the sun beating down on him, a chill started at the small of his back and snaked its way up his spine.

Coyote County Coroner, the simple black script read. With trembling fingers, he tore open the envelope.

Dee dropped three subdued children off at the Xaviers' and headed back to the office. She checked her watch and stepped on the gas. She had a case-planning meeting in half an hour.

The sun's heat filtered through the windshield, and even with the air conditioner running, it was hot and humid. Her cotton blouse clung to her skin, and she felt irritable and out of sorts.

Visitations often left her feeling disconcerted and mildly depressed, knowing that, too often, children would be integrated back into a home situation that was far from ideal. In some cases, they would suffer for it the rest of their lives. Her visit to the Parnell kids' home had been unsettling as well, but not for the usual reasons.

As far as she could see, the children adored Wade Sullivan. It was obvious they felt completely at home in the farmhouse, and Wade appeared competent and comfortable with the kids. Maybe that was what bothered her. It seemed rather odd that a single man would take such an interest in three children to whom he had no blood relationship.

She thought of the way little Dani had run to Wade and cried on his shoulder. A fleeting image of Mick Cranston flashed through her mind. Her stepfather had babied her the same way when she was younger. It wasn't until she was older that his affections had turned sinister. Or maybe there had always been something perverse underlying his interactions with her, and she just hadn't understood until it was too late.

She tried not to think too much about that time in her life. But sometimes her job seemed to throw her past in her face through the eyes of the children she worked with. Those were the times when she realized how much her past had influenced her career choice. And on good days she recognized it as one of the ways God had redeemed her past, allowing her to be part of the "rescue" that had come too late for her.

Her thoughts turned to her own father, and again she found herself comparing Wade Sullivan. She had to admit that the affection Wade expressed toward the Parnell children was as much like her natural father's as it was like Mick's. There had been nothing perverse about her dad's love for her. It had been a tender, beautiful thing—and the greatest of her losses in her parents' divorce.

Contrasting the two father figures in her life, she was reminded of the need to be constantly wary of how easily her past could color her perceptions in this business.

The truth was, Wade Sullivan seemed far more at ease with the kids than their biological father did. Of course, that was understandable. Darrin Parnell had been separated from his children for several years. It would take time to build relationships with them again. She had to admire the man. He'd returned to his insurance job in Minneapolis, but he was still making the eighteen-hour round trip to see his kids almost every week. As much as Dee knew her own father had loved her, Darrin's effort to see his kids was more than her father had done when her mother had moved Dee a mere six hours away from John Thackery.

Darrin Parnell's obvious devotion went a long way to convince Dee that, whatever problems he'd had in the past, he was strongly committed to making things work with his kids this time. This case would likely turn out to be a real victory for the family preservation movement Social and Rehabilitation Services championed. And it was her privilege to be part of that process. Sometimes she had to remind herself it *was* a privilege to be part of the healing of fractured families.

Dee eased the Taurus into the cramped parking lot at St. Joseph's. Clay Two Feathers' old Chevy was gone from its usual spot under the only shade tree on the lot adjacent to the brick building. She smiled as she thought how Clay made sure to be the first one to work every morning just to claim that spot. Never mind that he lost parking dibs mere hours into every workday the minute he had to transport a kid or put in an appearance at the courthouse. Chuckling to herself, she pulled into "his" space. She parked there whenever she could, just to get his goat. As soon as he got back to the office, he'd seek her out and give her what for.

It was a silly, juvenile game they played, but it was a fun diversion from the heaviness this job sometimes held.

Dee rolled her windows down a crack against the heat, locked her car, and went in the back door of the agency. A welcome blast of cool air hit her. She headed down the narrow hallway to her office, mentally composing her case report about this morning's visit to Wade Sullivan's place in the country.

Sophie wiped off the four-top and straightened the containers holding the Sweet'n Low and sugar packets. Before moving on to the next table, she stopped to stretch, kneading the taut muscles in her lower back. Brushing back a strand of hair that had escaped her ponytail, her fingers grazed the wound on her cheek. It was healing nicely, and her bruises had faded to a faint yellow green. But even though Darrin Parnell had supposedly gone back to Minneapolis, Sophie was still looking over her shoulder.

He'd warned her he would return on a regular basis to visit the kids. And he'd promised she hadn't heard the last of him.

After spending almost a week at Lydia's apartment, Sophie had finally gone back to her own place. Not that she was sleeping well at night. All her dreams were nightmares starring Darrin Parnell.

She'd only talked to Wade twice since the kids had gone into foster care. She knew it was killing him to see them only once a week. Truth was, she missed the little snots too. More than she'd ever thought she would. Wade had told her she was welcome to come over whenever the social worker brought the kids out for a visit. He'd sounded as though he really wanted her there.

Wade didn't deserve everything that had happened. And it wasn't over yet. Apparently, unless Darrin gave up his rights to the kids, this was going to court. What if Darrin ended up with the kids?

The thought brought a sharp pang of guilt. She still hadn't confessed to Wade—or anyone else, for that matter—that it was Darrin who beat her up that night in the parking lot. She would have told him if she thought it would mean they'd lock Darrin up and throw away the key. But she knew better. For all the times he'd worked Starr over, he'd spent a total of one night in jail, and that only resulted in his giving Starr a worse beating when he got out of the slammer than the one she'd called the police for in the first place.

Sophie had never seen anyone hoodwink people the slick way Darrin Parnell could. She considered herself a pretty good judge of people, and yet he'd snowed her. Boy, had he snowed her. But then, even Starr hadn't seen the man for what he really was—until it was too late.

Sophie moved to another table and scrubbed the bar rag hard on the Formica surface, trying unsuccessfully to push the thoughts from her mind.

She thought about what Darrin had asked her to do. Correction: Darrin never asked anybody for anything. He demanded it. Or he saw to it that you owed him one. And he wasn't subtle about calling in his chits. She rubbed her jaw and, out of habit, looked over her shoulder toward the front door of the café. Silly, since she'd locked up and put the Closed sign in place thirty minutes ago.

Twenty-Six

Wade read the stark words again. It still seemed unbelievable that he could be holding an autopsy report for his beloved Starr. She was still so fully alive in his memories. Even now, more than three months after he'd discovered her lifeless body on the floor of the bedroom they'd been so eager to share, it was still hard to fathom that she was gone forever from his life.

He stared at the two folded pages the coroner's office had sent. Though he didn't understand most of the pathologist's report, one sentence stood out like a billboard: "In my opinion the cause of death was cerebral aneurysm secondary to the presence of phenylpropanolamine."

The toxicology lab report attached to Starr's autopsy report shouldn't have contained more than perhaps a trace of caffeine from the cup of coffee Wade had made her the morning she died. The caffeine was there all right, under the column marked Drug Confirmation Results. But there was the technical-sounding word again.

Phenylpropanolamine (PPA) detected in blood.

Why couldn't they just write these things in plain English? Wade had no idea what this PPA was, but why would Starr have had a foreign substance in her blood? Something strong enough to contribute to her death, if he was reading the report correctly.

Could the paint fumes have been strong enough to get into her bloodstream? He knew nothing about this sort of thing, but it didn't seem likely. Yet it was equally unlikely she had actually ingested something that would kill her.

Though Starr had experimented with alcohol and even drugs during a rebellious youth, she had been ashamed of the fact, and up-front with Wade about it from the start of their relationship. Many times she'd lamented that Sophie had gone down the same path. She'd told Wade she felt responsible, since she had set such a bad example for her little sister.

But she'd given up that lifestyle when she became a Christian. And as long as Wade had known her, she had to be feeling pretty lousy to take so much as an aspirin.

In all the speculation over Starr's death, he'd never had a deep need to know. Now he felt differently.

He scooped the mail off the porch and went into the house, his mind reeling. He pitched the junk mail into the trash can under the kitchen sink. Taking the envelope from the coroner's office, he went to the desk in the dining area and pulled an ancient dictionary from the bottom drawer. Turning to the *P*'s, he ran a finger down the columns. The technical-sounding word wasn't listed, and he searched without success for the abbreviation PPA.

He threw the dictionary back in the drawer and scanned the autopsy report, searching for the phone number of the coroner's office. He picked up the phone and dialed the number, steeling himself.

"Coyote County Medical Examiner."

Wade faltered. "Yes...um...I just received an autopsy report from your office. It was for my...my fiancée. She died in March. Is there someone there who could explain this to me?"

"Well, I'll try. This is Doug Satherton. I'm the county ME. What is it you have questions about?"

"Well, this says the cause of death was cerebral aneurysm. But there's something in the toxicology report...something about..." He stumbled over the syllables, then shook his head. "I can't even pronounce it. The abbreviation looks like PPA... I'm not sure..."

"Oh yes. Phenylpropanolamine." The word rolled easily off the man's tongue. "I remember the report you're referring to. I don't remember the exact levels now...but toxicology found the drug in the bloodstream. Hemorrhagic stroke is consistent with certain levels of PPA."

"Wait a minute..." Wade shifted the phone to his other ear. "You're saying she might have taken a drug that caused her death?"

"The levels found probably would not indicate an intentional overdose or illegal drug use. They're probably more consistent with an over-the-counter drug. PPA was mostly found in diet pills and cold medications, but it was recalled a few years ago when studies showed a connection between high levels of PPA and intracerebral hemorrhage or aneurysms—especially in young women. But a lot of people keep old medicine around. You don't remember if your fiancée had a cold or maybe a respiratory infection at the time of her death, do you?"

Fresh pain assaulted him. Starr was always so cheerful and upbeat. When she was sick, she'd rarely let on. And she'd always bragged about having a high pain threshold. But a disturbing memory brushed a corner of his mind. Starr *had* been fighting a cold the week she died. Wade remembered sending her to his medicine cabinet for some sinus tablets. Was it possible something she'd taken for a stuffy nose had actually killed her? Something *he'd* given her?

"Sir? Hello?" The medical examiner's voice broke through Wade's haze of confusion and disbelief.

"Yes. I…I'm here. So…it could have been a reaction to some medicine she took that killed her?"

"That would be the most likely scenario, yes. It was the pathologist's opinion, apparently."

Wade was silent, his mind racing.

The medical examiner's voice cut through his thoughts once more, his tone impatient. "Sir, do you have any other questions about the report?"

"Um…no. No…thank you." He had thousands of questions, but he didn't even know how to phrase them right now.

His breath came in shallow huffs, and he felt lightheaded as he rose from the desk and went back to the bathroom. He flipped on the light over the medicine cabinet and opened the mirrored door, feeling numb as he pulled a bottle of sinus tablets from the top shelf.

He vaguely remembered buying them. It seemed like eons ago. He'd taken two of the capsules and hated the way they made him feel—groggy and disoriented. He'd never taken another dose. But for the amount of money he'd paid, he hadn't been about to toss them out.

Now he picked up the plastic bottle with trembling hands and brought it close to read the fine print. The first thing that caught his eye was the expiration date stamped on the label. The date had expired over two and a half years ago.

A wave of guilt rolled over him. Holding the bottle to the light, he read the list of ingredients.

There it was. *Phenylpropanolamine.* Listed under active ingredients.

Wade felt like the breath had been sucked out of him. He had bought these pills. Encouraged Starr to take them. Had his negligence at having out-of-date, toxic medication in his medicine cabinet killed the woman he loved? Had he unknowingly caused Starr's death? The thought made his stomach roil.

He went back to the desk and slumped into the chair, feeling the strength drain from him. Who else might have received a copy of the autopsy report today? His heart lurched. He needed to talk to someone.

Dialing Pete Dolecek's cell phone from memory, Wade tried to think how he would ever explain what had happened. The phone rang twice, and Pete's voice mail kicked in.

Wade hung up without listening to the rest of the message. He stuffed the autopsy report in his pocket. He held out his hands and discovered they were trembling violently. Grabbing his keys on the way out the door, he headed for the pickup.

Pete removed his K-State ball cap and swatted at a pesky horsefly before replacing the cap. Wade knew his partner well enough to know he was weighing his words carefully before he responded.

The two men sat side by side on the newly shingled roof of the addition they were building. Below them, a patchwork of prairie grasses and ripening wheat fields rippled in the breeze like an ocean.

With forearms propped on raised knees, Wade felt the sun bake his skin, felt the prickle as his arms turned a deeper shade of reddish-brown. It stung and it felt good at the same time. He had shown Pete the autopsy report, explaining what the medical examiner had said, and confessing that *he* had bought the pills, *he* had let them sit on that shelf for years past their expiration date.

Finally Pete looked up at him. "Wade, even if this pathologist is right, there's no way you could have known about this PPA stuff. Shoot, I've sure never heard of it. For all I know, there might be something like that sitting in our medicine cabinet at home right now."

"I should have been more careful."

Pete shook his head. "It was a fluke. It could have happened to anyone."

"But why did it happen to me?"

"I don't know, buddy. I wish I did."

"What if Parnell's lawyers try to make something of this? What if it jeopardizes my chance at getting custody of the kids?"

"Hey. That's not going to happen. Anybody who hears about this will realize it could just as easily have been them as you. Anyone who knows you at all knows you would never let something like that happen intentionally."

But it *had* happened. Just like Starr's death had happened, and just like he'd lost the kids. Why was it all hitting at once? *Are you punishing me, God?* He didn't ask the question flippantly. He truly wanted to know.

Pete took a swig from the grimy water jug beside him. "I'm sorry, man. You don't deserve this. I wish I could…I don't know…do something. But I'll be honest, Wade. I don't understand why things are happening to you the way they are."

"Yeah, well…if you figure it out, would you let me in on the secret? Because I've had about all I can take." He dropped his head to his knees and raked splayed fingers through his hair. "I'm supposed to see the kids again next week. I'm not sure I can face them."

"What do you mean?"

"How can I ever tell them what I did?"

"Wade, you didn't *do* anything." Pete's voice rose in frustration. "If anything, it's the drug companies that are to blame. Besides, the kids are too young to understand any of this. They don't need to know any of this junk."

"Pete…I…I'm about ready to give up." He looked up and met his friend's eyes. "But I don't even know how to do that. How to let go…"

Pete stared at him. "You mean with the kids?"

"Maybe that's what this is about. Maybe God's trying to tell me to give up on trying to get them back."

"No." Pete yanked off his cap and slapped it against his knee, causing a little cloud of dust to rise. "You know better than that. You're fighting a just cause, Wade. Don't let this dampen your resolve. Those kids need you." Pete's eyebrows shot up. "Hey, wasn't this the day you were supposed to see them?"

Wade nodded. "They came this morning. I had them for one lousy hour."

Pete gave a sympathetic wince. "But they're doing okay?"

"They're fine. Man, it was good to see them, but it about ripped my heart out to let them go again."

"So, did the social worker leave you be?"

"She was there the whole time. But she was okay. It wasn't as bad as I expected. The kids like her."

"Good…good."

Absently, Wade picked up a triangular scrap from a shingle and flung it like a Frisbee off the roof. "Do you know how fast an hour flies by, though? It seemed like the kids just got there, and before I knew it, she was telling me she had to get them back."

"What about the foster home? Everything okay there?"

"It seems to be. The kids didn't say much." Wade suddenly felt weary to the bone. He dropped his head to his knees again, feeling the strength seep from him. "It's only been two weeks… Locke says this could drag on for months. Is it right for me to put the kids through this?"

"*You're* not putting them through this." Pete's voice rose. "Come on, Wade… Quit talking like this."

He looked up at his friend. "Should I even be fighting this custody deal, Pete?"

"You don't have a choice, man! You can't just let their father have them. You know that." Pete clapped him on the back. "Hey…hang in there. I know God's with you through it all, even if it doesn't feel like it right now. Margie and I are here for you too. You'll get through this. We're praying for you—every day. You know that."

"I know."

It was a good thing, too. Because he couldn't pray for himself right now if his life depended on it.

Twenty-Seven

In spite of the sunshine spilling in through the multipaned windows of the St. Joseph's Children's Services, the air in the spacious playroom was chilly. Dee stood in the arched doorway and watched Darrin Parnell. He was perched on the edge of one of the child-size chairs that furnished the room. Leaning over Lacey's shoulder, Darrin looked on as his daughter chose a new crayon from the tattered green and yellow box that sat open on the low table in front of her.

"That's pretty," he said, pointing to the picture she was coloring.

"Thanks," Lacey said without looking up.

"You like to draw, huh? Your mama was a good artist."

"Uh-huh, I know." Lacey's eyes never moved from the page of the coloring book.

From where she stood, Dee could see the girl's furrowed brow and the firm set of her mouth.

Though Darrin was polite—even charming at times—Dee noticed that all the children remained rather aloof from him. And from what she could observe, he seemed acutely aware of their reticence. Dee watched him flit from one child to the next, like a bee searching, without luck, for a blossom to pollinate. It was painful to watch, but she had to give the man credit for trying.

As if demonstrating her musings, Darrin eased off the seat and went to stand over a beanbag chair in the corner where Beau was flopped, a magazine spread open in his lap.

"What are you reading there, son?"

Beau turned over the colorful cover and held it up for Darrin to see.

"*Boys' Life*, huh? I used to read that when I was a kid. What's that article about? Are you in Scouts?"

Beau grunted something unintelligible and shrugged before opening the magazine again.

Darrin knelt on the floor beside the beanbag chair. He pointed to a page of Beau's magazine, whispered something, then laughed. Dee couldn't hear what he'd said, but he had Beau's attention now. Beau's eyes went to his father's face, and his mouth went slack. Darrin whispered something else. Beau's expression didn't change, but he squirmed in the chair, and Dee thought he seemed uncomfortable at whatever Darrin had said.

She stepped away from the doorway and moved closer to where they sat. She cleared her throat. "No whispering, please," she said.

"I can't talk to my own son?" Parnell said evenly.

"Of course you can. Just...please don't whisper."

Darrin shot Beau an exaggerated wink. "I think the lady is a little cranky this morning, what do you think, son?"

Beau shrugged and went back to his magazine.

Darrin turned and flashed a smile at Dee. He had white, even teeth and a dimple that gave him a boyish look. He smelled of some spicy aftershave and wintergreen chewing gum.

"I'm just kidding," he said, giving her the same wink he'd given Beau.

Dee ignored his comment and went to sit at the table near the door to catch up on some paperwork she'd brought. She looked at her watch. There was still half an hour left of their visit. It was going to be a long morning. She thought to suggest an activity the family could do together, but something made her hold back. If things didn't go better next time, she'd intervene, but she wanted to give Darrin Parnell a chance to proceed at his own speed. It couldn't be easy trying to woo his children on foreign turf and in front of watchful eyes. And he *was* trying.

Wade shifted in his chair, crossed one leg over the other, and tugged at the knot in his tie that threatened to choke him. The conference room was stuffy, and they were seated too close around the wobbly table. Every creak of a metal folding chair, every scrape of a heel on the grimy tile echoed through the sparsely furnished room.

The meeting hadn't even started, and Wade felt weary from averting his eyes a dozen times to avoid the inquisitive gazes of Betty Graffe from SRS, Ben and Karen Xavier, and the guardian ad litem, an attorney appointed to represent the children. Dee Thackery, the caseworker who had supervised Wade's first visit with the children, was chairing the meeting. She sat with a legal pad and a stack of papers in front of her, alternately checking her watch and the door. Today her business attire and staid demeanor felt threatening. Wade tried unsuccessfully to picture her as she'd been that day at his house, casually dressed, playing with the kids, making small talk with him.

He felt as if he were already on trial. And in a sense, he was. Frank Locke was in court this morning and hadn't been able to make this meeting, but he'd warned Wade that the impression he made in the case-planning meeting today was crucial.

Beau, Lacey, and Dani had been taken to the playroom down the hall. But when the kids had first seen him in the corridor a few minutes earlier, they'd squealed and jumped on him as if he were a long-lost puppy dog. It had done his heart good. Right now he wanted nothing more than to get rid of all these people and just spend a few minutes with his kids. But that wasn't on today's agenda.

He pulled back his sleeve and looked at his watch. The meeting should have started fifteen minutes ago. They were still waiting on Darrin Parnell. Wade allowed himself to entertain a fragile hope that the man would not show up, that he had given up on trying to get his children back, that he'd gone back to Minneapolis forever. At the very least, Parnell had made a bad impression by being late for this crucial meeting. Wade hated the way the vindictive thoughts made him feel.

A commotion in the hallway brought him back to the present. St. Joseph's receptionist appeared in the doorway and behind her stood Parnell and a man Wade assumed to be his attorney. Like his lawyer, Darrin Parnell was dressed in a blue suit and tie. His hair was neatly combed, and he was freshly shaven, bringing the scent of Old Spice into the room with him.

Wade suddenly felt like a slouch.

"Terribly sorry to be late," Parnell said with a warm smile. He nodded to each person in the room, his eyes darkening briefly when his gaze swept over Wade. "We got stuck behind a train."

Everyone nodded sympathetically, and the tiny glimmer of hope Wade had nurtured vanished. In Coyote County, where alternate routes were few and far between, the Santa Fe Railroad trains were a famous and legitimate—excuse for tardiness.

Everyone shifted to allow Parnell and his attorney a place at the table. Parnell put his briefcase on the table and took a seat beside his attorney.

Dee Thackery cleared her throat and picked up a sheaf of papers from the table. "Is everyone here now who's expected?" When no one spoke up, Dee looked at her watch. "Well, then, let's get started, shall we?"

For the next half-hour she went through one page after another, asking for input from those present, outlining goals for each child, stating the agency's requirements for Wade and Darrin Parnell, and answering queries—mostly from Parnell's attorney and the guardian ad litem.

Throughout the meeting, Parnell's attorney slid notes to his client and whispered asides, apparently explaining the legal terms and agency jargon that were used with abandon.

Wade felt incompetent to ask an intelligent question and kept quiet, wishing he'd been more insistent about Frank Locke's presence at this meeting.

"Now about visitation…" Dee tamped a stack of completed forms on the table and picked up the next sheet, aiming her remarks at Betty Graffe and the other personnel from SRS. "I've already attended successful visits with Mr. Parnell and Mr. Sullivan. The plan calls for continued once-weekly supervised visits. After the next hearing we can revisit the issue if necessary. Since Mr. Parnell is commuting from out of state, his visitations take place here at St. Joe's on Friday afternoons. Visitations with Mr. Sullivan occur on Tuesdays, and at the request of Mr. Sullivan and his attorney, the children are being taken to his home for visitation."

Darrin Parnell rose from his chair. "I object to that," he blurted. His attorney reached out and tugged at his client's sleeve, but Parnell shrugged him off. "I don't want my children out there. There's no reason for it. He can see them here at the agency like I have to."

Dee Thackery leafed through several pages before looking up. "It's my understanding the request for in-home visits with Mr. Sullivan was made for several reasons. Mr. Sullivan's house has been the children's home since their mother's death, so understandably there are many memories there for them."

"I know they've missed being out in the country," the foster mother chimed in. "We have a nice fenced yard, but there's not much room for them to explore. They have a dog out there too that they're always talking about. I think those were big considerations when the decision was originally made."

"I don't think it's necessary," Parnell said, wagging his head, still on his feet. "Due to circumstances I can't control, I don't have the same privilege to see my kids in my home. They're going to have to make the break at some point. It seems like this is as good a time as any."

Wade sat forward on his chair and put his elbows on the table in front of him. "Please…" He aimed his remarks at Dee Thackery. "If this is truly about what's best for the children, as you all keep saying, it seems like it's not asking too much for them to be able to see their dog once a week—and to be at the house they've called home since…since their mother died. Besides, most of their things—their toys and stuff—are still out at the house, and—"

"Then get their things out of there." Parnell's voice was even, but a line of red crept up his neck. "There's no reason their toys can't be moved to the foster home—maybe even the dog—"

"Oh no. We can't have a dog," Karen Xavier objected. "And we… really don't have a lot of storage space, either. They already brought a lot with them…"

"Then I'll take their things back to Minneapolis with me," Parnell said. "They do not need to be at *his* place." He angled his head sharply in Wade's direction.

"But the kids couldn't have access to their things if you take them to Minneapolis." Wade struggled to keep his voice steady. "It seems you're assuming the kids will end up with—" Feeling an internal, holy restraint, he clipped off his words and set his lips in a tight seam. He didn't know anything about legal strategies, but he was fairly certain Frank Locke would not want him getting into the subject of the court's final decision. Even if he did have a good point. Whatever the reason, he somehow knew he was to be quiet for now.

"Listen, buddy," Parnell said, his voice rising an octave. "Those are my kids and you better not forget it. You're lucky you even get to—"

"Darrin—" Parnell's attorney stood and put a hand on his arm. "Come on...calm down." His tone was hushed, but it was obvious everyone in the room heard him.

Parnell brushed him off, but he did sit down, putting his elbows on the table and smoothing a hand over his hair.

Parnell's attorney turned to face Dee Thackery. "The visit was supervised, correct?"

"Yes, I supervised it."

"And you felt it went satisfactorily?"

"Yes, I did."

The lawyer nodded and jotted something down on the legal pad in front of him.

Dee turned to Parnell. "Are we okay, then, with leaving visitation as it is presently?"

Parnell didn't respond, but his lawyer nodded approval for him, as did everyone else around the table. Wade was surprised at the immense sense of triumph he felt. A minuscule victory, but victory nevertheless.

Twenty-Eight

A weekend rain had left the countryside lush and green, and Dee felt her spirits lift as she laughed and joked with the Parnell children on the drive out to Wade Sullivan's place. This would be the fourth time she'd supervised a visit there, and the route was becoming familiar.

On either side, field after field of wheat stubble waited to be plowed under or burned off. Twice Dee had to slow the car as tractors pulling wide implements hogged the road en route to fields that were most likely still too damp to work. She looked at the clock on the dashboard. Wade would be wondering where they were. At his request, they'd changed the visitation time to eight in the morning, but she'd gotten a bit of a late start today.

Finally they pulled into the drive. Dee couldn't help but contrast this tidy farmhouse with the typical homes she visited—run-down apartment houses, mobile homes in weed-infested trailer parks, and ramshackle bungalows on the proverbial wrong side of the Santa Fe tracks. Wade's house seemed to welcome visitors with its wide front porch spilling over with pots of colorful geraniums and faded impatiens. The lawn was neatly cut, and the sidewalk leading to the front door was swept clean.

Without having to be reminded, Dee drove around back and parked. The kids threw off their seat belts and scrambled out, calling Wade's name and whistling for the dog.

Dee locked the car and started across the driveway. But before she reached the walk, she heard the back door slam and looked up to see Wade coming to meet the children.

The three of them squealed with delight and raced to his side. Dee stayed in the background, watching their joyful greetings. In what had become their ritual, Wade lifted each little girl high into the air before capturing her in a hug, then he turned to Beau and rubbed his knuckles affectionately over the boy's spiky, sun-bleached hair.

In spite of her initial reservations about Wade, Dee was beginning to wonder why these kids had ever been taken from his home in the first place.

Lacey's gaze panned the yard, and a flicker of worry crossed her face. "Where's Shadow?"

"He's probably down taking a swim…trying to stay cool." Wade whistled, and they all waited expectantly. When the dog didn't appear after a couple of minutes, Wade put an arm across Lacey's shoulder. "Don't worry, he'll be up to see you before you leave." He looked at the sun, shading his eyes against the glare. "It's already pretty hot… Maybe we better find something to do inside."

Dee watched him, noticing the crinkled lines the sun had baked into his skin. With his neatly trimmed hair streaked with gold highlights, she realized that in a rugged, outdoorsy way Wade Sullivan was quite attractive. She wondered what his relationship with the children's mother had been like. Watching Wade with the children now, she had a feeling he had loved their mother very much. She shook her head to clear the thoughts, wondering why they were so unsettling.

Wade caught her staring at him and cocked his head, a question in his blue-gray eyes.

She looked away, embarrassed.

She felt his eyes on her briefly before he turned to the kids. "Maybe we could put a puzzle together or—"

"I know!" Beau said. "Let's play spoons!"

"Yeah, spoons! Spoons!" the little girls squealed, as though their brother had just suggested a trip to Disneyland.

"Okay, spoons it is." Wade turned to Dee. "Do you know how to play?"

She shook her head. "I've heard of it, but I've never played."

Wade winked at the kids. "I think somebody's in for a treat. What do you guys think?"

They laughed conspiratorially, and Dee shot them a wary glance, but Wade seemed to ignore her and ushered them all into the house.

Until today, the majority of their time here had been spent outdoors—

playing catch or Frisbee on the lawn, romping with Shadow, or just sitting under the shade of the front porch, talking.

Now Wade led the way through the entryway and up several steps to the kitchen. As Dee's eyes adjusted to the light, she was reminded again of her first impression of Wade's house. It really was quite charming—tidy and cozy, and still showing evidence of a woman's touch. Lace curtains hung at the kitchen window, and here and there the walls were stenciled with tendrils of ivy.

"Wow!" Dani said, her upturned gaze sweeping the kitchen. "The house is *clean!*"

Wade shot Dee a sheepish grin, then tickled Dani under the chin. "Of course it's clean," he said. "*You're* never here to mess it up." He knelt and wrapped her in a hug. "I'd rather have it messy," he said in a stage whisper.

Dani rewarded him with the sweetest smile this side of the Mississippi. Dee was struck again by how unspoiled these children had remained, in spite of the upheavals and tragedy in their short lives. Karen Xavier was smitten with all three of them and had even made noises about adopting them if somehow neither man managed to gain custody. That possibility was highly unlikely, but the mere fact Karen had broached the subject spoke volumes of her love for the children.

Beau walked over to a desk in the corner of the room and rummaged in a drawer, coming back to the table with a tatty deck of Winnie-the-Pooh playing cards.

"Get the spoons, Lacey Daisy," Wade said, pulling out a chair. "We'll need four of them."

Dee took a step back, folded her arms, and leaned against the kitchen counter, glad the visit was turning out so well, despite the fact they couldn't be outside. Often it was like pulling teeth to get family members to interact. Too many of them thought an hour of reality television or video games qualified as "quality family time."

Wade went to the living room and came back with another chair. The kids scampered for seats, and Wade pulled out a chair for Dee. She took it but pulled the chair away from the table before she sat. She wouldn't intrude on their family time, but she did need to be close enough to observe.

Lacey arranged the four stainless-steel spoons in a starburst pattern in the center of the table. Wade expertly shuffled the deck of cards and handed it to Beau. "Wanna deal first, buddy?"

Beau went around the table, methodically counting out four cards for each person. When he laid the cards in front of Dee, she put up a hand. "That's okay, Beau. I'll just watch."

"No!" Lacey pleaded. "You hafta play."

Dee tipped her head toward the table. "But…there're only four spoons."

The kids giggled, and Wade quieted them with an upraised hand. "Hang on. We forgot to explain the rules." He turned to Dee. "It's kind of like musical chairs. There's always one less spoon than there are people. When you get the right cards, you grab a spoon." He demonstrated, snapping up one of the spoons with a curvy *S* engraved on the handle. "As soon as the first person grabs a spoon, it's everybody get a spoon or—"

"Or sing a tune!" the kids yelled in unison, clapping with glee.

Wade tipped his head to one side and rubbed his chin, looking almost shy. "It's a little different twist that Starr—their mother—put on the game. If you're the one left without a spoon, you have to sing one line of a song."

Dee laughed nervously and folded her arms again. "Then I'm definitely not playing. I can't carry a tune in a bucket."

"Mama said Wade can't carry one in a pickup truck," Dani said matter-of-factly.

They all laughed as Dani looked from one to the next with a what's-so-funny expression on her face.

Wade gave Dee a pleading look. "Come on… It's not so bad. And if you're really good, you'll never have to sing anyway."

"Wade, it's better if just you and the children interact. My job is to be an observer, not a participant."

He bristled visibly. "Well, I'm sorry, but it's a little difficult to interact naturally when we have an audience. It would be more comfortable for all of us if you'd just pretend to be our guest and play the game with us." His tone was resolute, but not unkind.

She stared at him for a minute before reluctantly scooting her chair up to the table. "Okay. I'll play. But how about giving me an out this first game? If I lose, I don't sing."

He eyed her, and a slow grin came to his lips. "Fair enough. But only the first time." He picked up the cards Beau had dealt him and arranged them in a neat fan shape. "Okay, here's how it works: We're going for four of a kind. You can save numbers or face cards, and the first one to get all four grabs a spoon. As soon as one spoon gets picked up, everybody goes for a spoon, and the one left without gets to serenade us."

"But I get an out," she reminded him.

"Everybody hear that?" He looked around the table at the kids, that same sly grin on his face. "Dee doesn't have to sing the first time she loses."

"Aw, no fair," Dani pouted.

"Hey…" Wade whispered conspiratorially. "We'll get her on the second time around."

Dani rubbed her hands together and giggled. "Okay," she whispered back.

Three rounds later Beau had sung twice and Dani once, and Dee was feeling guilty she was still in the game, but also a little smug that she'd managed to escape the dreaded solo so far. And she still had that free pass Wade had proffered.

"Your turn to deal," Beau said, handing her the deck. She brushed her bangs away from her face and shuffled the deck. She probably shouldn't have agreed to play the game with them. As she'd told Wade, her role was simply to be an observer—and mediator, if necessary. The whole idea of these visits was to give the family an opportunity to interact. But she hadn't wanted to upset Wade. And he did have a point. It had to be awkward for him to have her scrutinizing everything they did. Even with her in the game, they were interacting beautifully. It seemed to come easily and naturally for Wade and the children.

Dee was surprised at how welcome they'd all made her feel. As though she were an honored guest here rather than the loathsome intruder most parents she supervised—and even sometimes the children—perceived her to be.

She dealt the cards and another fast-paced round began. Within minutes she garnered two aces to add to the one she'd dealt herself. All she had to do now was watch for the ace of spades to come her way. Piece of cake. Watching closely, she took the cards Lacey laid beside her and passed them on to Beau.

The sound of raucous laughter jolted her aware. She looked around the table, and her mouth dropped open when she saw Wade and each of the children hold a spoon up in triumph.

"Sing! Sing!" the children chanted.

"No." Wade came to her rescue. "Remember, she gets one out."

She really should bow out of the game, let them play by themselves. But if she purposely lost this round, she'd be forced to sing. It was not a possibility she relished.

She squeaked safely through four more rounds before glancing at her watch. "Oh! I've got to get you guys back. Karen is going to wonder what in the world happened to us."

"Just one more round!" Dani yelled.

"We really can't, honey. Karen will be worried. Besides, I need to get back to the office." She couldn't believe she'd let the time get away from her like this.

"You just don't want to sing," Beau accused. But the impish grin on his face told her he was teasing.

Wade tipped his head toward the phone on the desk. "Do you need to make a call?"

"Thanks, but I can call from my cell on the way back." She pushed her chair away from the table.

"Be careful. Those things are the biggest hazard on the road as far as I'm concerned."

The playful mood had evaporated, and she thought Wade sounded rather peeved with her. "I think I can handle it, thanks."

He drew back. "Okay…sure."

She hadn't meant her words to come out so tersely, but she felt unaccountably defensive. She had gotten so wrapped up in the card game—in her own enjoyment of it—that she'd forgotten she was working. She shouldn't have let her guard down. "Come on, guys," she told the children, avoiding Wade's eyes. "We need to hustle."

"Beau, girls…you heard what Dee said. You need to hurry." Wade went to the back door and held it open for them.

They filed outside and started for the car, Wade following behind.

"Wait!" Lacey cried, turning with a look of desperation on her face. "We never got to see Shadow!"

"Oh, dear," Dee said. She looked at her watch, and then at Wade. Well, he *had* promised them. There was no school today on account of a teachers' in-service, and she didn't have any meetings scheduled until the afternoon. "I guess we can stay a couple more minutes."

Without warning, Wade put his fingers to his mouth and let out a piercing whistle. The children looked expectantly toward the back of the house where the yard ambled down to the river. Within seconds, a graceful black form came bounding up the hill.

"Shadow!"

Like vultures, they swooped down on the black Lab. Dee let them love on the dog for a few minutes before looking pointedly at her watch. "Guys, I'm sorry, but we really do need to get you back now. Tell Shadow good-bye. Oh, and Wade, too."

"Gee, thanks," he said with a wry grin.

"I didn't mean that the way it came out," she said, returning the grin. She felt bad to have raised her hackles with him before.

The kids had the routine down by now, and the good-byes were no longer teary. While Dee unlocked the car, they each gave Wade and the dog one last hug before piling into the backseat.

"See you next week," Wade hollered, stooping to look into the car window. He raised a hand, then dropped it quickly to his side as she backed the car around.

Dee watched him in her rearview mirror as she maneuvered the car down the lane to the main road. He stood in front of the house with one hand on Shadow's neck, the other raised to shade his eyes. His head was slightly bent, and there was a slump to his shoulders that hadn't been there earlier.

Compassion and sympathy were emotions that had always come easily toward the children she worked with. But Dee realized she was feeling something that, until now, had been foreign when it came to the parents of those children. Yet there was no denying it.

Her heart ached for Wade Sullivan.

Twenty-Nine

Wade went back into the house and quickly changed into work clothes. Poor Pete had been pulling more than his share of weight in the business for weeks now. *One more thing to feel guilty about.*

Back in the kitchen, he fixed a jug of ice water, grabbed an apple from the fridge, and dashed out to the pickup.

The cab of the truck was like a sauna. Sinking his teeth into the apple, he tore off a chunk and chewed, letting the sweet juice cool his parched mouth. He rolled down the windows and pulled out of the drive, not caring that the dust blew back into the truck, coating his skin with a film of grit and peppering the damp flesh of the apple where he'd taken a bite.

Dear God, I miss the kids. I miss them like crazy. They'd been in foster care for almost six weeks. If he were honest, in some ways his life was easier now. No more worrying about picking them up at day care on time, no more keeping up with Beau's ball games, no more dentist appointments or frantically prepared suppers. Of course the meetings with caseworkers and his attorney and the initial hearings at the county courthouse had eaten up a lot of that time.

But he missed the constancy of having Beau and Lacey and Dani around. Their voices, their laughter, even their childish arguments. They had become the thing that mattered most to him in life. His family. They were the inheritance Starr had left him, and they'd added a cadence to his days that comforted him in ways he hadn't realized until he'd lost it.

Thoughts of Starr filled him with remorse again. In spite of Pete's compassionate counsel, Wade still had trouble shaking the guilt for the way she had died. No one questioned that it had been purely accidental, but never had he regretted anything so deeply as his carelessness at leaving those pills in his medicine cabinet. Every time he thought about it, something twisted inside him.

Oh, for the chance to go back and change things. He'd cleaned out that cabinet a thousand times in his mind, visualized himself flushing the pills and tossing the bottle in the wastebasket beside the sink. But when he shook himself back to reality, Starr was still gone. Her children were still lost to him. He was still alone.

"Oh, Father," he whispered. "I can't do this anymore." His words vanished in the hot wind that rushed past the open window, scattered with the dust of the road. He couldn't seem to pray anymore. He could never find the right words.

He flipped on the radio and cranked up the volume. Garth Brooks's voice carried over the wind. As the chorus repeated for the second time, Wade listened to the words. He was taken aback by the lyrics. They wove a story from the old cliché "Blood is thicker than water." But it was the last line of the song that caused his throat to tighten and a knot to form in his gut. "But love is thicker than blood."

He hoped a certain judge at the Coyote County courthouse believed that.

Some twenty miles later he pulled in behind Pete's truck at the work site and cut the engine. Thankfully, the combination great room and master bedroom addition was enclosed now. Pete had planned to work on the plumbing in the master bath while he waited on Wade to help put up the Sheetrock. On a scorcher like today it would be a relief to work inside, out of the sun.

He could hear the steady rhythm of his partner's hammer even before he opened the French doors leading into the great room. Inside, two large box fans hummed and rattled the plastic tarp hanging between the house proper and the new addition.

Pete greeted Wade with his easy, perpetual smile. "Hey, buddy. How'd it go today…with the kids?"

"Good. It went real good. We played spoons."

Pete looked up. "Spoons, huh?"

"Yeah. It was fun. She played with us."

"You mean the social worker? Dee?"

Wade nodded.

Mischief tinged Pete's grin. "Did she have to sing?"

Wade returned the grin. "Not yet."

The Doleceks had often been included in rowdy games of spoons with him and Starr and the kids. It had been a great way to pass the dreary winter months last year. More often than not, their card parties turned into true sing-alongs. Pete and Margie both sang in the choir at church and had beautiful voices. Wade had relished those times, regardless of his own lack in the musical department.

He was grateful to find the recollection sweet now, the accompanying ache not quite so sharp as memories of Starr often were. But he was surprised to find a new wrinkle to the remembrance.

Dee.

It had been good to have a woman at his table today. Almost as though he had a family again. He thought Dee had enjoyed it too. He shook his head, startled at the emotion her name evoked. What was wrong with him? He'd buried Starr barely six months ago. He hardly knew Dee Thackery.

He sloughed off the thoughts and looked at Pete. "We'll get her next time. She'll have to sing eventually." He paused, then shook his head. "Just so it's not *me* that has to sing."

Pete cocked his head and eyed Wade. "You like her, don't you?"

Wade grabbed the other end of the piece of Sheetrock his partner was manhandling. With practiced precision, they jutted it up to the one Pete had just finished nailing down.

"What do you mean?" In spite of the cool air billowing over him from the fan at his feet, he felt his face grow warm.

"Seems like I've heard her name an awful lot lately."

"She…she's my connection to the kids…that's all." He grabbed his hammer and went to work.

Together they beat out a rhythm as familiar to Wade as his own heartbeat. *Bam. Bam-bam-bam. Bam.*

Finally Pete spoke. "I'm wondering if it's more than that…"

Placing another nail, Wade aimed his reply at the wall. "Forget it, Pete. Sure…she's nice. I was expecting to hate her, and I'm glad I don't.

She's made it easier for me. For all of us. But don't go making this out to be something it's not."

Pete didn't push the issue. But all afternoon Wade thought about what he'd said. He did like Dee. Though they'd only spent a few short hours together, there was a sort of bond between them. It was the children, of course. He knew that, knew it would never be anything more. Still, it was a pleasant surprise finding an unlikely friend in the midst of this whole ordeal with the kids.

Like a well-oiled machine, he and Pete hoisted another unwieldy slab of Sheetrock into place, and in a comfortable absence of conversation, they resumed their steady hammering.

Sophie Braden was surprised to realize she was trembling as she drove her decrepit Plymouth out to Wade's place. She turned the air conditioner down and took her hands off the steering wheel long enough to rub her bare arms vigorously. But she knew it wasn't the cool air causing her hands to shake and her insides to flutter.

Keeping one eye on the road, she reached over and flipped open the glove compartment, rummaging around in the cluttered space until she found a smashed pack of Marlboros. She stripped off the cellophane, tapped the package, and eagerly slid out one slim cigarette. It had been almost four years since she'd given up her two-pack-a-day habit, but this thing with Darrin had provided all the excuses she needed to fall off the wagon.

She jammed the cigarette lighter in.

She hadn't seen Starr's kids since they'd gone into foster care. Or Wade, for that matter. Wade had called several times to let her know the kids would be at his house for visitation and to invite her to come and see them.

But she couldn't do it. She couldn't face him, knowing all that she knew, knowing what the future probably held for Wade and the kids. Because of the mess she'd made of her past. Because of her cowardice. She thought she'd escaped all that when she came to Coyote. But now, it seemed her past had caught up with her, and she was finally going to have to pay for everything she thought she'd gotten away with. It made her sick to her stomach. And yet she seemed powerless to change any of it.

Starr had always told her that God couldn't erase her past, but he could forgive her of it and make her into a new person. Well, she didn't feel like a new person now. She felt like the same old Sophia Braden who had screwed up her life in a thousand ways. Only worse. Because now her mistakes weren't just hurting her. They were hurting the people she loved. It seemed she'd even defiled the memory of her sister—the one good thing in her life.

She lit the cigarette and took a long drag, waiting for the sense of well-being and calm she'd learned to expect. But it never came. Leaning over the steering wheel, she peered into the cloudless Kansas sky. "Starr?" she said aloud, exhaling a stream of bluish smoke.

The sound of her voice over the drone of the car's engine startled her, and she dropped it to a whisper. "I don't know if you can hear me where you are, but I need help. I've messed up bad this time. I've messed up really bad—" A sob caught in her throat. She mashed her cigarette in the empty ashtray and slammed it shut. "I don't think your God can get me out of this one. I think I'm in too deep. Forgive me, Starr. I'm sorry…I'm so sorry. But I don't have a choice. I…I don't know what else to do."

Wade's mailbox appeared on her left at the end of the drive. Sophie took a deep breath and slowed the car. As she turned into the drive, she peered into the rearview mirror and frantically swiped at the smudges of mascara under her eyes. She'd scare the kids to death looking the way she did now.

A blue Taurus with state tags was parked near the back door. She pulled up behind the car, put the Plymouth in park, and cut the engine. She dug in her purse for some chewing gum and opened the car door wide in a futile effort to get rid of the smoky stench. Slinging her purse over one arm, she got out of the car, shoved the door shut with one hip, and went up the walk.

It felt funny to knock on Wade's door. He'd always had an open-door policy. But it had been so long since she'd been out here. She rapped tentatively before opening the outer door. "Hey! Anybody home?" She climbed the short flight of steps in the entryway and knocked on the door that led to the kitchen.

Suddenly the door swung open. Dani stood there with a quizzical expression on her pixie face. Then recognition came to her eyes, and her face lit up. "Aunt Sophie!" She turned toward the dining room and cupped small hands around her mouth. "Hey everybody! Aunt Sophie's here!"

As she realized how much she'd missed Starr's kids, Sophie's heart swelled. Then it pounded an erratic rhythm and constricted in her chest at the thought of the betrayal to come.

Thirty

"Hey, Dani. How's it going, sweet pea?" Sophie couldn't ignore Danica's outstretched arms as she stood in the doorway of Wade's kitchen. "Wow, baby, you're getting tall." She picked up her niece and swung her around, feeling lightheaded as her heart warred against itself.

Wade pushed his chair back from the table and came toward her, eyebrows raised. "Hey, Sophe." He sounded surprised to see her. "Glad you came. How's it going?"

"Okay, I guess."

From the corner of her vision Sophie saw a woman get up from the table and come to stand behind Wade.

Wade turned and motioned the woman forward. "Sophie, this is Dee Thackery." He turned to Dee. "Sophie is…the kids' aunt—Starr's sister."

Businesslike, Dee extended a manicured hand. Sophie looked down at her own ragged nails and chapped, red hands. She hesitated before she shook the woman's hand.

"Hello, Sophie. Nice to meet you. Wade's probably told you, I'm with the foster-care agency."

"Yeah, I guessed that… Saw your car outside." Anxious for the introductions to be over, Sophie looked past Dee to Lacey and Beau.

They were still sitting at the table, each with a handful of playing cards fanned out in front of them. She moved toward the table, anxious to avoid further conversation with the social worker. "Hey, guys…what're you playing there?"

"Spoons!" Lacey said. "Wanna play?"

Beau looked up at her from under bangs that needed a trim. He gave her a shy smile. "Hey, Aunt Sophie."

"Come and join us, Sophie," Wade said, going over to grab his desk chair and carry it to the table.

"Oh…here…"—the social worker moved quickly to pick up a handful of cards from the table—"why don't you take over my hand?"

Sophie waved her off. "That's okay. I'll just watch."

"No, please, I insist. I'm scared to death I'm going to have to sing." Dee gave Wade a peculiar smile. Something unspoken passed between them.

This Dee person knew about Starr's game? She seemed to be on awfully familiar terms with Wade. Without meeting her gaze, Sophie took the cards from Dee's hand and took her place at the table.

"We could just deal a new hand," Wade said, looking from Sophie to Dee. "Then we could all play. Beau, why don't you get another spoon."

Dee held up a palm. "No, really…I'd rather…just observe."

"Well, okay…if you're sure," he told the social worker.

Wade stood beside the table with one hand on the chair he'd brought in. He shifted from one foot to the other. Sophie eyed him. Why did he seem so nervous? Was he suspicious of her reasons for coming?

Dee took the chair from him and set it a short distance from the table. Sophie watched as the social worker crossed her legs elegantly and folded her arms over her crisp lime-green blouse. Oh, this was going to be pleasant. An audience. Maybe she didn't want to play the game after all.

But then she heard Darrin Parnell's voice echo in her head. Okay, okay…it wasn't like she really had a choice.

Wade sat down again and fanned out his cards. Sophie turned her chair slightly, looking over her shoulder to make sure Dee Thackery's face wasn't going to be in her line of sight every time she glanced up.

She riffled her cards and steeled herself with the memory of her last encounter with Darrin Parnell. "Okay, let's see what we've got here? Whose turn is it?"

The following Monday night, Wade walked through the house, turning off lights and checking the locks. The kids would be here again tomorrow, and he'd spent the evening running the vacuum and tidying up. He had a routine going now. And Tuesdays had become the highlight of his week.

He wondered if Sophie would come again tomorrow. He wondered what had prompted her to finally come and see the kids after so long.

She'd looked good. Compared to the last time he'd seen her, anyway. Then, she'd been recovering from the mugging in the café's parking lot, her face still bearing traces of the bruises and cuts some nameless assailant had inflicted on her. He still thought there was something fishy about that whole deal. But Sophie never wanted to talk about it. The few times he'd brought it up, she quickly changed the subject.

Even though things had been a bit tense between Dee and Sophie, he was glad she'd come to see the kids. She was Starr's only living relative, after all. It was good for them to stay connected. And Frank Locke was counting on her presence in the kids' lives to provide the motherly image the court would be looking for. Locke had talked about having Sophie testify, if it came to that. He wanted her to speak both to Wade's competence with the kids, and to Darrin's abuse of Starr. Wade hoped that wouldn't be necessary. He wasn't sure what kind of an impression Starr's sister would make on a judge. She could be pretty rough around the edges. Sometimes he wondered how Starr had turned out to be so different from her sister.

He'd been reminded of it last week, seeing the contrast between Dee's grace and poise, and Sophie's lack of sophistication. He'd never noticed Sophie's shortcomings so blatantly before. He felt guilty judging her in his mind now. Starr would have chided him soundly for that. But, sadly, appearances would count heavily when it came to a judge's decision about the kids.

Wade's hopes of getting the kids back grew dimmer with each day that passed, though Frank Locke continued to convey reserved confidence that the court would eventually rule in his favor. "Parnell's history of abuse and drug use will doom him," he'd assured Wade just last week.

"But couldn't the judge decide foster care for the kids is preferable to either of us having custody?"

Locke had scratched his head and sighed. "I won't tell you that's not a possibility, Wade. But wouldn't that be better than letting the kids go with Parnell?"

Wade agreed, but it was small comfort to him. He didn't think he could bear it if he lost the opportunity to share a life with Starr's children.

A shadow of worry crossed his mind as he thought of the bills that were piling up. How he was going to support the kids if he got them back, he wasn't sure. Between Frank Locke's bills, old medical bills for the kids, and the time he'd lost at work, he'd dug a pretty deep financial hole.

Pete had told him yesterday that he'd promised a client they'd have a remodeling job finished before Christmas. If they lost even one more workday, they'd never be able to make that deadline. And he was to blame for them being behind. He'd left Pete high and dry more often than not since this whole mess with the kids started.

Sighing, feeling overwhelmed, he turned out the last light and went to wash his face and get ready for bed. He opened the medicine cabinet and grabbed the tube of toothpaste. Glancing up, he saw a bottle of aspirin on the shelf. His vision blurred, and his veins turned to ice as his imagination played tricks on him and the plastic container became a bottle of cold capsules. How innocently Starr had reached her hand to this same shelf and picked up the poison that killed her.

He closed the door and stared at his reflection in the mirror. How had his life gotten so messed up? He'd lost his only love by his own carelessness. His business was in jeopardy, and he'd let down his dearest friend in the bargain.

He thought about the kids at the foster home. What made him think he had any business trying to gain custody of three small children? They seemed to be thriving with Ben and Karen Xavier. What did he have to offer them that was any better than where they were now? How could he even consider pulling them back into this craziness?

Maybe he'd been blinded by his grief over Starr, his love for the kids. He *did* love them. Fiercely. That was never a question. But true love sometimes demanded sacrifice.

Was that what God was trying to tell him?

Maybe it was time to stop fighting. Maybe it was time to let go. If he gave up his right to the kids, he could get his business back on its feet, fulfill his obligations to Pete and their clients.

But if he bowed out, did he trust the courts to do right by Beau and Lacey and Dani? He didn't know. The kids seemed to be doing fine with the Xaviers, but there was no guarantee they'd be allowed to stay in that home. Who knew where they might ultimately end up.

No, he didn't trust the courts. Not with a decision like that.

He thought of the long-ago promise he'd made to a hurting little boy. Was there any way he could keep that promise now?

Still, he trusted God to do right by the kids. Didn't he? Treasonous thoughts ripped through him. Wasn't God the one who'd allowed all this to happen in the first place? Why should he expect God to suddenly bail them out now?

He buried his face in his hands and groaned. *I'm sorry, God. I'm sorry. But what should I do? I don't know what you want from me. Where am I supposed to be? I don't know what you want me to do. Show me. Please…I'm begging you to show me.*

Thirty-One

Wade knelt by the back door and let Beau and Lacey and Dani envelop him in kisses and hugs. Oh, what healing power their little arms had for him.

He became aware of Dee standing on the walk nearby, observing the reunion. Struggling to stand, he extricated himself from the tangle of children and led the way into the house.

Without prompting, Beau ran to the desk for the playing cards, and the girls counted out the spoons, giggling and chattering back and forth.

Dee stood in the middle of the kitchen and looked at Wade, her gray-green eyes swimming with compassion. She glanced toward the children and lowered her voice. "Is everything okay? You don't look like you slept a wink," Dee said, peering deeper into his eyes.

He shook his head and shrugged, unnerved by the kindness in her voice. "I guess I didn't sleep very well. I…I've got a lot on my mind."

"Is everything okay?" she asked again.

Suddenly all the confusion and frustration of last night came rushing back, and before he could think better of it, he found himself pouring out his troubles to her. "We're so behind at work I'm afraid we're going to start losing contracts. Pete—my business partner—has covered for me beyond what any friend should be expected to. But I just…I can't miss any of these visits with the kids, either. Maybe I'm just being selfish, but…I needed to see them. For me."

Dee looked at him thoughtfully, as though trying to decide whether to say something or not. Finally she said, "Wade, it's not my place to say this, but…I don't think there's a selfish bone in your body." The words seemed to spill out of her.

He was touched deeply and didn't know how to respond. Dee cleared her throat and looked away, and he felt the warmth from their brief exchange subside.

"Hey, you guys…are you gonna play or not?" Lacey's insistent voice gave them both a chance to escape the awkward moment.

Wade went to the desk and brought a chair to the table for Dee. "We'll play a couple of hands," he told the kids. "But then let's go outside and get some sunshine. It's not quite so hot today."

One of the kids had already dealt the cards, and the four engraved spoons were neatly arranged in the middle of the table. Wade picked up his hand and fanned out the cards. "Okay, who's first?"

"Me!" Lacey declared. She took a card from the top of the deck, looked at it, and put it facedown on the table beside Dee.

Beau and Dani followed suit. The game picked up speed as the cards got passed around the table. Within minutes, Wade had three sixes in his hand and almost forgot to keep his poker face on when Beau passed him the winning card.

But he casually discarded his fifth card and slid his fingers across the table to pick up a spoon. The kids were on to him in a millisecond, each grabbing a spoon with lightning speed. They all turned to stare at Dee, who was still going through the little stack of cards that had collected in front of her. She glanced up briefly, and the kids erupted, crowing and laughing.

Her gaze shot to the middle of the table and then to Wade's face.

He tried not to gloat.

"No!" she said, slapping her forehead. "No way! Not on the very first round."

Lacey and Dani started chanting, "Sing! Sing!"

"Come on, you guys. Give me a break. I haven't had my coffee yet this morning."

"Uh-uh," Wade said, grinning and wagging his head. "We've been trying to get you for over a month now. No way are you getting out of this one. Right, kiddos?"

"Right!" they chorused, grinning like jack-o'-lanterns.

"I don't know what to sing," she whined.

"Sing anything." Wade sat back and crossed his arms, waiting.

" 'Row, Row, Row Your Boat!' " Dani shouted.

Dee hung her head. She looked up and brushed her hair off her forehead. A blush of pink climbed her neck. "This is hard," she said.

"Oh, just get it over with," Wade teased. "The first time's always the worst."

"Yeah, easy for you to say. You've never had to sing!"

"Yes, he has!" Beau said. "He always sings 'When You Wish Upon a Star.' And he's *terrible!*"

"Hey, you!" Wade polished his knuckles on Beau's head. "Watch it!" He hoped the kids wouldn't mention that he'd chosen that song for *his* Starr.

Dee opened her mouth and took a deep breath. But before one note peeped out, she clamped her lips together, giggling like a four-year-old. "Just one line, right?" she said, when she finally gained control.

"Just one line," Wade said, enjoying her misery immensely and making sure she knew it.

She took another breath. "Maryhadalittlelamb." Dee squeaked out the tune like it was one word, one musical measure.

Wade squelched a laugh. "Now, see? That wasn't so hard, was it?"

"It was awful!"

"Your singing?" he teased. "Aw, it wasn't *that* bad."

"Yeah, Dee," Dani said. "It wasn't so bad. Not as bad as Wade's singin'."

"Watch it there, Dani Banany," he said, reaching over to tickle her under the chin.

"Yeah, watch it," Dee told the little girl, obviously feigning offense.

Wade turned to Dee, laughing. "Ready to play another round? Maybe you'll get a chance to redeem yourself."

"Hey!" She reached over as if to give his arm a playful swat, but stopped in midswipe and drew her hand back as though she'd been stung.

"What's wrong?" Wade asked, wondering at the stricken expression on her face.

She shook her head, almost imperceptibly. "Nothing." She turned to look at the clock over the desk. "If you want to play outside…with the kids…maybe we should go now. It's getting late."

Wade followed her gaze to the clock. It was almost eight thirty.

Sensing her need to escape—for a reason he couldn't fathom—he scooted back his chair and gathered up the playing cards. "Let's go outside, kiddos …before our time is up."

Thankfully, the kids didn't protest. They climbed off their chairs and raced through the kitchen, calling Shadow's name before they'd even opened the back door.

The back door slammed, and the kitchen was suddenly uncomfortably silent. Dee pushed chairs up to the table, stacked the spoons in a neat pile, and put them on a kitchen counter.

Wade waited to catch her eye, but when she refused to look at him, he put a hand on her arm. "Hey…is everything okay?"

She nodded and moved away, still not looking at him. "Fine."

"You…you act like something is bothering you."

"I'm fine, Wade. It's just…" Her voice trailed off, and she turned and started out the back door.

Wade followed her out onto the stoop. "It's just what?"

The children were romping on the hill, Shadow barking joyfully at their heels. Dee took a step back and looked at Wade, her mouth set in a firm line. "Wade, I think things are getting a little too—familiar. I'm supposed to be here as an objective observer. Not a friend. I'm sorry. I've not respected that like I should."

He stuffed his hands in the pockets of his jeans and leaned against the railing, eying her. "I'm glad you feel welcome here," he said. "It…makes it easier. For all of us. I couldn't stand it if we had some…spectator… watching everything we did."

"Yes, but I think we've—*I've* carried it a little too far."

"What do you mean?"

She looked down, rubbing the toe of her sandal on the rough boards of the stoop. She crossed her arms. "I…I really can't explain it. We just…" She held up a hand. "I'm sorry. I just need to take my time here a little more seriously."

He narrowed his eyes. "Is this about your singing?"

She looked up. "What?"

"Are you upset because you had to sing? You know"—he pointed toward the house—"spoons? I'm sorry if we embarrassed you, Dee."

She waved him off. "No, Wade. You're missing the point."

"Then could you kindly draw me a picture, because I'm apparently not even close."

"Wade, do you understand that at some point I have to make a recommendation to the judge about where your kids—Darrin Parnell's kids—should be? I have to be able to make an objective, impartial statement."

"What? You think I'm trying to sway you?"

She shook her head. "No. It's not that."

He threw her a hint of a smile and spread his arms in an exaggerated shrug. "Am I getting warm? Can you give me a clue here?"

"I think maybe I'm getting too close to the situation. We...I need to back off a little. I...I need to explain to the kids that I can't play cards with you guys anymore. I should...just observe."

"What? What does your playing games with us have to do with anything? That makes no sense to me, Dee. Everybody keeps saying this is all about what's best for the kids, what's best for the children. Do you honestly think it's best for them to have you suddenly...back off like this?"

"Just look at us now, Wade. Here we are..." She threw up her hands. "You should be out playing with your kids. Your time is almost up, and you've spent most of it—" She let out a little growl before leveling her gaze at him. "You've spent most of it flirting with me!"

He stared at her for a long minute, incredulous, trying to absorb what he thought he'd just heard her say. "Is that what you think? That I'm trying to...put the moves on you?"

She stared at him, not responding.

"What?" He fought to keep his voice low so the kids wouldn't hear them. "You think I'm trying to coerce you into 'voting' for me or something?"

She shook her head vigorously, then brushed a hand through her hair. "I'm sorry...that came out wrong. And...I'm just as guilty as you are, Wade."

"I don't know what you're talking about." As soon as the words were out, he felt sick. Here she was being honest with him, and he'd thrown her sincerity back in her face. Maybe he had been flirting with her, but was that such a bad thing? She made it sound like something terrible. Like the laughter and the warmth they'd shared were somehow wrong.

For him, it had felt like the most natural thing in the world. The most natural progression. They had become friends over the weeks she'd been bringing the kids here. Yes, he could admit he was attracted to her. Dee had brought back some of the light and laughter that had left his house when Starr died.

But he'd done nothing inappropriate. Until he briefly laid a hand on her arm a few minutes ago, he'd never touched her, never said anything that could be interpreted as improper. But how could he explain these things to her now? He knifed a hand through his hair. For crying out loud, it wasn't like he was hitting on her.

"I'm sorry, Dee," he finally blurted, "but I'm not sure what there is for either of us to feel guilty about."

She pushed away from the railing and stood up straight. "Wade, there is a code of conduct I'm held to as a social worker. I can't have a…friendship with you. I'm here as a professional, for the kids. My only job is to be an impartial observer while you spend time with your kids."

He felt strangely deflated at her words. As hard as it had been for him to lose the kids, Dee had somehow made it easier. She had become the one bright spot in this whole mixed-up fiasco. And now she was telling him they couldn't even be friends.

His heart felt like a stone in his chest. The things she'd said hurt deeply, but if he told her that now, it would only make things worse. Instead, he narrowed his eyes at her. "So what exactly does that look like, Dee? This 'impartial observer' thing? No more smiling at each other? No more laughing? Do we each just put on our poker faces as soon as you walk in the door? I mean, heaven forbid we should be nice to each other. Or accidentally have a moment of fun together."

Her face fell. She hung her head, and her chin quivered.

He winced. He hadn't meant to make her cry. "Dee, I'm sorry. I think I…understand what you're saying. I'm sorry if I've caused you to cross a line you're not comfortable with. But please, I'm asking you not to change the way these visits go. I honestly couldn't stand it if you sat back and observed the way you did when Sophie was here last week."

"I don't know, Wade. I…I'll have to think about it."

"Can I ask you something?"

She looked at him warily. "That depends…"

"Strictly business," he said, attempting a smile. "I promise."

She nodded.

"I—" To his chagrin, his voice caught, and he had to swallow back a lump of emotion. He stared out past the kids playing tag on the hill, to the calm waters of the Smoky Hill River in the distance. "I'm thinking about…giving the kids up. I'm not sure I have what it takes to do right by them. Especially with everything that's going on with the business…" He turned his gaze to Dee. "Do you think they're happy at the foster home? Do kids…*can* kids come out of that kind of situation…intact? They seem happy where they are. They seem to—"

"Oh, Wade. No." An expression akin to horror clouded her features. "Don't give up. Karen and Ben are wonderful foster parents. The kids are doing fine there, but…you understand that's just temporary, don't you?"

"Yes, but it could become permanent, couldn't it? I mean, the judge could decide that, couldn't he?"

Dee closed her eyes.

"What? What's wrong?"

She looked around as though there might be spies behind the stand of cottonwood trees. "I can't really discuss this with you, Wade. But you need to know there's a huge"—she bit her lip, seeming to grasp for the right word—"*push* to get kids back with their natural parents. Unless there's something I don't know, that's the direction this judge is going to be headed right from the start."

Wade remembered what Frank Locke had said about Judge Paxton having lost his own son in a custody battle. "But they wouldn't put these kids back with their father, would they? There are people who can testify to what he did to Starr—to their mother. Dee, you don't understand what he's capable—"

She held up a hand. "Stop, Wade. Please. We really should not be discussing this at all."

He dared to ask one more question. "Are the kids' visits with Parnell going okay?"

She merely nodded.

"You…you think he might actually get them back?"

She hesitated, and in her eyes Wade clearly saw the conflict waging inside her.

"I'm just saying…please don't give up." She turned and gazed out to where the children were playing. "These kids need you, Wade. Fight for them."

Thirty-Two

After leaving Wade's house, Dee had several meetings, along with an after-hours visitation to supervise. It was nearly dusk before she pulled into her driveway. She parked under the carport and walked back down the drive to retrieve the empty trash cart at the edge of the street.

She waved at her neighbor as she rolled the cart up the drive. "Hi, Jewel."

The elderly woman was bent over a pansy bed in front of the tidy little ranch-style home. Only Jewel Frederick could keep pansies thriving through the scorching heat of the summer.

"Your flowers sure look pretty," Dee shouted across the yard.

Jewel straightened, patted her forehead with a white hankie, and turned to smile at Dee. "The secret is to water them three times a day," Jewel said.

"Well, they're beautiful. How's Don doing? I haven't seen him around for a few days."

"Oh, he's fine. He just wilts like a pansy in this heat. And he won't let me water *him* three times a day."

Dee laughed. "Well, tell him 'hi' for me," she said, grabbing the evening paper off the lawn as she walked by. Pushing open the front door, she escaped into the cool of the house.

Phog sashayed into the kitchen to meet her, tail high. He looked up at Dee, meowed pitifully, then sauntered off to stand in front of his empty dish.

"You're getting too fat, kitty," she crooned, sliding one hand down his silky gray fur. But she poured some cat food into his bowl anyway.

The refrigerator yielded a small bowl of leftover tuna salad. She made herself a sandwich and plopped down at the kitchen table. She opened the newspaper and smoothed out the creases. The headlines melted together on the page, meaningless. All day, her mind had been consumed with thoughts of her conversation with Wade Sullivan this morning. Setting the plate with her half-finished sandwich on the floor for Phog, she sighed and pushed the paper away. Maybe it had cooled off enough that she could take a walk. That always seemed to clear her brain.

She hurried back to the bedroom and changed into shorts and a T-shirt, then grabbed her sneakers and went out to sit on the front porch steps to put them on. Jewel had gone inside. The street was quiet.

She gave her shoelaces one last tug, then jumped up and started down the street at a brisk pace. The cicadas and crickets sawed out a monotonous chorus, and here and there a lawn sprinkler added to the symphony.

As she walked, Dee relived her day. She thought about this morning at Wade Sullivan's and giggled to herself, remembering her pathetic rendition of "Mary Had a Little Lamb." But she quickly swallowed back the laughter, thinking of the discussion that had followed. Did Wade understand what she'd tried to tell him? But how could he? She wasn't sure she understood it herself.

In the five years she'd been supervising visitations for children in foster care, she'd never been in such an awkward situation. There had been a few families that made her feel more welcome than others. But never had she come to feel as she did with Wade and the Parnell kids. They had truly come to be friends. She felt almost like a part of the family. Why was that so wrong?

But that was just it. It didn't *feel* wrong. It felt wonderfully right. And wasn't that a problem in itself? This wasn't supposed to feel right. There were professional boundaries she'd crossed today that could not be ignored. And if she were honest with herself, she'd have to admit it wasn't just today. She had violated certain lines long before this day—at least in her mind.

The sun was dipping quickly below the horizon as she crossed Blakely Street and headed west down the shady, brick-paved avenue. The air instantly felt ten degrees cooler. Dee quickened her pace to match the rate at which her mind was whirling.

She'd walked half a dozen blocks, barely aware of her surroundings, when the sound of a car's horn startled her. She turned to see Clay Two

Feathers' rattletrap Chevy tooling slowly beside her. She waved, and Clay pulled over and rolled the window down.

"Hey there, need a lift?"

She laughed. "Believe it or not, Two Feathers, some people actually walk for exercise and enjoyment."

"Yeah, but you're a long way from home. You look like you could use a nice cold drink. Hop in. I'm headed to Sonic."

"Yeah, right." She rested a hand on her hip. "The nearest Sonic just so happens to be back that way." She hooked her thumb in the direction from which Clay had come.

He had the decency to hang his head. But a second later he was looking at her with that eager puppy dog expression that always got to her. "You've got to admit an ice-cold root-beer float sounds pretty good," he said.

"Oh no you don't. Get thee behind me, Clay Two Feathers. I am not going to chase all these miles of exercise with ice cream."

He rolled his eyes. "A Diet Coke, then."

"Okay, sure. But I hope you're treating because I don't have any money on me." She looked at her watch. "And I don't want to be out too late."

She walked around the back of the Chevy. He had the passenger door open and waiting for her.

"So how was your day?" he asked as he made a U-turn and headed back east toward the Sonic.

She shrugged. "It was okay, I guess. Busy."

"Yeah, tell me about it. I don't see how they can avoid hiring somebody soon. I put in almost fifty hours last week."

"So what's new? You've been putting in fifty hours a week ever since I met you."

"No. Not fifty. It's never been this bad."

"Yeah, well, why don't you just use your comp time?" She knew he wouldn't miss the sarcasm in her question. Comp time was a joke. If any of them ever made up their overtime, their caseload would come crashing down like a house of cards.

He smirked. "I'll use mine as soon as you use yours."

Dee rolled her eyes and flashed him a knowing smile. They rode in silence for a few blocks. She debated whether to tell Clay about her encounter with Wade this morning. It might help to get his perspective on things. Clay always seemed to have a wise word when it came to professional matters. Yet, something kept her from sharing her thoughts with him—or anyone else.

The neon lights of the Sonic Drive-In flashed ahead. Clay pulled up beside the lighted menu board, cut the engine, and pushed the order button. "You're sure you don't want a float?"

"Diet Coke," she said in her sternest voice.

He placed their order, then unbuckled his seat belt and casually angled his body toward her. She did the same.

"So how are things going with you?" he asked.

"Workwise?"

"Anywise. It seems like I haven't talked to you for a long time."

She fretted with a frayed edge of the seat's upholstery, weighing again the consequences of telling him what was happening with Wade. What could it hurt? Maybe Clay would put her worries to rest. Maybe he'd tell her she was making a big deal out of nothing. She was aware of his eyes on her, waiting for a response.

"What are you thinking about?" he said finally.

"Oh…it's not that big of a deal…" Her words were far from the truth. The whole episode with Wade was all she'd thought about today. She took a deep breath and plunged in. "There's a…situation with one of my families. They're different from anyone I've ever worked with."

"How's that?" Clay leaned closer, curiosity vivid in his hazel eyes.

"They've just made me feel…I don't know…like part of the family."

"What do you mean? Wait, who is this we're talking about?"

She hesitated, unsure how much she wanted to reveal. "The Parnell kids. You know…the three siblings we placed with the Xaviers."

He nodded. "I remember."

"Their birth father and their mom's fiancé are both trying to get custody."

"I assume it's no contest. Dad will get them, right?"

"I'm not sure he *should*, Clay."

He raised an eyebrow. "Really? Why? Is he abusive?"

She shook her head. "Not with the kids anyway. I guess he had a history of abusing their mother, but that was a long time ago. He's been through anger management, and he seems like he really is trying hard with the kids."

"But you still have reservations?"

"I do. They just seem so happy with Wade...Sullivan. The fiancé," she explained.

"So you think they'd be better off with him? Are you going to recommend it?"

"I don't know. The next hearing isn't until next month, but if I had to make a recommendation today, yes, I think I'd vote for the fiancé. The kids just seem so much...happier with him. It's not that I have anything against the birth father. I think he really is trying, but it's just so obvious the kids are more comfortable with Wade. That he's far more of a dad in their eyes than their own father is. I mean, he's practically raised them for the past three years."

She stopped and waited for Clay's response. Met with only silence, she went on. "I've gotten to know them surprisingly well. They just...they include me. We play cards and stuff—and the kids insist on dealing me in. Have you ever had a family like that, where they just sort of opened their arms and took you in? I'm so used to being the despised 'observer'... But I've got to say this feels good, Clay. I wish there was a way it could always be like this...with our clients."

He narrowed his eyes. "So I take it this happy, feel-good, 'part of the family' thing"—he drew quote marks in the air with long, slender fingers—"happens at this Wade character's house?"

The cynical tone he'd taken raised her defenses. "It's not just him. It's the kids, too. It's weird, but it's like I'm—I don't know...a favorite aunt or something." She looked away, then back at Clay. "Have you ever felt like you were crossing the line with a client? You know, like you were becoming friends? Good friends?"

"Why?" He cocked his head. "Is that what's happening?"

She shifted uncomfortably in her seat. "Kind of. I mean, Wade and the kids are totally involved with each other when they're together, but they just bring me in...into the circle like it's the most natural thing in the world. I know it sounds strange, but it's almost like I'm in the middle of it before I know how I got there. We talked about it one of the first times I took the kids out there. I was going to watch them play a card game, and Wade got all upset and said how they couldn't interact naturally with an audience." She took a deep breath. "I think he's right, Clay. For the first time, I could imagine how awkward it would feel to be on the receiving end of what we do. And I truly don't feel like I'm distracting from their time together."

Clay shot her a look that said he was skeptical.

"I did say something about it to him—to Wade—this morning. I told him again that I really should just be observing. It ticked him off."

"Well, sure it did."

"What do you mean by that?"

"Think about it, Dee. Either he's buttering you up so you'll go to bat for him with the judge, or he's coming on to you. And by the starry look in your eyes, I'd bet on the latter."

She glared at him—and hoped he'd mistake the heat she felt on her face for the pink neon sign that flashed outside the car window.

To her relief the carhop brought their drinks just then. Clay paid the girl and handed Dee her Coke and a straw, turning an accusing eye on her. "Well?"

She unwrapped her straw and took a long sip. "No, Clay. It's not like that," she said finally. "This guy...he's not like most of the deadbeat dads we deal with. He's really not. I can't explain it, but he's just...a nice guy. He's a natural with the kids, and they adore him. It's so different than when they're with their birth father. Like night and day."

He gave her a searching look. "Do you know how unlikely it is that this guy—this Wade—will end up with those kids, Dee?"

"I know. But haven't you ever had a gut feeling about something?" She didn't tell him how leery she'd been of Wade's motives the first time she'd met him. But she knew him now. And she just couldn't believe he was anything other than the caring, wonderful man she saw every week.

"I don't know, Dee. It just…" He shook his head. "Never mind."

"No. What? I want to hear your opinion, Clay. That's why I brought it up."

"You like the guy, don't you?"

"I already said that. He's great with the kids."

"No. You know what I mean, Dee. I think it's more than that. You can't let this go anywhere, you know. You could lose your job."

"I'm not letting anything *happen*. It's not like that. I'm just saying what's wrong with being friends with our clients? Just friends."

"What's wrong is, you can't possibly be objective if you're friends with one of the parties. Not to mention it could easily go further than mere friendship. Those safeguards are there for a reason, Dee."

She nodded slowly. Of course, Clay was right. But how could she back off from Wade and the kids now, after they had such a great relationship? The very word—*relationship*—startled her, even as it entered her thoughts. She couldn't *have* a relationship with Wade Sullivan. Not any kind of relationship. Not if she meant to honor the ethics of her profession.

"So you think I need to back off?" she asked, dreading what Clay might say.

"Only you can say what you need to do, Dee. All I know is… Well, I just wish I saw half the light in your eyes for *me* that I see there for Wade Sullivan."

She turned away from his scrutiny and fidgeted with her straw. Finally she muttered, "I don't know what to say, Clay."

He set his empty cup in the cup holder, buckled his seat belt, and turned the key in the ignition. Dee straightened in her seat and fastened her own seat belt.

When they were out on the street, headed back toward Dee's apartment, Clay looked over at her. "You don't have to say anything else, Dee. I'm sorry. I wasn't a good one to broach this subject with. I have too much at stake personally to be giving you advice about who you should or shouldn't love."

"This isn't about love, Clay." She gave an exasperated sigh. "Man! How did this get so blown out of proportion?"

"I just calls 'em as I sees 'em," he said, not looking at her.

She knew Clay was trying to smooth things over. It was their way. He always pushed and tried to get her to talk about "them," when there was no them. She liked Clay a lot. But she wanted him for a friend and nothing more. Like Wade.

No. Not like Wade. Not like Wade at all. She knew Wade Sullivan better than any man she'd ever been close to. And he stood head and shoulders above all of them.

Even Clay. Maybe *especially* Clay, with whom she'd shared more of her life than any other man. But with Clay, as with any man who'd ever shown an interest in her, there had always been a certain tinge of fear. She'd always held back parts of herself, afraid of revealing her past. Fearful of allowing the relationship to go beyond friendship.

But Wade was different. Why was she suddenly thinking of him in a context beyond friendship? Was it because she *couldn't* have a relationship with him? Had she subconsciously chosen him because it was forbidden for him to touch her?

Her question was answered by the startling realization that she longed for Wade Sullivan to touch her. To hold her in his arms. To kiss her. Heat rose to her cheeks at the thought. She'd never felt this way about any man.

She pressed two fingers lightly to her lips. *Was* she in love with Wade? Was it ridiculous to think she could be falling in love with a man she'd only spent a few hours with over the course of a few short seasons?

She was afraid to search her heart too deeply, terrified of the answer to that question.

Thirty-Three

Wade put the pitcher of lemonade in the refrigerator and wiped off the kitchen counter for the third time. He didn't know what to expect this morning. Things with Dee Thackery hadn't ended on a very good note last week.

He went outside and hooked up a sprinkler to the garden hose on the back lawn. Maybe if they stayed outside all morning it would be less awkward. Wade walked to the side of the house and turned on the spigot.

The sun was already hot, even though it was September, and the cool mist that reached him as the sprinkler sprang to life felt good. Shadow came running, and pranced through the water, lapping at the spray and sloshing in the mud it quickly produced.

He heard tires on the gravel, and his heart gave a little lurch. Dee was here with the kids. He went to greet them.

The kids spotted the sprinkler the minute they climbed out of the car.

"Can we run through it?" Lacey asked.

"But we didn't bring our suits," Beau said, scowling.

"I know," Wade said, nodding hello to Dee over Beau's head. "But you've all got dry clothes here. You can change before you go." He looked to Dee. "Is that okay?"

"Sure, as long as they have stuff to change into. Sounds like fun."

The words were barely out of her mouth when Shadow trotted to where they were standing. Shadow panted and gave a doggy grin, then shook himself like a wet rag. Dee and the children squealed as a torrent of water hit them.

The kids raced after Shadow to land in the middle of the fountain the sprinkler created.

Wade turned to Dee, then gasped and stared at her in dismay. Rivulets of water ran down her face, making trails in the spots of mud Shadow had flung. Her beige pants and peach-colored shirt were covered with dark spots.

He put a hand to his mouth, first to express his horror, then to stifle a laugh. She looked like an appealing street urchin with her droopy hair and muddy clothes. "I am so sorry, Dee," he told her. "Wait right here... I'll get you a towel. Or do you want to come inside and try to wash off some of the mud?"

She brushed a sodden lock of hair off her forehead and looked down at her clothes. She giggled. "I really did take a shower *before* I came," she said, waving him off. "Don't worry about it. I'll just wash off in the sprinkler." She brushed a hand across her cheek and stooped to inspect her face in the car's rearview mirror. "Oh, dear! Maybe I will take that towel."

"Are you sure you don't want to try to wash off some of that mud? It's hard as the dickens to get mud out of anything."

She looked down at her shirt. "Well..." She hesitated, then gave a wave of her hand. "Oh, it'll be okay. But I will take that towel."

"I'll be right back." Wade ran to the house and grabbed a thick bath towel from the load of clean laundry in the dryer. He started back outside, then hesitated. Dee might not be worried about the mud now, but when she tried to wash those clothes later tonight, she might feel differently.

His eyes lit on the tall cupboard beside the washing machine. Starr had always kept a couple of changes of clothes at the house so she could shower here after a day of painting. Wade opened the door and pushed back a row of his winter work shirts. A sleeveless cotton blouse and a pair of black pull-on slacks hung there alongside several of Starr's sweatshirts. A lump formed unexpectedly in his throat, but before he could change his mind, he pulled the blouse and slacks off the hangers and draped them over one arm.

When he got back outside, Dee was leaning over the sprinkler, dabbing water on her face and laughing with the children as they played in the spray.

Wade took the towel and clothes and went to stand at the edge of the sprinkler's reach, holding them out to Dee like a valet.

She wiped the water out of her eyes and turned to him, still spotted with mud and water, but wearing a smile that melted him.

"Oh, thank you," she said, breathless. She took the towel and blotted her face, then bent at the waist to rub her hair dry. When she finished, she handed the towel back to him. "I'm not sure if that made it better or worse, but at least I got the mud out of my ears and—" She stopped suddenly, noticing the clothes Wade held. "What's this?"

"Some…extra things to change into. If you don't wash that mud out of your clothes right away, they'll be ruined." He held them out. "Please. I'd feel better. You can change inside, and I'll throw your stuff in the washer. You can bring these back next week."

Her expression softened, and understanding shadowed her features. "These were…hers?"

He nodded.

"Are you sure…you don't mind?"

"I'm sure."

She gave a slight nod, took the clothes from him, and went into the house. She was back in minutes, her muddy clothes wadded in one hand, her hair neatly combed and tucked behind her ears. Wade's breath caught, seeing her in the familiar outfit.

"I would have started the washer myself," she said, "but I was afraid I'd mess something up."

"I'll do it," he said, taking the muddy laundry from her. "I'm sure sorry about this."

She laughed. "Hey, don't think a thing of it. This is the most exciting thing that's happened to me all week."

"Well, thanks for being such a good sport. Maybe the sprinkler wasn't such a good idea."

She looked out at the children laughing and splashing in the sprinkler, then back at Wade. Tipping her head to one side, she smiled softly. "It was a good idea, Wade. A very good idea." She motioned toward the stoop. "I'm going to go sit over there and let the sun dry my hair while you play with the kids."

"Sure. Here, take this." Wade tossed her the towel again and ran inside to start the washer.

When he came back outside, he kicked off his sandals and walked across the wet grass to join the kids at the edge of the sprinkler. He sent up a prayer of thanks as he went. Dee's generous, forgiving attitude had enabled them to sidestep whatever had been troubling her before. He still didn't understand what had changed for her so suddenly the other day, but he was grateful for the moment of comic relief that had seemed to smooth things over.

"Hey, Wade!" Dani chirped when she noticed him. "Are you gonna play in the water with us?"

Grinning, he ducked under the geyser of water, scooped Dani into his arms, and spun her around. She shrieked with delight, and soon Lacey and Beau were lined up for turns on the Wade-A-Whirl. The landscape spun by him, and from the corner of his vision, he saw that Dee was laughing right along with the children.

By the time the kids needed to change into dry clothes for the trip back to the Xaviers', Wade was as soaked as they were. He turned off the water and went to get more towels.

As he climbed the stairs, Dee looked up at him from her seat on the bottom step. There was a glint in her eyes. "You look a little wet behind the ears there."

He laughed and shook his wet head over her, misting her with a considerably cleaner version of the shower Shadow had given her.

She tilted her head back and closed her eyes. "Mmm...that actually feels good now that I'm all dried out. At least you're not muddy."

The kids stood on the walk, dripping onto the concrete. He threw Beau the towel Dee had hung over the rail. "Hang on, girls. Let me get some more towels, and then we can go in for some lemonade."

Inside, he transferred Dee's clothes to the dryer, grabbed a stack of beach blankets, and took them out with him. He gave one to each of the girls, and while he dried off, Dee helped the girls dry their hair. When she finished with Dani, wrapping her in folds of bright turquoise terrycloth, Dee looked up at Wade. "That was fun."

He hesitated, immensely pleased with her comment, but not sure how this sudden friendliness fit with what she'd told him last week about things getting too familiar between them.

The silence stretched between them, grew awkward. "I'll bring out some lemonade," Wade said, giving his hair one last pass with the towel.

Dee didn't offer to help the way she would have last week. He went into the house and poured five cold glasses of lemonade and carried them outside on a tray.

Dee took a long draw from the glass he offered and sighed like a thirsty farmhand. "Mmm...that's good stuff."

"Fresh squeezed from lemons I grew myself, and sugar cane I processed out in the barn." He gave the kids an exaggerated wink.

"No, you didn't, Wade!" Lacey said, striking her familiar hands-on-hips pose.

"Shh... Don't give away my secrets."

"It's Kool-Aid!" Dani shouted. "The yellow kind."

"Aha! So Martha Stewart you're not," Dee said.

Wade took a swig from his glass and licked his lips. "I don't know. I think even Martha would approve."

Dee laughed and drained her glass. But then she looked at her watch and turned serious. "Hey, guys, drink up. You need to get changed and in the car in about three minutes." She took the tray from the railing and started collecting glasses.

"I'll run up and help the kids find dry clothes," he said. "Come on, guys, hustle up."

"Wade..." Dee stood looking at him, biting her bottom lip as though she were trying to keep from giving him bad news.

"Is something wrong?"

"I...probably should go with the kids. I'm really not supposed to—"

"Leave me alone with them?" He fought back an unwelcome surge of anger. Cocking his head, he frowned at her. "Do you trust me, Dee?"

She met his gaze head on. "Yes. I do. Completely."

Her answer satisfied his ire. "Thank you," he said quietly. He let out the last of his resentment on a deep sigh. "Okay...I'll clean up here while you help them get changed."

He added his empty glass to the tray and took it from her, saluting her with a wink before she shepherded the kids into the house.

If today was a demonstration of what she meant by "backing off," he thought he could handle it.

Dee didn't recognize the thirty-something brunette sitting in the playroom at St. Joseph's, but the minute the woman saw Beau and Lacey and Dani come through the door, she bolted from her seat and started toward them.

"Oh, my!" The woman put a hand to her mouth, her eyes misting. Her makeup was flawlessly applied, her lipstick matching her long, red fingernails perfectly. Not a hair on her head was out of place. "Oh, my," she repeated almost reverently. "I'd have known you anywhere." Her voice held a vague hint of the south. Texas, Dee guessed.

Puzzled, Dee opened her mouth to introduce herself, but before she got out a word, she heard Darrin Parnell's voice from the hallway behind her.

"Ah, good morning! I see you two have met."

Dee turned to greet him. "Well, no, actually we haven't." She turned again and held out a hand to the brunette. "You must be Darrin's fiancée."

The woman smiled warmly and took Dee's hand. "Yes, I'm Carma. Carma Weist. And you must be Dee."

"Dee Thackery. Nice to meet you. Glad you could get in on a visit. This is your first time to meet the kids?"

"Yes, but I would have known them anywhere." She moved to put a hand on Beau's shoulder and stooped to his eye level. "You are the spitting image of your daddy. But you probably hear that all the time."

Beau looked at the floor, silent.

Darrin stepped in and knelt between the two little girls. "Lacey, Danica...Beau, I'd like you to meet Carma. She's my fiancée. She's going to be your mama in just a few months."

"Well, your stepmama, anyway," Carma said, with a nervous laugh.

Dee watched the children carefully.

Beau ducked out from under Carma's hand and moved toward the bookshelves in the corner. "I'm gonna go put a puzzle together," he mumbled.

"Great idea," Darrin Parnell said, catching his fiancée's eye and giving a shrug before starting after Beau. He turned back to Carma for a moment. "Honey, why don't you and the girls come help us."

Carma slid her handbag off her shoulder and laid it on the coffee table near where she'd been sitting. She took Dani's hand. "Come on, Danica, Lacey. Is there a favorite puzzle you like to work?"

Dani looked up at Dee with wide eyes, as though asking permission to go with the woman.

Dee smiled and gave an encouraging nod. "I'll be right over here. You go on ahead and play with the puzzles, Dani."

"Oh, I'm sorry." Carma knelt and faced Dani. "I called you Danica. Would you rather go by Dani?"

The little girl gave a slight lift of her shoulders and nodded.

"Well, it's a pretty name either way. Now, let's go see what those boys are doing."

Dani giggled. "Darrin isn't a boy."

Carma rolled her eyes. "Well, you'd have a hard time proving it by me. He sure acts like one sometimes," she said, laughing at her own joke. She pulled up a child-size chair beside Darrin Parnell, patting his knee under the table.

Dee watched as Lacey and Dani hung back, apparently not quite sure what to make of this new wrinkle in their weekly visit with their father. Beau had plopped in a chair in the corner, head down, concentrating on a piece of the easy jigsaw puzzle. Every few seconds, he glanced up through a curtain of long, blond bangs, eyeing Carma warily.

"Come on, girls, pull up a chair," Carma said, scooting out the chair on the other side of her. She patted the seat. "Come and sit beside me."

The girls sat down and quickly became involved in the puzzle. The five of them worked together in silence for a few minutes. When Lacey snapped a corner piece of the puzzle in place, Carma purred, "Ooh, good job, Lacey. I've been looking all over for that piece. You're pretty good at this."

"I'm good at puzzles too," Dani said.

"Yes, you are. Just look! We're almost finished with this puppy."

Wrinkling her nose, Dani tilted her head and looked at the puzzle. "It's not a puppy," she said. "It's a merry-go-round."

Carma burst out laughing and leaned in to give her a squeeze. "It's just a figure of speech, sweetie."

Carma Weist wasn't the least intimidated by the children. Dee looked on as the woman asked them questions and made little jokes. Soon the girls and even Beau were laughing right along with her. Carma seemed to bring out a softer side of Darrin, too. Dee watched with interest as he followed his fiancée's lead in interacting with the children.

It struck Dee that they really did look like a family sitting around the table enjoying their time together. There was no doubt Beau Parnell was his father's son, with their matching hazel eyes and dark blond hair. And even with their pale yellow hair, the two girls could have been Carma's daughters as she bent her head between them, joining in their giggling.

Dee thought about how very quickly October—and the date for the next hearing—was approaching. And watching this broken family together, seemingly mending before her eyes, she knew that, with this woman by his side, Darrin Parnell would easily be granted full custody of his children.

Dee thought of Wade, and her heart broke for him.

Thirty-Four

The early weeks of fall took on a dreary familiarity for Wade, punctuated only with brief moments of happiness each Tuesday morning when Dee brought the kids out for their weekly visit. She was bringing them earlier now that school had started. She usually had them at his place around seven. He fixed breakfast for all of them, and then she dropped them off at school on her way back to work.

He and Pete had finally finished the addition south of town and were beginning another project just a mile from his place. It was nice not to feel like he was wasting so much time on the road.

This morning he had a case planning conference at St. Joseph's at ten o'clock, but he'd gone to the site early and put in a good three hours with Pete before he had to come home and clean up for the meeting.

Now, freshly showered and shaved, he hopped in the pickup. He turned the key in the ignition. Nothing. He tried again. The starter had been acting up lately, but he'd always been able to get the engine to finally turn over. He yanked at his tie and looked at his watch. The meeting would be starting in fifteen minutes. He didn't have time to mess with the truck now.

He slammed the driver's side door harder than necessary and ran into the house for the keys to Starr's car. He'd only driven her car a few times since he'd lost the kids. He never had changed over the title or insurance, not feeling quite right about even having Starr's car in his possession, though he'd continued to pay her auto insurance bills every month.

He backed out of the garage and raced down the drive, quickly reaching sixty on the gravel road.

The only good thing about these meetings was that they gave him a chance to see Dee Thackery. After their rough start, he and Dee had settled into a comfortable routine. They'd seemingly reached a compromise, with her joining into his games with the children occasionally, and him being more careful to respect the professional distance she needed to keep between them.

Ironically, he'd learned to know Dee even better since she'd told him she needed to back off. Maybe she'd just needed to make sure *he* understood the boundaries. Whatever it was, she had begun to open up and share more of herself with him, and he'd felt comfortable doing the same with her.

After she'd brought the kids out for their visit last week, he finally admitted to himself that, were it not for the constraints of professional integrity keeping them apart, he would definitely ask Dee for a date.

The realization was unsettling. He felt almost as if he were being disloyal to Starr. Yet it brought with it an awareness that Starr—and her children—had changed him in ways he was only beginning to understand.

"What have you done to this confirmed bachelor?" he whispered into the emptiness of Starr's car. He wasn't sure if he meant the question for Starr or for God. He'd spoken to the former less often as the months went by, and to the latter far more often. That it took tragedy to bring him closer to his Savior shamed him, and yet how grateful he was to have a place to take his sorrow.

He'd started attending church on Sunday mornings again. Pete and Margie always saved him a place, and though it was still hard to walk through the front doors every week knowing he would be inspected and probably pitied, he'd found comfort and fellowship there too.

As he turned onto the blacktop, he looked at the clock and punched the accelerator harder. He did not want to be late for this meeting.

A mile and a half from town he was making good time when he glanced in his rearview mirror and saw the dreaded flashing red and blue strobe lights of a Coyote County police car behind him.

Wade hit the brakes and slammed the ball of his hand on the steering wheel. He did not have time for this. He pulled over and dug in his back pocket for his wallet. As Wade watched in the side mirror, the officer strolled to the side of the car. It was Bill Etchison. He and Wade had graduated from the same class at Coyote High.

Wade rolled down the window. "Hey, Bill. How's it going? I guess I was driving a little fast, huh?"

"I clocked you at seventy-five," Bill said in the slow drawl that made him the most-impersonated cop in town.

"I'm sorry. My truck wouldn't start, and I was late for a meeting. Not making excuses, just giving you the facts."

"I understand," Bill said, reaching into his pocket. "Happens to the best of us."

As Bill slowly folded back the cover of the citation pad, Wade held his breath, hoping to see the word *Warning* at the top of the page.

"Hate to do it, Wade, but I'm gonna have to give you a ticket," Bill said. "I'm gonna need to see your driver's license and some proof of insurance."

"I understand." Wade sighed under his breath, and dug his license and the red and white State Farm Insurance card out of his wallet.

While Bill carefully copied the information onto the ticket, checking every little bit to see if the carbon was going through, Wade tapped an impatient rhythm on the steering wheel and watched the clock mark off the minutes. Great. Now, besides being late for the meeting, he could add a traffic ticket to all the strikes against him.

"I see you've still got the car insured in...her name. You probably ought to get that changed over."

Wade rested an arm on the open window. "Yeah. Yeah, I've been meaning to do that."

Bill tore the ticket off the pad and handed it back to Wade, along with his license and insurance card. "You have a good day now." He gave a half-mast salute.

Wade resisted rolling his eyes. "Thanks, Bill." He waited until the cruiser had disappeared over a hill before he pulled the car back onto the road. It was an effort to stay within the confines of the speed limit as he drove the last mile into Coyote.

Frank Locke was supposed to be at the case planning meeting. Wade would ask him what he should do about Starr's auto insurance. There went another hour of work time down the drain.

Sophia Braden grabbed two meat loaf dinners—the Monday lunch special—off the pass-through and headed for the booth in the corner. "There you go," she said, sliding the plates onto the table and removing the soup bowls. "Holler if there's anything else I can get for you."

The two elderly gentlemen nodded over mouthfuls of mashed potatoes and waved her off.

As Sophie headed back to the kitchen, she noticed Wade Sullivan waiting to be seated. She hadn't seen Wade since that day she'd gone out to see the kids at his place. She turned and walked over to him. "Hey, Wade. How's it going?" She hoped the slight quaver in her voice didn't give away her apprehension.

"It's going okay. Do you have a minute?"

Her stomach turned a somersault. She tossed her bangs out of her eyes and cleared her throat. "Um...sure. Let me get rid of these dishes." She tipped her head toward an empty section of the restaurant. "Go ahead and have a seat over there. We're not busy. I'll sit with you for a minute. You ordering?"

He gave a nod. "I'll just have iced tea." He walked back to the table and sat down with his back to the door.

Wade hadn't been in the café in months. Sophie knew he'd been working out of town, but still, he used to bring the kids in for supper once a week or so. Maybe coming in here reminded him too much of the kids—and Starr. After all, this was where they'd met. She closed her eyes and tried to push the thoughts of her sister from her mind. It was still sometimes hard to believe Starr was dead.

She dumped the dirty bowls in a dishpan, poured an iced tea, and went over to sit across from him.

"Thanks," he said, when she set the glass in front of him.

She eyed him carefully. "Is everything okay?" He looked different. Thinner and pale, almost—in spite of his deep year-round tan. "How are the kids?"

He brightened a bit. "They're okay. They're handling the whole thing pretty well, I think."

"That's good. You still get to see them every week?"

"Uh-huh. It…it'd be nice if you'd come and see them sometimes. Since school started, they're usually there around seven. I know that's kind of early for you, but…I'll fix you breakfast." He ran a finger through the droplets of condensation that had formed on his glass.

She didn't respond. Didn't know what to say.

"I had a meeting with my attorney this morning," he told her. "You know the hearing comes up next month? The big one."

"Yeah, that's what I heard." Oh, had she ever heard it. Hadn't Darrin Parnell reminded her of the fact every single week for the past three months?

Wade took a swig of his iced tea, then put the glass down and looked at her. "Frank Locke—my lawyer—says it would be really helpful if you could spend some time with the kids—until the hearing anyway. Parnell's engaged now, and Locke says it would help a lot if we could show that I…that the kids have a…you know—a female role model in their lives."

She opened her mouth to protest, but he held up a hand and cut her off.

"I know it's the worst possible time for your schedule, Sophe, but…I'm begging you. Locke won't come right out and say it, but I know he thinks Parnell is going to get the kids."

"Really?" Her heartbeat quickened. If that were true, why did Darrin need *her* so all-fired bad? "He really thinks you'll…lose?"

Wade's voice rose half an octave. "I'll make it up to you, Sophie. I don't know how. We're behind at work, and this lawyer is costing me an arm and a leg. But I promise I'll make it up to you somehow—when this is all over."

"You don't owe me anything, Wade. And"—she hung her head, genuinely ashamed—"it's not like I don't want to see the kids. I do. I love them. But—" Her throat filled, and she motioned for him to wait.

Wade reached out and put a hand over her wrist on the table. "Is something wrong? What is it, Sophe?"

Her mind raced to come up with a response that wasn't a lie. "I'm not the best role model for Starr's kids. You don't know the…junk I've done."

"I know most of it. And I know it's in the past. Those kids don't give two hoots if you had some rough years. They love you anyway. And"— his grip on her wrist tightened—"if Starr were here she'd tell you that's exactly the way God loves you."

She pulled her arm away, rubbing the place where he'd touched her. "No, Wade. I'm not buying it. You think you know what I've done…what I've been. But you don't know the half of it."

He looked at her, a question in his eyes.

She turned away, shunning his gaze.

"I don't care," he said finally. "The kids won't care. It doesn't matter, Sophie. Love doesn't keep score. There are no degrees of sin."

"Yeah, right." She'd heard that line before. It never had made sense. He wouldn't be saying that if he knew the truth about her.

"Sophie, will you help me? I don't want to lose them." Wade's voice broke.

Sophie felt a hard place inside her soften ever so slightly. "I…I can't make any promises. I'm working extra shifts every chance I get. I can't keep that up if I don't get some sleep, and I can't pay my bills if I don't work the hours." That, at least, was true.

"I know. I'm sorry. Maybe I could work out something in the evenings. I don't know how flexible Dee can be. I've already changed the time on her once."

"I'll see. I'm not making any promises," she said again.

"All I'm asking is that you try. For the kids' sake."

She gave a slight nod, avoiding his eyes. Laughter floated in from the entry, and Sophie looked up to see a group of women from the office across the street waiting to be seated. She slid her chair back and stood. "I've got to go." She started toward the front of the restaurant, grateful for an excuse to end their conversation.

"Tuesday morning's the next visit," he called after her. "Seven o'clock."

She pretended not to hear him.

Thirty-Five

Wade opened the door to the State Farm Insurance Agency and let out a short breath as the blast of chill air hit him.

A ponytailed college-age girl looked up from behind a computer on a cluttered desk. "Good afternoon. How may I help you?"

Wade took his wallet from his pocket and slipped out his proof of insurance card. "I'd like to cancel this account." He laid the card on the only clear spot on the desk.

The girl pushed some papers out of the way and picked up the card. "Starr Parnell?"

Wade nodded.

"And your name?"

"Wade Sullivan. I'm... I was her fiancé. She's...deceased."

The girl's head jerked up. She stared at him. Wade prepared himself for an embarrassing display of sympathy, but after a moment, she pulled her keyboard closer and began keying in information from the card. "And are you still..." She stopped and looked up from the computer. "Oh, sorry. Please have a seat."

Wade pulled out the molded plastic chair in front of her desk and sat down.

"Now, are you still driving the vehicle? We could transfer the policy over to your name if you like."

"Um...no. It's—" He cleared his throat. "It's kind of complicated. Her estate hasn't been settled yet, and my lawyer advised me to just cancel the account for now. No one is going to be driving the car."

The girl turned back to the computer, clicked a few buttons, and leaned in to read the information that appeared on the screen. Wade was not computer savvy, but he instinctively sat forward on his chair to gaze at the screen. The computer was sitting at an angle, so he had a clear view of the screen, but the glare off the overhead fluorescent light obscured the page.

"Okay, here it is," the girl said, clicking a button on the mouse. She ran her finger down the screen, then looked up. "You're Wade? Sullivan?"

"That's right."

She tilted her head to one side and gave him a look he couldn't quite read. "Did you know there's a life insurance policy on this account, along with the coverage on the vehicle?"

"Life insurance?"

"Yes. With a fifty-thousand-dollar benefit."

His mind raced. Fifty thousand dollars? Why would Starr have bought life insurance when she already had a policy at the nursing home? "When…when was that policy added?"

The girl scrolled down the page. "It looks like it was part of the original policy we wrote. With a term life policy like this added with the auto, it was only eleven or twelve dollars a month. A pretty good deal, really." Her lips suddenly welded into a tight line, and she looked down, fiddling with a stack of papers on the desk, as though she'd just realized how insensitive her remark was. "So…um…do you still want to cancel the policy on the vehicle? Either way, we can fill out a statement of death certificate, and that check will be issued in a couple of weeks.

"Who is the beneficiary?"

"You're Wade Sullivan, right?" she asked again.

He nodded.

She looked back at the computer screen. "Well, it says here it's you."

Dee sat in front of Betty Graffe's desk, absently unraveling a loose thread from her cardigan. She usually brought a sweater whenever she visited the SRS office because they kept the air conditioning turned so low, but it had suddenly grown very warm in Betty's office.

"I'm not making an accusation, Dee," Betty said, tapping her pencil on the desktop, obviously as uncomfortable with the conversation as Dee was. "I just want to give you a chance to talk about this if you need to."

Dee floundered for a response. Betty might say this wasn't an accusation, but Dee could not make the words the social worker had flung at her a few minutes ago into anything else. "There's only one place this could have come from," she said finally.

Betty remained silent.

Dee sighed. Heat crept to her cheeks. "Betty, I can only assume you got this from Clay Two Feathers."

"I promised I would keep it confidential, Dee."

But Betty showed no surprise at Clay's name, which told Dee all she needed to know.

She felt her embarrassment drain away, to be replaced by anger. "First of all"—she struggled to unclench her jaw—"you need to know that Clay has been trying to get me to go out with him practically since the day he started work at St. Joe's."

Betty gave a thin smile. "There isn't anything in our code of ethics that says you can't date a coworker, Dee."

"That's not the point!" Dee gripped the arms of the chair and forced her voice down an octave. She silently counted to five. "I'm just saying that Clay obviously has ulterior motives for reporting me for something like this."

"He didn't *report* you for anything, Dee. He's just concern—"

"So it *was* Clay."

Betty's face flushed deep crimson. She sighed and closed her eyes briefly. "He's concerned, that's all. And rightly so, if what he told me is true."

"What exactly did he tell you?"

"Dee, please don't be angry with Clay. I...I hope you won't say anything to him about this. I didn't mean to break his confidence."

"What exactly did he say?"

Betty folded a corner of her desk calendar back and forth until it tore off. "He...he's just concerned that you've become overly involved with Wade Sullivan. That you've struck up a friendship with him that goes beyond what's acceptable. He feels perhaps you can't be objective in this case anymore."

Dee stared at Betty. "Is he going to ask to...have someone else assigned to the case?"

"I told you, Dee. He was just voicing his concern. He would have gone straight to Jeff Russell if he really thought you needed to be off the case. I just think he was afraid you wouldn't listen to him if he approached you about it. Possibly because of what you said…about his attraction for you."

Dee's heartbeat galloped, and yet she felt numb. "Betty, I'm not going to sit here and tell you I don't like Wade Sullivan. He's a nice guy, and I do enjoy my visits out there with the kids. But we have no…*relationship.* We've never seen each other outside of work. We've maintained a very…a good working relationship and nothing more."

"He's never acted improperly toward you?"

"Never." She grimaced at the implication. "He has never been anything but a perfect gentleman, and he's a wonderful father. Frankly, if I was making the decision, I'd give those kids to him tomorrow. I think the only thing he was guilty of in the first place was having a broken heart and being a little inexperienced at being a father."

Betty leaned forward, elbows on the desk, a knowing look in her eyes. "It sounds to me like you know him pretty well."

Dee looked away.

"And what about Darrin Parnell?" Betty pressed. "Why would you give the kids to Wade first? Is Darrin not a fit parent?"

Dee hesitated. "I'm not saying that. I just… It's obvious the kids are happier with Wade. That they see *him* as their father. Not Darrin. Darrin Parnell just does not connect with them. I think…he tries. But there's nothing there. And the kids know it."

"That doesn't sound like a very objective evaluation, Dee."

"Betty…I'm not saying that's what I'd recommend. I'm just saying if I were the judge, knowing what I know now—" She cut off her words, feeling she was digging herself into a hole.

The older woman clasped her hands in front of her and studied Dee. "Unfortunately, you know as well as I do this judge is not going to see it that way."

Dee sighed. "I know… And it just makes me sick."

Betty tipped her head to one side. "Well, we just won't recommend for one or the other. This is a hard call to make. It would be…regardless."

"I'm trying to be objective, Betty. I…think I *am* being objective."

"It'll be okay, Dee…" She let out a long sigh and shook her head. "But you'll go crazy if you let yourself get too involved. You know that. This is a rip-your-heart-out business, and if you let stuff like this get to you, you'll burn out so fast your head will spin. I've been here twenty years. I know what I'm talking about."

Dee recognized genuine kindness in Betty's eyes and in her gentle smile. She nodded her understanding. Betty was right, of course. Even if her warning was too late.

But Clay had no right to discuss this issue with Betty Graffe. This was none of his business. Anger welled up in Dee again, even as she realized it was her own fault for confiding in Clay. She loved the guy like a brother, but he'd blown it this time. And she intended to let him know it in no uncertain terms.

She pushed back her chair. "Thanks, Betty. I know Clay meant well, but I think he had ulterior motives in talking to you. And…well, this is between him and me."

"I understand." She dipped her head. "I didn't know about…well… about him having a thing for you."

"No, and I'm sure he didn't bother to tell you, did he?"

Betty shook her head and gave a little laugh. "No, he didn't."

"Don't worry, Betty. I'm not going to let this get to me. I love my job. I'm not going to do anything to jeopardize it."

"That's good."

Dee looked pointedly at her watch. "Oh! I need to go," she said. She waved and hurried from the office, letting Betty think she was late for an appointment. And in truth, she was. An appointment to give Clay Two Feathers a piece of her mind.

Dee was still fuming when she pulled into the parking lot of St. Joseph's ten minutes later. As luck would have it, Clay was pulling in at the same time. Ordinarily, she would have raced him for the only shady space, but today she ignored the goofy smirk he gave her as he raced ahead of her, revving his engine. She parked on the other side of the lot and got out of the car.

"I win. Again," he hollered back across the parking lot. He turned and grinned, waiting for her to catch up.

She didn't respond and hurried past him, suddenly afraid of what she might say.

"Hey?" She heard him behind her, jogging to catch up. "You having a bad day or something?"

When she felt Clay's hand on her shoulder, she whirled around and glared at him. "Yes, I am having a bad day, thank you very much."

"What happened?"

The compassion in his voice that usually touched her brought her temperature to boiling today. "As if you don't know."

He drew back, a question in the exaggerated knit of his brows.

"I just got back from talking to Betty Graffe."

Clay glanced away for a fraction of a second. "Oh?"

"Don't 'oh' me, Clay Two Feathers." She ground out his surname as though it were a curse word.

Clay winced.

"I hope you're proud of yourself."

His gaze bored a hole in the asphalt. "So…what did she say?"

"I'm not going to stand here and give you a play-by-play of all the gory details, but I—" A sob worked its way up her throat. She clenched her teeth and swallowed it back. "Why did you go to Betty, Clay? Why didn't you come to me first?"

His head jerked up. "I *did* come to you first," he practically hissed. "I told you I thought you were on thin ice with this Wade character. I told you I was worried about you. And if—"

"For your information, I'm a big girl. I can take care of myself. And I'll thank you to stay out of my personal business from now on."

He tucked his hands in the pocket of his jeans. "Dee, you *asked* my opinion. I gave it to you."

Dee remembered that night at the Sonic Drive-In. Though she

couldn't recall exactly how the conversation had gone, she was afraid Clay was right. "Even if I did," she said lamely, "that doesn't give you the right to go blabbing to Betty. What I told you was in confidence."

"Yeah, and I thought what I said to Betty was in confidence," he said under his breath. "So much for that idea."

She narrowed her eyes at him. "Betty didn't tell me it was you. I guessed. Who else would it have been?"

He shook his head. "I'm sorry, Dee, but I had to talk to somebody."

"Why? What does it matter to you, even if what you told Betty is true?"

"What did she say I said," he asked, wiping the sweat from under his beaded headband with the back of his hand. "It's too hot to stand here. Do you want to go somewhere?"

She turned her wrist over and looked at her watch. "I can't. I have a meeting in fifteen minutes." She started for the building. "I don't know what there is to talk about."

He caught up with her, then hurried ahead, walking backward and facing her as he spoke. "Dee, let me take you to dinner tonight. Nothing fancy. Not a date. Just…let's talk this out. I don't want you to be mad at me. I want to explain why I went to Betty."

She stopped a few feet from the back entrance. He did likewise. She stared past him, thinking.

"Please, Dee?"

She hesitated. "Not dinner." She didn't want to give him any excuse to think she was warming to the idea of a date with him. "But if you want to go walking with me tonight we can talk. Be on my front porch at eight o'clock." She glanced at her watch again. "I really have to go."

"Okay. I'll see you at eight."

She stepped around him and went into the building. She closed the door and turned to look out the window. Clay was still standing where she'd left him.

Thirty-Six

Clay's old Chevy pulled up to the curb at exactly eight o'clock. From her kitchen window, Dee watched him get out of the car, then ran outside before he could ring the doorbell.

When he saw her, he dipped his chin and held a hand up, looking terrified that she might bite his head off.

Poor guy. He had no way of knowing she'd cooled off considerably since her diatribe this afternoon. She crossed the lawn but stopped halfway to the curb, flashing him a half smile. "Do you need to go potty or anything before we go?"

A slow grin came to his face, and he wagged his head, making the feathers in his headband bob. "I…uh…went before I left home, thank you very much. You've obviously been in the company of a few too many little kids today."

She grinned back. "True. So I'm ready for some adult company. Think you can handle that?"

He drew back and held his palms out in mock surrender. "Hey, I'm not the one who stomped off in a huff this afternoon."

She led the way, and they headed down the street at a brisk pace. "I guess maybe I was a little over the top. I'm sorry, Clay. But I…I don't think you should have talked to Betty."

"I didn't know who else to talk to, Dee. You ought to just be glad I didn't go to Jeff and ask him to take you off the case."

She shuddered to think of him talking to her supervisor. "Why did you have to talk to anybody?"

"Because I'm worried about you." He glanced at her from the corner of his eye. "I don't think you realize how…involved you are, Dee."

"What do you mean by that?" She picked up her pace.

He matched it without missing a beat. "Dee, I see how you look when you come to the office on Tuesday mornings after your visits out there."

She didn't dare pretend not to know where "out there" was. "How do I look?"

"You know," he said, "all happy and bubbly with this certain glow on your face."

"Hey, they're adorable kids."

He let out a short harrumph. "It's not the kids, Dee. And I think you know it."

She skidded to a halt in the middle of the road. Clay had to jog back a few steps to meet her. When he did, she propped her hands on her hips and glared at him. "Okay. I'm going to lay it on the line here. Yes, without meaning to, Wade Sullivan and I have become friends. And yes, I like him a lot. Maybe more than I should, and maybe in a way I shouldn't. But I have done absolutely nothing to act on that fact. And neither has he. And I have no intention of jeopardizing my job by doing so—now or in the near future."

She turned and took off walking again, wishing she hadn't added that "in the near future" line. She couldn't imagine what the coming days might hold for her, but she felt a wave of profound sadness whenever she realized how slim the chance was that Wade might be a part of her future. More and more, she found herself praying that he would.

Clay caught up and fell into step with her. "Dee, don't you think it would be best if you let someone else take this case? Just so there's no question."

She had actually entertained that possibility recently, though not for the same reasons Clay was probably thinking. He merely wanted her away from Wade. But she had started to feel she needed to remove herself from any temptation where Wade was concerned. As much as she longed for an even deeper friendship with Wade, what she'd told Clay was true—she didn't want to do anything to jeopardize the job she loved.

"I considered that, Clay. I honestly did. But the final hearing is just a couple of weeks away. It will be a moot point after that."

She wanted to cry every time she thought about it. Partly because she felt in her heart that Wade would lose the children. But mostly because, one way or another, the judge's decision would mean an end to the precious hours she spent with Wade and the kids.

Clay wiped his brow with the tail of his T-shirt. "Dee…I don't know how recently you've reviewed the code of ethics, but you might want to glance over the section on unprofessional conduct. This isn't just an ethical issue. There are legal ramifications for this kind of thing."

Her breath caught. "What do you mean?"

"I'd never really had reason to look it up before, but there are strict regulations about dual relationships with clients, and they're—"

"You looked it up?" Was he actually considering filing a report against her?

Even in the dim evening light, she could see him flush.

"I was just curious."

"Yeah, right."

"Well, I didn't see *you* bothering to check it out. Do you know the law prohibits you from having any type of dual relationship with a client—and certainly not a sexual one—for a full twenty-four months after the client-professional relationship ends?"

She stopped in the street again, turning toward him, fuming. "Clay. How many times do I have to tell you: There *is* no relationship. He's never so much as touched me." That wasn't quite true, but in essence it was. Wade had been a perfect gentleman.

"Okay, okay," Clay said. "I just want to be sure you're not getting in over your head."

She took off walking again, but what Clay had told her shook her to the core. She *hadn't* realized there were such strict rules in place. She'd never dreamed she'd be faced with such a question. She filed the information away in the back of her mind to deal with later.

"So what kind of recommendation are you making in this case?"

She sighed. "I don't know yet. I… Even now there's that still, small voice—" She sensed him bristle beside her. "I know, I know…you don't put any stock in that. I do. And something just tells me these kids belong with Wade Sullivan. But there's not one logical thing I can say against their father. And if *you* have a problem with the still, small voice thing, you can imagine how that reasoning would go over with a judge."

He shook his head and gave a wry smile. "No…I don't think I'd bring that up in court."

They traversed the evening shadows to the rhythm of their labored breaths and the *scritch-scritch-scritch* of their tennis shoes on the pavement. Here and there the streetlights started to come on.

They walked in silence for a few minutes before Clay spoke again. "I may not buy into the still, small voice you talk about, Dee, but I do trust your instincts where kids are concerned. But…how can you advocate for Wade *against* the biological father? How would you support your argument?"

She tried to inhale and fought against a smothering weight in her chest. It was becoming a familiar sensation—one she felt every time she thought how it would make Wade feel if she were to make a recommendation for Darrin Parnell. Would he see it as a betrayal? How could he possibly feel otherwise? Now Clay had added this new burden to her worries. Could there actually be legal repercussions if her friendship with Wade were to become more? She was anxious to look up the statute Clay had referred to.

It terrified her to think her growing feelings for Wade were no longer a secret, private thing she held in her heart. She couldn't afford to appear prejudiced in any way now. But neither could she bear to think of making a recommendation that would take those children away from Wade. She stopped and bent over, hands on her knees, trying desperately to catch her breath.

"Hey, are you okay?" Clay stopped and took a similar stance, leaning in to study her face. "Let's sit down and rest for a minute."

He plopped onto a patch of thick grass at the curb. She eased down beside him, still breathing hard.

"Clay, if the judge gives those kids to their father, Wade will be lucky if he ever sees them again. Darrin Parnell and his fiancée live and work in Minneapolis. There's no way they are going to bring those kids back here to see Wade. And that's assuming the judge even grants him visitation rights." Hot tears welled in her eyes. She swiped them away with the back of her hand. "Sometimes I hate this business."

Clay stared straight ahead into the darkness. "I know. I know," he whispered.

Dee was touched by the genuine compassion in his voice. More than once, she'd comforted him when he was lamenting a child's situation. He really did understand how she was feeling. She shouldn't have been so harsh with him this afternoon. In some ways it was a relief to have things out in the open with Clay and with Betty. Except now she knew they'd both be watching her. Well, maybe that was a good thing. Though it sure wouldn't make it easy to face Clay after her next visit with Wade and the kids. The thought brought a wry chuckle.

Clay looked at her askance. "What's so funny?"

"I'm just trying to figure out how I'm going to keep from glowing on Tuesday mornings."

He didn't return her laughter.

She huffed out a short sigh. "I didn't go looking for this, Clay. And it feels silly even to say that because *this* isn't…anything…"

"But you admit the attraction is there?"

"I already told you it was. I'm not sure a person really has any control over something like that. But just because a person feels an attraction for someone, she doesn't have to act on it."

"I agree." Clay bobbed his chin.

His voice carried a whiff of triumph that irritated Dee.

"But I'd take it one step further," Clay said. "I'd say if a person were wise, she would remove herself from a situation that had potential for temptation."

She conceded his point with an exaggerated sigh. "Well, if it's any comfort to you, this won't even be an issue in two weeks. I…I'm going to tough it out until then."

He shrugged. "Whatever."

"Wade, you can't tell me that—" She let out a little gasp. Heat rushed to her face in waves. Had she just called Clay by Wade's name?

He unfolded himself from the curb. "I rest my case," he said, his voice void of emotion. He turned and started walking in the direction they'd come from.

"Clay, wait…" She jumped up off the curb and jogged to catch up with him. "I'm sorry. I'm sorry, Clay. Maybe I am proving your point. I'll…have to think about it. Maybe you're right."

"No…" He bent his head and slowed his pace. "I'm not being fair. You do what you have to do, Dee. I trust you. I just…I don't want to see you get hurt."

"Thank you, Clay. I appreciate that. And thanks for listening."

After a long minute, he turned to her. The streetlight cast his face in shadow, but there was no mistaking the sadness in his eyes. "Sure," he said. "What are friends for?"

Frank Locke's voice held more optimism than Wade had heard in weeks. "This could be very important, extremely helpful…" Locke said, looking up from the insurance documents State Farm had given Wade. He put the papers in a neat stack, rested his elbows on the desk, and steepled his fingers. "What this will say to a judge is that the children's mother, in effect, chose you as the executor of her estate. And by natural progression, it makes you her unspoken choice of guardian to her children."

"So you think we might have a chance?"

A brief grimace contorted Locke's face. "I'm hoping that, at least, we might be able to work out joint custody."

In spite of the fact he'd begun to fear he would not get the kids, Wade reeled at Locke's words. Joint custody seemed like an impossibility, dragging the kids back and forth between here and Minneapolis. He'd probably get them during the summers, his busiest time at work. And what kind of life would that be for Beau and Lacey and Dani—taking them away from their new friends to put them in day care? He wasn't sure he could do that to them. But could he trust that Darrin Parnell had reformed his ways? That the kids would be safe with him? Though Locke saw the fiancée as a strike against Wade's getting custody, at least she would provide a safety net for the kids. And, yes, a feminine influence in their lives.

The temptation to give up and concede to Parnell raised its ugly head again. Then he thought of Dee's plea that he fight for the kids.

He pushed the thoughts from his mind, trying to focus on the reason he'd come to Locke's office.

"If we can get joint custody," Locke was saying, "it might untie some funds from Starr's policy at the nursing home for you to help with the kids' expenses."

"I don't care about the money," he said.

Locke gave him a stern look. "Well, if you get the kids, you *should* care about it. You're taking on a huge financial responsibility."

"What would be the best way to handle this State Farm money?" he asked, dodging the attorney's lecture.

"Definitely use it to pay your attorney first," Locke said, laughing.

Wade didn't quite see the humor. He owed Locke and Locke a sizable chunk of change, and he doubted he had much choice other than to use the proceeds from Starr's insurance to pay the bill. "Of course, I will do that," he said, unsmiling. "But I want to put as much as possible into a trust for the kids. Something Darrin Parnell can't get his hands on if he does get the kids."

"Of course," Locke said, sobering. "I can help you set up a trust fund."

For the next twenty minutes, Locke walked him through the likely scenario for the next hearing. He coached Wade on how to answer questions Parnell's attorney or the other parties might raise, and he prepared him for each possibility.

Locke's words made things all too real. Less than a month from now Wade's fate would be decided. He would have his kids safely home, and this would all be a distant nightmare.

Or he would have lost them forever.

Thirty-Seven

Wade felt like the defendant in a murder trial as he sat behind the table at Frank Locke's left. Tugging on his too-tight tie, he tried not to look at Darrin Parnell—or at Dee Thackery—as the judge introduced the parties present in the courtroom.

Dee sat in the gallery to his right. Even though she was two rows behind him, he couldn't seem to keep her out of his peripheral vision. Nor could he help noticing how pretty she looked in a peach-colored pantsuit, with her hair caught up in a silver clasp. He dared to imagine what it might be like to celebrate with her when—*if*—he won his kids back. He knew it was unlikely the judge would actually announce his decision today, but this deposition hearing was an important one—probably the one that would ultimately decide the fate of Starr's children.

Wade turned and searched the gallery directly behind him, hoping to see Sophie, but not surprised that she wasn't there.

Judge Richard Paxton was imposing in his long black robe, even if the small county courthouse didn't boast a bailiff—or even the bang of a gavel—to announce him.

The judge finished his acknowledgments and looked briefly over the docket. "This hearing is for the purpose of deciding custody in the matter of minor children Beau Parnell, Lacey Parnell, and Danica Parnell. Mr. Baze, would you please speak to the recommendations of Social and Rehabilitation Services and St. Joseph's Children's Services?"

Wade's palms grew damp and his heart galloped. So much hung on the words this man would speak.

Marcus Baze, the young county attorney, pushed back his chair and rose. He didn't look like he could be over twenty-five, but he spoke with authority when he presented a brief overview of the case, reminding the judge how visitations were being handled. "Your Honor," Baze said, his tone turning almost apologetic, "at this time, the agencies don't feel comfortable making a recommendation for or against either Mr. Parnell or Mr. Sullivan. This decision has been a dilemma for SRS and the foster-care agency."

What did that mean? Wade looked to Frank Locke, but the attorney's expression was unreadable.

Baze paused and bent to shuffle some papers on the table in front of him before continuing. "Numerous observations of each man's inter-actions with the children have been made during supervised visitations, and it is the opinion of the case managers that both men seem equally able to fulfill the parental role for these children. Any preference we might cite for Darrin Parnell would be in the interest of family preservation, based, of course, on the fact that he is the children's biological father. An addi-tional consideration would be the fact that his fiancée, Carma Weist, has developed a close relationship with the children and is a positive female role model in their lives."

Wade's shoulders sagged, and a tight knot formed in his chest. In spite of Marcus Baze's claim of indecision, it sure felt like the recommendation leaned in Parnell's favor.

The county attorney picked up a legal pad and read from his notes. "A congruent preference for Wade Sullivan would rest on the fact that he has been a father figure to the children for the past three years. They have lived in his home, which contains tangible memories of their mother. Also, their mother's sister, their only other living relative, resides here in Coyote, which would play into a preference for Mr. Sullivan having cus-tody. The agencies feel recommendations for either party would essentially carry equal weight and, as such, have presented a dilemma. We look for-ward to hearing the decision of the court."

The county attorney's statement seemed awfully ambiguous. Frank Locke had explained that Baze represented SRS and St. Joseph's, and that those agencies had compiled their recommendations. Wade wondered what Dee's professional recommendation had said. Did she really think it didn't matter who got the kids? But the question was barely formed in his mind when her words of a few weeks ago echoed through him. *These kids need you, Wade. Fight for them.*

As Marcus Baze took his seat, Judge Paxton called on Ruth Cadena, the attorney appointed as guardian ad litem to the children. She gave a statement that reiterated much of what the county attorney had said. Wade had been impressed with the woman in previous meetings and hearings. She had a way of making the children—and everyone around them—feel at ease. He'd felt the kids were in good hands under her representation, but he was disappointed she didn't speak more adamantly in his favor now.

He shouldn't have been surprised. Locke had warned him that the goal of the social services agencies would be to preserve the family of origin if at all possible.

Judge Paxton slipped on a pair of reading glasses and looked at the papers in front of him for a minute before recognizing Darrin Parnell's attorney. "Mr. Hinson, the court will hear your statement."

The attorney stood and stepped from behind the table. "Your Honor, Mr. Parnell has worked very hard over these last months to prove to this court that he is dedicated to regaining custody of his children. Not only has he sacrificed income and time away from a lucrative and stable job to travel here from Minneapolis each and every week for visitation with the children, but he has invested countless hours completing parenting classes and other training that will benefit him as a father to his children."

Wade wanted to gag at the way Parnell's attorney couched his client's mandatory attendance at anger-management classes. He waited for Frank Locke to point that out, but his lawyer remained silent while Jonathan Hinson continued.

"I'm happy to report that in the interim Mr. Parnell has become engaged." The attorney smiled and turned to where Carma Weist was seated in the gallery behind Parnell. "As noted in the acknowledgments, Ms. Weist is present in the courtroom today and has been attending Mr. Parnell's visitations with the children for several weeks now. Ms. Weist has a degree in early childhood education, has managed a day-care center in Minneapolis for several years, and is looking forward to being a mother to these children."

Hinson paused, walked back to his place, and checked his notes.

"One of Mr. Parnell's greatest concerns is that, with the death of their mother, these children have lost the influence of a woman in their lives. Carma Weist will provide—in fact, has already begun to provide—that influence and is eager to continue doing so."

From the corner of his vision, Wade could see Parnell's fiancée bobbing her neatly coifed head in agreement.

Hinson took a sip of water from the glass on his table, then continued. "It is a concern to Mr. Parnell that the children have been left with a single man who has no blood relationship to them whatsoever. Much of the children's time while under his care has been spent in day-care facilities. And again, they have lacked, under his care, the influence of a mother figure in their lives. We strongly believe that, while Mr. Sullivan has made an effort to provide the children with food, clothing, and other material needs, Mr. Parnell is in a better position to provide these things, along with the loving devotion a birth father naturally feels toward his flesh and blood. For all these reasons, we firmly believe it is in the best interests of Beau, Lacey, and Danica Parnell for full and permanent custody to be given to their biological father, Darrin Parnell."

Parnell's attorney sat down, and the judge recognized Frank Locke. Wade sent up a prayer that Locke would be given the right words to speak.

"Your Honor," Locke began. "While I fully agree with the philosophy of family preservation and believe, whenever possible, children should remain with their family of origin, the overriding consideration in any custody case must always be what is in the best interest of the children. What *is* in the best interest of these three children—Beau and Lacey and Danica Parnell? Is it that they be separated from the only man they have ever really known as 'Dad'? Wade Sullivan has been an integral part of these children's lives for three years. Until recently the children have had no contact whatsoever with their birth father. Lacey Parnell was a baby when she last saw Mr. Parnell, and until a few months ago, Danica Parnell had never laid eyes on her birth father. Even Beau has very few, if any, memories of Mr. Parnell as his father, and sadly, what memories he does have are distressful ones."

A hush fell over the room.

But Locke went on without explanation. "The children have never received one penny of child support from their father. He has not been a part of their lives in over four years. In every sense of the word, Wade Sullivan has been the only father these children have ever known. And though their mother was not yet married to Mr. Sullivan at the time of her death, a wedding date had been set, and they were actively building a life together that included these children in the strongest way possible."

Frank Locke's words gathered steam, and for a minute Wade almost forgot it was his own story being told with such passion.

Locke took a step toward the bench as he continued. "Together, Mr. Sullivan and Starr Parnell were refurbishing a house in the country—the house Mr. Sullivan freely offered as a home to these children after their mother's death. Beau, Lacey, and Dani find great comfort in being in the house their mother was so excited about moving to—a home where each of them has a bedroom waiting—a room lovingly painted by their mother with artwork and calligraphy designed especially for them. In spite of the financial hardship and the time commitment, Mr. Sullivan lovingly took in these children and cared for them, providing for their every need. And again, this was at considerable financial sacrifice, since the insurance money from Mrs. Parnell's employer has been held up pending the naming of a guardian. Those monies are still in limbo.

"However…" Locke drew out the word and took another step toward the bench. "It was recently discovered that Starr Parnell, the children's mother, had purchased a life insurance policy in the amount of fifty thousand dollars, naming Wade Sullivan as primary beneficiary and naming her children as successor beneficiaries. Mr. Sullivan has selflessly placed the bulk of that benefit in a trust to be used for the children's education."

A soft buzz rippled through the courtroom as surprised glances were exchanged. Parnell and his attorney conferred in whispers.

But Frank Locke wasn't finished. "In spite of his grief over his fiancée's death, not only did Mr. Parnell provide for the children's physical needs, but he went many steps further—seeing that they participated on sports teams, coaching them on the weekends, making sure they had time for outings with their school friends, taking them to church and Sunday school."

Wade felt a twinge of guilt. Locke was making him out to be a saint, when he had rarely taken the kids to church after Starr's death. He wondered if Parnell and his fiancée were involved in a church.

Frank Locke continued, "Let's look, Your Honor, at the factors Kansas statute considers in deciding custody." He ticked them off on his fingers. "The considerable length of time the children have already been in Mr. Sullivan's care, the desires the children have expressed to remain with Mr. Sullivan, the positive interaction and interrelationship these children have with Wade Sullivan, the admirable adjustment the children made—under his guidance—to their home, school, and community after their mother's death."

Locke stopped and cleared his throat. He studied the floor for a moment, then his gaze rose with purpose. "Unfortunately, Your Honor, another factor in Kansas statute—one that can't be ignored in this case— is evidence of spousal abuse. As police records in two different Minneapolis jurisdictions testify, Mr. Parnell has a history of abuse toward the children's mother."

At that, Parnell and his attorney immediately put their heads together. Hinson raised a hand and the judge nodded.

Hinson spoke through clenched jaws. "Your Honor, this has no bearing on the case we are discussing. It happened years ago under a very stressful, unique set of circumstances. Mr. Parnell has successfully completed anger-management classes, and he has never—not even one time— laid a hand on his children. This is irrelevant to this case and should not be a factor in this decision whatsoever, Your Honor."

The judge picked up a pen and scratched something on a notepad before motioning for Frank Locke to continue.

Locke moved ahead as though he hadn't noticed the interruption. "Always, first and foremost in a case such as this, the ultimate consideration must be 'What is in the best interest of the children?' I don't believe it could be any more clear that, in the case of Beau and Lacey and Danica Parnell, their best interest is served by having them remain permanently in the care and custody of the man who has been a father to them in the best sense of the word for as long as any of them can remember. Their memories of their mother are invested in the home they shared with Wade Sullivan. Their friends from elementary school and Sunday school and from the community are here in Coyote. Their only other living relative, their mother's sister, Sophia Braden, lives here and has helped Mr. Sullivan in various ways with the children's upbringing."

Again, Hinson waved a hand, asking the judge to recognize him.

Judge Paxton nodded. "Mr. Hinson?"

"Your honor, it's unfortunate this has to be brought up, but I believe it is important to note that Sophia Braden is anything but a good role model for the children—and especially for Mr. Parnell's daughters. She has a history of drug abuse and..." He hesitated, dropping his head for a moment. "Well, let's just say that her morals as a woman leave much to be desired."

A wave of nausea rolled over Wade. It was all he could do not to turn around and scan the courtroom to see if Sophie had come after all. Now he prayed she wasn't there. It would kill her if she knew her past was being used against him and the kids this way.

Wade waited for Locke to speak in Sophie's defense, to argue that Sophie's sins were in the past and also irrelevant to this case. But of course, he'd never told Locke about Sophie's history. It had seemed too deep a breach of loyalty, especially when it *was* in the past. He felt hot anger rise in him. He sent up a prayer that Parnell's attorney wouldn't take his comments any further.

Wade let out a grateful sigh when the judge nodded, motioning for Locke to continue.

"Thank you, Your Honor," Locke said. "I will counter by saying that Mr. Sullivan has seen to it that the children have many positive female influences in their lives. They spend a good deal of time with female teachers and day-care givers, women much like Carma Weist." He glanced pointedly back toward Darrin's fiancée. "As well, they have spent many hours with the wife of Mr. Sullivan's business partner." He turned to Wade. "I'm sorry, her name slips my mind..."

"Margie...Margaret Dolecek," Wade filled in.

"The children are not lacking for a feminine influence in their lives, as anyone who has spent any amount of time with them could testify." Locke pointed a stern finger at no one in particular. "As I was saying, if this is truly about what is best for the children, it would take a stretch of the imagination to see how it could possibly be in Beau and Lacey and Danica Parnell's best interest to move them from their home in the country to a faraway city with two people they barely know. To take them away from the only man they have ever known as a father, and the house where so many memories of their mother reside. To take them away from the friends and teachers at their schools and church. Away from their beloved pet dog. Away from everything dear and familiar to them. I pray the court will see that the only decision that can possibly be in the best interest of these children is for them to remain here in Coyote with Wade Sullivan."

When Frank Locke sat down, Wade let out a breath he hadn't realized he was holding. He was pleased with Locke's speech. If the judge was listening at all, surely he was convinced. Wade risked a glance over his shoulder to see Dee's reaction. She met his gaze, then looked away quickly, her expression divulging no emotion.

The judge pushed his reading glasses back up on his nose and shuffled the papers on his desk. "I'd like to ask a few questions of Ms. Thackery, the foster-care social worker."

Everyone turned to the gallery to look at Dee. She straightened and sat forward in her seat. "Could you describe for me the children's interaction with Mr. Parnell during visitation?"

Dee hesitated, clearing her throat. "Well, those visitations have taken place at St. Joe's—St. Joseph's. Usually the kids work on puzzles or play games, look at magazines, that type of thing. Mr. Parnell usually…tries to talk with them about whatever they're doing. They…they're pretty quiet —shy, I guess—with him. But they seem to get along okay."

"And Ms. Weist?" the judge asked.

Dee wrung her hands in her lap. "They seem to like her. She…she's very good with them, trying to draw them out…" She shrugged, letting her words hang in the air.

"And Mr. Sullivan? Can you describe his relationship with the children?"

Wade watched Dee closely. Did the others see the way her face brightened, the spark that flickered in her eyes? Or was he imagining it?

"Well, it's obvious the children feel very much at home with Wade—Sullivan, Mr. Sullivan." She looked at her lap and cleared her throat again. "Usually he plays games with the kids…card games, or they do puzzles. A lot of times they play outside. He'll throw the baseball with them, or they throw the Frisbee for the dog. The kids are always eager to go to visitation with him. They laugh a lot when they're with him. It's like…well, it's like they're home."

The judge nodded slowly. "So, from what you've observed, you would not have reservations about the children being in the care of either Mr. Parnell or Mr. Sullivan."

Her gaze flitted in Wade's direction. Before their eyes met, she looked quickly to the judge, but Wade didn't miss her slight hesitation.

"No, Your Honor…I wouldn't have reservations…about either of them."

Thirty-Eight

Dee parked behind Wade's pickup in front of the house and stepped out of the car to help the kids with their seat belts. As soon as she turned them loose, Beau and Lacey raced to greet Wade, who was waiting for them on the porch. Going around to the other side of the car to help Danica, Dee heard Shadow's happy yipping and the older kids cooing at the dog as though he were a new baby.

Dee knelt by the car door and started to unbuckle Danica from the child safety seat. The sun felt good on her back, and she thought what a happy routine this had become for her. She heard Wade's voice behind her and turned to glance over her shoulder at him.

"Good morning." He gave a quick wave and flashed her a smile—a smile she knew she'd spend the rest of the day chasing from her thoughts.

He bent beside her. "Need some help there?"

She moved out of the way and let him lift Dani from the car seat.

"Hey there, Dani Banany! How are you?" He gave the little girl a quick hug, then swooped her over his shoulder and blew raspberries on her neck.

"Wade! That tickles!" Dani's squeals of glee floated away on the newly crisp autumn breeze.

Dee stood by the car and watched them, thinking how sharp the contrast was between Wade's way with the children and Darrin Parnell's. Darrin's interactions with his children were more like business meetings, with him giving polite lectures or interviewing them about their activities.

A shadow of guilt moved over her, and she wished for the hundredth time that she'd been more specific when the judge asked her about the children's interactions with Darrin Parnell. But she'd been afraid. Afraid that her feelings for Wade would be exposed. Afraid that her prejudice for Wade had colored her judgment of Darrin. Clay had been so right. Why hadn't she listened to him? Well, it was too late now. Monday the judge would hand down his decision.

"Dee? You coming?"

Wade's shout drew her from her musings. He was standing on the front porch, waiting for her.

"I'll be right there." She slammed the car door and pressed the lock mechanism on the key chain.

"Okay with you if we stay outside today?" he asked as she came up the walk.

"Sure. It'd be a shame to waste this beautiful weather."

He shaded his eyes and looked up at the sky. "We had almost two inches of rain yesterday."

"That's great. Ought to make the farmers happy."

"Well, it sure makes me happy. Hang on a sec..." He disappeared around the side of the house and came back with his hands behind his back. He winked at Dee, then hollered for the kids. "Hey, you guys!"

All three came running, Shadow in tow.

"Looky what I found," he said, grinning and producing a brand-new soccer ball with a twist of his wrist.

"Cool!" Beau said, reaching for it.

"Here..." Wade motioned for him to go long and winged the ball in the air. Beau's gaze followed the ball's path, and he ran after it, leaping in the air to bounce it neatly off his head.

Wade gave a whoop. "Great shot, buddy!"

The girls dashed out on the lawn, and the game was on.

Dee plopped onto the porch steps and watched, laughing at their antics, cheering when one of them managed to put the ball between the two old elm trees Wade had designated as goalposts.

With Wade at goalie, Beau dribbled the ball down the lawn for a third score.

"Oh, man! Not again!" Wade moaned as the ball sailed between the trees. "That's it for me, buddy. You're too good for this old man." He tackled Beau, and they wrestled on the ground for a minute.

Groaning, Wade struggled to his feet, brushed the grass off his jeans, and lumbered over to the porch. "Gee, thanks for all your help," he told Dee, plopping down beside her on the steps.

"Sorry, but soccer is definitely not my game. Now if it was spoons, we'd be in business."

He gave her a sidewise smile and turned back to watch the kids.

Feeling suddenly vulnerable at his nearness, she rubbed her arms and changed the subject. "It's chilly sitting out here. That's sure a switch."

"Here, you can have this…" He stood and peeled off his sweatshirt, tugging at the white T-shirt he wore underneath. "I'm burning up after all that running." Before she could protest, he lopped the sweatshirt over her shoulders and ran back to join the kids on the lawn.

Dee brought one sleeve of the sweatshirt to her face and breathed in the heady mixture of autumn grass and laundry soap. And Wade's aftershave. The slightest tremor whispered through her. She wrapped both sleeves around her, then felt almost guilty, as though it were Wade's very arms embracing her instead of a silly sweatshirt.

The girls' shrieks and laughter made her look up. The soccer ball sat in the middle of a puddle at the edge of the driveway. Beau and Wade attempted to fish it out with a forked tree branch. Lacey and Dani stirred the smaller rain puddles with sticks, splashing and giggling together.

After a minute, Dee noticed Dani shivering, standing rigid with her arms folded over her midsection, hands tucked under her chin. Dee eased off the porch and pulled Wade's sweatshirt from her shoulders. "Here, sweetie, let's wrap this around you." She draped the thick sweatshirt over Dani's slender shoulders. It engulfed her, reaching below her knees. Dee crossed the sleeves in front and pulled them snug, giving the little girl a quick hug. She looked up to find Wade's eyes on her.

He quickly went back to helping Beau wash off the ball. But in that instant, a memory from her childhood pierced Dee's mind.

She must have been about eight or nine. They were living in Michigan then, and a thunderstorm had turned their backyard into a swamp. She'd fallen into a puddle and started to cry. But her dad ran to help her up. Then, to her surprise, he stepped into the puddle beside her. Before she knew it, her mother joined them, and soon all three of them were splashing and laughing together.

It was a rare, sweet memory, before the bad times had started. She hadn't thought of it in years. But now, watching Wade play with the kids and feeling such a part of his little family, she realized how badly she wanted this for herself, and for any children she might someday be blessed to have.

"Are you okay?" Wade bent to peer into her face.

She shook away the wistful thoughts and gave a little laugh. "I'm fine. I was just remembering…playing in the puddles when I was little."

"It's kind of fun, isn't it?"

She nodded, then looked pointedly at the kids. "Except…maybe we'd better start drying everybody off. I need to take them to school in about fifteen minutes."

He checked his watch and shook his head. "Is it my imagination, or does this hour go by faster every week?"

And now it's almost over. Oh, Wade. Tears came abruptly to her eyes, and she turned away, pretending to brush some imaginary bit of dirt or grass from her slacks. She squeezed her eyelids tight, struggling to compose herself.

Wade ran to the house for towels, and Dee remembered another day they'd romped in the water and laughed together. It seemed like a lifetime ago. She could hardly remember a time when this man and these children had not filled her thoughts, her heart. She'd had some clients over the years who tugged at her heartstrings a little more than others. But this family—for they *were* a family, in the best sense of the word—had captured her heart and changed her forever.

She heard the back door slam. Wade came jogging around the corner of the house with a stack of towels. He tossed one to each of the kids and handed one to Dee.

Looking at Beau, Wade laughed. "Man, you look like you've been swimming. How did you manage to get that soaked?"

Beau shrugged, then grinned. "Makin' all those goals, I guess."

Wade gave a growl, threw a towel over Beau's head, and started rubbing.

"Hey!" Beau yelled. But Dee noticed he wasn't trying too hard to get away.

She started in on the girls, who had at least managed to keep their hair dry. She gave one last rub of the towel and stood back to inspect Lacey. "Not bad, kiddo, but I think you're going to have to lose the socks. They're soaked."

Dee helped her untie the shoes and peel off the damp cotton anklets, then moved to Dani, who was already tugging at her shoelaces. Dee helped her with her socks and ordered both girls up to the porch to dry their feet and put their shoes back on.

Wade sent Beau to the house with the dirty towels, then turned to Dee, his gaze seeking hers. She saw desperation in his eyes, and it nearly tore her apart.

"Will I... If things don't go like I hope on Monday...at the court-house...will I get a chance to tell the kids good-bye?"

"Yes. Yes, you will, Wade. I'll make sure of that." If anyone dared to refuse Wade that, she would personally tear them limb from limb.

Wade reached out and touched her arm briefly. "Dee...whatever happens on Monday, I want you to know how much I appreciate everything you've done to make it possible for me to...be with the kids like this. You've made a terrible time bearable, even happy, for me. I...I appreciate that more than you could ever know."

The tears came again, and she could only nod over the lump in her throat.

He looked down, rubbing circles in the grass with the toe of his tennis shoe. "You've made a difference in my life at a very rough time. You've been a bright spot...a blessing. In spite of everything, I'd like to think... we've become friends. And I hope...I hope I can see you again, and—"

She held up a hand. "Wade...please. Don't. Thank you... Thank you for telling me, but...I can't think about that right now."

"I know...I know." He closed his eyes. "I'm sorry. I just...I didn't want you to leave without knowing how I feel."

She nodded. "I have to go. The kids are going to be late for school."

He stepped back and turned to the porch, cupping his hands around his mouth. "Come on, guys. It's time to go. Hustle up."

They came running. While Dee buckled Dani in, Wade helped the other two with their seat belts. It was a routine they'd developed over the weeks. After the first few visits, the kids had seemed to accept that their time with Wade would be short. They'd adjusted amazingly well and rarely complained anymore when it was time to go.

She looked from Beau's face to Lacey's to Dani's. What would their lives be like this time next month? She looked up at the house where the sun reflected off the windows. Two weeks from now would they be waking up in their bedrooms here—the rooms their mama had painted special for each of them? Or would they be on their way to Minneapolis?

Thirty-Nine

Wade banged on the door again. "Sophie!"

He looked around the parking lot. Her car was sitting in its usual spot, but he'd practically pounded the door down, and still no response. It was four o'clock in the afternoon. Usually, Sophie was awake and getting ready for work by now. Maybe she was in the shower. But he'd been knocking and ringing her doorbell for almost ten minutes now with no answer. He shuddered inwardly, thinking of the day he'd hollered for Starr, wondering why she didn't respond.

It had been weeks since he'd talked to Sophie. She never had come out to see the kids since that day he'd confronted her. He'd been to the café twice hoping to catch her, but she hadn't been there. Last time, Lydia told him Sophie had the day off, but he wasn't sure he believed her. Ever since Sophie had been assaulted in the parking lot, he suspected Lydia was covering for her. About what, he didn't know.

He rang the doorbell one last time before walking around to the back of the building. From the rear, the row of cookie-cutter porches stopped Wade short, but then he recognized the colorful plastic banner tacked to the back of one door. Dani had made it in Bible school last summer and insisted on giving it to her aunt Sophie. He was strangely touched to see it hanging there.

He knocked on the door, then edged to the window and peered inside. Glancing around, he hoped the neighbors wouldn't think he was trying to break in. It was hard to tell looking into the darkened kitchen, but nothing seemed amiss. But why would her car be here? Maybe Lydia had picked her up.

He was just about to turn away when a movement inside caught his eye. He pressed his face closer to the window, cupping his hands around his eyes. Someone darted into the kitchen before ducking out of sight.

Wade suddenly realized how little he knew about Sophie's life lately.

He regretted he hadn't made more of an effort. Especially when he'd judged her so harshly for not keeping in touch with the kids.

Once more, he raised his fist and pounded on the door. Maybe Sophie had a boyfriend over, and she was embarrassed for him to know it. The guy who had beat her up?

A tinge of fear skittered through him. He pounded again, louder. "Sophie! Come on, open up!"

He shielded his eyes and peeked in the window again. There she was, walking toward him. Wade stepped back and waited.

Slowly the door swung outward. "Wade."

He stepped into the house, dispensing with the niceties. "Good grief, I've been banging on the door for ten minutes. Did I wake you?" She didn't look like she'd been sleeping.

"No." She shut the door behind him and flipped on a light switch.

"Where were you, then?" He looked around the apartment, looking for a clue to her odd behavior.

She turned her back to him, filling a teakettle at the sink.

"Are you okay?" he pressed.

"I'm fine. You want some tea?" She carried the kettle to the stove and switched on the burner.

"No. Thanks. You haven't been out to see the kids."

Silence.

"They miss you, Sophe. They—"

She spun to face him. "I'm not going to see them, Wade. Please stop asking."

Wade drew back. "But...why? I don't understand."

"And I can't make you understand. I'm just telling you the facts. I'm not going to see the kids. So you can forget about me being your token female role model."

His anger flared. "Don't you even care that I might lose the kids?"

"Stop it, Wade." Her voice was flat. "It's not like I was what you had in mind for a role model for the kids, anyway. It's just that I was all you had." She pulled a stained mug from the cupboard and plunked a tea bag into it.

"Sophie, I didn't mean it that way. You're their aunt. You're the only living relative they have now—"

"Lucky kids," she said, rolling her eyes.

"Come on, Sophie. You know what I mean. They love you. Don't you get that? They miss you, and they don't understand why you haven't made an effort to see them."

"I came to see them."

"That was eons ago as far as they're concerned." A pang of guilt sliced through him as he realized he wasn't being altogether truthful. The kids rarely asked about Sophie. Wade was always the one who brought up her name.

The teakettle whistled, and Sophie grabbed it off the stove and poured the steaming water over her tea bag. She carried her mug into the living room.

Wade followed.

Sophie set the mug on the coffee table and plopped onto the sofa. He stood, leaning against the archway between the two rooms. She picked up the remote and aimed it at the television. Oprah Winfrey's voice filled the room.

Anger roiled inside him. Sophie's selfishness would likely cost him the children. He didn't know what was going on with her, but something wasn't right. If he had to guess, he'd say she'd been dragged back into the world of drugs and alcohol that had almost done her in a few years ago.

He hated the thoughts that bubbled up, but he seemed unable to stop them. What had God been thinking when he'd taken Starr from this world and left Sophie? He felt a flush of guilt for the ugly question. But his anger remained. He walked to the television and hit the Power button. She just sat there, staring into space.

He turned to confront her. "What is wrong with you?" he shouted. "Are you on something?"

Her head shot up and she glared at him. "No, I'm not *on* something."

"Then what is it? You're acting totally irrational."

She set her mouth in a hard line. Finally she looked at him. "No,

Wade. I'm not acting irrational. It's just that I'm acting on information you don't have. So you can stop judging me now. I know what I'm doing."

"Then would you mind telling me just what that is?"

"Yes, I would mind."

He threw his arms up and paced into the kitchen and back, trying in vain to let off some steam. "Sophie…what is with you? I don't understand why you're doing this to me."

She folded her arms over her stomach, as though she were physically protecting herself. "I'm not doing anything to you. I'm…I'm doing something *for* you."

"What?" She wasn't making any sense at all.

Without warning, Sophie burst into tears. Wade stood there for a minute in shock before he finally went to the sofa and sat down beside her. "Sophie? What is it? What's wrong?"

She leaned forward and rested her head on her knees. Her shoulders shook.

Feeling awkward, he put a hand on her arm. "Sophe? Tell me what's wrong."

She sat up and looked at him. The rims of her eyes were red, her nose running. She sniffed and wiped away smudges of mascara with her fingertips.

Wade looked around for a tissue. Not finding one, he grabbed a crumpled dinner napkin off a tray on the cluttered coffee table. "Here." He thrust it at her.

She blew her nose and took a ragged breath. "Wade. I have nothing to offer the kids, nothing to offer you. It…it would only hurt your case if I got involved."

"That's not true, Sophie. The kids—"

"Stop!" she practically screamed at him.

He pulled back and stared at her. Maybe she *was* high on something.

Sophie jumped up and started pacing the length of the tiny room. "Listen to me, Wade. For once, just listen and quit offering your sorry little platitudes. The kids don't need me, and you know it."

He didn't try to deny it.

She sat back down on the sofa beside him. "I tried to tell you once before, and you wouldn't listen. I'm going to tell you now, and I don't ever want to discuss it again."

He waited.

"I've done some unforgivable things in my past, Wade. You know some of it. But you don't know the worst of it. When I came to Kansas I thought I was running away from my troubles. But now… Well, I guess it's impossible to run away from some things."

Wade opened his mouth to protest, but she held up a hand.

When she spoke, her voice was strong, determined. "I couldn't be in your kids' lives because…because Darrin Parnell—anything he could say would only convince a judge that the kids should be as far away from me as possible."

He wondered if someone had told her what Parnell's attorney had said at the deposition hearing. "Sophie, if Darrin said one word about your problems back in Minneapolis, he'd be cutting his own throat." He studied her. "You're not back into that—the drugs—are you?"

She shook her head. "No. But it's not just the drugs, Wade. There's stuff you don't know. Bad stuff. Things…even Starr didn't know. Thank God, Starr didn't know." The last words bled out from her, full of remorse and regret.

"Like what?" Wade was almost afraid to hear.

She hung her head. "It…it's too awful."

"Sophie, I know you're sick of hearing this, but it's true. There is nothing so terrible that God can't forgive."

Usually, Sophie bristled whenever he or Starr had brought up the subject of God, but now she sat quietly, seeming almost to lean in to his words.

He brushed aside his curiosity long enough to continue. "Aren't you tired of running? Aren't you ready to give up? Turn it all over to God?"

She put her head in her hands and started crying again. "Oh, Wade. Even if I could, it wouldn't make any difference. There's nothing I can do to help you now, to help Starr's kids. Oh, God…"

To Wade's ears, the word sounded like a prayer rather than the curse she usually meant it to be. *Oh, Father,* he prayed, *make yourself real to Sophie. Let her feel your presence. Let her open her heart to you, Lord.*

She beat her fist impotently on a faded throw pillow. "I was so stupid. So incredibly *stupid.*"

Wade put a gentle hand on her back. "Let it go, Sophie. It doesn't matter. He's already forgiven it. All you have to do is reach out and accept it." He sensed her vulnerability. And for now he truly didn't care about anything but Sophie's soul.

"Wade...I..." She straightened and turned slightly to look at him.

He folded his hands in his lap, waiting, praying.

"I did something terrible...to Starr." Her voice trembled.

"What, Sophie? What do you mean?" Wade's pulse quickened. For one blinding minute, he thought Sophie was confessing some unspeakable crime surrounding Starr's death.

But her voice took on a flat, dead tone, and the truth poured out. "I had an affair with Darrin. While he was married...to my sister." The last word rose in a sorrowful wail, and Wade put an arm around her, stunned, yet limp with relief that she hadn't said what he feared more.

"He...Darrin was getting me drugs, and I...I couldn't pay him. So he...found another way for me to pay off my—" She sucked in a gasping breath and collapsed against him, burying her face in his chest.

Wade put a brotherly arm around her, his heart breaking for all the years she'd harbored such a terrible secret. Trying to keep the shock from his voice, he whispered, "It's okay, Sophie. It's over now. It's all in the past. She would have forgiven you. Starr would have forgiven you and kept right on loving you. You know that." A lump came to his throat, knowing how true his words were. Starr had had the purest, most forgiving heart of anyone he'd ever known.

"How, Wade? How could she do that? I don't understand. I think it's true, but I don't know how. I want to be like that. I want what she had."

Hope soared in his chest. "You *can* have it, Sophie. It's what Starr wanted for you more than anything in the world. All you have to do is accept the gift."

"It's Jesus, isn't it? That's what she always said."

"Yes, Sophie. It's Jesus."

Her eyes narrowed, and he saw fear reflected there. "It's too easy," she said. "That can't be all there is to it."

"That's all. The work was finished when God sent his son to die—for you."

"I want it, Wade. I want it so bad. But I'm afraid. What if God says no?"

Wade gave a soft laugh. "Sophie, this is the one prayer God has never said no to. Never in all eternity."

"Then I want it," she said simply. An eager light shone in her eyes. "Will you help me ask?"

His throat was too full to respond with words. He could only nod and bow his head next to hers.

Forty

Wade spotted Sophie the minute he walked into the café. She had her back to him, but when she turned to pour coffee at a booth across from the door, he immediately noticed there was something different. Her face shone as she spoke to the elderly couple in the booth. And her eyes had a sparkle to them that he didn't remember seeing there before.

It had been a long journey to faith for her, but watching her now, he guessed her commitment was real, that it had already made a difference in her life.

Sophie poured coffee for another customer and looked up from the booth. When she saw Wade, she beamed and started toward him. His heart filled with gratitude. *Thank you, Lord.* How he wished Starr could have lived to see her sister's transformation.

"You're all dressed up," she said, looking him up and down. Then her face fell. "Oh…did you have another hearing?"

"Just a meeting with my lawyer. Can you take a break?"

She glanced around the café. "Sure. Give me two minutes. You can take a booth." She motioned him to a corner by the window.

He slid onto the bench seat and sat there watching her make the rounds to her tables, before bringing the coffeepot over. "You want some?"

"Please." He studied her as she filled his mug. "You look…good," he said when she caught him staring.

She smiled softly. "I am good, Wade. Real good. I've got a long ways to go, but I think…I think I get it now."

"I'm glad. Starr would have been so happy."

"I think she knows." She looked at him, a question in her eyes. "Don't you? I…I've been reading…her Bible. There's a lot of stuff I don't understand, but I think Starr knows about me."

He nodded. "I think she does too."

She fiddled with a packet of Sweet'n Low. "I've been wanting to tell you. I know it's probably too late for me to help you—you know, as far as the kids are concerned. I'm sorry about that. Sorrier than you could ever know. But if…if everything goes like it should, I'd like to see them more."

"They'd like that, Sophie. And so would I." *Oh, Father, please don't let Sophie down. Give her another chance to get to know the kids.*

"So when will you find out? Soon, right? Don't you have to go to court again?"

"Yes. A week from next Monday."

A shadow crossed her face. "You scared?"

He toyed with his napkin. "A little bit. Parnell could get them, Sophie. It's a strong possibility."

"I don't think God would let that happen."

Oh, for such a pure, fresh faith. He hesitated, not wanting to quash her newfound hope. "Sophie, God's not… He doesn't always work things out the way we think they should work out."

"But I know God loves those kids. And he's watching over them. He knows they've had more than their share of heartache."

"Yes. He does."

Sophie reached across the table and patted his hand. "I'm praying hard, Wade. I'm trusting God. I know he'll answer our prayers. I just feel it."

"I hope so, Sophie." *Oh, dear God, I hope so.*

Wade stood in the doorway of Beau's room and let his gaze rove from the Kansas City Royals pennants between the windows to the denim quilt hanging on one wall and, finally, to the frieze of stars and planets Starr had painted on the wall across from the bed. Would that straw-headed, ornery-eyed boy ever sleep in this bed again? *Please, God…please.*

He flipped off the light and moved to the bedroom the girls shared. He remembered the night Beau had helped him haul Dani's bed and mattress in here because she didn't want to sleep by herself. It seemed like an eternity ago. Would Lacey and Dani ever giggle together in this room again? Would he ever have the privilege of throwing up his hands in frustration over a clutter of baby dolls and dress-up clothes scattered from one end of the room to the other? *Please, Father. Please don't let me lose them.*

He looked up at the ceiling Starr had painted with glow-in-the-dark paint. When he switched off the light, the words twinkled to life: "Cast all your care upon Him, for He cares for you."

Could Starr have known as she was lovingly tracing words of wisdom on these walls that they would be her legacy to her children—and to him? But if Starr's children never slept under his roof again, could he bear to walk into these rooms and look at her handiwork? *Cast all your care upon Him, for He cares for you.*

I'm trying, Lord. Help me to lay it all at your feet.

He plodded down the hallway and put a hand on the doorknob of the room where he'd found Starr's lifeless body. The room that was to have held so much love, so much laughter. He opened the door and flipped on the light. Here, Starr's words held no comfort for him, no happy memories. Instead, they were only a sharp reminder of all he'd lost. "Grow old along with me! The best is yet to be." He stared at the phrase for a long moment, his throat constricting. Her beautifully scripted calligraphy seemed to taunt him.

The empty room was much as he'd left it the day he'd found her lying here. It was ridiculous for him to still be sleeping on a sofa bed downstairs while four perfectly good bedrooms went to waste upstairs, but he could not bring himself to sleep in this room and be surrounded by these mocking words.

His gaze was drawn to the can of yellow paint Starr had used on the walls in the master bedroom. It was still sitting on the floor under the windows where she'd left it, ready for touch-ups.

Suddenly knowing what he needed to do, Wade went downstairs and out to the garage. Shouldering his load back upstairs, he set the stepladder up in the corner by the bedroom door, then reached for the paint can. The lid was stuck tight, but he pried it off and carefully set it aside. The pungent smell that drifted to his nostrils brought memories of that terrible day careening back. But a spirit of resolve came over him, and he pushed away the awful images. He plunged a flat wooden paint stick into the can and stirred until the paint was the texture of thick cream.

He climbed the ladder and began to apply thick strokes of yellow over the moss-green words that crept around the top of the wall. He had to slap the paint on thick to cover the craft paint she'd traced her penciled calligraphy with. At first it pained him to be obliterating what Starr had meant as a surprise for him. To destroy her meticulous work of love. But with each stroke of the brush, he felt the wound in his heart lessen, and healing begin.

After an hour of steady work, painstakingly blending the new coat of paint with the old, he climbed down to move the ladder again. Looking up at his work, he read what remained on the wall. "The best is yet to be."

His breath caught in his throat at the promise Starr had unknowingly left for him. *The best is yet to be.* It was as though God had made the words of the poem brand-new, infusing them with meaning that was for him, right now, in this season of his life.

He thought of the scripture that promised a day when God would wipe away every tear, when there would be no more death or mourning or crying or pain. How he longed for that day. Maybe this was what "the best is yet to be" meant for him. Maybe it wasn't to be on this earth. But suddenly it didn't matter. Whether on this side of heaven or the other, it was a promise he could grasp, a promise to live by.

He scooted the ladder to the next wall and began to brush paint over the words in long, smooth strokes. He didn't need them on his wall as a reminder, for now they were imprinted on his heart.

Tomorrow he would plane the closet doors and rehang them, then wire the new light fixtures Starr had selected. He would ask Pete to help him move the queen-size bed down from the attic. He would bring his things up from the den and make this room his own. It was time to move on.

Maybe the best *was* yet to be.

Wade turned and watched the sun peek over the hedgerow to the east. Dee would be here with the kids in a few minutes, but before they arrived, he wanted to load some tools he'd borrowed from Pete into the pickup.

He went to the garage and lifted the heavy old door. He hoisted Pete's miter saw and sawhorses into the truck bed, then backed the truck out onto the drive.

He'd tried to put the significance of this day out of his mind. But it barreled back over him like a steamroller. Today would be his last visit with the kids before the final hearing. His last time with Dee.

In less than a week the judge would announce his decision and grant custody to him or to Darrin Parnell. Either way, Wade's life would be forever changed. He faced it with an odd mixture of peace and trepidation. For the children's sake, it was time for this to be over. Though they'd proven remarkably resilient, it couldn't be easy on them living in a temporary home and bouncing between visitations with him and Parnell every week.

A longing for Dee rose in his chest, an ache that was almost physical. He hoped he might have a chance to talk to her today, to again express his appreciation for everything she'd done. And to let her know how much he had come to care for her. Of course, he couldn't exactly come out and say those words without violating the boundaries of propriety as far as she was concerned. But he thought—he hoped—she could read between the lines.

When this whole, ugly custody thing was over, he hoped Dee would still be a part of their lives. Or a part of his life. If his worst fears came true, and he lost the children, he hoped it wouldn't mean he'd lost Dee, too.

She was always cautious when they talked about anything related to the custody hearings, but he sensed that she feared the worst for him.

Wade parked the truck at the side of the house and went to close the garage door. He breathed in the scent of rain. The October day held a crisp promise that autumn might actually visit Kansas after all. The summer had been one of the hottest and driest on record, but an overnight rain had rinsed the dust from the trees and given everything a sheen of newness.

He walked to the end of the long drive for the morning paper, glad to have to sidestep several puddles. Shadow pranced beside him, stopping to lap murky water from each pool.

Wade picked up the paper and started back to the house. Behind him, Shadow's deep bark pierced the air, and Wade heard the crunch of tires on gravel. His heart soared, even as it ached. And a smile lifted the corners of his mouth as he hurried to greet the people—the *four* people—he loved most in all the world.

Forty-One

The theme song for the ten o'clock news played over the credits. Wade switched off the television and checked the locks before heading upstairs.

Five minutes later he crawled into the big old bed and lay staring at the ceiling. It was quiet and peaceful in this upstairs room. He'd slept surprisingly well since moving up here. But tonight sleep eluded him. All day long he'd tried to put tomorrow's hearing out of his mind, not wanting to think about what might happen.

Tomorrow he would know. One way or the other.

He lay awake for a long time, praying for the kids. Praying for God's will to be done in the courtroom tomorrow. Praying for Dee.

Downstairs, the clock in the foyer chimed eleven times. Feeling a strong compulsion, he threw off the covers and eased his legs over the side of the bed. He dropped to his knees and rested his elbows on the bed, his head in his hands.

"Father," he whispered into the dead quiet of the room, "in my heart, I only want what you want. I want your will done in my life. And in the kids' lives. I honestly do. But, Lord, I can't believe it could be your will for Darrin Parnell to get my kids. Maybe he's changed, Lord. Maybe I'm judging him wrong. But even if that's true, it doesn't seem right for the kids to be uprooted from everything they know and love here. Show me if I'm being selfish, Lord. Give me your peace. Please, Lord. I can't do this alone."

He prayed until the hardwood floors made his knees ache and his back scream for relief. Finally he crawled back into bed. He waited for peace and felt numb instead. *Oh, Father. Give me strength.*

It had been a long time since he'd taken to his knees. Only when Starr died had he felt as strong a need to pelt heaven with his prayers. But that had been different. Then, he had not expected even his most fervent prayers to bring Starr back.

Tonight he hoped his prayers would turn a judge's heart.

As Frank Locke led the way to the front of the courtroom, Wade glanced around the nearly empty gallery. Pete and Margie were near the front, behind where Wade would sit. Sophie was there too, beside Margie. Sophie caught his eye and gave a soft smile, nodding almost imperceptibly. He knew they were all petitioning heaven for him and the kids, and he felt their prayers like a warm blanket around him.

Dee was seated on the other side of the gallery near the aisle. She was deep in conversation with Betty Graffe and didn't look up as Wade walked by.

After a few minutes, the scraping of chairs and rustle of papers gave way to sudden silence when Judge Paxton entered from the door behind the bench and ascended to take his seat. Somewhere in the back of the room, a clock ticked off the seconds.

As in past hearings, the judge made preliminary introductions and acknowledgments. Then he cleared his throat. "I shall precede my decision today by saying that I can sympathize with the difficulties the county attorney and social workers had in making a recommendation in this case."

He glanced at the stack of papers in front of him. "It appears Darrin Parnell has satisfactorily demonstrated his commitment to his children. By all appearances, he has made every effort to do what's necessary to be a good father. He has completed various training to that end and has gone to great lengths to attend each and every visitation."

Wade had to remind himself how to breathe. He drew a shallow breath—a slow, strangely conscious effort, as if holding his breath could influence the outcome of this hearing.

The judge slipped off his glasses and looked out over the gallery. "In spite of a rather rough start, it appears that Mr. Sullivan has made an admirable effort to provide the Parnell children with a home after the death of their mother. Under the circumstances, I believe he has done a very commendable job."

Judge Paxton shifted the papers on his desk and continued. "However, another important consideration for this court, given the young ages of the children, is the fact that Mr. Parnell's fiancée has shown a willingness, indeed an eagerness, to be a mother to the children. This is something Mr. Sullivan—granted, through no fault of his own—is simply unable to offer."

Beside him, Wade heard the air go out of Frank Locke's lungs.

In that moment he knew he had lost.

He strained to hear the judge's final words over the blood pounding in his ears.

Judge Paxton looked from Wade to Darrin Parnell. "It is the studied opinion of this court that, whenever possible, children belong with their biological parents. Therefore, this court grants full custody of Beau Parnell, Lacey Parnell, and Danica Parnell to their father, Darrin Parnell."

Wade's shoulders sagged under the crushing weight of the decree. His neck suddenly seemed unable to support his head. He put his face in his hands and leaned against the hard table. He had a strange sense this was all a dream. It couldn't really be happening.

But the judge wasn't finished. "It is my strong recommendation," he continued, "that Mr. Sullivan be given generous visitation rights. However, given that Mr. Parnell lives in Minneapolis, and because of the financial hardship it might cause either party to do so, this court will make no legally binding ruling to that end. The details are to be worked out at Mr. Parnell's discretion."

The judge's voice droned on with words Wade couldn't make sense of. He sucked in a breath and felt as though he were breathing water. He was vaguely aware of Frank Locke's hand on his shoulder. He forced himself to sit up straight.

The court was apparently dismissed, for the room became a quiet buzz of activity around him. Wade rubbed his face and turned to find Pete and Margie standing behind him. Pete patted his shoulder, consoling without words. Margie seemed to be in shock, her face ashen and slack.

Wade could only nod and remind himself again to breathe. Suddenly he remembered Dee's promise. "I've got to find Dee Thackery," he told Locke. He turned, searching the gallery frantically for her." She said I'd be able to talk to the kids before…before he takes them."

"I'll find her," Locke said, starting up the aisle.

Where were the kids? Had they been brought to the courthouse, ready to go home with whoever was decreed the winner?

He felt a hand on his arm and turned to see Sophie. Even through the haze of his grief, he could see the peace etched in her features.

"I'm so sorry, Wade," she said. "But I know God will work everything out."

He didn't know how to respond, how to tell her that everything had already been "worked out." It was over. He'd lost his children. Didn't she understand that?

From the corner of his eye, he saw Parnell and his fiancée heading out the door with Parnell's attorney. He had to get to the kids before they took them away.

Sophie squeezed his arm. "It'll be okay, Wade. God has everything under control." She hesitated and glanced toward the door that led to the corridor. "I'll be right back," she said.

She slid past Pete and Margie, hurried up the aisle, and disappeared through the wide doorway.

The door swung open again, and Dee appeared. She walked down the aisle toward Wade, her face grim.

"Just a minute." Wade excused himself and hurried toward her.

"I'm so sorry, Wade," Dee whispered when they met in the middle of the aisle that split the gallery.

Though it was obvious she was near tears, Wade brushed off her sympathy. "Where are the kids? You said I could see them."

She nodded and held up a hand. "Yes, we're trying to work it out. Mr. Locke is talking to Darrin Parnell right now."

"I have to see them. I can't just let them go without explaining what's happening."

"I know. We're working on it. Karen Xavier will answer their questions. And the guardian ad litem will be talking to them soon. But we're doing everything possible to make sure you get to see them."

"Where are they now?" He heard the panic rising in his own voice.

"Karen is on her way here with them."

"They still have stuff out at my place. They'll get to take their things with them, won't they?"

"I'm sure someone will make arrangements for that." Her voice was measured and steady, as though she were speaking to a small child.

And indeed that's how he felt—stunned and confused, his mind spinning out of control. His knees felt ready to buckle. He grabbed on to a bench and doubled over, struggling for breath.

Dee bent to look into his face, her voice low and laced with concern. "Are you okay? Do you need to sit down for a minute?"

He squeezed his eyes shut and shook his head.

"Stay here," she said. "I'll go see if Karen's here with the kids yet."

Sophie stepped into the corridor and turned to look both directions down the hall. There they were, near the entryway, laughing and celebrating. Darrin and his attorney stood with their backs to her. Carma Weist sat on a bench along the wall, looking dazed, as though she were just beginning to realize what this ruling meant for her.

As Sophie studied her, Carma stood and whispered something to Darrin. He nodded, obviously distracted, and she started toward the women's rest room midway down the corridor.

Sophie waited until she'd gone in, then followed her. Carma stood at the mirror, applying lipstick to already crimson lips. The three stalls stood open and empty. Good. They were alone.

Sophie cleared her throat, and Carma glanced up, lipstick poised. Their eyes met in the mirror. Carma looked away quickly, replacing the lid on the tube of lipstick and tossing it into her purse. She turned to leave, but Sophie stepped into her path.

"I want to talk to you about something," Sophie said, surprised at how steady her voice was.

Carma flounced a shoulder. "There's nothing you have to say that I want to hear," she said. But she didn't try to leave.

Either Carma knew who Sophie was, or she was merely aware that Sophie was somehow a part of Wade's camp. Sophie tipped her head and studied the prim, well-dressed woman in front of her. A woman so different from Starr.

Even though they were alone in the rest room, Sophie lowered her voice. "I don't know if he's started hitting you yet or not. It didn't start with my sister until after they were married."

Carma narrowed her heavily shadowed eyes. "I don't know what you're talking about."

"Ask him about the visit from the police the night of Beau's third birthday. Ask him how many times he put Starr in the hospital. Ask him—"

"You're crazy! I don't have to listen to this." Carma huffed out a breath and pushed past Sophie.

Sophie followed her and ducked between her and the door. Carma's flawlessly made-up face was just inches from hers. Sophie started, as the light above the door cast one side of Carma's face in shadow, while brightly illuminating the other. Beneath the layers of cosmetics on the high, porcelain forehead, Sophie thought she saw the greenish-yellow ghost of a bruise.

She stared pointedly, a wave of sadness coming over her as she remembered what Starr had endured. "Don't be a fool," she whispered. "It only gets worse, Carma. I can promise you that. It will only get worse."

"Get away from me. Let me through."

Sophie opened the door. But she stayed firmly planted in front of it, refusing to let the woman pass yet. She lowered her voice. "Carma, I am begging you. Get help. For yourself and for my sister's kids. Get help before it's too late."

Carma gathered herself to her full height and spoke between clenched teeth, her eyes spitting fire. "I love those kids, and I would never, ever let anything happen to them." Her eyes narrowed further. "And I'd say you have plenty to worry about in your own life without worrying about mine. Now let me through."

Sophie felt anger rise in her chest. She pointed a finger and shoved it in Carma's face. "If he ever… If *either* of you ever lays one hand on those kids, I will personally see to it that you pay, and pay dearly."

"Get out of my way!"

Sophie moved aside. Carma brushed past her and hurried down the corridor.

Sophie stepped into the hallway and let the door swing shut behind her. She watched as Carma glided to Darrin's side, a smile pasted on her face as though nothing had happened. They made a handsome couple.

Sophie leaned her head against the cool marble wall outside the women's room and let out a deep breath. Her hands trembled like leaves in a breeze. She wanted to fall to the floor and weep. Maybe she should have had more compassion on Darrin's fiancée. Starr had been infatuated just the way Carma was—before she knew the truth about Darrin Parnell. And even after he started abusing her, Starr had made excuses and continued to claim she loved him.

Sophie shook away the memories. She didn't understand why God had allowed the judge to hand down the decision he had today. It made no sense. There was nothing just or fair about it.

But the amazing thing was the peace she felt in the face of it. Even now, peace washed over her like a comforting shower. She had never known such a feeling before. No drug, no relationship—nothing she'd ever tried had offered the serenity she felt now. And somehow she knew that, no matter what happened, God *was* in control. Of her life. And of Beau's and Lacey's and Dani's.

If God had stayed with her through this darkest hour, she knew he would be with Wade and the kids, too. They just had to keep trusting.

Forty-Two

"There they are." Dee stopped on the stairway and turned to look back up at Wade, deep relief on her face. "They're with Karen."

He turned the corner in the wide stairwell. Beau and Lacey and Dani stood in a knot beside Karen Xavier in the center of the corridor. She hovered over them like a mother hen, wings outstretched to protect her brood. They were all dressed up in their Sunday best, faces scrubbed pink, pale hair neatly combed.

Wade was afraid his heart might stop beating as he descended the last flight of stairs. He held back, collecting his emotions, letting Dee greet them first.

She walked toward them, her back straight, her stride purposeful.

Lacey saw her first, then they all rushed to greet her.

Beau looked past Dee and spotted Wade. He stormed toward him, and the girls followed, laughing and shouting Wade's name. He met them in the middle of the corridor and knelt, bracing for their attack. As they threw themselves against him, he wrapped his arms around them.

"Hey, guys! How's it going?" He acknowledged each one in turn with a tweak of their nose or a pat on the head. His senses were heightened, and their soft skin and silky hair seemed almost to burn his fingers. His gaze darted around the nearly empty corridor. "Let's go sit over there," he told them, pointing to a bench along one wall.

They followed him and lined up on the bench, jockeying for position. From the edge of his vision, Wade saw Karen Xavier and Dee talking softly across the hallway.

He turned and rested on his haunches in front of the kids. *Give me strength, Lord. Help me say the right words to help them understand.*

He looked from one precious face to the next. They gazed back at him with such anticipation. He remembered the night he'd gathered them in the living room to tell them SRS was coming to take them into foster care.

Their faces had worn this same look of eager expectancy that day. It amazed him that through the past months of heartache and emotional upheaval, their spirits hadn't been broken. Wade wasn't sure he could say the same of himself.

He swallowed hard. "Wow. You guys look pretty spiffy." He touched the hem of Dani's sweater. "I see you ladies got new outfits."

"Me, too, Wade," Beau said, grabbing the crisply ironed collar of his blue cotton shirt and thrusting out his chin.

"Whoa, you're lookin' pretty handsome there, bud."

"Karen took us shopping," Dani said.

"Well, that's nice. Did Karen... Did she tell you what's going to happen now?"

Beau's eyebrows drew together. "She said the judge decided we're s'posed to go live with...Dad—and Carma."

"That's right. Do you understand what that means? Your..." He gulped and started over. "Your dad and Carma are going to be taking you back to Minneapolis with them to live."

"But we'll still come visit you every Tuesday," Lacey said, smiling and bobbing her head.

"Yeah, and Shadow, too," Dani said.

Wade closed his eyes. "No, guys...I'm afraid... Well, Minneapolis is a long way away. Darrin...your dad had to drive a long time every week to come and see you. Even in an airplane, it takes a few hours."

"Cool! We get to fly on a airplane?" Beau said, eyes wide.

Wade pressed hard on the bridge of his nose where a dull ache had started. "Beau...Buddy, it's not going to work that way. You're going with your dad and Carma...for good now. I...I hope I'll get to come and visit you sometimes. But we won't get to see each other every week anymore. You'll be in school up there and probably playing on a new soccer team," he said, trying to inject an enthusiasm he didn't feel.

"But we can still come and see *you* sometimes too...right?"

Lacey's voice held a waver that told Wade she was starting to figure things out. "I don't know, Lace..." He sighed. "Probably not for...well, for a long time. We'll just have to see."

"But what about you, Wade?" Dani's voice echoed the quiver in her sister's. "Are you gonna be all alonesome?"

Sorrow rolled over him in waves. He struggled to keep his face from contorting, but the hot tears rolling down his cheeks gave him away.

"Why are you cryin', Wade?" Dani's voice broke. She reached out and touched his cheek, then brushed away his tears with the pudgy palm of her hand.

He swallowed a sob and pulled her to him. "Because I'm going to miss you guys." *Oh, God, let me say everything I need to say.* He stretched his arms to encompass them all once more. "I love you guys more than I've ever loved anyone in my life except for your mama."

"When *can* we see you again?" Beau's spine had turned rigid under Wade's hand.

Wade leaned back and looked at him, pressing his lips together while he fought for composure. "I honestly don't know, Beau. That…that'll depend on what your dad says. It's going to be up to him now. And Carma. You guys be good for them, okay?"

The girls nodded solemnly, but Beau stood stiff and straight, his arms crossed over his chest. "I don't want to go to Minneapolis. I wanna stay here."

"Buddy, you don't have a choice. What the judge says is the law. We have to go by what he says."

"I don't care. I'll run away. I'll run away from home. I'll do it this time. I will! You can't make me go."

Wade stood and put a firm hand on Beau's shoulder. "Beau, I'm sorry. I know this is hard. I don't like it, either. But I—"

A light came to Beau's eyes as if he'd just remembered something. Then his face turned dark and his jaw tensed. "You promised!" he exploded. He pounded his fists on Wade's chest. "You promised me everything would work out okay!"

At that, the girls started crying. Karen and Dee hurried to their sides and bent in unison to comfort them.

Wade took Beau aside, trapping him with his back to a wall. Beau kept swinging as Wade knelt in front of him. "Beau, listen to me. Stop."

Beau flailed some more, hitting harder. Wade grabbed his wrists, but Beau struggled to get loose from his hold.

"Beau, stop it! Stop it right now. You're as bad as he is!" He felt sick the minute the words were out. What had possessed him to compare a confused, hurting little boy to the monster Darrin Parnell had been?

Beau's head jerked up. He glared at Wade for a minute, then the fight went out of him. He slumped against Wade, sobbing. Wade wrapped his arms around the boy and held him tight, drawing strength from Beau's need.

"I'm sorry, Beau. I'm so sorry, buddy," he said over and over. "I love you. You know that. I did everything I could. You have to believe that. I don't want this any more than you do."

Beau leaned harder against him. Wade shifted his weight to keep his balance. "Listen to me, buddy... Look at me." Wade tipped the narrow chin up. Beau's eyes were red-rimmed and swollen. "I want you to know that I will love you as long as I live. No matter what happens, I will never, ever forget you. You were a gift God put in my life, and I thank him for that every day. God is going to be with you in Minneapolis just like he was with you here. He'll be with you every step of the way. And if you ever need anything, you call me. I think your dad has...changed. But if things ever get—bad...like they were before, you call me. Do you understand what I'm saying to you? You know our phone number, right?"

Beau sniffed and nodded.

"Okay. Good. I need to go talk to your sisters now, okay? You all right?"

Again he nodded.

Wade let him go and rose slowly.

"Wait!"

Wade bent to Beau's eye level. "What is it?"

"What about Shadow? When can we see him?"

"I don't know, bud. We'll...have to figure something out. Let's go see the girls." He put a hand on the thin shoulder, and together they walked over to where Karen Xavier and Dee were standing with Lacey and Dani.

Dee's eyes glistened with tears. "We'll be right over here," she told Wade. She motioned Karen to a nearby alcove.

He watched them walk away, then knelt beside the girls, while Beau stood looking on. Pulling them to himself, one in each arm, he kissed the top of Lacey's head. "I love you, Lacey Daisy."

He repeated the ritual with Danica. "I love you, Dani Banany. You guys go with Dee now, okay? She's going to take you up to your dad and Carma. I…I'll send you a letter soon. You be good, you hear? Say your prayers every night."

They nodded in unison, their faces serious.

He wanted to make this moment last forever, and yet, with every second that passed, it only grew more difficult to turn and walk away.

He pulled all three of them into one final embrace, breathing in the scent of them, committing it to memory. He struggled to his feet and turned to find Dee and Karen watching, tears streaming down their faces.

He went to Karen Xavier and held out a hand. "Thank you…for everything. The kids were"—his voice broke—"very happy with you and Ben. Thank you for opening your home—and your hearts to them."

Karen nodded in acknowledgment, her cheeks still damp with tears.

Turning to Dee, he asked, "Can you keep them down here for a little bit? I…I want to speak to Parnell. Give me ten minutes, okay? I'll leave by the upstairs entrance."

Dee's brow lifted in a question.

"I can't do this again. When I walk away, I'm not turning back."

She swiped at a tear and nodded. "I understand."

He started to turn away, but Dee's hand on his arm stopped him. "Take care, Wade. I…I'll be praying for you."

He nodded and moved slowly to the stairs. It felt as though he carried a thousand-pound burden on his back as he ascended the wide steps. He rounded the corner and trudged up the last half of the flight. He didn't dare turn around and look back.

Darrin Parnell's smile faded when he saw Wade approaching. Carma Weist and Parnell's attorney turned to follow Parnell's gaze. Seeing Wade, they parted like the Red Sea.

Wade curled his fingers into fists at his side, then forced them to unclench. He reached out a hand. Parnell hesitated for a long second before accepting Wade's handshake.

"Could I talk to you for a minute?"

Parnell's expression remained dour. "Go ahead. Anything you have to say can be said right here."

"I...I'd like to write to the kids. Will you allow them to accept my letters? And maybe a phone call now and then?"

Parnell stuffed his hands in the pocket of his suit pants and looked at the floor. "I don't think that would be wise. The sooner they make the break, the better off everyone will be."

"A Christmas card then? And on their birthdays? Please. I don't want them to think I've forgotten them."

Parnell started to speak, but Carma put a hand on his arm. "Darrin..."

"I suppose a card now and then would be okay."

An idea had been forming in Wade's mind, and he risked voicing it now. "Would you mind if the kids took Shadow—their dog—back to Minneapolis with them? He's a black Lab, very gentle. He's well trained. He wouldn't be any trouble. It...it would mean so much to them." He gave a humorless laugh. "They've cried more over him than they have over me."

But Carma was already brushing at her expensive-looking suit jacket, as though it were crawling with dog hair at the very thought.

Parnell put an arm around her and practically sneered at Wade. "If I want to get my kids a dog, I'll get them a dog. I don't need any suggestions from you."

"I was just—"

Carma took a step toward him. "Thank you for offering, Mr. Sullivan, but the children will be fine. Kids are very resilient creatures. They bounce back from this kind of thing quicker than you might think. They'll be fine. We'll see to that."

Forty-Three

The driveway was still littered with rain puddles when Wade arrived back at the house. As he dodged them in his pickup, he remembered the day he and the children and Dee had splashed and played in them. How he wished he could turn back the calendar and relive that day just one more time.

The scenes from this morning's hearing overflowed his brain, yet he felt drained and empty. He parked the pickup in the garage, pulled down the heavy door, and headed for the house. Shadow raced up the hill from the river to prance beside him.

Wade patted the dog and looked up at the empty house. Its darkened windows stared blankly back at him. He couldn't go inside. Dropping down on the back stoop, he unknotted his tie and stripped it off, then hung it loosely around his neck. Shadow plopped down beside him, panting and nudging his head onto Wade's lap, begging for a good scratch. Wade put a hand on the brawny head, letting the warmth seep into him.

"Well, fellow…it's over. They're not coming back." Speaking the words brought the reality thundering home. The kids were probably on their way to Minneapolis right now. And he had lost even the right to get a phone call saying they'd arrived safely.

But would they be safe once they got there? That was the question tormenting him now. He'd been given no choice, but if those kids had been put in harm's way, he would never forgive himself.

Shadow pressed against his hand and lifted his head, his ears perking. A few seconds later, Wade heard a car on the drive. He didn't want to see anyone right now. Maybe not for a long time. He pushed the dog aside and scrambled for the back door, but before he could open it, a car pulled around behind the house. He was stuck.

He didn't recognize the dark green Toyota, but whoever it was seemed familiar with his place. The car pulled smoothly into the spot where friends and family always parked.

Before he had time to wonder any more, Dee Thackery stepped from the driver's seat.

Shadow lumbered off the porch and trotted to greet her.

Dee patted the dog's head. "Hey, boy…" She rubbed behind Shadow's ears, looking up at Wade with a mournful smile. "Hi."

He lifted a hand and sat back down on the stoop with a sigh. She stood in front of him, seeming uncertain what to do or say. Did she see the same grief in his eyes that was reflected in her own?

"I'm so sorry, Wade," she said finally. "I'm so very sorry."

To his surprise, she began to weep. He jumped up and, without even thinking, put his arms around her, tucking his chin on top of her head, the way he might have comforted one of the kids. No—the way he would have held Starr. He wanted so badly to be able to comfort Dee and to find solace for himself here in her arms. But he felt her tense even as the possibility crossed his mind.

Reluctantly he let his hands drop to his sides.

She did the same and took a step back, wiping her cheeks with the back of her hands. "The kids should be with you. It's so unfair. It's not right."

"But it happened, Dee. It's over. And now I've got to deal with it." He eased his frame back onto the steps.

"I wish I could have done something. You…you don't know how badly I wanted to just tell the judge that *you* should get the kids."

"Why didn't you?" he said softly, not meaning it as an accusation, afraid of what might be behind the door he'd opened with that question.

"Oh, Wade…if there'd been one tiny reason to destroy Darrin Parnell's right to those kids, I would have grabbed it with both hands. But there wasn't anything. He was"—she shrugged—"I don't know…awkward with the kids. He didn't really know how to interact with them. But he was their father. That's the bottom line."

"Are you convinced he's changed? That the kids will be safe with him?"

She looked at him, thoughtful. "As convinced as I can be. He was good to them, Wade. I really think he was trying. And Carma seems to genuinely love them. I think maybe she tempers Darrin a little."

"I hope you're right. I'm sure I'm just being selfish. I…I truly do want what's best for them. I know they need a woman's influence in their lives. The girls especially. It would have been harder as they got older, you know…to give them what they need."

He stared down to the river, where the maples and cottonwoods were just beginning to turn scarlet and gold. "Maybe I was wrong to fight for them at all. But knowing what Parnell did to their mother, well…it just didn't seem right to give them up without a fight. I only want them to be happy, Dee. Do you…do you think they'll remember me? Dani's so little…" He could almost hear her silvery little-girl laughter. He tried to fathom what it would be like to never hear that again, never see her again. Unexpectedly the tears surfaced. He rested his elbows on his knees and put his head down, embarrassed to have Dee see his emotion.

He felt her hand brush his arm. He looked up into eyes that were gray-green pools of compassion.

"Of course they'll remember you! You were—you *are* a wonderful father to the kids. You helped them through the worst possible time in their lives." She turned and her gaze swept the house behind them. "You created this beautiful home for them—filled with love and laughter. They will always carry that with them, Wade. It's a part of them now— everything they had here with you. They'll never forget that."

He nodded, his throat constricting. The words meant a great deal coming from her.

"No matter what happens after today, you—" Dee's voice broke. She put a fist briefly to her mouth, obviously fighting her emotions. "You made a difference in their lives, and you'll always be a part of who they are. Always." A smile dawned on her face. "I probably told you this before, but they were always so excited to see you whenever I picked them up from Karen's. You'd have thought I was taking them to Disneyland every Tuesday."

She *had* told him, more than once. But it was a balm to hear it again. "They were good kids, weren't they?"

"They *are* good kids, Wade. They're angels. And I'm not just saying that. I see a lot of children in similar situations, and yours were more resilient than most. And I know you had so much to do with that."

"I wish I could have just one more day to spend with them."

"I know," she said. "I understand. But what would you do differently than you did every day you had them? You spent quality time with them, you played games, you taught them important things they needed to know…"

Wade frowned. "I wish I'd taken them to church more, after…after their mom died. I should have seen to that. Starr would be furious with me if she knew what a slacker I was in that department."

"Maybe. But they knew what you believed, Wade." She gave Shadow a pat and sat down across from Wade on the top step. "Even in the short times I was here with you and the kids, I saw the way you prayed with them and answered their questions about God. You lived out your faith in the everyday things. They saw that. Don't think they didn't." A spark came to her eyes. "Remember that time you caught Beau cheating at spoons?"

Wade nodded, grinning at the memory.

"I was so impressed with the way you handled that. You didn't just mete out a punishment, but you explained why it was wrong. And you made sure he knew it was what he did, not who he was, that made you angry."

Wade looked at her from the corner of his eye. "We had some fun times here, didn't we?"

She nodded. "Remember that time we were playing spoons, and Dani kept telling everybody she was collecting sevens and aces, so—"

"So Beau started hoarding sevens and aces," he finished for her, laughing. "Oh, man, I'll never forget the look on his face when he realized there was no way he could win since she had the very cards he needed."

They laughed together at the memory.

"Yeah," he said, "but my most memorable game is still the one where you *finally* had to sing. Oh, did the kids ever get a kick out of that."

Her face turned the same peachy shade it had that day. She hid behind the visor of her hand. "You would have to bring that up!" But she was laughing.

She sat beside him and listened as he talked about the kids, remembering each of their unique traits, the special relationship he'd had with each one.

"Thank you, Dee," he said when he felt he'd burdened her enough.

"It was my privilege, Wade. To be a tiny part of your life with the kids. I…I would have given anything to have a relationship with my stepfather like Lacey and Dani had with you."

She'd told him about her parents' divorce, but she'd never mentioned that her mother remarried. "You grew up with a stepdad?"

"If you could call him that. My parents divorced when I was nine. Just about Beau's age."

Wade tried to picture Dee as a little girl. He could almost see her—a gangly, honey-haired child with big green eyes. "I bet that was tough."

A shadow swept her face, and she looked away. "The man my mother married…abused me. In a horrible way. I finally got the courage to tell her before things got…" She rubbed her temples and let out a harsh breath.

Wade caught his breath. His stomach clenched. "I'm sorry, Dee. I didn't know."

A sad smile touched her lips. "Of course not. How could you?"

"I suppose you see that type of thing a lot in your work. That must be really hard. To be reminded."

She nodded. "Yes. But…well, it's one of the reasons I went into social work. I think maybe God is using what happened to me so maybe I can help prevent it from happening in someone else's life."

"I'm sorry for what happened, Dee. But I'm so glad you're allowing God to turn it into something good. Because that means you were there for *my* kids." He corrected himself. "For Starr's kids."

"They *were* your kids, Wade. In every way that mattered. You made a big difference in their lives."

Oh, Father. Let that be true. Don't let this all have been for nothing.

"That means a lot. It really does. I don't know how any of us would have gotten through this if it weren't for you, Dee."

"I was just doing my job. Anyone else would have done the same."

He shook his head. "No. I don't think so. You...you just clicked. With the kids—and with...well, with all of us."

She dipped her head. "I'm glad you feel that way."

An awkward silence grew between them. Finally Dee stood and stretched. "Well, I probably ought to go. I...I really shouldn't have come out here in the first place, but—"

"Why did you come?"

She drew back, her brow knit. "Why did I come?"

He tilted his head and narrowed his eyes. "Is this part of the package? Some sort of complimentary consolation visit all your clients get when the case is over?" He tried to keep his tone light, but instead it came out sounding sarcastic.

She crossed her arms, and her tone held a defensive edge. "No, Wade. I...I shouldn't even be here. You know that. We've talked about the boundaries I have to set where clients are concerned."

"But here you are. What does that mean?" He knew he was backing her in a corner, but he needed to know.

"I...I'm not sure—" She shook her head slowly. "I...knew you were hurting. I'm sorry. Maybe I shouldn't have come," she said again. She turned and started toward the car.

"Dee." He struggled to his feet and stepped off the porch.

She whirled to face him, her eyes bright with tears.

He blew out a breath. "Listen. I've already had three people walk out of my life today. If you're going to do the same, the least you can do is tell me what you're feeling." He put his head in his hands and combed his fingers through his hair. Then he looked up at her and held his palms outward, tacitly pleading forgiveness. "I'm sorry, Dee. That wasn't fair."

She glared at him. Her voice took on a hard edge. "You want to know what I'm feeling? All right. I'll tell you what I'm feeling, Wade. I'm feeling like I just lost everything I love most in this world, and I don't even have the privilege of mourning it, because I wasn't supposed to love it in the first place."

He drew back and studied her, amazed—and deeply moved—by her confession.

"Wade, in case you think I fall in love with all my clients the way I fell in love with you and the kids, you're wrong. You guys…you were something special." The edge that had been in her voice softened. "I can't explain it, and it's probably best if I don't try."

He stared past her, trying to wrap his mind around her words. *The way I fell in love with you…* How did she mean that? Had she truly fallen in love with him? Or was he just part of a package with the kids? A package that had now been irreparably broken?

She wrapped her arms around herself, shivering visibly, in spite of the October sun shining down on them. "When I drive out of this driveway, it's forever, Wade."

The finality in her voice caused his stomach to churn. He cocked his head. "Forever?"

"Well…it might as well be forever."

"Why do you say that? I'm not your client anymore." He picked up a twig that had blown onto the porch and absently broke it in two. "I…I'd like to see you again, Dee. I'd like you to be a part of my life. To continue being part of my life."

A look of chagrin crossed her face. "You don't understand."

"What?"

"Wade, the code of ethics for my profession doesn't allow me to have a relationship with you. At all. At least not anytime in the near future."

"Then I'll wait. I'm a patient man."

She shook her head. "No. I mean a long time. Two years."

He felt like she'd slapped him. But he reached out and touched her arm. "I'll wait, Dee."

"No." She took a step back. "Two years is a long time, Wade. You'll find someone else."

"Or you will."

"I…I don't think so. Wade…we shouldn't even be talking about this.

I've already said more than I should." A look of panic flashed in her eyes, and she turned and started toward the car.

"Dee! Wait…"

"I have to go, Wade." She sucked in a ragged breath. "I have to go…"

She ran to the car as though someone were chasing her.

Without thinking, he ran after her, grabbed her shoulders, and pulled her into his arms. For one brief moment, she melted against him, let him hold her.

Then, with a little cry of dismay, she pushed away and ran around the car to the driver's side.

He let her go. Turning his back to her, he heard the car door slam, the engine rev, the gravel crunch as she drove away.

And he was alone again.

Forty-Four

Dee guided her car down the road, nearly blinded by tears. She'd gone to Wade's meaning to comfort him. Instead, she'd been immature and unprofessional. And selfish. She'd made it all about her and her feelings, her loss.

How could she have been so insensitive? Clay was right. She should have asked to have someone else assigned to the Parnell kids the minute she realized how deep her feelings for Wade had grown. But it was too late for that now. She'd cut him to ribbons when he was already deeply wounded.

She wanted to turn the car around and go back and throw herself into his arms. Code of ethics be hanged. But that was irrational. She loved her job and deeply respected the profession she was a part of. It would be foolish to throw away everything she'd worked so hard for. Besides, it wasn't like she was independently wealthy. She couldn't exactly support herself working at McDonald's while she figured out what to do about her feelings for Wade.

She grabbed a tissue from the box in the console and dabbed at her cheeks. What had she gotten herself into? Her mind churned. Even without the barriers her profession placed between them, how could she be sure she and Wade really had anything lasting between them? Yes, she loved what she'd seen in him over the months she'd spent time with him and the kids. She admired his commitment and compassion for children who were not his own. His faith and work ethic, his integrity and sense of humor were all exactly what she longed for in a man. And things she'd seen so little of in the few men she'd dated or even been acquainted with.

Never mind the fact that Wade's winsome smile made her heart beat a little faster, or that the spark in his eyes made butterflies dance inside her. She loved his honest emotions and his playful spirit. Did they really know enough about each other to feel the way they did?

But how could she ignore the feelings she had for him? The way she'd felt when he put his arms around her? She took one hand off the steering wheel and rubbed her shoulder where his hand had rested. Was the physical attraction she felt for Wade wrong? She'd never felt for any man what she'd felt in his arms today.

And yet, the fact that, until today, he'd never touched her beyond a chaste brush of the hand was one of the things that drew her to him so strongly. She had always been timid at a man's touch—even when it was innocent. Too many times, she'd bolted and run like a skittish colt when a man wanted to kiss her good-night or hold her hand. She'd never felt comfortable explaining the reason for her fears. Until today.

The words had come so easily with Wade. And his reaction had been one of utter compassion and gentleness. It seemed important that she'd grown to love a man—and he her—completely outside the physical realm. It seemed so right. So exactly the way God would desire. Especially for her.

She longed to tell Wade her thoughts and feelings, longed to go to him and apologize for her selfishness, and to have another chance to be a true comfort to him. But they were both too vulnerable right now. She knew that.

God was so hard to understand sometimes. Why would he have brought Wade into her life, when the very work to which God had called her forbade their being together? It didn't make sense. Nothing made sense anymore.

The mailbox was stuffed with catalogs and bills. Wade tucked everything inside his jacket and zipped it to his chin. The air had taken on a nip overnight. He breathed in the crisp, smoke-scented air. But autumn didn't fill him with the hopeful anticipation that its advent usually brought.

Today was Tuesday—the second Tuesday he hadn't gotten his "fix" of the kids. Instead, he'd climbed into his pickup at six thirty this morning and gone to work, like it was any other day.

He slammed the mailbox shut and turned to look across the patch-work of fields that stretched beyond the Smoky Hills to the north as far as the eye could see. As he had every evening of the week, he cast a whispered prayer toward Minneapolis. "Father, be with them. Keep them safe. Help them make the adjustment. Let them know your presence every single day. Please don't ever let them doubt my love for them. Or yours. And, oh, Father…if it be your will, please allow me a chance to see them again. Please soften Darrin Parnell's heart. Give him patience with the kids. Hold back his anger, Lord. Let Carma be a good mother to the kids." The tentacles of fear that always latched on to him when he reached this part of the prayer grabbed tight again. If he ever found that those precious children were in danger, he wasn't sure he could live with himself. He shook away images that made his stomach knot.

"Help me bear this grief in a way that honors you, Father. And be with Dee. I don't know what you had in mind with her. I don't know why you allowed her into my life, only to take her away. You know how much I care for her… If she has no place in your will for my life, Lord, please take away these longings…"

And as it did every evening, his prayer brought tears. But they were cleansing tears, and he was grateful for their release. He whispered an "amen," then turned and trudged back to the house.

Shadow came up from the river and trotted beside him. Wade filled his bowls with food and water before he went into the house. The kitchen was dark. He switched on the lights and waited in vain for their glow to chase off the chill of loneliness. He unzipped his jacket and tossed the mail on the table.

He pulled out a chair and sat, automatically culling the junk mail from the bills. An ivory-colored envelope caught his eye. His name and address were scrolled across the front in a decidedly feminine hand. There was no return address, but the letter bore a Coyote postmark. Probably another sympathy card. He had received many notes and letters of encouragement from friends and acquaintances from the church and community. He hadn't realized how many people were aware of what had happened in his life. It comforted him to know people understood his loss and were praying for him. In spite of his grief, he was learning to rely on God more deeply than ever before.

He ripped open the envelope and pulled out a letter written in the same flowing script. It was long. Two pages. He turned the last page over in his hand. His pulse quickened at the signature.

He hadn't heard from Dee since she'd come to see him after the hearing. Her exit that day had been painful, leaving him feeling as if there was serious unfinished business between them. Perhaps she was feeling the same. He began to read.

Dear Wade,

I want to apologize for the way I behaved last week. I was selfish and insensitive and completely thoughtless. Please forgive me. I hope you'll believe me when I say that I truly only meant to offer a listening ear and the comfort of a friend. But somewhere I got terribly off track, and I know I offered neither. I am so sorry.

I have thought of you so often. I'm praying for you, Wade. I can't even imagine how much you must be missing the children. But I know God loves them even more than you do and that he has his eye on them every minute of every day. When I was reading my Bible last night, I came across the verse in Matthew that talks about how not one sparrow falls to the ground without God knowing and caring about it. I thought of your three little "sparrows" and how precious they are to God. I found deep comfort in that. I hope you do too.

Wade, I fear anything else I say will only make matters worse than I've already made them, but I do want you to know the time we spent together while I was the children's caseworker was precious to me—both for having had the privilege of knowing such sweet, unspoiled children, and for having known a man like you. I'm certain I overstepped some professional boundaries. Perhaps this letter does the same. (And I admit that, because of the code of ethics I must follow, I'm a little hesitant to even put my thoughts in writing.) If the result of either is hurtful to you, I am sorry.

But selfishly, I have no regrets. I am honored to have known you and Beau and Lacey and Dani, and to have been even a small part of your lives these past few months. I admire your strength of character and your integrity, and I wish for you only God's very best in the days ahead. You and the kids will always be in my prayers.

Dee

Wade put the letter down and rubbed his eyes. He wasn't sure if it made things better or if it only made him miss her and the kids more.

If he'd thought life was lonely after the kids had been put in foster care, now it was beyond any kind of isolation he could imagine. Of course, he'd brought some of it on himself. As much as he knew he needed to go to church, whenever Sunday rolled around he simply couldn't face it. He didn't feel ready to handle all the well-meant condolences and sorrowful stares.

Pete and Margie had issued a standing invitation to dinner at their house, but even that seemed too difficult, and he'd yet to take them up on it.

There were days he was glad Darrin Parnell had been so quick to say no to letting the kids have Shadow. The dog had become his trusted confidant.

He read Dee's letter again. He heard her melodic voice in the sweet, thoughtful words she'd written. But he didn't detect an ounce of hope for the future in them. Even reading between the lines. Sweet as it was, it was still, in essence, a Dear John letter.

He folded it carefully, slid it back in the envelope, and tucked it in the desk drawer atop a stack of the children's drawings and the yellowing newspaper announcements of his and Starr's engagement.

Forty-Five

Wade threw another log in the wood-burning stove and brushed off his hands. Outside, the first snow of the winter swirled around the house and piled up inside the window sills.

He went into the dining room and sat down at his desk. He stared at the phone. For three days he'd been trying to get up the courage to call Minneapolis. On the advice of Frank Locke, he had let the holidays go by without making an effort to contact the kids. He agreed with Locke that Darrin Parnell would be more amenable to his call if he first proved that he didn't intend to be a pest.

To Wade's surprise, a week after the final hearing Carma Weist had sent a note to Frank Locke, informing him that the children were adjusting well, and asking Locke to pass the news along to Wade. He'd hoped Carma's note might be the first of many regular updates, but he'd not heard one word since.

The Christmas lights and decorations had gone up on Coyote's Main Street the week after Thanksgiving. And the tellers at the bank started handing out the candy canes the kids had loved so much. It seemed that everywhere he turned reminders confronted him.

Santa Claus had visited the café one night while Wade shared a cup of coffee with Sophie. Wade watched the cager expressions on the faces of the children who came to sit on Santa's lap. Oh, how Dani's eyes would have sparkled at hearing the jolly "ho-ho-ho." Even Sophie choked up a little, talking about how excited the kids would have been for Christmas to come to Coyote.

He'd spent a lonely Christmas with Pete and Margie. And an even lonelier New Year's Eve at home.

He took a deep breath and exhaled a stream of air. He lifted the handset and punched the number into the keypad. The insistent burr sounded on the other end. Once, twice, three times. He'd rehearsed what he wanted to say a dozen times, but he went over it one more time now.

"Parnell residence."

It was Beau.

Wade's heart thudded out an uneven staccato, and his throat grew thick. "Beau?"

"Yeah?" His voice was lower than Wade remembered.

"Hey, it's Wade. How're you doing, buddy?"

There was a long silence on the other end. He heard Beau's uneven breathing.

"Wade?"

"Yeah, buddy. It's me. How are you?" His spirits lifted just hearing the familiar voice.

"Where are you? Are you here?"

"In Minneapolis? No, buddy, I'm home. In Coyote."

"Oh." The word dropped on a dull note.

"I just called to see how you and the girls are getting along."

"When are you coming, Wade? We— The girls are always cryin' for you."

Wade's thoughts immediately flew to Parnell. "Is everything all right?"

More silence.

"Beau?"

"It's okay, I guess. But when are you comin'?"

"Well…I don't know, buddy. I'd love to come and see you…soon. So, he's treating you okay?"

"I guess."

"Do you get to see Carma quite a bit?"

"What do you mean? She lives here."

"Oh. I thought they weren't getting married until next spring." He'd hoped he might offer to keep the kids while the newlyweds honeymooned.

"Yeah, the wedding is in March or something. Or maybe it's May. I forget."

"Oh, I see." So she'd moved in with him. He wasn't crazy about the example it set for the kids, but at the same time, it was rather comforting to think of Carma being there as a buffer. Wade grasped for something to say. "Did you get the Christmas presents I sent?"

"No…I don't think so. Not yet. Is Shadow okay?"

Wade brightened. "Oh yeah! He's doing great. We have snow here, and he was down by the river chasing snowflakes when I got home from—"

"Hey!"

The shout caused Wade to pull the phone away, but he immediately pressed it to his ear again.

Beau sounded angry. "No, wait! Carma! It's—"

There was a commotion. Then a brusque feminine voice interrupted. "Hello? Who is this?"

"Yes…um…is this Carma?"

A cautious pause. "Who is this, please?"

"Oh, I'm sorry. It's Wade Sullivan…from Kansas?"

"Oh. Did he call you?"

"Beau? No…no, I called there, and he answered the phone."

"Well, the kids aren't supposed to use the telephone without permission."

"No, I don't think you understand. He didn't call me."

Silence.

"I…I was just calling to ask about the children. I wonder if I might speak to the girls? Just for a minute. Are they there?"

"The children are fine. They're doing very well…adjusting quite well. I…we sent a note to your attorney."

"Yes, I got the message."

More silence.

"Would it be okay if I talk to the girls?" he asked again, trying to keep his frustration at bay.

"Um…let me talk to Darrin. Hold on just a moment, please."

Wade heard the drone of a television and muffled voices in the background.

A long minute passed before a deep voice barked in his ear. "Sullivan?"

"Yes. Darrin? I was telling Carma that I just wanted to see how the kids were—"

"The kids are fine."

"Could we…find a time I could come up and visit for a couple of days? I thought it might be easier if I traveled up there. I was thinking maybe the kids could come here while you two honeymoon…"

"Oh, we've got those arrangements all worked out."

"Well, another time then? Over their spring break?"

"I don't think so. Maybe after they get adjusted a little better. It's too soon now."

"But Carma said they were adjusting well. Is everything okay?"

"I told you, they're fine. We'll talk about this in a few months. I'll give you a call."

His heart sank. "Well, then, could I talk to the girls? Just for a few—" The dial tone buzzed in his ear.

A cauldron of anger simmered inside him. He jabbed at the redial key. But before the number finished dialing, he hung up the phone. It would be foolish to try to reason with Darrin Parnell in this frame of mind. No use making the man angry and risk having him turn it on the children.

He pushed back his chair and paced the floor. At least Beau had sounded okay. But he'd said the girls were crying for him.

Why did that image break his heart and warm it at the same time?

Wade climbed out of the pickup, zipped up his insulated coveralls, and pulled his stocking cap down over his ears. He looked up at the roof where Pete was perched high on the rafters. He had the radio cranked up as loud as it would go, and Wade heard him singing along to Gary Allan's raspy vocals.

It was cold, but the freezing rain had finally quit. The February sun had warmed things enough that they could work outside again.

He started up the ladder, tools in hand. "Yo, Pete!"

His partner looked up and, seeing him, reached around to turn down the volume on the CD player balanced precariously on a beam. "Hey."

"How's it going?"

"Goin' good. Nice to have the sun out for a change."

"You got that right." Wade straddled a rafter and set to work. They'd gutted this old house and were remodeling it from the ground floor up for a group of investors that planned to open a bed-and-breakfast here. As he'd watched the project take shape, Wade gave thanks for a job in which he found such satisfaction. It had kept him sane over the months since he'd lost the kids. Since he'd lost Dee.

As though his partner had read his mind, Pete slammed home another nail and glanced over at him. "So, what are you doing Saturday night?"

"The usual," Wade said, instantly suspicious. "Hot date."

"Yeah, right." Pete rolled his eyes and chuckled. "When was the last time you had a date?"

Wade held his hammer aloft. "Don't even go there, buddy. Just change the subject right now."

"No, I'm serious, man. Margie met this new teacher at the elementary school. I've seen her a couple of times. She's a real looker. And sweet as she is cute, Margie says. Margie can't wait for you to meet her. We were wondering if you wanted to come over for supper Saturday night. Amber's spending the night with a friend, and we thought the four of us could play cards or something…maybe rent a movie?"

"I appreciate the thought, Pete, but I don't think so."

"Come on, man. What have you got to lose? It's not like a date. Just a chance to meet a new friend, that's all."

"You know better than that. Margie's probably already got the wedding invitations picked out." He was kidding, giving his partner a hard time. But he wasn't going. It didn't matter how hard Pete pushed. He'd been blessed to have two precious women in his life. He would be content with that. That, and the whisper of a hope he didn't dare to voice.

As he sought the Scriptures early each morning, one truth had begun to sink deep into his spirit: This life was only a whisper of a breath to eternity. God was far more interested in making him ready for the life to come than he was in seeing that Wade was happy on this finite planet.

This constant ache of loneliness was only for a season on earth. And in spite of it—perhaps *because* of it—he had become ever more aware of an overwhelming sense of peace in his life—a peace undergirded by something he could only describe as joy.

The Wal-Mart parking lot was jam-packed on a Saturday afternoon. Wade hadn't realized Easter weekend would be such a big shopping day. He parked the pickup in the closest spot he could find—half the length of a football field away—and jogged to the front entry.

A jovial, six-foot-tall Easter bunny met him at the door with a basket of foil-wrapped chocolates and coupons for Easter-egg dye. Lacey and Dani would have been in hog heaven over the encounter.

Wade wondered how the kids were celebrating this Easter. It startled him to realize it would be their second without their mother. Last Easter had gone uncelebrated, so close on the heels of Starr's death. The year before, Starr had spent a small fortune putting together colorful, treat-filled baskets for each of the kids. The girls got new dresses for Easter Sunday, and Beau got his first bow tie. The girls made corny jokes about Beau wearing a bow. Much to Starr's chagrin, Beau had retaliated by ripping off the tie and refusing to put it back on. How oblivious they'd all been then to what lay ahead.

Taking the shopping cart the elderly greeter offered, he headed toward the automotive department. He planned to change the oil in the truck this weekend, and he needed windshield wiper blades and brake fluid too.

He pulled a case of oil from the bottom shelf. When he straightened and turned to put the box in the cart, he found himself looking into Dee Thackery's eyes. "Dee…"

She put a hand to her throat. "Wade. Hi." She fidgeted with the strap of her purse. "How are you?"

He lowered the case of oil into the cart and stood with his hands gripping the handle. The cart formed a barrier between him and Dee—one he was grateful for, since he found himself desperately wanting to give her a hug.

"I'm doing good," he told her, trying not to stare. She looked beautiful. Her hair was longer, and she'd done something to the color—highlights, he thought they were called. She was wearing jeans and a pale yellow sweatshirt, and she had a fresh, girl-next-door look about her.

"How are the kids?" A note of compassion crept into her voice. "Do you get to see them often?"

He bit his lip. "I haven't seen them since…since they moved to Minneapolis."

Her forehead furrowed, and she leaned toward him. "Oh, Wade. I'm so sorry. Have you at least gotten to talk to them?"

"I called there and got to talk to Beau for a little bit. It's hard to tell over the phone, but he sounded like they were doing okay. Carma's written Frank Locke twice, asking him to let me know the kids were okay."

"That's good," Dee said.

"Yeah, I guess. I talked to her for a few minutes the night I called Beau." He paused, remembering the frustration of that night. "But then she put Parnell on the phone, and that was the end of it. She'd moved in with him. I think they were supposed to get married this spring."

Dee shook her head and clucked sympathetically. "I'm so sorry it hasn't worked out differently for you, Wade."

"Yeah. It…it's been kind of rough." He forced a smile. "So how are you? Still working at St. Joe's?"

"Oh yes."

"And it's going well?"

"Very well. I enjoy my work."

He dipped his head. "Well, you're good at it."

A flush bloomed on her cheeks. "Thank you. Are…are you still living out west of town?"

"Still there. Me and Shadow."

"Oh yes, good ol' Shadow." She grinned. " The dog that gave me my first mud bath."

He laughed with her. "I'd kind of forgotten about that." Not true. He'd relived every moment with her a hundred times. "I bet that made a good first impression."

"I've had better," she said, a teasing glint coming to her eyes. "You redeemed yourself, though."

An awkward silence grew between them, and Wade shuffled his feet on the shiny tile floor. Should he take those words at more than face value? Had the feelings she'd once had for him remained strong, as his had for her?

"Oh, hey," she said, snapping her fingers and looking into his shopping cart. "You're buying oil. Maybe you can help me."

He tipped his head. "Depends. What's the question?"

"My neighbor's going to change my oil for me this weekend, but I have no clue what kind to get."

"Oh, well, you probably want petroleum-based—conventional—not synthetic. It's cheaper. Probably 10W30."

She shrugged and smiled sheepishly. "You're speaking a foreign language. Sorry."

"Here…" He found the right grade and stooped to pick up a case. "This should work."

"Oh…I guess I should have brought a cart." She wrinkled her nose. "Does it take that much?"

"Well, no. You could buy individual quarts. I'm just used to buying it by the case because it's cheaper that way."

"Oh, okay."

He set the case into his cart. "I'll take it to the checkout for you. Were you done shopping?"

"I'm done. Thank you. I…I'm glad I ran into you."

He wheeled the cart around in the narrow aisle, and they headed toward the checkout, walking in silence. She went through the checkout first, then waited while he paid for his purchases.

He loaded her case of oil back into the shopping cart. "Show me where you're parked, ma'am." He flashed a grin. "Here at Wal-Mart, we aim to please."

She laughed and led the way past the Easter bunny and out to the parking lot. "Sorry…I'm parked way down at the end."

"Hey, you couldn't be any farther away than I am. Isn't this a madhouse?"

She nodded, suddenly seeming distracted and distant. She stepped ahead of him and unlocked the trunk of her car.

He hefted the oil and set it inside, scooting the box around to make sure it wouldn't shift while she drove. He slammed the trunk lid, painfully aware that it was time for him to make a graceful exit.

Turning to her, he breathed her name. "Dee."

She looked up, expectancy in her eyes.

"I…I never answered your letter, but…thanks. I appreciated it."

"I thought maybe it made you mad," she said, glancing away. "Since I never heard back."

He paused, not quite sure how to respond. "Well, not mad exactly. It just sounded pretty…final."

Now she studied him, shaking her head slowly. "It had to be, Wade. It's not what I wanted."

He cocked his head. "I don't suppose the rules have changed by now?"

She hesitated. "Rules?"

"You know, the two-year thing." For one awful moment he was afraid he'd totally misread her. Maybe he was assuming far too much. Maybe she hadn't given him another thought since she mailed the letter. What if there was even somebody else? He took in a short breath at the thought and voiced it before he could chicken out. "Is there someone… Are you seeing someone else?"

"Oh…" She seemed thrown by the question. "No, there's no one."

"Good."

She looked at him askance. "Good?"

"I haven't given up hope, Dee." He stared at the asphalt, afraid of what he might see in her eyes.

"Oh, Wade. It's…such a long time."

"Seven months down, seventeen to go."

"You're crazy," she said. "That's forever." But Wade liked the flash of anticipation he saw in her soft smile, the lilt in her voice when she said it.

"I told you, I'm a patient man."

The look of near panic he'd seen in her eyes that day at his house flitted there again. But there was something else there now too. Something that gave him hope.

"I have to go," she said. "Before I do something I'll regret." She rummaged in her purse for the car keys. When she looked up, tears brimmed in her eyes. "Thank you, Wade…for helping me…with the oil." She backed toward the driver's side door, her gaze holding his.

He tipped an imaginary hat. "My pleasure, ma'am."

Forty-Six

Not yet fully awake, Wade hunched over the kitchen sink and pushed back the lace curtains to look across the road. The sky was pink with dawn. Spring was late coming, but down by the river, the naked gray branches of the cottonwoods had grown a distinct haze of green, seemingly overnight.

May More than a year since he'd found Starr's lifeless body on the floor upstairs. So much had happened in those four brief seasons.

He took a can of Folgers from the cupboard, measured the dark grounds into the coffee maker, and filled the reservoir with cold water. The machine started sputtering and hissing almost as soon as he pushed the button. He dropped two slices of wheat bread into the toaster and pushed the lever. Soon the kitchen filled with the mingled aromas.

He filled a large mug with coffee, buttered the toast, and took it to the table. As he'd done every morning since October, he began his morning by praying that God would keep the kids safe and help them forget all the trauma they'd endured over the past year. Wade prayed they wouldn't forget him in the process. That they would always remember how much he loved them.

But today he felt an odd urgency as he prayed. Beau's face came to his mind, as sharply as though the boy's photograph were imprinted on his eyelids. He tried to move on and pray about other things, but Beau's image kept pestering him. *Father, be with Beau in a special way. I don't know what's going on with him today, Lord, but you do, and I trust you to take care of him. Please let him know how much you love him. Let him remember how much I love him. Give him strength to get through whatever he might face today…*

His Bible lay there beneath last night's *Coyote Courier*. He pushed aside the newspaper, opened to Psalms, and began to read. "God is our refuge

and strength, an ever-present help in trouble. Therefore we will not fear."
A little farther down the page he read, "Be still, and know that I am God."

He closed the worn leather cover, rinsed his dishes in the sink, and
headed outside. But even as he went about his morning, feeding Shadow
and working on the truck, the urgency to pray for Beau kept snaking its
way back to the forefront of his mind.

Why was Beau so heavy on his heart this morning? If things had
turned sour with Parnell, how would the boy ever learn to trust people?
Wade thought of the long-ago promise he'd made the night Beau had
tried to run away. Would Beau ever be able to trust a loving Father God,
when two earthly fathers had let him down?

The thoughts troubled him as he went through his chores. He was
repairing the light fixture in the entryway when the jangling of the phone
broke the silence. Letting out a growl of frustration, he climbed down
from the stepladder and hurried to answer the phone.

The young voice quavered just above a whisper. "Wade?"

"Beau? Is that you?"

"Wade? You gotta help me. He's hittin' her again."

Adrenaline flooded his veins. "Who's he hitting, Beau?"

"Carma. He's hittin' her again."

Wade exhaled his relief. For one horrifying second, he'd feared for
Lacey and Dani.

"She's cryin' really hard this time—" Beau's voice broke.

Wade didn't like the sound of it. He had rarely seen Beau shed a tear.
"Beau, where is Carma right now?"

"They're in the kitchen. He...he knocked her down. She's tryin' to
talk to him now. But he won't say he's sorry. He always tells her he's sorry,
and then it's okay. He quits hitting. But it's not working this time. He just
keeps yelling and yelling."

"Where are the girls, Beau?" Wade struggled to keep his own voice
even.

"They're in there with Carma. Lacey tried to help, and he told her she
better shut up or he's gonna hit her, too."

The strength drained out of Wade, and he leaned against the wall for support. He held his breath, willed calmness into his voice. "Is Lacey okay? *Did* he hit Lacey, Beau?"

"No. Just Carma. But I'm scared, Wade. He's never been this mean."

"Where are you now, Beau?"

"I'm at his house."

"Okay, but where? What room?"

"Oh. In their bedroom. I brought the phone in here. He'll kill me if he finds out I called you."

"It's okay, Beau. You did the right thing. I'll tell you what…" Wade's mind raced. "I'm going to call the police. They'll come and make sure—"

"No!" Beau's voice squeaked up an octave. "Don't call the police! He'll be really mad. Carma did that once, and he said he was gonna kill her. You can't call them. You can't! You need to come, Wade. You've gotta come and help us!"

The terror in Beau's voice made Wade's blood run cold. "Beau, listen to me, buddy… Quiet down… Is there a neighbor you can call? Somebody who can come over right away?"

"I…we don't know the neighbors. We're not supposed to talk to them."

"Okay…just hang on. Stay right there. We'll think of something." He grappled with what he should do, what he should tell Beau. Far in the background he heard a commotion—crying, and a man yelling. The voices got louder. "Beau? What's going on?"

No answer.

"Beau?" His heart lurched, and his breath came quicker.

Suddenly a masculine voice was clear in Wade's ear. A stream of curses came through the receiver. Curses aimed at a nine-year-old boy. Wade's heart broke even as it pounded with anger and fear.

"What do you think you're doing? How dare you snoop around in my room!" The line grew scratchy, the voices muffled.

At first Wade thought Parnell had discovered the telephone and covered the receiver, but Beau apparently had stuffed the phone under a pillow or something because the ranting continued. Muted now, but still clear enough that he could understand every word.

"What are you doing in here?"

A woman's pleading interrupted Parnell's voice. Carma. "Darrin. Stop it. Leave him alone. Please...this doesn't have anything to do with him."

"Shut up!"

"Darrin, please..."

The sickening sound of flesh hitting flesh came through in spite of the fuzzy connection.

Beau's high-pitched wail pierced the line, and Wade nearly doubled over, feeling the blow almost physically himself.

"Darrin! Stop it!" Carma sounded hysterical.

Panic jump-started Wade's heart. He shouted into the phone. "Parnell!"

But the shrieking on the other end of the line continued.

"Parnell! Darrin! Listen to me!" He screamed Parnell's name into the phone until he was hoarse.

Suddenly he thought he heard the little girls' cries added to the chaos. Feeling utterly helpless, he continued trying to distract Parnell across five hundred miles of telephone wire.

The words Darrin was bellowing now didn't even make sense. It sounded like the man was completely out of control.

Wade glanced wildly around the room. He needed to call the police. Now. But if he hung up the phone, he might not be able to dial out, and he'd lose his one tenuous connection to Beau and the girls.

In a frenzy, he laid the handset down and ran to the kitchen where he'd left his cell phone charging on the countertop. He raced back to the desk phone with it, dialing 911 as he ran.

"Coyote County 911," a woman's calm, low voice answered. "Do you have an emergency?"

With one ear to the phone thinly tying him to Beau, Wade gave his name and address to the dispatcher and tried to describe what was happening. He was forced to put down the other phone while he dug frantically through the desk drawer, looking for Darrin Parnell's address.

Finally, unearthing it from under a pile of bills, he read it off to the dispatcher, along with the phone number he had for Parnell.

"Okay, Mr. Sullivan," the dispatcher said, her voice maddeningly calm. "I have the information. I'm contacting the Minneapolis police right now. They'll send someone to check things out."

"Tell them to hurry. He's hitting them! I can hear them right now!"

"I'll request an ambulance," the dispatcher said. "I want you to stay on the line and try to distract him, Mr. Sullivan? Can you do that?"

"Yes. Yes, okay."

"I'm going to hang up now. We'll get someone to the address in Minneapolis. Please stay by the phone in case we need to contact you again."

"Yes. I'll be here." The noise on the other phone distracted him momentarily. "Will you call and let me know—"

But her line had already gone dead. Wade punched off the cell phone and turned his full attention to the other phone. Darrin was still ranting nonsensically. It sounded like he was drunk.

He pressed his ear harder to the receiver, straining to catch something that would assure him Beau and the girls were okay.

A sudden bark sliced through his eardrum. "What the—" Parnell. His voice no longer muffled.

Wade heard static through the line. Parnell had obviously discovered the phone. There was a split second of dead silence, and then Parnell roared. "Who were you talking to?"

Beau's voice came through strong. "Nobody."

"Liar! You tell me now! Who were you talking to?"

"Parnell?" Wade shouted into the receiver again. "Parnell? Listen to me..."

Again his voice fell on deaf ears.

"How dare you deceive your dad, you worthless little—" Parnell sneered an epithet.

Wade heard a whimper. Then Beau's voice, unwavering this time. "I'm not worthless... And you're not my dad!"

Wade could almost picture him with his chest stuck out, skinny arms akimbo. He would have felt proud had he not been so terrified.

Another slap.

Beau's howl of pain was cut off abruptly as the line went dead.

Wade stood in front of his desk, knees turned to jelly, hands trembling, while a dial tone buzzed in his ear.

He grabbed the paper with Parnell's address and dialed the phone number written there. It rang half a dozen times before Parnell's smooth, composed salesman's voice came on the line. "This is the Parnell residence. We are unable to take your call at this time. At the sound of the tone, please leave your name and number, and we'll return your call as soon as possible."

Wade waited for the tone. "Parnell? Darrin? Please pick up the phone. Carma?" He waited, drumming a panicky rhythm on the desk with his knuckles.

Silence.

He quickly weighed his options. "Beau, if you can hear me, pick up the phone." He felt on the verge of hysterics. "Beau? I'm sending help. Do you hear me? Beau? Take care of the girls. Help is on the way. I love you. Don't ever forget that."

He waited for an eternity, praying desperately that someone would pick up the phone. Finally a shrill *breep-breep-breep* cut him off, and he was left with the drone of the dial tone.

Again he punched in the number, and again he got the answering machine. Not waiting for the message to finish playing, he slammed down the phone. Striding from the dining room through the length of the kitchen and back, he raked his fingers through his hair, trying desperately to think what he should do.

He went back to the desk and dialed Sophie. Maybe she would know someone to call in Minneapolis. The phone rang a dozen times. She apparently didn't have her answering machine turned on.

He put down the handset and paced again. The clock ticked off the minutes. Fifteen of them. He tried Sophie again. Still no answer. Another ten minutes dragged by.

He picked up the phone and dialed 911 again. The dispatcher he'd talked to earlier answered. Wade asked if she'd heard anything from Minneapolis.

"No, Mr. Sullivan. We turned that call over to the police department there. You'll need to contact them directly."

"Do you have the number I should call?"

"One moment, please." She came back on the line a minute later and read a number to him.

His hand was poised over the telephone when it started ringing. He grabbed the receiver and barked into it. "Hello?"

"Mr. Sullivan?"

"Yes?"

"This is Sergeant Brian McCullough from the Minneapolis Police Department. I understand you made a 911 call earlier this morning from Coyote County... Is that Kansas?"

"Yes... That's right. Is everything okay? Are my kids all right?"

"You haven't heard back from them?"

"No," Wade said. A chill crawled up his back.

"Well, Mr. Sullivan, we confirmed the address you gave the dispatcher as the current address of Darrin Parnell. We dispatched an officer to that address, but there was no one at home."

Dee was on her way out the door when the telephone rang. Blowing out a huff of frustration, she slid her purse off her shoulder, dumped the pile of clothes for the dry cleaners on the counter, and grabbed the handset. "Hello?"

"Dee? It's Wade Sullivan."

"Wade." She pulled out a chair and sank into it, her pulse fluttering erratically. "Hi..."

"I need your help, Dee. The kids are missing."

She could hear the fear in his voice, and a spike of alarm went through her. "Missing? What do you mean?"

"Beau called me here about an hour ago, terrified because Parnell was beating Carma. While we were on the phone Parnell came in and started slapping Beau around—" Wade's voice caught, and he finished with a tremor in his tone. "I could hear everything that was going on, but then Parnell apparently discovered the phone and cut us off."

"Oh, Wade. How awful!"

"I called 911, and they sent the Minneapolis police to the house, but they just called and said when the police got there, there was no one home."

"But…where would they have gone?"

"I don't know. Maybe they found out Beau was talking to me. I…I left a message on the answering machine telling Beau I was calling the police. Maybe they just ran."

"Are the police looking for them? What can *I* do?"

"That's why I called, Dee. Would there be any information in St. Joseph's records or the SRS files that would tell us where they might be headed? Parnell's work address or where Carma used to live maybe? I… I'm at a loss to know what to do next, and the police don't really have anything to go on."

"I don't know what we might have, Wade, but I'll find out. I…I probably can't give the information directly to you, but there's a network I can go through with social services… Maybe there's someone in Minneapolis who can help."

His sigh of relief was audible. "Thank you, Dee. Will you keep me posted?"

She didn't like the sound of this new development one bit. Just last week in Topeka a man had shot his wife and daughter over a custody ruling. She shuddered, the images from the newspapers too fresh in her mind. "I'll do whatever I can, Wade. I promise."

Dee disconnected and immediately dialed Betty Graffe at home.

A lump swelled in her throat. Wade had suffered so much already. And those precious kids. *Please, God. Please. Don't let this end in tragedy.*

Forty-Seven

Wade had spent almost forty-eight hours with a telephone glued to his ear. Now Monday morning was dawning, and he still had no word from Minneapolis. Dee had called late last night to say that Social Services seemed to be hitting dead ends as well.

Where could Parnell have taken the kids? He threw up his thousandth prayer for their safety and picked up the phone to call Sophie again.

He'd finally gotten hold of her at the café last night. As soon as Wade told her what had happened, Sophie started to cry. "Oh, Wade, you've got to find them. You've got to. You don't know what he's capable of."

Something in her voice had clamped his heart like a vise. "What do you mean, Sophie?"

"He beat me, too, Wade. It…it was him…that night in the parking lot. Darrin did that to me. I should have said something, but I… Well, he had his reasons with me. But what if he does that to Beau? I'll never forgive myself."

Just thinking about her revelation brought Wade to the edge of hysteria. Her answering machine picked up now, and he left a brief message.

He hung up and slumped over the desk, clutching the top for support. "Please, God," he whispered. "Wherever they are, be with the kids. Protect them, Father. Put your angels around them. Please."

His heart felt like a lead weight in his chest as he plodded to the kitchen. Like an automaton, he measured the ground coffee into the basket of the coffee maker.

It was all he could do not to hop in the pickup and head north. But besides the fact that it would take him nine hours to get there, it was foolish to think he could do anything the police weren't already doing.

While he waited for the coffee to brew, he went to the laundry room and threw in a load of work clothes. He turned the dial, and the washing machine sprang to life.

The clothes in the dryer were wrinkled beyond hope, so he started the dryer again—a guilty shortcut to ironing he'd learned from Starr. He felt helpless and foolish doing laundry while his children were missing. But he needed to stay by the phone, and he would go stark mad if he didn't do something.

Over the swishing of the washer's agitator, Shadow's sharp yelp pierced the air outside. It sounded like he was headed down to the river. He barked again, the deep, happy yap that usually signaled he was on the trail of a squirrel or a raccoon.

The *woof-woof-woof* grew louder. Wade turned off the washing machine and cocked his head, listening. There was a slightly different timbre to the dog's bark this morning. And something else. A high-pitched squeal. There it was again. Somebody must have dumped a litter of pups or a batch of kittens in his yard. It happened from time to time—one of the dubious rewards of living in the country. But usually people waited for the cover of darkness to make the drop.

Wade started, hearing footsteps on the front porch. He hadn't heard anyone drive in. But then the washer and dryer had been running. Shadow's yipping grew more insistent.

The doorbell chimed, and his heart leapt. Maybe someone had news. He hurried through the living room and looked out the window. He didn't recognize the black sedan parked in front of the house, but the lid of the car's trunk stood open, and a man was unloading something from the back. The man had his back to Wade as he wrestled with a large cardboard box, hoisted it from the trunk, and set it on the ground beside the car. He pulled out a smaller box and stacked it atop the first. The pile of boxes grew as Wade watched from the window. Then came a black suitcase.

"Shoot-fire," Wade said under his breath. He didn't have the time or the patience to mess with some vacuum cleaner salesman today.

He went to the door and jerked it open. He stepped out onto the porch. "Can I help you?"

The man popped from behind the trunk lid.

It took Wade a minute to realize who it was. "Parnell? What...what's going on? Where are—"

"I brought you your kids." Darrin Parnell slammed the trunk shut and walked toward the house.

Wade looked around the yard, his skin suddenly growing clammy. "What…are you talking about? Where are the kids?"

Parnell stopped at the bottom porch stair and hooked a thumb in the direction of the backyard. "They're back there. With the dog," he said matter-of-factly.

Wade turned to look toward the river, but the house blocked his view. He wondered if he was dreaming. Still, Shadow's excitement made sense now. Did he dare to hope? "They're here? Beau? And the girls? Are they… okay?" His throat clogged with emotion. "Where have you been? We've been looking every—"

Parnell's head jerked up. "Who's been looking?"

Wade cleared his throat, his mind reeling, trying to gauge Parnell's mental state. "Never mind. I'm…glad you're here. The kids are okay?"

Parnell kicked at a pebble with the toe of his shiny black dress shoe. "They're fine. But it's not going to work out. I think…they're better off with you." He sighed heavily and pulled a thick envelope from his breast pocket. "I've got all the papers here. Anything else you need should be in the mail to you soon. Hinson—my attorney—said it was all in order. It might take a couple of weeks to get the rest of the paperwork sent, but if you have any questions, his number's in here." He slapped the envelope against his thigh, then held it out to Wade.

Wade grabbed on to one of the columns that supported the porch roof. He steadied himself, then descended the steps and cautiously took the envelope from Parnell's hand. He looked at the outside. Blank, except for Jonathan Hinson's embossed return address. "What about Carma?"

Parnell hung his head. "Carma's…not in the picture anymore. Everything you need is in that envelope."

Wade pressed two fingers hard against the throbbing space between his eyes. He shook his head. "I don't understand." He could scarcely imagine what had brought about this surreal turn of events.

"They're better off with you," Parnell repeated. He looked up and studied Wade. "I may not have been the best father, but I want…what's right for my kids."

Wade nodded. He didn't dare press his luck by asking any more questions. He only wanted to run to see his kids. Make sure they were really all right. "Do you…want to come in for a minute?" The words were out before he had time to consider them. What was wrong with him? He should be calling the police, not inviting the man to coffee.

Parnell rubbed his jaw where the shadow of a beard sprouted. "No… I've been on the road all night. I need to get some breakfast and head back."

"I have coffee on."

Parnell tipped his chin, as though he were considering Wade's invitation, but then he wagged his head. "No. I don't think so."

Wade knew he should let the authorities know what had happened. Make sure Carma was okay. But he wasn't about to risk doing anything that might cause Parnell to change his mind.

Parnell moved toward the car, then turned back to face Wade. His face darkened, and his forehead furrowed, as though he were in physical pain. "I'd like to know how they're doing…once in a while. You will take them, won't you?"

Wade nodded with his whole upper body. "Of course. Sure."

"Listen, Sullivan, I just want you to know… I never meant—" He looked away, then shook his head slowly. He motioned to the envelope in Wade's hand. "You've got my number." He turned again, shoulders slumped, and trudged back to the car.

Wade nodded, still reeling in amazement and disbelief. "Parnell… Darrin?"

Parnell looked up, leaning one forearm on the roof of the car, a question in his eyes—and something else. Anguish and loss. The same potent mixture Wade had seen when he looked in the mirror this morning.

He closed his eyes briefly, overwhelmed. "Thank you, Darrin. I promise I'll do right by them." He choked on the end of his sentence, utterly grateful, yet aching to run to the backyard, where hauntingly familiar laughter now rang out.

Parnell gave a hard nod and climbed into the car, suddenly seeming far older than his years. The engine revved, and the car turned a wide curve and drove away. Wade watched it disappear in a cloud of dust.

Was he dreaming? But the pile of boxes and suitcases sat in the driveway as testimony to the miracle that had just happened.

The children's laughter wafted to him from behind the house, and Shadow barked now and then, as if welcoming them home. Wade turned and took two steps before his knees buckled. He crumpled, as if someone had wrestled him to the ground. First kneeling in the tender grass, then bowing, face in his hands, he wept like a child.

Never had he imagined God would answer his prayers in this way, after all this time, after all his anguish. He could not yet fathom that it was real. He remained with heart and knee bent before the Lord for what seemed an eternity, unable to find the words to express the overflowing of gratitude and joy that welled up inside him.

Finally he struggled to his feet. Like a newly mobile toddler, Wade half ran, half stumbled to the back of the house and stood on the rise of the hill, watching the children—*his* children—play on the lawn with their dog.

They looked healthy and whole. He could scarcely wait to call out their names, one by one. To watch them turn and spy him, then race one another to his arms.

At the same time, he wanted time to stand still. To savor this moment for as long as he could make it linger.

Beau broke the spell. He threw a stick for Shadow to retrieve and turned, his gaze following the stick's path. His eyes widened and he gave a little gasp. "Wade!" He ran helter-skelter from Lacey to Dani and back again. "It's Wade, you guys! He's here!"

The girls screamed his name and came tearing up the hill, just as they had in his daydreams. In his prayers.

He knelt in the grass again, this time with open arms. And an open heart. They jumped on him, tumbling him over like a bowling pin in the soft grass. He tussled with them gently, speaking their names, one at a time, then running the syllables together as if it were one beautiful word: "Beaulaceydani."

Soon, out of breath, they all sat in the grass, spent, panting, and clammy with sweat, wearing smiles as wide and shimmering as the distant Smoky Hill. Shadow plopped down inside the circle they'd made.

"Are you guys okay?" Wade put a finger under Beau's chin and tipped his head into the light. No bruises were apparent. "Beau?"

The boy's eyes clouded, but he nodded. "I'm okay."

Wade turned to the girls.

"He didn't hurt them," Beau said. "I took care of them like you said."

Wade put a hand on his shoulder, unable to speak.

Slowly they started talking. Reluctant at first, then their words came in torrents, like the river at flood stage.

"Did your dad tell you why he brought you here?"

"Carma made him," Beau said. "She said she was gonna tell the police."

"Oh," Wade said, piecing the story together. "Is she okay?"

Beau nodded. "She made him bring us back."

"Oh?"

"She moved back to her house." Beau's eyes narrowed. "He was always hittin' her. Just like Mom."

Wade's heart twisted like a knife in his chest. No little boy should have such memories. "You're sure he didn't…hurt you guys?"

They shook their heads solemnly, each one, and Wade let out a breath he hadn't been aware of holding.

"We get to live here," Beau said. "All the time."

"Yeah," Dani piped up. "Every day. Not just to visit with Dee on Tuesday."

Dee. Wade couldn't wait to give her the good news.

Beau cocked his head and eyed Wade. "We can stay here, can't we? He said we didn't hafta go in foster care anymore. His lawyer said so."

Wade tousled Beau's hair and swallowed the boulder in his throat. "Yeah. You can stay here."

Beau stuck out his neck and made a squinty face at Lacey. "See! Told ya!"

Her cheeks flushed pale pink.

Wade reached over to wrap an arm around her slender shoulders. He pulled her next to him. "You're here to stay, Lacey Daisy," he whispered against her silky hair.

Watching them, he was struck by how much they'd grown. How much they'd grown *up*. He'd missed so much in such a short space of time.

One at a time, reverently, he laid his hand atop each blond head, needing proof they were really here. That they were finally, truly his. *Oh, Starr...*

A sharp hook of bitterness pricked him, prodding his mind for entry. But he refused to let it sink in, refused to be reeled in to dwell on what was past. He would not waste one minute of whatever time he had with these kids. God willing, his next good-bye would be as each one, in turn, packed a suitcase and headed for college. The very thought brought the lump back to his throat. But that kind of lump he could live with.

Forty-Eight

"Macaroni and cheese!" Dani yelled, pumping her arm in the air.

"Yeah, macaroni!" Lacey and Beau echoed.

Wade stared at them, mouth agape. "You've got to be kidding! After all the grief you always gave me about my gourmet macaroni-and-cheese dinners, *that's* what you want for lunch?"

He laughed, then found himself choking up again, still amazed he could have awakened this morning to an empty house, and now, six hours later, he was about to fix a box of macaroni and cheese for three hungry kids, as though this were the most ordinary day in the world.

He would never take another moment of life for granted. He would never again feel hopeless about any situation. Miracles still happened, and today, he had been on the receiving end of a big one.

He'd contacted the police in Minneapolis and assumed they were looking for Darrin Parnell en route to the city. He'd set up a meeting with Frank Locke to go over the papers Parnell had brought him. Everything from Hinson's office looked official, but Wade wanted to make sure. He wasn't about to risk losing the kids again.

He'd also called Margie and Sophie with the good news. Everyone was coming out to the house tonight to see the kids and celebrate. What a reunion it would be!

Dee came to the forefront of his thoughts. She was the one he longed most to share the news with. He smiled, imagining the joy he would see on her face when she heard. He'd tried to reach her all morning but had only gotten her answering machine. This wasn't the kind of news you left on a machine.

He was tempted to invite her to tonight's celebration, but this didn't change her situation. The boundaries between them remained. Still, she had played a cherished role in their story, and he wanted her to know that.

He felt a tug on the tail of his sweatshirt.

"Wade?" Dani looked up at him, her blue eyes wide.

He bent and cupped her face in his hands. "What is it, sweetie?"

"Can I set the table?"

"You sure can. But hang on a sec… Let me make sure I have some macaroni. We might be eating cold cereal." He opened a cupboard and rummaged around behind boxes of Hamburger Helper and cans of soup. He pulled out a dusty box of macaroni and held it aloft. "Ta-da!"

The kids cheered.

"Okay, we're set." He pulled four plates from the cupboard and gave them to Dani. "Here you go, squirt. Set these around, and I'll get the glasses down." He couldn't remember the last time he'd used four plates at once. It felt wonderful to be setting a full table again.

Lacey filled a pot with water and set it on the stove while Beau put chairs up to the table. As they went about the little things that had been part of their everyday life before, a sense of euphoria threatened to render Wade useless. He never wanted to lose the awe he felt over what had happened here today, but he was eager to settle back into a routine. Happily, he realized the kids were doing just that. As he watched them bustle around the kitchen, intent on their jobs, he wondered how they were doing emotionally.

For more than a year, they had endured one tragedy or disruption after another, things that would have laid low many adults. There were sure to be deep psychological wounds. He should ask Dee about that. Maybe she could suggest a counselor.

"The water's boiling," Lacey announced.

He turned to smile at her. Tomorrow would take care of itself. Today he was making macaroni and cheese for his kids.

When they sat down to the table a few minutes later, Wade offered a hand to the girls on either side of him, and they all joined hands around the table. He bowed his head. "Father, thank you that this table is full again—" His voice broke. How long would he choke up every time he thought of what God had done? He swallowed hard. "Thank you, Father, for answering my prayers and bringing my kids back."

"Help us through the next days as we adjust to each other again. We love you, Lord, and we thank you. In Jesus' name. Amen." He squeezed the two little hands tucked securely in his.

Dani squeezed back and peeked up from under her bangs. "You forgot to pray for the macaroni," she whispered. She quickly bowed her head again.

Laughing, Wade did likewise. "And thank you, Lord, for good ol' macaroni and cheese. Amen."

He'd forgotten how noisy his house was with three kids under the roof. There'd been a time it had gotten on his nerves. And there'd probably come a time when it would again. But today it was music to his ears.

"Carma doesn't make macaroni and cheese," Dani said over a mouthful.

"Oh?"

She wagged her head. "She said it's not good for you."

Wade cringed. "Well, Carma might have a point there. But once in a while won't hurt you."

The kids chattered throughout the meal, and slowly Wade put together bits and pieces of their life back in Minneapolis. It sounded as though Carma had been the glue that held things together for the kids— and then just barely. Wade hoped she would be all right.

After lunch they worked together to clean up the kitchen.

"When the dishes are done, why don't we go finish unpacking the rest of your stuff," he said. "We don't want it in the way tonight when everybody gets here."

"What are we gonna do tonight?" Lacey asked.

"Aunt Sophie's bringing pizza, and then we'll probably just play cards or something."

"I know!" Beau said, "We can play spoons! Like we used to."

"Yeah," Lacey said, grinning. "With Dee."

Wade sighed. "Dee won't be here tonight, honey."

"Hows come?" she pouted.

"Well...she just won't."

"Can't we call her and tell her?" Beau asked.

Wade bit his lip. He didn't know how much to tell the kids. But suddenly an idea took shape. "You know what?" he said, turning the possibility over in his mind.

They all waited with eager eyes.

"You guys go wash your faces and brush your teeth. Let's go see if Dee is home."

"All right!" They bounced like jumping beans.

"Now, she might not even be home," he warned. "And even if she is, we can't stay long. Just long enough to say hi and let her know you're back."

His words were lost in the clomping of feet on the stairs as they raced for the bathroom. A minute later Wade heard the water pipes begin to groan and clank. He smiled. The old house had come to life again.

In the bathroom off the kitchen, he washed his own face and ran a comb through his hair. He felt energized at the prospect of seeing Dee again. Inspecting his jaw line in the mirror, he decided he could get by without shaving again, but he opened the medicine cabinet and splashed some aftershave into his hand. He rubbed his hands together briskly and slapped the lotion on his face.

Was he doing the right thing by taking the kids to her house? He thought about calling her first, but he didn't want to put her in a position where she'd feel obligated to say no. If he just showed up on her doorstep, she would be blameless. And she couldn't be angry with him once she realized his reason for coming.

He hollered for the kids, anticipation building as he thought about seeing her again. As he walked back through the kitchen, his eyes fell on a deck of cards the kids had been playing with earlier. Inspiration struck, and he chuckled to himself as he slid open the silverware drawer. He took out a single spoon and tucked it in his pocket.

"Come on, you guys," he hollered up the stairway. "Hustle up!"

They wouldn't stay long. Just for a minute, so she could see the kids. And so he could see her.

Dee had spent the morning at the office, searching for some clue that might indicate where the Parnell kids could be. She'd contacted Social Services in Minneapolis, but they didn't have any records on file for Darrin Parnell. Finding little to go on, she finally drove home, deeply disappointed that she didn't have better news for Wade.

She hadn't been home five minutes when the doorbell rang. It was probably Jewel from next door. She loved the elderly woman, but she wasn't in the mood for company today. Walking through the living room, she mentally composed a polite excuse.

But when she opened the door, her breath caught. "Wade…" His eyes held an odd gleam.

"Hi, Dee."

She gripped the doorknob tighter to steady herself. If he'd come to her house, the news must not be good. "Have you…heard anything?"

Expressionless, he held up a hand and turned toward the street where his pickup was parked. Putting two fingers to his mouth, he let out an ear-piercing whistle. "Hey, guys," he shouted. "She's home."

The passenger-side door burst open, and Beau and Lacey and Danica spilled out onto the lawn.

Her heart swelled as she understood the sparkle in his eyes. "Oh, Wade! They're here! You found them!"

He beamed as the kids scrambled up on the porch.

She caught his eye over their heads. "Oh, Wade…I'm so glad they're all right!" *Thank you, Lord.*

Lacey caught Dee in a hug from one side, and Dani snuggled on the other. She bent to hug them back.

"Hey, you guys! How are you?" She struggled to contain her emotions.

Looking up, she noticed Beau standing to the side, an embarrassed grin on his face. She straightened and put a hand on his shoulder. "Look at you, Beau. You've gotten so tall!"

He shrugged, but his grin grew into a full-fledged smile. "Oh, it's so good to see you guys. I've missed you!" She glanced up at Wade, hoping he knew how much those words were meant for him, too.

A meow sounded from inside the door, and they all turned to look.

Dee reached back and opened the screen door to let Phog out. The cat sauntered onto the far end of the porch under the swing. The kids ran to pet him.

"Be nice to him, now," Wade called after them.

She turned to Wade, angling her head toward the kids, who had the cat stretched across all three of their laps in the swing. Dee could hear him purring from clear across the porch. "What happened?" she whispered.

His voice dropped. "They're mine, Dee."

"What?" Her breath caught.

He nodded. "Parnell literally dumped them on my doorstep this morning."

"You're kidding?"

He told her what had happened, a smile blooming on his face, as though he were hearing it himself for the first time. "Darrin left me with an envelope full of legal papers that basically say the kids are mine."

"Oh, Wade, that's unbelievable. That's wonderful!"

"Starr's life insurance money is conspicuously absent from the envelope, but I don't care. It doesn't matter to me."

"You're not going to fight him for it?"

"No way. The money is probably long gone by now, anyway. And the last thing I want to do is end up in another legal battle with him. We'll get by okay." He studied her for a moment. "I'm never going to be a rich man, Dee. Just so you know."

"I think you're already a rich man," she said quietly.

He closed his eyes and nodded. "Yes…I am."

"You're not worried that he'll…come back for them."

"No, I think he knows he doesn't have a chance at them now. Not after what's happened."

"Oh, Wade, this is so incredible!" It was all she could do not to throw her arms around him. Instead, she folded them in front of her and glanced over at the kids. "Are they…doing okay?"

He shook his head. "I think so. I'm sure we're not out of the woods yet, but so far, this day has felt like they never even left."

"I am so happy for you. Thanks for coming by to tell me."

"Thanks for all your help."

She waved him off.

He looked at the kids and back at her. "We won't stay long," he said.

She grinned. "Yeah, that's what you said." She wanted to invite him in. Oh, who was she kidding? She wanted to propose to him right here and now. But she wasn't about to jeopardize the eight months she'd already invested in waiting for him. "I'm so glad you came by."

As if he'd read her mind, he shuffled his feet and took a step back. "Well, I guess we should go. But...the kids wanted to see you."

"I'm so glad, Wade," she said again. "I...I've missed them."

"That's good," he said. "Because... Well...when you're considering this over the next sixteen months...it's a package deal now. You get all of us."

A tingle worked its way up her spine at the vulnerability in his eyes. She risked her next words. "You're still waiting?"

"Yes. I'm still waiting." He held her gaze. "And not as patiently as I once claimed."

Something stirred inside her. She closed her eyes for a moment, trying to collect herself. "You'd better go."

He grinned. "I'm going. But...we know our way back." He went to the swing where the kids were still fussing over the cat. "Hey, guys, it's time to go. Tell Dee good-bye."

"Aw! Do we have to go now?" Dani said. "We just got here!"

"I told you we weren't staying long. We have to go get the house cleaned up for tonight."

Dani looked over at Dee. "We're havin' a party tonight. With pizza."

"Oh, that sounds like fun." Dee suddenly felt lonelier than she had in a long time.

Wade reached out and touched her arm briefly. "I wish you could be there."

She shivered under the warmth of his hand. "Yeah. Me, too."

He looked toward the ceiling of the porch. "Lord, help the next sixteen months to fly."

"Amen," she whispered.

He rounded up the kids, and she watched from the porch while he buckled them into their seats. As he opened his door and started to climb in, a blanket of gloom settled over her.

But then Wade turned and jogged back to the house. He stood on the step below her, grinning. "I almost forgot," he said. He dug in the back pocket of his jeans and pulled out a stainless steel spoon. A spoon with a curvy *S* engraved in the handle.

"For you," he said, placing it in her hand. A glint lit his eyes. "Maybe you should practice." He turned and jogged back to the truck.

The engine revved, and he pulled away from the curb. The pickup disappeared down the street. But she stood on the porch for a long time, rubbing the smooth, cool metal against her palm, tracing the *S* again and again with her finger, a soft smile caressing her face.

"You guys be good now. Don't give your Aunt Sophie any trouble, you hear? And go to bed when she tells you to." Wade winked at Sophie over the kids' heads and opened the door to leave. "Thanks, Sophe, I owe you one."

"You owe me more than one," she said with a teasing smile. "Now, get out of here. You've got better things to do than stand here and make small talk with the baby-sitter."

Wade gave her a quick hug, closed the door behind him, and jogged through the leaf-strewn lawn to his pickup.

The October air was laced with the scent of wood smoke, and he breathed in its sharp chill. He felt as nervous as he had on his first date the night of his senior prom. A wry smile tugged at the corner of his mouth as he thought of his gangly, awkward seventeen-year-old self. He sure hoped this night ended better than that one had.

Fifteen minutes later when he turned onto her street, his pulse quickened. The lights were on in the windows. Good. She was home.

He parked his pickup along the curb in front of her house and walked across the lawn and up onto the front porch.

Sixteen long months had passed since the day he'd first brought the kids here.

He smiled to think of the covert front porch visits they'd made since that long-ago day in May. They never talked about it, never made a date. He hadn't wanted Dee to feel responsible for breaking the code of ethics that bound her. But once in a while, every few weeks or so, when he couldn't stand being away from her another minute, he would load up the kids and bring them to see her.

He'd knock on her door, and the kids would yell, "Surprise!" Then they'd play in the yard or on the porch while he and Dee talked. He'd never stayed more than an hour. They'd never gone inside her house—

even one January day when it was so cold he feared they'd all get frostbite standing on the porch, watching their breath form clouds in the air.

He'd never touched her—except in his dreams. Their conversations were always punctuated with "I really should go" and "Yes, you really should." Yet they'd learned more about one another in those precious stolen minutes than they had in all the hours they'd spent at his house.

And he grew more in love with her every time he saw her.

It had been almost two months since he'd been here last. He felt almost sad that this would be the last time he'd sneak up on her porch. It was the first time he'd come alone, without the kids.

He wiped sweaty palms on his jeans, raised his hand to knock, and almost fell through the doorway when the door swung inward.

Dee stood there with a serious expression on her face. "Yes," she said. It wasn't *yes* with a question mark. But simply *yes*. As though it were an answer to a question he was pretty sure he hadn't asked yet.

"Huh?" he said.

"I said yes. Whatever your question is, my answer is yes."

He wondered if the grin splitting his face looked as silly as it felt. Apparently so, because she started laughing.

He cocked his head and grew sober. "Are you sure, Dee? Because my questions are pretty serious."

"Yes," she said again. She gave an exaggerated bob of her chin that made him think of an old *I Dream of Jeannie* rerun. "Yes. I will. I am. I do… Does that about cover it?"

Now it was his turn to laugh. "I'd say that pretty well covers it. So…I take it you know what day today is?"

"Yes, I do. And you're eight hours, seventeen minutes and"—she looked at her watch—"forty-three seconds late. You had me worried."

He seemed unable to do anything but stand there and beam like an idiot.

Suddenly her eyes misted. "Oh, Wade, I can't believe you're really here. I thought this day would never come. And then I was afraid when it did come, you'd somehow forget or maybe you'd change your mind or—" Her face crumpled, and she started to cry.

He reached for her hand and pulled her out onto the porch. Gently he pressed his fingers over her lips. "Shh. I'm here. How could I ever forget you?" he whispered against her hair. "I didn't wait this long for nothing."

He pulled her into his arms then and felt her heart beat against his. And though he had never touched her like this, never held her before, it felt as though she belonged here. As if she was made for him. And he for her.

"You're sure about this, Dee? I'm asking you to share my life with three noisy, rowdy, ornery kids. I'm asking you to be a pauper with me. I...I want you to be sure."

She reached up to caress his face, and her eyes locked with his. "I've had two years...two long, lonely years to think about this, Wade. I know exactly what you're asking, and I've never been so sure about anything in my life."

He pulled her closer and took her face in his hands. As they shared their first kiss, all the long months of waiting melted into nothing. Pulling away, he looked into her eyes, then placed the palm of his hand on her head, the way he had with each of the children that day they'd come home to him. He felt the warmth of her hair against his skin, the realness of her.

And suddenly he knew that she, too, had finally come home to him.

Acknowledgments

Once again, I come to the end of a book, and the daunting task of trying to thank the many, many people who so generously gave of their time and expertise to help me bring a new story to life.

In researching the topic of this book, I am deeply indebted to those who granted brief first interviews, those who endured second and third interviews, and especially those who allowed me to pester them with frequent phone calls and to interrupt office hours— and sometimes leisure hours— throughout the many months I worked on the manuscript: James Scott Bell, Medical Investigator Megan Branson, Tamara Cooper, Terri Downin, Susan Downs, Meredith Efken, Mary Friesen, Alton Gansky, Dr. Melvin Hodde, Ron Hoffman, Marci McCullough, DiAnn Mills, Wayne and Melanie Phillips, Denese Purcell, Linda Rondeau, Marlo Schalesky, Trish Rose, Terry Stucky, Judge Sam Sturm, Max Teeter, Carrie Turansky, Toby Tyner, Sandy Villines, Eric Wiggin, Marilyn Wilder, and Judy Young, along with those who, because of the sensitive nature of their work, preferred not to be named.

Special thanks go to Melanie Bender. This story could not have been written without your knowledge and insight into the profession of social work. For the many hours you spent answering my questions, poring over the manuscript, and researching my questions, I am extremely grateful.

As I spoke with dozens of people—foster parents, social workers, judges, attorneys, those who serve as guardians ad litem, and various other employees of Social and Rehabilitation Services and foster-care agencies— I was deeply impressed with the level of dedication to and compassion for children caught in the middle of shattered families.

This book was extremely difficult to research. Because legal procedure and office procedure of the agencies portrayed in my book vary from county to county and state to state—and because they are constantly changing with the enactment of new laws and policy—information I received often seemed contradictory. Fortunately, I was somewhat at an advantage writing about a fictitious case in a fictitious county. Any mistakes, however, are my own.

For reading my manuscript in its early stages and offering excellent advice and direction, I am grateful to Tammy Alexander, Debbie Allen, Lorie Battershill, Meredith Efken, and Terry Stucky.

Gratitude is owed to my talented editors, Dudley Delffs and Terry McDowell, along with the incredible staff at WaterBrook Press—especially Mark Ford, who designs the beautiful covers for my books.

To the wonderful Midwest contingent of my authors' group, ChiLibris —Colleen Coble, Mel and Cheryl Hodde a.k.a. Hannah Alexander, Annie Jones, Nancy Moser, and Stephanie Grace Whitson—you brainstormed this novel brilliantly.

To my family—my husband, Ken, and our four children, my parents and siblings, in-laws and extended family—how can I ever thank you all for the enthusiasm, encouragement, and love you have shown me? You have made this journey one of deep joy.

To my Lord and Savior, Jesus Christ: I owe you my all.

I love hearing from my readers. To e-mail me or to learn more about my books, please visit my Web site at www.deborahraney.com, or write to me in care of WaterBrook Press, 2375 Telstar Drive, Suite 160, Colorado Springs, Colorado 80920.

Deborah Raney is the award-winning author of eight novels, including the RITA award winner *Beneath a Southern Sky, A Scarlet Cord,* and *A Vow to Cherish,* her first novel, which was the inspiration for World Wide Pictures' highly acclaimed film of the same title. Deborah has also written nonfiction books and articles and often speaks at writers' conferences and women's retreats. Deb and her husband—illustrator and children's book author Ken Raney—have four children and make their home in Kansas. Please visit Deborah's Web site at www.deborahraney.com.

Engaging fiction from award-winning author
Deborah Raney

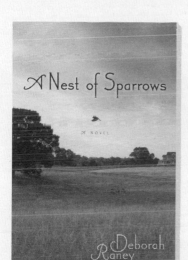

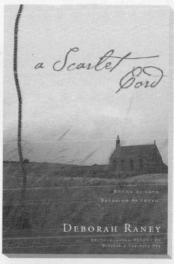

Available in bookstores everywhere.

WATERBROOK PRESS
www.waterbrookpress.com

To learn more about WaterBrook Press and view
our catalog of products, log on to our Web site:
www.waterbrookpress.com

WATERBROOK
PRESS